THE CREW

Margaret Mayhew

CORGI BOOKS

THE CREW
A CORGI BOOK : 0 552 14492 4

First publication in Great Britain

PRINTING HISTORY
Corgi edition published 1997

3 5 7 9 10 8 6 4 2

Set in 10/12pt Linotype Baskerville by
Kestrel Data, Exeter, Devon.

20 Corgi Books are published by Transworld Publishers,
61–63 .... W5 5SA,
a division of The Random House Group Ltd,
in Australia by Random House Australia,
and in New Zealand .... NSW 2061, Australia,
and in New Zealand .... by Random House New Zealand Ltd,
and in South Africa by Random House (Pty) Ltd,
Endulini, ... Road, Parktown 2193, South Africa.

Reproduced, printed and bound in Great Britain by
Cox & Wyman Ltd, Reading, Berkshire.

Papers used by Transworld Publishers are natural, recyclable
products made from wood grown in sustainable forests.
The manufacturing processes conform to the environmental
regulations of the country of origin.

For Mary and Keith

And in memory of Jack

Acknowledgements

I am greatly indebted to the late Squadron Leader Jack Currie, DFC, the author and Lancaster bomber pilot, for all his kind and generous help and advice.

Also, to my editor, Diane Pearson, for her invaluable encouragement and guidance. And to my husband, Philip Kaplan, for his constant support.

Finally, to the very young crews of World War Two Bomber Command whose courage and self-sacrifice in the cause of our freedom remain an inspiration to us all.

Foreword

A Lancaster bomber required a crew of seven men: pilot, navigator, bomb aimer, flight engineer, wireless operator, mid-upper gunner and rear gunner.

During the Second World War, the average age of a crew was twenty-four and, at the height of RAF Bomber Command's strategic offensive against Germany, their chance of surviving a tour of thirty operations only one in three. By the end of the war 55,573 men in aircrews had died and the casualty rate in Bomber Command was the heaviest of any British Service.

In the words of Winston Churchill: *They never flinched or failed. It is to their devotion that in no small measure we owe our victory. Let us give them our salute.*

This novel tells the story of seven such men. And their women.

PART I

PART 1

One

They were lost. Again. Christ only knew where Piers had got them to this time, because he sure as hell didn't. Even if the whole damn countryside hadn't been covered in cloud, he wouldn't have known without some obvious landmark. The crazy jumble of fields and woods and villages all looked the same to him – when you could see it at all, which wasn't often.

Jesus, the weather they had over here! Cloud, rain, fog, sleet, snow, more rain, and still more rain, and still more cloud. And it was supposed to be spring. Bad enough on the ground. Up here, bloody murder.

By now they should have landed safely back at base, be stripping off their flying gear, lighting up, cracking jokes, acting the confident, close-knit crew – the jolly old comrades they were supposed to have become. Instead, they were still wandering hopelessly about the skies. Van peered downwards, trying to see something – *anything*. About fifteen minutes ago, when there'd been a gap in the clouds, he'd caught sight of the sea, which meant they were very likely heading in the general direction of Holland. Any moment now some Jerry fighter was probably going to appear and make it the end of a perfect day. The end of everything.

He flicked the mike switch on his mask and tried to keep the worry and irritation out of his voice. 'Pilot to navigator. What's our position, please?'

'I'm frightfully sorry, skipper. I'm not absolutely sure. Can you possibly hang on a moment?'

God help us, he thought. We're lost and Piers is *frightfully* sorry. At the moment, all we're doing is stooging around in broad daylight. When we stop playing games and have to go and drop bombs on the enemy in the dark, the Jerries won't need to waste shells bringing us down, we'll do the job ourselves.

He could sense his flight engineer's seething impatience beside him. Jock must be cursing his luck at being assigned to them – which Van had a strong suspicion had been done in the hopes of improving their performance. Tough deal, Jock! Top of his course and stuck with a Yank pilot who had yet to show he could make a halfway decent landing, a navigator who didn't seem to know north from south, an Aussie bomb aimer who'd flunked the new bomb sight exam, a mid-upper gunner who evidently couldn't hit a rat in a barrel, a wireless operator older than God and a kid rear gunner who read poetry. When some guy had told him in friendly fashion over a beer in the Mess that they were odds-on favourites to be the first crew to get the chop on ops, if not before, he hadn't been a bit surprised.

Nothing from Piers. What the hell was he doing back there? It wasn't that difficult, for Christ's sake. He was about to press the mike switch again when the clouds suddenly parted and he saw Lincoln Cathedral down below the Lancaster's port wing, its three big towers sticking up cheerily from the city hilltop: a landmark he knew and was learning to love the hard way. Not even Piers could get lost – they were only twenty miles from base.

Now it could be *his* turn to screw up. He brought

the Lancaster bomber down steadily, praying he'd manage a passable landing this time and not give them all something else to worry about. The runway lay ahead, a mile-long, straight concrete scar across that mishmash of English fields. All he had to do was get her down onto it in one piece. All twenty-five tons of her.

At a thousand feet, Flying Control gave him permission to join the circuit downwind.

'Undercart down, please, engineer.'

Jock acknowledged curtly. 'Undercart down.' His hand reached for the lever. After a few seconds the green lights came on. 'And locked.'

He made all his landing checks and turned cross wind.

'Flaps twenty, please, Jock.'

'Flaps, twenty.'

He was driving eight thousand horses. Under the thick flying clothes, his body felt clammy with sweat, his muscles rigid. Six lives in his hands, besides his own. He could take advice from the rest of the crew, but he was the guy who had to make the final decisions. And they'd better be the right ones.

Control crackled again in his ears. 'You're clear to land, G-George.'

'Thank you. Pilot to crew. Stand by for landing.'

He turned on finals at seven hundred feet, pointing the Lanc's nose straight at the runway. The heavy bomber roared over the Lincolnshire farm land, sinking gradually. All tickety-boo, as the RAF said.

The airfield boundary was coming close.

'Full flap, Jock.'

'Full flap.'

They were over the boundary hedge and the

15

rubber-streaked runway rushed up at them. Too fast. The Lanc's port wheel hit it first – hard and with a loud squeal. She bounced high, lurched, and bounced and lurched again as the starboard wheel crunched down next, the wing dipping horrifyingly close to the ground. There were two more bounces and a thud-thud as her tailwheel slammed down. The nose reared and yawed in front of him. Shit, shit, *shit*!

They were halfway down the runway before she'd settled and he had full control. He should have given her the gun and gone around again. Wrong decision. Total screw-up. Nobody said anything. Not a word. They were probably too bloody frightened to speak. Or too disgusted, like Jock who was wagging his head slowly from side to side.

At dispersal, when the Merlins had died, Van un-fastened his harness, pulled off his helmet and wiped the sweat from his forehead. The others were clatter-ing and clanging about in the metal fuselage behind him, making their way aft. He didn't blame them for being keen to get out. When he joined them outside nobody said anything to him then either. They were huddled in a foot-stamping, arm-swinging group at the edge of the tarmac, faces turned into the teeth of the wind away from him, looking for the crew bus – Jock, Piers, Stew, Harry, Bert and Charlie.

Van fumbled for his cigarettes and lighter. His hands were still shaking, and he had trouble getting flame and cigarette tip together in the lee of his Irvin jacket. When he lifted his head he saw the Bedford coming along, speeding round the peri track towards them, a WAAF driver at the wheel. It had started to rain again.

*   *   *

16

'Reckon he'll kill us all, if Jerry don't first,' the wireless operator, Harry, said in his flat Yorkshire. 'We could have gone off the runway and gone arse over tit, Bert. Blown oop in bloody flames.' He stood by the bar in the Sergeants' Mess, a pint of beer clutched in one large hand, his pipe in the other. He was a big fair-haired man – built like a brick shit-house, Bert always told him affably. The mid-upper gunner, dark and with a wide grin like a monkey, barely reached his shoulder. Side by side, they looked and sounded like a music hall act.

'Be fair, mate, you don't do such a good job twiddlin' the old knobs neither. Blimey, you got that dance music once, remember? I was doin' a quick-quick-slow up in the turret. Let's face it, we're none of us so bloomin' marvellous.'

Harry nodded. 'Aye, that's true enough. How you got through gunnery school with your eyesight, I'll never know.'

'Luck an' bluff, cock. That's 'ow,' Bert said chirpily.

'And what 'appens when you're supposed to shoot down a Jerry fighter for us? I'll tell you what's goin' to 'appen, Bert, you're goin' to miss 'im.'

The gunner grinned. 'We'll 'ave to find Germany first and that's not goin' to be so easy with our nav.'

'Aye, we'll end up in Timbuctu, more like. You'd think with all the education he must 'ave 'ad that he could do a better job.' Harry took a swig at his beer. 'Oh, well. No good worryin', I s'pose. There's nowt we can do about it. Can't change horses in mid-stream.'

'Mid-air, you mean, mate.'

Charlie, the rear gunner, who was even smaller than Bert, sipped his beer, listening to them. With every sip

17

he tried to hide his shudder at the taste. Everyone in the Mess seemed to be downing pints of the stuff. He watched Harry take another swallow and the level in his mug sink rapidly. It would soon be time for the next round and they'd wonder why he hadn't half-finished his first one yet. He took another desperate gulp. He was still feeling a bit sick from the flight, which didn't help either, and the smoke from Harry's pipe and Bert's cigarette was making things even worse. He'd bought some Woodbines himself, hoping he'd look older if he smoked, but every time he lit up it made him feel dizzy.

He hadn't said anything, but he was just as worried about the skipper. There was a lump on his head where it had hit the turret roof on that dicey landing. He'd thought they'd had it for a moment. Going to do a ground loop and not much chance of him getting out. None at all if the doors behind him went and jammed. The rear turret wasn't the safest place to be. Someone had told him that Tail-End Charlies were the ones most likely to cop it. There were always blokes who liked to put the wind up you. Got a kick out of it most probably.

He hadn't exactly chosen to be a rear gunner. 'With a name like yours,' they'd said to him at gunnery school, 'you haven't got much option, have you lad?' But he was very proud of his AG badge with its one wing, and of his three stripes, and he didn't much mind being all on his own in the tail, being dragged backwards in his fish bowl through the skies. It gave you a lot to look at and a chance to think about things. And sometimes he recited poems to himself. They'd teased him about his book of poetry, of course. It had fallen out of his pocket once and Stew had picked it up and turned the pages over, as though he couldn't believe his eyes.

'Jesus Christ, Charlie, what's this? *Poems?*' The bomb aimer had read a bit aloud in his Aussie accent.

> *My heart leaps up when I behold*
>   *a rainbow in the sky*
> *So was it when my life began;*
> *So is it now I am a man;*
> *So be it when I shall grow old,*
> *Or let me die!*

He'd handed the book back, shaking his head. 'Strewth, if you're going to be beholding bloody rainbows, kid, we'll all be dying with you.'

Charlie took another small sip of beer. Harry's mug was nearly empty now. How on earth could he get it down so quickly? Must be all the practice. He was really old, Harry. More than thirty – *years* older than the rest of them. Bert was nineteen, Jock twenty, Stew twenty-one. He wasn't sure about Piers and the skipper, but they'd be somewhere around that. He was easily the youngest himself, as well as the smallest, which was handy as it was a bit of a squash in the rear turret.

Bert tipped up his mug and drained it. 'Time for another.'

'Your shout, Bert,' Harry said firmly.

'OK, OK. Get it down, Charlie, and give us your glass.'

'Not quite ready, thanks.'

'Blimey, come *on* . . . you won't grow up to be a big strong man like 'arry if you don't drink up your beer like a good boy.'

He couldn't. He just couldn't. Luckily Harry saved him.

'Leave him be, Bert. The lad's takin' his time, but I don't mind if I do.'

Up the other end of the bar, the bomb aimer, Stew, was buying a beer for himself and a lemonade for Jock. He handed over the glass of lemonade to the flight engineer with a grimace. 'Don't know how you can drink that muck, sport.'

'Och, it's no so bad.'

'Have a fag?'

'No, thanks.'

Strewth, the bloke didn't booze and didn't smoke, and didn't chase sheilas either. What the hell sort of a life was that? No flaming fun at all. Stew stuck a cigarette in his mouth and flicked the wheel of his lighter with his thumb. As usual the bloody thing was playing up. If it hadn't been his lucky mascot he'd have chucked it away long ago. He went on flicking the wheel harder and harder.

'What d'you reckon our chances with our Yank driver, then, Jock?'

'Not too good.'

'He was fair enough when we were on Wimpeys, but seems to me he just doesn't get it with the heavies.'

'Aye, you could say that.'

'Think he'll get any better?'

'I certainly hope so.'

The lighter suddenly burst into flame and Stew bent his head to it. He took a drag at the cigarette and blew smoke upwards.

'Anyway, far as I can see, it's not going to make a blind bit of difference. It's odds-on we won't be coming back to land at all. We're the favourites for the chop, did you know that?'

'I'd heard something of the kind.'

Jock didn't look like he gave a bugger. He was a cool customer and no mistake. Must have ice in his veins instead of blood, Stew thought. Maybe it was the climate in Scotland that made them like that. Most Aussies, himself included, thought themselves pretty tough blokes, but he wasn't sure the Scots hadn't got the edge. He'd come across one or two others like Jock: steel eyes, voices like glass breaking, made of cast iron. They could generally drink you under the table as well, which made it even weirder that Jock never touched a drop. Didn't swear either, which was the weirdest bloody thing of all.

You couldn't tell so easily about the English lot. They hid it. Put up a smokescreen. They might have a streak of yellow a mile wide or be brave as hell for all he knew. He hadn't a clue how their four would turn out when it came to the real thing – when the chips were down. Harry and Bert were probably OK. Harry had one foot in the grave but he was one of those solid north country types, and if he ever learned to work the radio set properly he might do all right, and Bert was a wiry little cockney bastard who told some good blue jokes, even if he wasn't Dead-Eye-Dick. But Charlie was a worry, same as the skipper. For a start, seventeen was too bloody young for this caper; they ought to have rumbled him at the recruiting office. And any kid who read poetry about rainbows wasn't exactly going to be the killer type. He'd be dreaming away and gazing at the flaming stars, or something, and they'd go and get their arse shot off. The only thing he'd be any use for would be to keep the tail down on landing.

Stew took another drag at his cigarette. As for that drongo, Piers, getting them lost all the time . . . well, they might as well take up a ball of string next time. When it was time to go home, Charlie could wind it in from the rear turret and they could fly down backwards so the skipper could try landing that way for a change. How the hell Piers had got to be an officer he'd never know, unless it was the toff talk that had swung it. Or his posh family had pulled some strings.

He frowned. Not that he'd any right to throw stones when it came to cocking-up. He'd gone and failed that bloody exam at the Heavy Conversion Unit, hadn't he? No excuses, but it had been a snap test, after all, with no time to bone up for it, no chance to get all the facts on the new bombsight and fuses and detonators properly fixed in his memory, like he'd done with all the previous exams he'd passed OK. They'd sprung it on them and it had been a bastard. There'd been more blanks on his paper than answers, and when the chief bombing instructor had hauled him in and chewed him into confetti, he'd thought they were going to throw him out of the Unit then and there. Like a condemned man, he'd pleaded for another chance and they'd let him do a special two-day course to catch up. Now, he wasn't so sure he should have been so flaming keen. If he'd kept his mouth shut they'd've replaced him and he'd've ended up with another crew, not this lot. Still, too late now. Too bloody bad, sport!

Christ, what a way to crew-up! They stuck you in a hangar with a hundred or more other blokes you didn't know from Adam – pilots, navigators, bomb aimers, wireless operators, gunners – all milling about, and told you to sort yourselves out, chaps! You were expected to pick your partners like you were at a bloody dance. Only you weren't choosing partners for an evening's hoofing; you were trying to pick the men you were going to have to trust with your own sweet life.

He'd wandered about the hangar, not knowing what the hell to do for the best, and when he'd stopped for a fag his lighter had gone u/s on him. A bloke standing nearby with pilot's wings and a Canada shoulder flash had given him a light and it had seemed a good idea to join up with another colonial, not being too sure about the Poms, so they'd shaken hands on it. Later, of course, he'd discovered that Van was really a Yank in disguise. Pretty soon Harry had come by with the kid Charlie in tow, like a minnow on a line. They'd still needed a navigator, until Piers had come up, stammering and blushing like a sheila, and asked if they'd mind *awfully* if he butted in. If they'd known then that he couldn't find his way out of a paper bag, they'd've minded quite a lot. Bert had teamed up with them as mid-upper gunner when they'd gone on from Wellingtons to Lancs, and their flight engineer had been assigned whether he liked it or not. Poor old Jock, he'd had lousy luck to get stuck with them. Well, they were all stuck with each other and all you could do was bloody pray.

It was a frightful scrum in the Officers' Mess. Piers waited his turn patiently to order a sherry and stand his skipper a beer – the least he could do after the mess he'd made of navigating. 'I'm terribly sorry about making such a hash of things again today, Van.'

'Forget it. I'm just as sorry about that landing.'

23

'Gosh, that's all right. It can happen to anyone, I expect.'

'Not to most guys. Maybe we'll both improve, in time. Cigarette?'

'Thanks awfully. I rather like your American ones.'

He took one of Van's Chesterfields. The smoke felt good going into his lungs; so did the sherry going down his throat. They both made him feel better. After all, he wasn't the only one who'd messed up; that landing *had* been bloody awful. He'd really thought they were going to cartwheel, in which case that would probably have been that. He'd seen a Halifax do it: stand on one wingtip and flip right over like an acrobat before it had gone up in a mighty whoomph. No-one had got out. And he couldn't see them getting out of a Lanc quickly, either. If anything happened in the air, they were all supposed to bail out by the nose escape hatch so they didn't go and smash into the tail. On the ground, in flames, God knows if they'd be able to get to *any* exit in time. They'd probably be caught like rats in a trap. He tried not to think about that. Not much point. In fact, absolutely no point at all.

Just the same, he'd no regrets about volunteering. The parents would have preferred him to go into the Army, following family tradition, but he'd always liked the idea of flying. If he hadn't failed the course, he'd have been a pilot, but navigator wasn't a bad alternative. And it wasn't as though he didn't know his stuff – you couldn't get through the training unless you did – but when it had come to the real thing, he kept getting into a complete panic and losing his head; forgetting everything he'd learned.

The thought of letting the rest of them down – maybe getting them all killed, not just lost on a training exercise like today – filled him with a sickening horror. To get oneself killed was one thing, to be responsible for six other deaths along with your own, quite another. Of course, it was the same for each of them. Their lives depended on the other chaps doing their jobs properly. They were bound to each other like links in a chain – and a chain was only as strong as its weakest link. He hoped to God that link wasn't himself.

In a couple of weeks they'd be posted to an operational station somewhere and doing their first sortie. The first of the thirty. The chances of getting through the tour weren't terribly good, he knew, but he tried not to think about that either. After all, they could be one of the lucky ones. Survive your first five, he'd heard somebody chant, and double your chances of staying alive.

He wondered why Van had volunteered to fight in a war that hadn't been his country's problem. The skipper never talked about it – hardly talked about himself at all – but he must have joined up long before the Japanese had attacked the American fleet at Pearl Harbour. From the little he knew of America, mostly from films, they seemed to live pretty comfortably over there. Certainly a lot better than wartime England. Plenty of food and everything, and no bombs. Mad to come here.

'Think anyone'd mind if I played that piano?' Van said, nodding towards the beer-stained upright in the corner of the Mess.

'Golly, I shouldn't think so.' He watched his skipper make his way across the room, park his beer and cigarette and sit down at the keys. He played a few bars of a song that Piers recognized vaguely but couldn't put a title to. After a while he realized that Van was rather good. A lot of the chaps had stopped talking and were listening, and some of them gathered round the piano. Piers drank his sherry and smoked his American cigarette and listened. He felt a lot better now. With any luck they'd be posted somewhere decent – one of the pre-war aerodromes with proper buildings, not tin huts. And before that, there'd be some leave so he could get home for a few days. He was looking forward to that.

Two

In the fading light, the bombers were emerging from their dispersal pans and lumbering after each other round the perimeter track, like elephants in a circus ring.

Assistant Section Officer Catherine Herbert stood with the small group of station personnel beside the runway, watching the Lancasters and waiting to wave them off. Whatever the weather, every kite was seen off on every op, and every time she wondered which ones they were waving goodbye to for ever.

Although it was May, there was a cold wind blowing hard from the Wolds and she had to hang on to her cap. The hedgerows and a huddle of bent trees along the eastern edge of the aerodrome were the only protection on the piece of flat Lincolnshire farm land that had been turned hurriedly into a wartime bomber station. The ancient farm buildings lay at the northern perimeter and a raw group of Nissen huts and wooden shacks had sprung up among the trees to the east. Drab brown and green camouflage, ugly corrugated iron and asbestos, concrete paths linked across oozing mud, gigantic steel hangars, barbed wire, the deafening roar of heavy bombers, a ceaseless wind. That was RAF Beningby.

She had hated it at first, and then gradually got used to it. There was a war on, after all, which meant getting used to everything – including men dying.

The big four-engined bombers had only been with the squadron a few weeks, and they were an impressive sight. And an impressive sound. Mingled with the steady roar of the engines, the WAAF could hear the short extra bursts of power and the sharp squeal of brakes as the pilots steered along the narrow, winding track between the blue and amber lights. Once or twice she'd seen a bomber run off the concrete edge and bog down in the mud, which meant a long delay for everyone behind while the aircraft was hauled out. It was usually a sprog crew and there was one on this op. She'd spotted them at the briefing, as easy to pick out as new boys in a school class: not knowing where to sit or what to do, taking industrious notes, making neat little diagrams of flak and search-light batteries, and paying more attention than all the rest of the old hands put together. All too often she never saw sprog crews more than once or twice: the first five ops were known to be the trickiest for them. But if they got through those, they had a fair chance of surviving the remainder.

The target for tonight was St Nazaire, and they were off to lay mines in enemy waters. Gardening, the crews called it, and the mines were vegetables. Nobody called anything unpleasant or dangerous by the proper word. You didn't get killed, you 'bought it', and you didn't bomb the enemy, you 'clobbered' him. The atmosphere in the briefing room had been almost light-hearted. Not Hamburg, or Cologne or Stuttgart . . . just a milk-run. Piece of cake.

The leading bomber had reached the end of the peri track. When the red light from the controller's caravan winked to green, it rolled forward onto the

28

start of the main runway and swung round into the wind to face the flarepath lights. The engines howled and faded and the Lancaster hovered for a moment before she leaped forward with a mighty roar. She passed the waving group, engines bellowing. The tail lifted and further on down the runway the elephant rose slowly and majestically into the air, to become an eagle.

Catherine watched the first one climb away, red and green wingtip lights fading into the distance, and then turned back to the second, already in position at the end of the runway. One aircraft would take off every ninety seconds.

The sprog crew's rear gunner waved back as he went by. They were in S-Sugar, the ropey kite. She hoped they'd make it.

Charlie had seen the people waving to him and he'd held up his gloved hand awkwardly in reply, wondering if that was the right thing to do. They were distant shapes now, grey blobs getting smaller by the second as the bomber raced on, carrying him down the runway. The tail was already off the ground and he could feel it swinging; he prayed the skipper would keep her straight. They'd got six fifteen-hundred pound sea mines on board, and that morning one of the ground crew had told him a horror story about another new crew who'd gone careering off the runway when they were trying to take off, all loaded-up for their first – and last – op. The Lanc always wanted to go left, apparently, and once you got a bad swing with a heavy load, you'd more or less had it.

So far as he could tell, though, the lights flashing past looked at the proper angle to the tail. He kept his eyes fixed on them until, suddenly, they dropped away beneath and he knew they were airborne. The dark roof and chimneys of the farmhouse at the edge of the drome went by below, and he and his Brownings were pointing downwards to earth as they climbed. The flarepath became little pinpricks of light and RAF Beningby disappeared from view. He wriggled around on the seat pad to get more comfortable. It was a bit like being packed in a glass suitcase. The metal doors behind him formed a back rest, the control column, with hand grips and triggers, was between his legs. If he stooped his head a little, the gun sight lay immediately in front of his face. With the illumination switched on, he could see the red circle with a dot in the middle superimposed on the dark landscape below.

He reached down with his right hand for the lever and unlocked the turret on its rotating ring so he could swing round, searching the skies above and each side and below him. He was the eyes in the back of the crew's head. They'd been taught that over and over in training. He had to keep a constant look-out for anything and everything behind and report to the skipper instantly. And if it was an emergency, with a fighter suddenly attacking from the rear, he had to tell the skipper which way to turn fast to get away and not muddle starboard and port because he was facing backwards. You had to think fast and get it right. It was a big responsibility and he worried about it a lot. He must hold his ammo if the fighter was out of range, but if it came near he had to give it everything he'd got. Luckily, he was a good shot. It had come naturally to him in the training and, unlike Bert, his eyesight was perfect: like a cat in the dark. Bert could see all round from his turret, on top in the middle of the kite, but he hadn't got such a good view of what was happening at the rear, and none of them could see the blind spot right underneath without the pilot rocking the wings.

Charlie found it a bit nervy, not to be able to see anything forward. All he could do was listen to what the rest of them were saying about what was happening up front and hope for the best. He could hear them talking to each other over the intercom now: short, crackling exchanges in his headphones. The skipper's drawling Yank accent, Jock's Scottish, Piers's posh one, Stew's Aussie, Harry's Yorkshire, and Bert's chirpy cockney. Easy to tell which was which without them saying, though they nearly always did. You had to be quite sure who was talking so there were no mistakes.

He didn't understand why people kept on telling him horror stories. Maybe because they thought he was the kind to frighten easily. He *was* windy at times, but he wasn't going to show it if he could help it. Still, that take-off story had rattled him and when they were getting into the crew bus to go out to dispersal he'd gone and picked his parachute up by the release handle so it had come undone all over the place. They'd had to hang about while he went and got another, and he'd felt a right noddy. Then one of the other crew in the bus had leaned across, grinning, and asked if he could have his egg if he didn't come back. It was a joke, of course, and he'd managed a laugh with everyone else, but inside he'd felt a bit queasy.

It wasn't really the idea of dying that worried him, so much as the way it might happen. None of the possibilities was very comforting, except being blown to little bits, because then you wouldn't know a thing

31

about it. The thought of having to bail out was almost more terrifying than anything else. He wasn't too good with heights and the idea of throwing himself into space . . . well, he wasn't sure he'd be able to do it. Whatever happened, he'd be on his own unless he could make it all the way up to the nose escape hatch, which wasn't very likely. Nobody envied him being in the coldest and loneliest place on the kite, but the cold wasn't too bad with his electrically heated suit, and he could hear the others and they could hear him.

In training they'd been told that rear gunners were one of the most important members of the crew, and he had nearly twice as much ammo as the other two turrets put together to prove it. So he was proud of being Tail-End Charlie. And if it came to dying, what really mattered, to his way of thinking, was whether the cause was worth it. He thought it was.

> *We must be free or die, who speak the tongue*
> *That Shakespeare spake; the faith and morals*
> *   hold*
> *Which Milton held.*

That was out of his poetry book. By Wordsworth. He repeated the words to himself often. Some of them had to die to stop Hitler. *We must be free or die. Britons never, never, never shall be slaves.*

He wished Mum could understand, but the only thing she could really see was that she might lose him. He knew that would be hard because he was all she had, but it couldn't be helped. She'd never said a cross word when he'd gone off to the recruiting office and lied to them about his age, but he'd heard her crying in her bedroom and he'd felt very bad about it.

32

It was dark now – darkness and engine noise and vibration, all around him. The skipper's voice spoke suddenly in his ears: 'Pilot to rear gunner. OK back there, Charlie?'

He pressed his mike switch down carefully, still not easy with speaking out over the intercom. 'OK, skipper.'

He went on searching the night skies.

They dropped the mines in what Van hoped were the waters off St Nazaire, Stew letting them go at three-second intervals. For once Piers had sounded sure about their position, but that might not mean a damn thing. There was no flak and no enemy fighters; nobody seemed to be taking any notice of them at all. He had a feeling that it was never going to be this easy again.

They flew back over the Channel and crossed the English coast at what should have been Portsmouth but was probably somewhere else, because later they turned out to be at least fifty miles off course. Piers was frightfully sorry about it, as usual, and eventually got them back to Beningby after a circular tour of Lincolnshire. Van managed a reasonable landing with only a couple of bounces, and they were ferried back from dispersal in the crew bus. He sat in front beside the WAAF driver, a jolly, red-cheeked girl who made bright conversation about the weather as though they were taking a pleasure drive out in the country. Apparently it was going to be a nice day, or what passed for one. The smell of dew-damp grass reached him pleasantly through the half-open window. He wondered just exactly where they had dropped the mines.

Catherine saw the sprog crew come into the de-briefing room. All the other crews had already gone off for their breakfast and for a while she'd been afraid that they'd bought it on their first op. She watched them gather round a table: two pilot officers and five sergeants. They'd yet to do a really dicey trip, so they hadn't that dazed look she knew so well. That would come later. A fairly typical crew, except that someone had told her the pilot was an American. He'd be the tall fair one with the wings, chewing gum. The other officer, also fair-haired and wearing a navigator's badge, looked very English and very anxious. The bomb aimer was a stocky, aggressive Australian in the royal blue of the RAAF, and the flight engineer with the reddish hair and dour expression was probably Scottish. The two gunners were the smallest and youngest-looking of the crew, one of them scarcely more than a boy. The wireless operator, a big man, was obviously considerably older than the rest.

They were behaving like most crews at the start of their tour: like a group of virtual strangers with nothing much in common. Because it was their first op, they would try to answer all the de-briefing questions conscientiously in every detail. Later, they'd learn to rattle through it as quickly as possible and escape to their eggs and bacon and their sleep. If they lasted that long. Some said the first op was the diciest of all, and they'd survived it. Still, it had only been St Nazaire.

She watched them lighting cigarettes and drinking their cocoa. The wireless op was filling a pipe and poking at it with a match, the Aussie bomb aimer tipping back his chair perilously on its hind legs. She watched the navigator lean forward earnestly to answer a question from the intelligence officer, the dark-haired gunner speak up with a cheeky grin and the very young-looking gunner smother a tired yawn. Then the skipper glanced across the room in her direction and she turned back to her papers and picked up her pen.

'I'm afraid it's been empty for some time, Mrs Banks. It's rather damp.' The estate agent stood aside to let Dorothy into the cottage and she stepped past him into the dark front room.

She could smell the damp and see mildewy patches of it all along the bottom of the walls. Still, there was a nice fireplace with a good-sized grate, and if she could get a fire going and dry the place out, it would help. The few bits of furniture weren't up to much, but a good clean could work wonders. She followed the man into the kitchen at the back of the cottage. The range was thick with rust, the cupboards lined with old and yellowed newspaper. In the lean-to scullery beyond, there was a stone sink containing several dead spiders, some dead woodlice and a bath full of logs. A narrow wooden staircase, hidden behind a latched door, led to two bedrooms upstairs, with iron bedsteads and rickety chests of drawers. They clumped downstairs again.

'I'm sorry it's not in better order, Mrs Banks. I'd like to have been able to show you something more attractive, but it's all we have to let on our books in that price range at the moment, and you said it had to be in this exact area.'

He was looking at her in a worried sort of way, as though he hoped she wouldn't take the cottage. But she could see that she could make something of the place, with a bit of work, and she wasn't afraid of that. She moved over to the sitting-room window. The sill was littered with dead flies and bluebottles, the glass clouded with grime. She rubbed at it with her fingertips, clearing a patch.

The bomber station lay on the other side of the road, and if it hadn't been for the hedge she might have been able to see the runway. She could hear the sound of engines rumbling like distant thunder. The thunder grew louder and a big plane rose suddenly into view. As it climbed, she could see the black-painted underside of its body and wings. The window pane shook beneath her fingers. When the roar had died away, the estate agent apologized again.

'I'm afraid you'd get quite a lot of noise. Beningby is very close . . . the RAF bomber station.'

'Yes, I know,' she said. 'That's why I wanted to be here.'

'Oh?' He looked at her, puzzled.

'My son's just been posted there. He's a rear gunner. In the Lancasters.'

He looked even more puzzled. 'Forgive me for being personal, Mrs Banks, but you don't seem nearly old enough.'

'I was only seventeen when he was born.'

He smiled. 'That explains it. Well, I'm sure he'll be glad to have you near him.'

'He doesn't know yet. I haven't told him.' She hesitated. 'To tell the truth, I'm a bit worried he'll think I'm fussing. That it might embarrass him with the others . . .'

'I wouldn't worry too much, Mrs Banks. Anyone would understand. But won't it make it rather hard

36

for you? To be so close? To see it all going on. Wouldn't it be better to stay at home?'

She shook her head. 'I'd sooner be here and have more of a chance of seeing him . . . while I can. We live in Kent, you see. It's a long way away.'

'How does your husband feel?'

'I'm a widow. He died a long time ago. Charlie was our only child. He's all I've got.'

He said gravely, 'I know how you must feel. But are you quite sure you're doing what's best for *you*?'

'I don't care about myself,' she told him. 'I only care about Charlie. And I'll take the cottage.'

Peter was waiting for her at the bar of The White Hind. Catherine threaded a way through the RAF uniforms, past the beer swillers and the line-shooters . . . *came back looking like a colander . . . could've stepped out and walked on the bloody flak . . . can't have been me, old boy. I was over Bremen at the time . . .*

'The usual?' Peter asked when she finally reached him. He leaned across the counter and ordered the shandy. They clinked glasses. 'Another one chalked up,' he said. He'd been to Stuttgart the night before and two of the other Lancs hadn't come back. He wouldn't mention that, of course. It wasn't done to talk about the losses and the dead comrades. You pressed on regardless.

Somebody bumped into her and sloshed beer over her sleeve. Peter took hold of her arm. 'Let's get away from this bloody mob.'

They found some space in a passageway off the bar and she mopped at her uniform with her handkerchief.

'I hoped it'd be you de-briefing us, Cat.'

'Not my turn. Sorry.'

'We had that bastard Pilson. I think he takes pleasure in spinning it out as long as he can.'

'He's only doing his job, Peter.'

'Is he? Sometimes I think he just wants to throw his weight about – show what an important chap he is, safe and sound on the ground while we risk our bloody necks.'

The strain was getting to him, she thought. He never used to sound so bitter. Never took any notice of wingless wonders like Flight Lieutenant Pilson, who'd never flown anything but a desk in his life. He looked very pale, with dark marks under his eyes like bruises, and these days he rarely smiled.

She touched his arm. 'You need a break. Haven't you got some leave due?'

'Well, we've moved up a couple of places on the roster since last night . . .' He was referring to the missing crews – obliquely.

'Will you go home?'

'I'd sooner go somewhere with you, Cat.'

It wasn't the first time he'd asked her and she'd always refused. This time she couldn't have gone anyway. 'I can't get leave at the moment, Peter. It's too busy.'

'Surely you could get a forty-eight at least?'

She shook her head. 'Honestly, I couldn't.'

He looked hard at her. 'You could if you really wanted.'

'I've told you, I can't.'

'And I don't believe you.'

'I'm sorry but it's the truth.'

He stared down into his beer. 'I want a lot more than just a quick forty-eight somewhere, Cat. I'm

38

talking about us being permanent. I want us to get engaged and married – asap. You know that. I've asked you enough times.'

'I still think we ought to wait, Peter.'

'Because I'll probably get the chop?'

'No, that's got nothing to do with it.'

'Then why won't you?'

She said truthfully, 'I don't know. I just think we should be very sure. We've only known each other six months.'

'*I'm* perfectly sure.'

'Please try to understand. Don't make it so difficult.'

'It's you who's making it difficult. So bloody complicated when it's perfectly simple.'

'Oh, *Peter* . . .'

'Oh, *Catherine*,' he mocked her, and then smiled suddenly. The tension went from his face and he looked more like his old self. A different person. 'Oh well, I suppose I'll just have to learn to be patient.'

She smiled, too, relieved at his changed mood.

More people had come into the bar, and among them she noticed the American pilot with one of the Code and Cypher WAAF officers. Fast worker, she thought. She couldn't see any of the rest of the crew, but then he wouldn't want them around on a date, cramping his style. She wondered what the others were up to and whether they'd stuck together like crews usually did.

'Lend us five bob, would you, Harry. Just till pay-day.'

'*Five bob!* What for?'

'I've asked this WAAF from Parachutes out to the flicks in Lincoln, see. A real smasher, she is.'

'You shouldn't've asked her, Bert, if you can't afford it.'

'Aw, come on, Harry. You were young – once.'

'I've forgotten what 'twas like.'

'You'll 'ave it back next pay-day.'

'Aye, that's what you said last time, and it was two of 'em before you coughed up, lad. I don't know what you do with your money, Bert. You never seem to 'ave any. You ought to learn to manage it a sight better. Save some of it. That's what we do up north.'

'Blimey, I didn't ask for a lecture, Harry. Just five bob. Come on, do us a favour. She's a corker!'

'I don't know . . . you and your girls, Bert. You'll 'ave to settle down one of these days and stop your larkin' about.'

''Ave an 'eart, mate, I'm only nineteen. Don't want to lock myself up for life yet, do I . . . not if I've got any sense. Got to get about a bit first. Find out what's what. Part of me education, see. Come on, be a sport.'

Harry sighed. 'All right. Just this time. But no more, mind.' He handed over two half-crowns and Bert was out of the door faster than a greyhound out of its starting gate, leaving him alone in the hut. The other crew sergeants they shared with were away on leave, and even Charlie had gone off somewhere.

He sat down on his iron bed, beneath the line of threadbare RAF blankets slung to dry from the roof. Without the other lads around, the place got him down. It was a right slum and no mistake: what with the blankets overhead, the greatcoats stuck on pegs all along the walls, muddy boots lying around, Stew's girlie magazines strewn over his mattress, tin-lid ashtrays overflowing with cigarette stubs, unwashed

Thermos flasks left under beds, a sorry collection of broken old chairs, the empty coal bucket upside down in a corner, an oil drum for a rubbish bin – over-flowing. No wonder they got rats.

They tidied it up now and again, but on an operational station nobody bothered much about inspections and bull like that. Too much else to worry about. And you didn't notice the mess when everyone was there. It was different then – with all the talk going on and the joking and leg-pulling and the laughs they had.

He picked up a tattered paperback from the floor. *No Orchids for Miss Blandish*. It fell open where the saucy bits were. They'd all read it in turn but he wasn't sure that Charlie ought to have read it at all. Personally, he hadn't thought much of the story, but he'd kept that to himself. He rubbed his hands together. It might be May but he could have done with a bit of warmth from the coke stove – if there'd been any fuel. He felt cold and depressed, and Bert had set him off thinking about things again, which never did any good. There was no girl he wanted to take out. Once bitten, twice shy, that was the trouble. Perhaps if he'd got about like Bert beforehand, he might have known better.

He sighed and took the creased snapshot of his ex-wife and their daughter out of his breast pocket and stared at it for a while. It had been taken more than four years ago when Paulette had only been a toddler; Rita was holding her in her arms, turning her round to face the camera. When he'd taken the picture the two of them had been all the world to him. Now, he didn't want to look at Rita at all because the sight always gave him pain, but he hadn't a photo of

Paulette on her own, so he couldn't look at one without the other.

When he'd first set eyes on Rita she'd been working in a tobacconist's shop in Leeds. He'd gone in for some cigarettes, in the days before he'd taken up a pipe, and she'd been standing there behind the counter – all dressed-up like she was going to a party in a white frock and rows of beads. He'd fallen in love with her there and then. He'd gone back a lot more times and bought a whole lot of cigarettes he didn't need before he'd finally screwed up the nerve to ask her out. It'd been a couple of years, though, before he'd found enough nerve to ask her to marry him. Luckily he'd had his steady job with the toy company and a bit put by, so he'd got something to offer, and Rita was tired of working in the tobacconist's shop. She liked nice things and it had cost him a tidy penny to keep her happy because she got bored and restless so easily. He hadn't minded, though. He'd thought she was worth it. And when Paulette had come along he'd felt like he was the luckiest bloke alive. He'd sooner have called the baby something simpler – Susan or Joan – but Rita had found the name in one of her film magazines and he'd gone along with it to please her, same as he always did.

Then Rita had met another man: someone from down south with much more money than he had and with a house for her and Paulette to live in, not a poky rented flat. And that had been that. He'd let her divorce him because she'd said it would be best for Paulette, and he sent money regularly as clockwork for his daughter's maintenance. But he hardly ever saw her. At first he'd tried travelling down south every fortnight or so and taking Paulette out for a day, but after a time he'd come to realize that his daughter dreaded his visits. She hated wandering around the park, or sitting in tea-rooms, or doing any of the things he tried to think of that might please her, and when he returned her to the posh house in the avenue, she always ran in without a backward glance, as though she couldn't get away from him quick enough.

Sometimes he wondered what Rita had said about him to her, what stories she might have made up to set his daughter so much against him. One thing was very clear to him: he wasn't wanted in their lives any more and, except for the payments, he wasn't needed. He'd kept on visiting doggedly, but less often, and the older Paulette grew, the more she showed her contempt for him. Then the war had started and he had joined up. He'd given up the flat and spent his leaves at his parents' semi on the outskirts of Huddersfield, sleeping on a divan in the bleak little spare room. He'd only seen Paulette half a dozen times in the past two years.

Harry went on staring at the photo for a while before he put it away in his pocket. He pulled himself together. No point in dwelling on things. It wouldn't do any good. Brace up and cheer up. The hut was no place to spend an evening so he'd pop along to the Mess and sink a pint or two. Maybe Jock and Stew were there. Funny about young Charlie sloping off like that on his own. Maybe he'd got some girl on the quiet, too. Happen the lad would surprise them all.

Charlie got off his bike at the cottage gate. There was no name on it but it had a blue front door like Mum had said in her letter, and it was in the right place, on the other side of the drome. He leaned the bike against the front hedge and padlocked it so nobody could nick it while he was inside. As he pushed open the gate, the door opened.

'Hallo, Charlie.'

'Hallo, Mum.'

They stood looking at each other for a moment and then he moved forward quickly and gave her a hug. She searched his face. 'You're not angry with me?'

'*Angry*? Why would I be?'

'I know I shouldn't have done it – not without telling you, anyway. Without asking you. You might not want me here.'

'It's all right,' he said gently. 'I don't mind. I'm glad you're here. It's all right.'

The worry and guilt left her face and she smiled at him. 'Well, come on in, then. It's not much of a place, but I've given it a good clean and made it as nice as I can.'

He followed her inside and looked round the dingy little front room. He could tell how hard she'd tried. There was a smell of furniture polish and Brasso and carbolic, all mixed up with a fusty smell of damp, and jam jars of bluebells on the table and the mantle-piece and the windowsill. Upstairs, in what was, apparently, to be his bedroom, she had somehow transported some of his books, an old model aeroplane he'd made years ago, even – he blushed to notice – his old teddy bear, propped against the pillow on the bed. She picked it up.

'I know it's silly of me, but I thought he might make a mascot for you. I read in the newspaper that air crews have all kinds of lucky things they take with them – some of them toys – and I thought of Sam.'

She held out the bear to him and he took it

awkwardly. It had one ear and one glass eye missing and most of its light brown fur had been rubbed away. Sam had once gone everywhere with him – dragged by ear, arm or leg – badly treated for nearly seven years and, for the last ten, forgotten in some cupboard. He'd have to think of some excuse to leave him here. It was bad enough with the poems; if he turned up with a teddy bear he'd never hear the end of it.

Mum cooked him a huge supper of sausages and potatoes with baked beans and fried bread – far more than he wanted, but he managed it to please her. She didn't eat much herself, but then she never had. She kept on smiling and talking as they sat at the table, but he knew she must be worrying about him, and he didn't know what to say to comfort her. The fact was he could get the chop easily any day – with or without Sam.

She wanted to know about the rest of the crew, and what they were like.

'Oh, just ordinary sort of blokes,' he said.

'Is the pilot good?'

He thought of the skipper's kangaroo landings and some scary moments in the air. 'One of the best. He's American.'

'*American?*' She looked astonished. 'That's not ordinary. What's he doing with the RAF?'

'Not quite sure. He joined the Canadian Air Force and they sent him over. Our bomb aimer's Australian.'

'My goodness, he's come a long way as well.'

'There's quite a lot of Aussies in the crews. And New Zealanders. And Canadians. Some South Africans, too. From all over.'

'Goodness,' she said again. 'I'd no idea. What about the rest of your crew?'

'Well, one's Scottish – the flight engineer. But

45

the other four of us are English – the navigator, the wireless operator, the mid-upper gunner and me.'

She fiddled with the salt cruet. 'They didn't tease you – about my coming here? I wouldn't want that, Charlie.'

'Of course they didn't,' he said stoutly.

But the truth was that he hadn't told them, and he felt ashamed of that. He hadn't told them because he was afraid they'd pull his leg and that it'd get all over the camp. Charlie Banks's mum has come to hold his hand for him . . . He wished to goodness she hadn't come here, for both their sakes. It was going to make it twice as hard for him, knowing she was alone in this run-down place, and twice as hard for her, seeing and hearing the bombers coming and going the whole time. Probably counting them out and back.

'I'm just a bit worried about you, Mum, that's all. Being here on your own, not knowing anybody. I won't be able to get off the station to see you that much, and we only get leave every six weeks.'

'I'm going to get a job. They told me in the village shop that they want extra help in the kitchens up at that big army camp over the way. Shift work for civilians.'

'I don't like the idea of you going there.'

'I can't sit and twiddle my thumbs, can I? Not when everyone's doing their bit.'

He tried again. 'But what about leaving it empty at home?'

'The neighbours are keeping an eye on the house for me. And it'll only be for six months, or so, won't it? Just while you're doing your tour.'

'It depends,' he said. 'It could be longer or shorter.

46

It's according to how much we're stood down, with bad weather and everything.' He thought of something else, too. 'The Germans might bomb the station. It's not safe here for you, so near.'

She looked at him across the table. 'It's not very safe for you either, is it, Charlie? If you can take risks, so can I.'

He gave up then. There was going to be nothing he could say to persuade her to go back home to Bromley.

It was dark when he left the cottage, and she came to the gate to see him off on his bike. There was a half moon and a whole lot of stars. He could hear the noise of a lone Lanc taxiing out on the airfield – some blokes doing a Night Flying Test.

'Haven't you got a front light, Charlie?'

'Someone pinched it. Everything gets pinched if you don't watch out. I can see enough by the moon. Just have to hope I don't run into a copper.' He gave her a hug and a kiss. ''Bye then, Mum. I'll get over again as soon as I can.'

'Are you – are you going off anywhere soon?'

'I don't know. They don't tell us till the day.' He swung his leg over the saddle. 'Promise you won't worry? I'll be all right.'

'I promise.'

He started off slowly, trying to see his way ahead. Then she called out to him to wait and her footsteps hurried down the road after him.

'You forgot Sam.'

'Mum, I don't think—'

She was thrusting the bear at him. 'He'll look after you, Charlie. Bring you good luck.'

He rode away in the darkness with the bear dangling by one arm from the handlebars.

Three

'The fish tasted off at dinner, Miss Frost.'

'I'm so sorry, Mrs Mountjoy. I'll speak to the chef about it.'

'I insist on seeing Miss Hargreaves. She must be told.'

'I'm afraid she's not here at the moment, Mrs Mountjoy. She's gone out.'

She hadn't, in fact. Miss Hargreaves seldom went out in the evenings at all. She spent them up in her private sitting-room, listening to the wireless, and with strict instructions that she was only to be disturbed if one of the guests died or the hotel caught fire.

'Well, would you please inform me the minute that she returns.'

'Yes, of course, Mrs Mountjoy.'

'Fortunately, I only ate a small piece but when I told that useless head waiter about it, he didn't seem to take the slightest notice. If you're not careful you could have a food poisoning outbreak on your hands. It wouldn't do the hotel any good at all.'

'I'll go and deal with it at once, Mrs Mountjoy.'

'See that you do.'

Honor watched the old woman waddle her way into the Residents' Lounge, leaning heavily on her ebony stick. Mrs Mountjoy found something to complain about almost every day, in fact, complaining was

48

probably the only thing that kept her alive. She appeared to be completely alone in the world or, if she had any relatives, they certainly never came to see her. If she hadn't been such a difficult, cantankerous creature Honor might have felt sorry for her.

She left the reception desk and walked across the hall towards the dining-room. So long as she didn't have to hurry she could manage to walk so her limp hardly noticed.

Cedric, the head waiter, who was probably even older than Mrs Mountjoy, was bumbling about while Peggy, the new waitress, was serving soup timidly to a table of RAF officers. One of them was teasing her, making her wobble the plate and spill some of the soup as she set it before him. In the kitchens, beyond the swing doors, the chef was furious at any suggestion that his plaice fillets were off. He waved one of them under Honor's nose, swinging it by its slimy tail.

'Fresh in this morning. The very idea!'

She went back to the reception desk to find the phone ringing. 'The Angel Hotel . . .'

Somebody wanted to book a room and when she had dealt with that, Colonel Millis, the other elderly resident, announced that he had lost his room key, which meant a major search before it was discovered in his pocket.

The grandfather clock in the hall struck eight. She was supposed to go off duty at six but it was sometimes as late as nine before she left. The advertisement had been for a receptionist/secretary, but the truth was that Miss Hargreaves had wanted a maid-of-all-work. She answered the telephone, took the bookings, typed the letters, made out the bills, ordered the provisions, did the laundry lists, saw to the black-out, wound the clocks, watered the potted plants, stoked the fires, served behind the bar, helped lay the tables, made up the staff wages, calmed down the chef, dealt with the complaints. Miss Hargreaves sat in her private sitting-room upstairs, issuing orders like the captain of a ship, while Honor ran about the decks. Well, limped about them.

She was typing a letter when she heard the bombers. She stopped to listen to their distant drone, her fingers motionless on the keys, and thought of the men in them. It made her shudder to think of how they might have to die. She waited until the sound had died away before she went on typing.

The target was Mannheim and they were carrying a four-thousand-pound cookie, three thousand-pounders and thirteen canisters of incendiaries. The route took them across the Thames and out over the Channel by Beachy Head. The chalk cliffs were unmistakable, so Piers must have done his sums right for a change. On the last trip, to Duisburg, he'd used the wrong Gee co-ordinates and they'd gone waltzing off in completely the wrong direction. It had taken them a long time to catch up with the bomber stream.

He flicked down his mike switch. 'Pilot to crew. Let's have an intercom check, guys.'

They all acknowledged, except Charlie.

'Pilot to rear gunner. Can you hear me, Charlie?'

'Sorry, skipper. Yes.'

The kid always sounded self-conscious over the intercom – still wasn't comfortable saying his bit. He'd better speak up a lot smarter than that in an emergency. Piers gave him a new course at Boulogne and they turned eastwards on the long leg to Mannheim.

He scanned the luminous needles flickering on the dials in front of him and kept a sharp look-out for other aircraft, for the tell-tale blue glimmer from exhaust stubs that stopped you running into some other kite. Too bad it helped enemy night fighters as well. Whenever he caught sight of them on another bomber, glowing away like beckoning beacons, he thought, Christ, that's what *we* look like. *We're over here, Jerry. Come and get us. You can't miss.*

After three hours, the Rhine lay below instead of the Thames, equally identifiable in the clear, moon-lit night. Jolly good show, Piers! Bang on! Simply spiffing! The expected searchlights were ahead, milk-white beams sweeping to and fro, and flak explosions sparkled in the sky. Kind of pretty, from a safe distance. No Jerry fighters to worry about: the gunners wouldn't want to shoot down their own planes. But if the fighters don't get you, the flak will, or the other way around.

Still hard to believe this was for real: that down there a whole lot of folks were hell-bent on killing them. Nothing personal. It was all the same to them which British bomber they shot down, which crew they got. Nothing personal about the bombs they were going to drop on them, either.

They'd been wallowing along bumpily in the wake turbulence of an aircraft when a sudden shoot of flame appeared ahead, streaming earthwards like a comet's tail. He saw black twin-fins spiralling. A Lanc. *Jesus Christ, seven guys in there.* It was for real, all right.

He pressed his mike switch. Make it very cool and calm. Matter-of-fact. The tough skipper. 'Lanc going down on fire on the starboard bow. Log it, will you, navigator?'

'Roger.' Piers sounded shocked.

Van strained his eyes but couldn't see any parachutes. The comet was plunging fast, down and down and down, until it exploded far below in a big orange ball. Seven guys with no chance.

They started their run-in, weaving through the flak bursts. Shell shrapnel rattled on the fuselage and the stink of explosive clogged his nostrils. K-King was rocking and shaking violently; he gripped the control wheel harder. Nothing, he thought, prepared you for this, for flying straight into hell. Nobody could give you a clue what it was like to have to serve yourself up on a platter to the Jerries. Piers' mike clicked on, giving him a small course alteration, and he swung the wheel and touched the rudders, acknowledging. The Lanc headed straight for the target.

The flak was exploding all around them like some crazy Fourth of July party that had got way out of hand. Searchlight beams dazzled his eyes, wrecking his night vision. He flew the bomber as straight and level as he could and forced himself to concentrate on Stew's instructions: to blot out everything else, including his own terror. Do exactly as Stew was telling him in his ears.

'Left, left. Steady . . . Left, left . . . Holy shit! Dummy run. Sorry, skip. Have to go round again.'

Christ almighty, Stew had screwed up, goddamn him! They'd gone over the target without dropping a single bomb, and now they had to go round and fly through all the fucking flak again. He made a wide circle, teeth gritted, eyes peeled for other Lancs, and began a second run. This time the flak was even worse; they were probably the main target of every Hun battery within range. He was almost beyond fear now. Almost calm. 'Get rid of them this time, Stew.'

'Left, left . . . steady, steady, steady . . . Bombs gone, skip! Bomb doors closed.'

K-King, released from the heavy load of bombs, bobbed upwards, buoyant as a cork. Van closed the bomb doors and turned her hard to port, diving away from hell. They headed home to England.

Piers was dog-tired but he couldn't sleep. The noise of the engines was still ringing in his ears, but that wasn't what was keeping him awake. It was the thought that he'd messed things up so badly on the way back. Everything had gone absolutely fine until after they had crossed the English coast. Then somehow it had gone all wrong, and the G-box lattice lines that should have guided them straight to Beningby had led them miles away. Actually, *he* had, of course. He must have misread the signals. Made a complete hash of it all yet again. In the end, the skipper had had to put down at another airfield and ask where they were. The chaps there had thought it was frightfully funny. The others had been really decent about it, considering they were all pretty wacked and should have been home ages before.

Bert had clapped him on the shoulder. 'Put it this way, mate, we're just bloody glad to be back at all.'

God, that was true enough. He hadn't seen the flak or the searchlights, or any of it, closeted away behind his blackout curtain, but the Lanc had been thrown about all over the place and it had been jolly un-comfortable and frightening until they'd got clear of things.

He'd found out that the downed Lanc he'd entered

53

in the log had been B-Baker. He'd had a bit of a chin-wag in the locker room beforehand with their navigator who'd seemed a really decent type. When B-Baker's crew had got off the crew bus at their kite, the nav had given him a wry sort of grin and a thumbs-up. He kept seeing his face and the grin . . . kept remembering exactly how he'd looked as he went. Blot it out. Don't think about it, or about the shrapnel hits he'd noticed all over the fuselage of their own kite when they'd got back. It could have been them. Instead of lying safe and sound on his bed, back in England, he might just as easily have been a charred corpse lying somewhere in Germany. Or simply blown to bits with nothing left for anyone to find. *God, stop thinking about it . . .*

Well, they'd all been scared – not just him. He'd heard the fear in their voices over the intercom. *All* of them, even Stew. The other crews hadn't seemed to think it was a specially dicey trip, though. 'You ain't seen nothin' yet,' one chap had said to him. 'You wait.'

After the de-briefing, he'd tackled Van as soon as they'd got back to the cubicle they shared in the officers' hut. It was the only decent thing to do – to offer to get transferred. Give them the chance to get another navigator.

Van, tugging off his tie, had brushed the suggestion aside. 'Forget it, Piers, you were tired. We all were. None of us had been in the air that long before. We're just rookies. Look at Stew's dummy run. He screwed up like hell. But we'll cut it better in time – I hope.' With that, Van had fallen into his bed and gone straight to sleep, putting an end to any further discussion.

He *had* been very tired, but it seemed a poor excuse. He'd be tired again on the next op, most likely, and he couldn't keep letting them down. He'd simply *got* to do better.

Piers closed his eyes. B-Baker's navigator's face was there again, grinning wryly.

'You sneakin' off, Charlie?'

'Thought I'd just take a bike ride, Bert.'

'Got a popsie tucked away somewhere, then?'

''Course not.'

'No 'course not about it. You're gettin' a big boy now. Time you found out all about the birds an' bees. Ain't that right, Stew?'

'Yeah . . . not your birds, though, sport. That sheila of yours has lost a sight too many feathers.'

'Blimey, look who's talkin' . . .'

No ops tonight and they were all in good moods. Stew had got a food parcel from home and was sharing it around: cans of condensed milk and meat and cheese, and bars of chocolate. 'Long as it's not kangaroo, mate,' Bert had told him, inspecting a tin. They'd all been writing letters, or reading, or chatting, or arguing, and Charlie thought he'd be able to get away out of the hut without any of them really noticing. No such luck. They'd all stopped whatever they were doing now and were watching him as he went to get his cap out of his locker. He felt himself going red in the face.

'I reckon it *is* a girl,' said Bert, ''e's blushin'. Red as a beetroot, 'e is. Who is she, Charlie? Hope it's not Two-Ton-Tessie. She'll flatten you like a bloomin' pancake.'

They all laughed loudly at that. The WAAF driver

was three times his size and weighed about fifteen stone.

'Come on, spill the beans, Charlie, boy,' Stew flicked over the pages of one of his magazines full of naked women. 'What's her name?'

'Bet it *is* Tessie an' all.' Bert was chortling away. 'Cor, fancy our Charlie takin' 'er on.'

'Leave him alone, lads,' Harry said. 'Give him a bit of peace.'

But he knew it was going to be hopeless to hide it from them. They were going to find out sooner or later and it might as well be sooner. He couldn't help it if they pulled his leg and thought him a mummy's boy. Better to tell them straight out. 'It's not a girl,' he said. 'It's my mother. She's rented a cottage just near. I'm going to see her.'

There was silence in the hut and the four of them stared at him. Pins dropping could have been heard easy as anything. Let them laugh, he thought. I don't care.

'You taking the mickey?' Stew looked incredulous.

He shook his head.

Jock said quietly, 'She must care a lot about you. I reckon you're a lucky lad.'

'Can't see my old woman doing that,' Bert agreed.

'Good on you, kid,' Stew added, though more doubtfully. 'Off you go.'

He fumbled in the locker for his cap and as he did so Sam fell out of his hiding place onto the floor. Harry, who was the nearest, picked up the teddy bear. There was another silence. 'Yours, Charlie?'

'Mum brought him with her,' he said desperately. 'She thought he'd bring good luck.'

Harry held the bear aloft, showing him round the

56

hut. 'What do you say, lads? Let's make him our mascot. Take him along with us.'

There was unanimous agreement. Nobody seemed to care about the one ear and one eye.

'That's settled, then. Got a name, 'as he?'

'Sam.'

'Well, Sam's one of us now,' Harry announced. 'And I reckon he'll see us through.'

The mustard had gone all lumpy. No matter how hard she stirred it, the lumps wouldn't go away. Old Mr Cedric, the head waiter, wouldn't notice because he was half-blind, not to mention him fancying a drop, but Miss Hargreaves would if she did one of her snap inspections, and the guests might complain, especially Mrs Mountjoy. She thought wildly of throwing the whole lot away, but you couldn't do that with everything so scarce. Maybe if she went on stirring and stirring it would get better.

Miss Frost came into the dining-room. 'Is everything all right, Peggy? Do you want a hand with anything?'

She liked Miss Frost. She was always helping out, and you could trust her not to sneak to Miss Hargreaves. It must be awful having a crooked foot like that, with people staring at you all the time.

'It's the mustard, miss. It's gone lumpy.'

'Let me see. Oh, dear . . . I think we'll have to try getting rid of them with a whisk.'

Miss Frost fetched a whisk and another bowl and, working with a little of the mustard mixture at a time, smoothed out the lumps like magic.

'There you are. Next time, the way to do it is only to add a very little water at first and mix it well in before you add any more. Then you won't get lumps.'

'Thank you, miss.'

Peggy spooned the mustard carefully into the little pots and set them on the dining-room tables, together with the salt and pepper cruets. She arranged them in neat groups beside the vases of flowers in the centre of each table. Then she laid out the cutlery, cleaning off any spot marks with the corner of her apron.

When she'd first started a week ago she hadn't really known how to do anything much and she didn't think Miss Hargreaves would have given her the job if it hadn't been so hard to get help these days, with the war on. She had stared at her across her desk as though she didn't like what she saw one bit.

'How old are you?'

'Sixteen, madam.'

'Have you had any experience of waitressing?'

'No, madam. But I'm sure I could learn quick.'

Miss Hargreaves had frowned. 'You're very young for the post. My residents are accustomed to a high standard of service, and so are our non-resident diners. We have high-ranking officers coming here in the evenings.'

'I think I could manage, madam.'

'Hmm.'

In the end, she'd got the job and Mum had been pleased. Although it meant she wouldn't be home to help so much, there'd be a bit more money coming in.

She finished laying the cutlery and put out the table napkins in front of each place. Miss Frost had shown her how to fold them so they stood up like little wigwams. There was a strong smell of frying onions coming from the kitchens, to go with the liver on the lunch menu, and a lot of clattering and banging of pots and pans, too, which meant the chef was in another bad mood. She went round the tables again, checking to make sure she hadn't forgotten anything. She checked Mrs Mountjoy's table three times. Mrs Mountjoy insisted on everything being just so and she made a big song and dance if it wasn't.

The bombers were busy today. They'd been roaring around overhead while she'd been doing the laying – practising, she supposed. One was going over so low that it was making everything rattle – knives and forks and spoons and glasses jingling and tinkling on the tables. She ran to the window and looked out in time to see it flying past, a great black thing with huge wings and a long tail, like a fish with a fin sticking up each side. She could see guns poking out of the glass bit at the end.

There'd probably be some Air Force officers in again tonight and that made her nervous to think of. They were nice enough gentlemen, but they kept teasing her so she got in a fluster and made mistakes. She gave a last look at the tables and then hurried into the hall to the big brass gong standing in its corner by the stairs. It was her job to ring it for meals and she liked making it boom loudly. Before she could hit the first note, Mrs Mountjoy came stomping out of the Residents' Lounge, looking at her wristwatch.

'Five minutes late, girl. Can't you tell the time? Well, what's it for luncheon today, then? Not fish again, I hope.'

The cottage garden was a terrible mess: weeds and long, rank grass and overgrown shrubs. Dorothy could hardly see what plants there were for it all. Still, it would be nice to get it a bit tidy, for Charlie's sake –

more like home – and she could watch the bombers coming and going while she was out there working. She found an old fork and spade in a shed near the outside privy, and made a start on the small patch at the front. After a while she began to uncover the remains of what must once have been a pretty little garden with lupins and poppies and hollyhocks. She cleared away the tangled growth from around the plants, making a big pile of weeds on the brick pathway. From time to time she stopped to watch a bomber taking off or landing over on the aerodrome, wondering if it was Charlie's plane and if it was him up there, sitting in the tail turret with the guns, testing everything like he'd told her they had to do.

The old labourer from the farm up the road went by the gate. He'd stopped to pass the time of day with her before when she was beating the carpets outside, and he did so again, lifting his cap.

''Afternoon, Mrs Banks. Warm today.' He squinted up at the sun overhead. 'Wouldn't be surprised if we don't have a nice summer.'

She didn't know his name, but he knew hers. She was a stranger to the area, so they were all curious about her, of course, but she hadn't said anything about Charlie.

'Doin' some gardenin', then?' he went on. 'Bit of a job that for a young lady like you.'

People always took her for younger than she was. She wondered what he'd say if he knew she had a son serving in the RAF. 'I thought I'd try to tidy it up.'

'More weeds than flowers, I'd say. I could let you have some seeds, if you like. Fill in the gaps.'

'Could you really? I'd pay for them, of course.'

'They're spare,' he said. 'No payment needed. Plannin' on stayin' a while, then?'

'Six months or so, I expect.'

'Well, safer than down south – long as the Jerries don't take it into their heads to pay the aerodrome a visit. Too close for comfort, that'd be.'

He went on speaking, but the roar of a bomber taking off at that moment drowned his words. She put up her hand to shield her eyes and watched it climb into the sky.

'. . . always feared one'll fall on the farm,' the old man was saying, as the sound died away. 'I've seen 'em crash comin' back, all shot-up. An' t'other week one blew up takin' off with the bombs. You could see the blaze for miles . . . Weren't nothin' left but little bits. An' there's lots go off an' don't ever come back. More an' more, so they say, with all the guns those Jerries've got. Down they come over there, poor lads, an' that's the finish of 'em, 'less they're lucky.'

'Excuse me,' she said. 'I'm a bit thirsty. I think I'll get a drink of water.' She fled inside the cottage and stood leaning against the wall, waiting for him to go away and for the sickness inside her to pass, the trembling to stop. After a few moments she went to get some water from the kitchen tap and gulped it down. When she felt better she went back outside.

The old man had gone and another bomber was taking off. She remembered something else that Charlie had told her – that they always tested the planes on the day of an operation to make sure they were working all right. It meant they must be going tonight. Charlie might not be going with them, of course. It might not be his crew's turn, in which case there was nothing to worry about. He might even manage to get over this evening, just for a while. Or he might not. She might never see him again. *Lots go off an' don't ever come back.* That's what the old man had said. *More an' more of them.*

Stop it, she told herself sternly. Stop it this minute, Dorothy. You promised Charlie you wouldn't worry. You've got to stop thinking like this or you'll be nothing but a nuisance to him. He'll be all right. He's got a good crew, hasn't he? That's what he said. And he's got Sam now, and Sam'll bring him luck.

The waiting around always made them nervy. After the air test there was nothing much to do but hang about the station until briefing in the evening. No leaving base, no phone calls, no outside world.

Van wrote a letter home full of the usual lies. *Everything fine . . . great food . . . easy trips . . . home soon . . .* He doubted if they'd believe it but he could hardly give them the true facts: *everything stinks . . . filthy food . . . suicidal missions . . . unlikely ever to come home again . . .*

He'd thought several times of writing some kind of 'last farewell letter' to leave in his drawer in case he didn't come back, but had torn up the attempts. He wasn't sure what he could say that might make things easier for them and so he'd shirked the whole thing. He wondered if any of the others had written letters. Not Piers, he thought. Not quite the done thing. In the photographs that Piers had shown him of his parents, they had looked typically reserved English to their upper-class backbones: the mother in evening dress and jewels, the father in some kind of fancy army dress uniform with a row of medals. Not a glimmer of a smile on either face. If Piers got the chop, the upper lips would stay stiff without any embarrassing emotional outpourings from their son. He couldn't imagine Stew writing one either: *what the hell d'you take me for skip?* Or Jock, who never spoke of his family at all. Or Harry, whose wife had flown the coop. Or Bert, who'd never been seen writing any kind of letter to anyone. The only one who might have done was the kid, Charlie, to his mother; maybe with one of his poems.

He wandered out later to watch some guys playing cricket out on the Flight Line. Somebody had once tried to explain the rules to him, but he was none the wiser. Football was his game, but American football, not the kind they played over here. Watching the slow progress of the cricket match, he felt an outsider witnessing some unfathomable native ritual, beyond him to appreciate. It wasn't the first time he'd felt like that.

He biked over to the ops block for the briefing. The crews were already filing in through the double doors, and as he propped the bike against the wall, Stew came freewheeling up to park his with a crash.

'Got a nasty feeling about this one, skip.'

'Yeah . . . so've I.'

The rest of the crew were already sitting in what had now become their place. The curtain covered the map on the wall, concealing the target, and there was the usual guessing game taking place: Hamburg? Cologne? Rostock? Kiel? Beside him, Stew, cigarette parked in the corner of his mouth, started doodling in his notebook with his pencil, crude female outlines all down the margin.

They smoked and they waited. The Nissen hut buzzed with chat, and tobacco smoke thickened overhead like a London fog. The atmosphere was getting more tense by the minute. Towards the front, Van caught sight of the WAAF intelligence officer he'd noticed at de-briefing: not a hair out of place, not a sign of feeling. She was talking to the senior IO and he could guess how her voice would sound – a female version of Piers.

With the arrival of the Station Commander and Squadron Commander, the crews lurched to their feet, chair legs screeching. The Group Captain made his way between the rows towards his armchair below the platform. 'Be seated, gentlemen.'

More screeching and scraping and another, quieter, buzz of talk, dying away to an anxious silence. Men waiting to hear their sentence, Van thought. Prisoners in the dock, trying to disguise their dread. The curtain covering the wall map was tugged back to show the long piece of red tape pinned across it from England to Germany. Muttering from all round the room and some groans.

The Senior Intelligence Officer took the stage, pointer in hand. 'Tonight, gentlemen, you will be making history. The RAF is sending the largest number of bombers ever assembled to Germany.' The pointer tapped the map briskly. 'More than a thousand aircraft will converge on the city of Cologne to inflict the maximum possible damage to the enemy . . .'

Stew chucked down his pencil. 'Stone the bloody crows! Told you so, skip.'

'Are you for the flying meal, sir?'

'Oh, yes, rather. Thanks.'

The WAAF waitress smiled at Piers as she set the

plate of egg, sausages and chips before him. He didn't think he had the appetite to eat it, which would be a most frightful waste.

A thousand bombers! Lancs, Wimpeys, Stirlings, Halifaxes, Hamdens, Manchesters. It would be a miracle if they didn't collide with one of them, and no hope of taking the Huns by surprise. Navigation had given them a route to keep them well clear of the main flak barrage on the run-in. He'd written everything down, concentrating like fury, but if he got it wrong this time . . .

'Tea, sir?'

'Thanks awfully.'

They were always nice to you at flying suppers because they knew it might be your last meal ever, and he smiled back to show he wasn't a bit worried. He gulped down a mouthful of gristly sausage and drank some of the strong tea.

Two-Ton-Tessie drove them out to dispersal. Charlie was squashed up at one end of the bench in the back of the Bedford. They took up a lot of room in their bulky flying clothes, with their parachute packs and satchels. Next to him, Harry took up more than most, being so big, and with the pigeon in its yellow carrier on his knee as well. The pigeon was poking its head out of the hole, having a good look round. Just as well it didn't know where it was going.

Charlie was sweating uncomfortably in his thick suit, though that wouldn't last long once they'd taken off. As usual, he'd got the butterflies. To his way of thinking, this was the worst bit: just before you went, when you started to think about everything being the last time for something. Your last meal; your last cigarette – he'd got used to smoking now, and he'd almost got used to drinking beer too; your last view of England.

'Gum, Charlie, lad?' Harry was offering a piece of Wrigleys. Sam was tucked inside his Mae West, head sticking out like the pigeon.

'Thanks.' He chewed away as they swayed round the peri track. Like a cow chewing cud. Chomp, chomp, chomp. But somehow it calmed you down. He had his own gum, together with his bar of chocolate and his tin of orange juice and his barley sugar, as well as a flask of hot coffee and a sandwich, though last time the bread had gone so dry and curled up, he'd fed it to somebody's dog when he'd got back.

The Bedford came to a halt by the dispersal pan.

'All change for Cologne,' Bert sang out, as though he were a bus conductor. Nothing seemed to worry Bert.

Charlie jumped down out of the back of the truck, hauling his gear with him. D-Dog was waiting for them on the concrete pan, her bomb doors hanging open. Two fitters up on a gantry were still doing last-minute work on her starboard inner. Seen like this, from down on the ground, a Lanc always looked enormous. It still amazed him to think that she was going to soar up into the skies and carry them all the way to Germany and back – if they were lucky, that is.

He didn't know if he really believed in luck, but a lot of them did. When they'd been in the locker room Bert had nudged him and shown him a silk stocking he was wearing round his neck that Emerald, one of the WAAFS in Parachute Section, had given him for luck, and Stew always carried his Zippo lighter on ops. He'd seen other crews carrying all kinds of mascots –

66

charms and rabbits' feet and toys – and wearing funny things like cowboy boots, lucky scarves, even a top hat. They spat on the tail wheel and peed on it, touched or didn't touch things, got into the kite in a certain order, and one rear gunner had told him he always turned round three times before he went into the turret.

Harry, who had taken charge of Sam, was going to hang him up just inside the rear door. The idea, he had explained very seriously, was that everybody touched him in turn as they got in, which meant that Harry always had to get in first.

Charlie picked up his parachute pack, about to follow the others, when Two-Ton-Tessie leaned out of the truck window and called to him, beckoning. She wouldn't get out, he knew, because that was another superstitious thing. The crews didn't like the WAAFS on the dispersal pans – it was unlucky. He went over to the truck, but reluctantly, because he knew he'd be teased about it.

She smiled at him, but it was a motherly smile. Not the sort that Bert's Emerald gave. 'Thought this might help, Charlie. Make it a bit more comfortable for you.' She was offering him a cushion made of some flowered material with a frill all round the edge. He tried to refuse but she thrust it at him out of the window. From its squashed look he realized she must have been sitting on it when she was driving.

He said awkwardly, 'Thanks. I'll give it back.'

'No, keep it – till the end of your tour.' She stuck up her thumb with another smile, but she wouldn't actually wish him good luck in so many words because that was unlucky, too.

The fitters had come down and wheeled the gantry

away and Bert was waiting for him by the crew door, crushing his last fag out under his flying boot – one of Charlie's fags, in fact. Bert seemed to have more of them than he did. They weren't supposed to smoke near the aircraft, but Bert never took much notice of rules like that.

He looked at the cushion, grinning his monkey grin. 'Told you she fancies you, Charlie.' He prodded the cushion. 'Cor, you know where *that's* been, don't you? Still warm, an' all.'

He climbed up the short metal ladder after Bert, glad of the fading light that helped to hide his red face. D-Dog had been standing in the sun all day since the air test in the morning and it was still warm inside the fuselage. She smelled of glycol and petrol – the smell of all Lancasters, but her own particular one. Each aircraft, he'd found, smelled a bit different. You could almost tell D-Dog, say, from S-Sugar or R-Robert with your eyes shut, just by your nose.

Sam was hanging there by the crew door and he touched him on his one ear before he clambered his way aft in the darkness of the fuselage, past the Elsan, up over the tail spar and through the flimsy doors to the tail turret entry. He parked his chute and his Thermos flask and sandwiches outside the open turret doors and put the flowered cushion in place on the seat. Then he grasped the two handgrips in the fuselage roof to hoist his legs up and into the turret, ducking his head as the rest of him followed. With the steel doors shut behind him, he felt quite snug, sitting on the soft cushion.

After a while, he heard the engines firing, one after another, and the plane shook and shivered as they roared into life. He unlocked the turret and rotated it, twisting the handgrips to raise and lower the guns and sight. Everything OK.

The skipper's voice came over, checking the inter-com. 'Rear gunner OK,' he answered smartly in his turn. As they joined the procession of Lancs trundling along the perimeter track, he swivelled the turret and its loaded guns away from the aircraft behind them. Near the start of the main runway they stopped, waiting in the queue to take off – the part that always scared him most. The tail would unstick when they'd got going full-tilt so he'd be airborne before anybody else, so to speak. But he couldn't tell when they'd really left the ground, he just had to sit there and say his prayers.

D-Dog rolled forward and swung round to face the runway.

'Pilot to rear gunner. All clear behind?'

'All clear, skipper.'

He settled himself and waited.

Jock kept his left hand close to the skipper's hand on the throttles, ready to take them. They were running straight and approaching flying speed.

'Full power, Jock.'

'Full power.'

Timed exactly right, he slid his hand smoothly under the skipper's and took over the throttles, push-ing them to the gate and clamping them. Van had both hands on the control wheel now, easing it back, and the Lanc was off the ground, the concrete runway falling away.

'Undercart up.'

'Undercart up.'

At eight hundred feet, flaps up and trimmed, D-Dog

was climbing smoothly and steadily. No problems on this one. Not a moment's worry. The skipper was improving, he had to admit that. Maybe one day he'd even manage a decent landing.

Stew was down in the bomb aimer's compartment in the nose, through the opening by Jock's feet. Officially, he was supposed to stand behind them for take-off and landing, but Van turned a blind eye. If he'd been skipper, Jock would have insisted on it but the Yanks were slacker about things, he reckoned, not so disciplined. For himself, he preferred to stick to all the rules – everything to be done exactly by the book. There was usually good reason for it.

As each bomber took off, Dorothy waved a piece of white cloth torn from an old sheet. There were so many planes going that she was sure Charlie must be in one of them, and there was just a chance that he might be able to see it. Maybe she ought to have tied it to the end of a stick, but it was too late now. They were taking off so quickly, one straight after the other, that there wasn't time. The noise went on and on until she could bear it no longer and had to stop waving the cloth and put her hands over her ears.

She stayed by the garden gate long after the last bomber had gone, listening to the silence and watching the empty sky darken. Sleep would be impossible. She must stay awake to be sure to hear the first one returning so she would know if they'd all got back safely. It was only later on that she realized that, with all the noise, she had completely forgotten to count them.

* * *

70

Stew had seen the flutter of white below as the Lanc clambered skywards. The Perspex blister in the nose gave him a bonza view and he thought he had the best bloody place on the kite. And the take-off was the best bloody bit of all. It gave him a real thrill to be right out in front when they went roaring down the runway. Got to him every time, deep in his guts: the surge, the speed, the power, the climb, the earth falling away . . .

He watched Lincolnshire recede and finally disappear. His control panel was right beside him and the front turret with the two Browning guns immediately above. He could stand up and grab the triggers in two shakes if any bastard Jerry fighter showed up.

Charlie's voice came over the intercom: 'Rear gunner to skipper. There's another Lanc right behind us.'

'Roger, Charlie. Watch him, will you. Let me know if he gets any closer. Pilot to crew: keep a good look-out, guys. There's a hell of a lot of kites about.'

Too bloody right, Stew thought. And over the target it's going to be fucking murder with them *and* the Jerries to worry about. On top of that, he'd be worrying about not screwing up his part again.

It was almost dark when they crossed the English coast; the North Sea looked like shiny grey metal. It seemed flat calm from this height, but you couldn't tell and he wasn't keen to find out. The way the skipper kept cocking up on dry land, they wouldn't have a hope ditching.

D-Dog droned on and he kept a sharp watch through his Perspex window.

'Bomb aimer to navigator. Enemy coast ahead.'

Piers' voice answered him, 'Thanks awfully, bomb aimer.'

Strewth, Stew thought, I wish we'd got a nav who spoke like a normal bloke. Come to that, I wish we'd got a nav who could bloody navigate.

Piers checked and re-checked his calculations. If he'd got everything absolutely right he'd be taking them between two coastal flak batteries, slipping in unnoticed. And if he went on getting things right they'd make their bombing run away from the Cologne barrage. In his cramped cubicle behind the blackout curtain, the little Anglepoise lamp illuminating his charts, he felt secure for the moment. It wouldn't last, of course. When they got near the target, if not before, that would all change. The enemy would know they were coming, and night fighters were probably already up and searching for them. And over the target it was bound to be dicey. He needn't actually see anything of it, if he didn't want to – some navigators never came out from behind their curtain – but he felt he ought to see what was going on this time. It was like being compelled to look at something horrible, even though you knew it would appal you.

Harry passed him a scrap of paper with his latest radio fix. Piers went over everything again.

'Navigator to pilot. ETA on target is o three forty-five.'

'Roger, nav.'

In less than half an hour, he realized, it would be his birthday.

Sitting on his canvas sling seat, head and shoulders in the Perspex dome of the mid-upper turret with the rest of him, feet in stirrups, down in the draughty fuselage, Bert was thinking about Emerald and fancying his chances. She was a smashing bit of skirt, the best-looking bint he'd ever taken out. They'd had a good old snog in the back row at the flicks, and look how she'd given him the silk stocking – to bring him luck, she'd said, with one of her sidelong smiles – and if that wasn't a come-on he didn't know what was. He fingered it round his neck, grinning to himself. Next time he took her out . . .

Blimey, what was he doing, dreaming about that now? He was supposed to be keeping a sharp look-out for enemy fighters, and anything else that could get them into trouble.

He put Emerald out of his mind and rotated the turret slowly. Trouble was, when you went on staring out into the dark for long you started imagining all sorts of things. What was only a cloud started looking like a whole lot of Messerschmitts, and you could fire away at nothing and put the wind up everyone else, not to mention waste ammo. Sometimes he felt sort of trapped in the turret. You had to be a bit of a Houdini to haul yourself up into it, and getting out in a hurry'd be a bloody sight worse. And once he was there, there he had to stay unless the skipper ordered him to leave. He tried not to think about the turret having no armour protection, or about the RAF roundels painted just below and making a nice convenient bull's-eye aiming point for Jerry fighters, or about the fact that he couldn't wear his parachute and had to stow it down below. Most of all, he didn't think about all the stories of mid-uppers coming back from ops without a head.

Still, he wouldn't have swapped places with Charlie for anything – all on his tod at the blunt end there, out in the cold. Not for all the tea in China.

Piers couldn't see much until his eyes adjusted from the light of his chart lamp to the darkness of the cockpit, and when they did, it all looked far, far worse than he had expected. He stood behind Van, staring in horror at the glittering wall of exploding flak and searchlights ahead. Christ, they had to go into *that*! It was sheer suicide. They'd have no chance at all. He wanted to dash back behind his curtain, but a dreadful fascination made him stay and watch it all come closer and closer. A shell burst somewhere beneath them and he grabbed for a handhold as D-Dog plunged about wildly and shrapnel rattled hard on the fuselage. A searchlight beam swept the sky only yards away, and a second beam followed so close he thought they must surely have been spotted. Another shell exploding even nearer almost flung D-Dog onto her back. God, they'd never get out of this alive. It was hopeless. *Hopeless.*

A stab of orange fire flared suddenly away to port. As it grew he saw that it was a bomber on fire, flames flickering furiously along its wings. An almighty explosion lit up the sky and dazzled his eyes. Mesmerized, he watched blazing brands of wreckage spin earthwards.

'Bomb doors open, skip.' Stew's voice sounded perfectly calm.

'Roger, bomb aimer. Bomb doors open.'

'Right . . . steady. Left, left. Left, left. Steady . . . steady. Bombs gone, skip.'

D-Dog turned away from the target, heading for the dark. Back at his charts, hands shaking, Piers somehow pulled himself together.

Charlie could see the glow from the fires for a long while on their route back. They'd clobbered the place well and truly. Given the Jerries a taste of their own medicine.

It didn't do to think too much about the women and children and old people they might have killed and maimed in the process. The Jerries had done the same, after all. They were the ones who'd started it. That was what he told himself when he saw the burning buildings. He watched the crimson smudge getting further away until it vanished. Only another couple of hours and they'd be home. Another op done. He was looking forward to his egg and a nice long kip.

'*Fighter! Fighter! Corkscrew port! Corkscrew port – Go!*' Bert was yelling from the mid-upper turret; the skipper rolled D-Dog left. Charlie knew what was coming. They'd practised it lots of times. They'd dive port, then climb port, roll, climb starboard, dive starboard, roll and then dive port all over again – trying to get away from the enemy fighter.

They went down in a dive that turned his stomach worse than anything he'd ever been on at a fairground. His head was jammed up against the turret roof, vomit spewed up into his mouth. He screwed his eyes tight shut until he felt the Lanc slowing, levelling out.

'Climbing port, gunners.'

'He's still there, skipper. Two o'clock high.'

Bert's guns clattered from the mid-upper turret. 'Missed him, skipper. Going low astern. Watch out for him, Charlie.'

Charlie couldn't see him. Had never seen him. Where on earth was he? His night vision was good enough to see anything. Maybe the fighter had scarpered after Bert had taken that shot at him. Maybe Bert had only imagined him?

Then he saw a dark, winged shadow flash past below

the turret and skid into a turn. 'Rear gunner to mid-upper. I see him now.'

It was an Me110 – coming straight for them – still out of range, but closing fast. A stream of brilliant tracer snaked by the tail before he had him properly in his sights: lined up, smack on. Ready to fire. Then all of a sudden his fingers seemed to freeze on the triggers.

Bert's voice yelled in his ears. 'Shoot the bugger down, Charlie! *Get him!*'

He opened fire and the bullets from his guns curved away in a line of bright beads. He thought he saw a chunk of the Messerschmitt's port wing fly off before it flipped over on its back and dived away, vanishing into cloud below.

'Rear gunner to pilot. I think I hit his wing, skipper. He's cleared off.'

'Well done, Charlie. Good shooting.'

Bert was crowing away in his turret and the rest were really chuffed. He should have been feeling a bit pleased himself, too, but all he could think of was that if Bert hadn't yelled at him like that he might not have fired until it was too late, and the Jerry would have got *them* instead. And if he'd fired sooner, when he should have done, he could've scored a direct hit in the nose and finished him off good and proper, not just clipped him. He didn't know why he'd gone and frozen up like that. Gone rigid for those few seconds. He'd always thought it would be easy to shoot at the enemy but when it'd come to it, he'd funked it.

They crossed the English coast at Dungeness and flew north to Beningby in the cold grey light of dawn. Piers got it on the button this time, thank Christ, but they had to wait their turn to land, circling slowly over the fields with other returning Lancs. This was the ball-breaking part that Van hated most of all. He was tired. They were all tired. And they had to go around and around and around, waiting for the OK from Control before they could get down on the ground.

At last it was their turn and he brought D-Dog in a curve onto the downwind leg. He made himself concentrate hard. Wheels down, half flap, then full flap from Jock – pronto as ever. D-Dog sank obediently. Van brought the nose up a fraction as they crossed the threshold lights and she floated on down the runway. When he could feel her on the point of stall, he dropped her the last few inches onto the concrete. The wheels touched down all three together and with hardly a sound. *Wow, a greaser!*

Jock put his thumb up, eyes above his mask creased in a grin. First time that had ever happened. The grin or the greaser.

In the truck on the way back from dispersal, Piers spoke up bashfully. 'I say, chaps, it's my birthday. Would you mind awfully if I stood you all dinner?'

Four

'I hope that new girl is going to ring the dinner gong on time this evening, Miss Frost.'

'I'll see that she does, Mrs Mountjoy.'

'Just because there's a war on, it doesn't excuse unpunctuality. We should keep up standards, not let them slip.'

The telephone ringing saved Honor from another lecture from Mrs Mountjoy. She had listened to them on all subjects: the decline in good manners, the inefficiency of the Royal Mail, the vulgarity of ITMA, the laxness of morals, the disgraceful amount of noise made by the Royal Air Force . . .

By the time she had dealt with the call, Mrs Mountjoy had gone off into the Residents' Lounge where she would sit in her usual chair until dinner. Colonel Millis was already in there, slumped in *his* chair, but there would be no conversation between them beyond 'Good evening' and the colonel's inevitable comment on the weather which Mrs Mountjoy would ignore. Conversation with the colonel was difficult, in any case, because he was so deaf, but he had not lost his sense of time. In ten minutes, at six o'clock precisely, he would emerge to shuffle across the hall to the Oak Bar for his first gin and tonic.

She was busy in the inner office at her typewriter when he appeared at the reception desk and rang the bell. With his drooping moustache and mournful expression, he looked very like a bewildered old walrus.

'The bar's shut. It's after six and there's nobody there.'

She leaned across the counter and spoke into his better ear. 'I'll come and open it up for you, colonel.'

Ron the barman was late yet again, which meant she'd have to hold the fort for him, as usual.

The colonel followed eagerly at her heels across the hall into the Oak Bar, and she poured the gin from his private bottle of Gordon's. She knew how he liked it – up to a certain mark in the glass, just a splash of tonic and no ice. Sometimes he reminisced wistfully about the pre-war days when he had also had a slice of lemon. No more lemons now, or oranges or bananas . . . She carried it over to him at his place in the corner, careful not to spill any on the way. He raised the glass to her in his courtly fashion.

She was replacing the bottle in the cupboard under the counter when a party of RAF men came into the bar, making a good deal of noise. Two were officers, she saw, but the rest of them were sergeants – which Miss Hargreaves wouldn't care for at all. One of the officers approached her.

'I say, could we possibly order some drinks?'

'What would you like, sir?'

'I don't suppose you'd have any gin or whisky, or anything like that?'

She closed the door on the colonel's gin and locked it. 'I'm very sorry, sir, there's only beer or sherry available at the moment.'

'Oh, that's all right. I'll have a sherry, please.' He turned to the others. 'What'll you have, chaps?'

One of the sergeants asked for lemonade, but the rest all wanted beer. The officer paid for everything with a nice smile. 'It's on me. My treat. By the way, I'm Pilot Officer Wentworth-Young. I telephoned earlier about a table for dinner.'

'It's reserved for you, sir. A table for seven.'

Mrs Mountjoy was going to have something to say about sergeants in the dining-room, but she could hardly refuse them admission.

'Jolly good. We're a crew, you see.'

These, then, were men who were in the bombers that she listened to going overhead. She'd never seen a crew all together before – just the RAF officers who came to the bar and to dinner at The Angel and odd airmen she passed in the street.

'You wouldn't happen to have any champagne by any chance, would you?' The pilot officer blushed as he spoke. 'It's my birthday. Twenty-first, actually.'

Champagne, for heaven's sake! Some hope! 'I very much doubt it, sir, but I'll ask the head waiter for you in a moment.'

One of the sergeants came over to the bar. His uniform was a different blue from the others – royal blue – and the buttons were black. She'd never seen one like it.

'Got any matches, miss?' He looked her over as he spoke.

'I think so – somewhere.' She had to hunt hard for a box as Ron never kept anything in order. The sergeant was watching her all the time, irritating her. 'This isn't my usual job.'

'Yeah, I could tell that by the way you did the beer.' He pushed the pennies across the counter towards her. 'Thanks.' As he turned away she saw *Australia* on his shoulder.

Ron came hurrying in with a long story about a puncture on his bike – it was always a different excuse. She left him flitting about behind the bar and went off to see about the unlikely champagne.

Pity about the limp, Stew thought, watching the girl leave the room. Looked like something wrong with her right foot.

Not that she was his sort. All prim and proper in that frumpy blouse and skirt, hair done like a school-teacher's, no make-up. He went for the type that sent the message loud and clear, like the one he'd picked up on leave in London last time. Met her in the hotel bar, bought her a few drinks and taken her straight up to his room. Easy as that. They hadn't wasted time with the fooling around beforehand that some sheilas expected. Jesus, that'd been a night to remember, all right, and he could remember a few.

He lit his cigarette and stowed the box of matches away in his pocket. Bloody lighter! Still, so long as it brought him luck . . . He was feeling pretty pleased with himself after that last op. No dummy run this time. Dropped the bombs smack on the main target, or as near as he could get the buggers. Then the kid had clipped that Jerry that Bert had spotted, and Piers had even managed to find the way back. And to cap it all, the skipper had gone and done a three-pointer. Maybe they weren't such a mug crew after all. He looked round the bar, at the dark oak panelling and the pictures of foggy landscapes and long-horned cattle, the brown leather chairs, the drab velvet curtains. Strewth, what a mausoleum! Not a patch on the hotel his parents ran back home. This place looked as though nothing had been touched for a hundred years. Fat chance of any decent tucker, but with Piers footing the bill he wasn't going to grumble. He was going to drink, eat and be as bloody merry as possible.

There was no champagne in the cellar, of course. Cedric looked at Honor as though she'd asked for the moon. If there had once been any such thing left, she knew he would have polished it off long ago. She went back to the reception desk. There were more people in the Oak Bar now and a lot of male laughter reaching the hall. Fortunately, Mrs Mountjoy had gone into the dining-room and would be out of earshot. The colonel's ears wouldn't hear much anyway and besides it was nearly time for him to go in for dinner. On the dot of seven-forty, after slowly spinning out his customary three gin and tonics, he would come out of the Oak Bar and head towards the dining-room. And, sure enough, as the grandfather clock hands edged towards that time he appeared. Passing the desk, he paused and shook his head sadly.

'Officers and NCOs drinking together . . . never happened in my day. Not the thing at all. Don't know what the country's coming to.'

The crew didn't leave the bar until half an hour later and she could tell that, except for the sergeant on lemonade, they were all the worse for drink. The Australian who had bought the matches gave her a look that made her turn away hurriedly.

Peggy saw them come in and watched Mr Cedric conducting them to their table. They made quite a commotion about sitting down, and one of them knocked a chair over. She knew she was going to have a spot of bother with them. It looked as though they'd spent a long time in the bar before and as they were already ordering more beer, things were likely to get worse, not better. Mrs Mountjoy was looking daggers from her corner. If looks could kill, Peggy thought, the seven of them would have dropped down dead.

She went across to their table with the menus and her pad and pencil. Not that there was much of a choice: just the cock-a-leekie, then either something the chef called Chicken à la King (though she couldn't see what it had to do with His Majesty), or steamed halibut with a sprig of old parsley stuck on top. There was trifle for pudding, unless they fancied the mouse-trap.

She stood waiting behind the fair-haired one sitting at the end of the table. He only had one ring round his sleeve so she knew he wasn't very high up. Last night she'd waited on an old man with four rings and she'd been so nervous she'd gone and dropped a bread roll off the tongs right into his lap. She waited hopefully for a few minutes but they were all talking and laughing among themselves, not paying much attention to the menus and none at all to her, so in the end she thought she'd better say something to the one at the head of the table.

'Excuse me, sir, would you like to order now?'

He peered up at her, surprised to find someone standing there, and she could see he was more than a bit woozy. His hair was flopping over his forehead and his face was flushed, but he gave her a lovely smile.

'Gosh, I'm most frightfully sorry . . . don't actually think we're ready yet. I say, chaps . . . I say, *chaps* . . . do *listen*. What do you all want?'

It took a long time to sort it all out. She had to go round the table and ask each one in turn and of course a couple of them were a bit cheeky. Still, she was getting used to that sort of thing and it didn't fluster her quite so much. As she went off to the kitchen, Mr Cedric was bringing them the beer.

Later, they started singing *Happy Birthday*. Honor could hear it loud and clear from reception and it was followed immediately by *Twenty-one today* . . . When that had finished there was a lot of clapping and shouts of *speech, speech*!

Mrs Mountjoy came storming out into the hall and rapped her stick furiously on the edge of the desk.

'Miss Frost, I demand that you put a stop to this appalling noise at once! I've never seen or heard such disgraceful behaviour in my life. This is supposed to be a hotel, not a zoo.'

'I'm so sorry, Mrs Mountjoy—'

'Sorry is not enough, Miss Frost. Go and *do* something this minute. As for allowing *sergeants* in the dining-room . . . whatever next? I don't expect to have to eat with that class of person. I am seriously considering moving elsewhere.'

If only she would!

'I'm afraid there's no hotel rule about that, Mrs Mountjoy.'

'Then there should be. I shall speak to Miss Hargreaves in no uncertain terms.'

There was another burst of clapping from the dining-room and more loud laughter. Mrs Mountjoy brandished her stick.

'Listen to that! Well, aren't you going to put a stop to it?'

'If you insist, Mrs Mountjoy.'

'I most certainly do.'

Honor went into the dining-room. Pilot Officer

Wentworth-Young was on his feet, evidently making some kind of speech. Peggy hovered behind him, waiting to serve the trifle. The Australian sergeant was walking round the table, upside-down, on his hands. The youngest-looking of them had actually fallen asleep with his head on his plate. She saw scandalized faces all round the dining-room.

The rambling address petered out.

'Well, thanks most awfully all of you . . . jolly glad you all came. Jolly, jolly glad . . .'

The speech-maker collapsed suddenly backwards into his chair and when Peggy darted forward to set the plate of trifle in front of him he caught hold of her and dragged her down onto his lap. Sponge cake and jam and custard and mock cream flew about as she struggled to free herself.

Honor limped forward hurriedly. 'Would you please let go of the waitress, sir . . . and could I ask you *all* to be much quieter. You're disturbing the other guests. People are complaining. Please. Please. *Please*—'

They took no notice of her but started to sing again, one of them conducting vigorously, and this time it wasn't *Happy Birthday* but something far worse. She knew the tune but the words were quite different.

The Australian sergeant had reached her on his upside-down tour of the table. He righted himself clumsily. 'Come to join the party, sweetheart?'

The hotel wasn't on fire and nobody had died but she could see that the only thing to be done was to fetch Miss Hargreaves, who would probably go and call the police.

The Australian stumbled after her and caught her up as she reached the dining-room doors. He grabbed hold of her arm. 'Be a sport, miss. Don't make trouble.'

'You're the ones who've made the trouble.'

'It's his bloody birthday.'

'I can't help that.'

'He might not have another.' His fingers tightened their grip and he jerked her round to face him. He was looking furiously angry now, glaring at her as though *she* was at fault. 'None of us bloody might. Think about that, you stupid bloody sheila, if you can bloody think at all.'

She wrenched herself free. Mrs Mountjoy was waiting for her in the hall, leaning on her stick.

'Well? I hope you're going to have them thrown out this instant.'

'They'll be leaving soon, Mrs Mountjoy.' She went into the inner office, rubbing at her bruised arm. She was close to tears.

Five

Catherine saw the subtle change in them when they walked into the de-briefing room, back from a raid on Bremen. The strange alchemy that transformed a collection of very individual men into a crew was working its magic. They had to forget their differences, their dislikes, even their distrust. Their survival depended on it. She watched them collect their mugs of hot cocoa and tots of rum from the padre at the hatchway and light their cigarettes and talk together, waiting for their turn to sit down at one of the de-briefing tables. For the first time, they ended up at her table, dragging out their chairs and slumping into them – unshaven, red-eyed, dishevelled and dirty. She unscrewed the cap of her fountain pen and began her questions about the raid. The Aussie bomb aimer had black rubber mask marks on his cheekbones, like war paint. He looked positively aggrieved when she asked if they had bombed on target.

'Too right we did. I reckon we walloped those U-boat yards good and proper.'

She smiled at him placatingly. 'I only asked.'

He took a cigarette from the open tin on the table and scraped a match alight. 'Yeah, well . . . we did, didn't we, skip?'

'Sure.'

She turned to the skipper. 'How about flak?'

'Pretty much where they told us.'

'Was it heavy?'

'Guess you'd say moderate. Plenty of pitches but none of them in the strike zone.'

'I'm sorry?'

'They kept missing us.'

She cleared her throat. 'Any enemy defence tactics you hadn't come across before – decoys, weapons, anything different that you encountered?'

'I guess not. Nothing we noticed.' His expression was deadpan.

Maybe she was imagining it, but she suspected that he was mocking her and her questions. She said crisply, 'Any enemy night fighters in the target area? Or elsewhere?'

He shook his head. 'Not on this one.'

'Did you see any kites go down?'

He indicated his mid-upper gunner with one thumb. 'Bert saw one in trouble.'

The gunner nodded. He was the small, dark one with the cheeky grin, only he wasn't grinning now. He looked bone tired. She noticed, amused, that he had an extra free cigarette from the tin parked behind one ear.

'A Stirling. Over the drink on the way home – 'bout 'alfway across. Must've taken 'its in a couple of engines 'cos I could see two stopped an' they was losing 'eight. Went into cloud, then, so I didn't see what 'appened to 'em after that. Charlie spotted 'em, too, didn't you, Charlie?'

The little rear gunner agreed. He looked ridiculously young to be doing this ghastly job. No early-morning stubble on his boy's cheeks – only adolescent pimples very red against his pallor. He stifled a yawn.

She went through the rest briskly in her in-
terrogation voice, knowing that at times she must
sound like a bossy schoolmistress with a rather
slack class. When they got wearily to their feet she
caught the skipper's ironic glance before he moved
away.

'You seem a bit crook.' Stew, hands in pockets, fell
into step beside Piers as they left the ops block. The
nav looked like death warmed up. 'Still got that
hangover?'

'I think I must have. I feel absolutely awful—'

'The oxygen ought to've cured you. Still, a good kip
and you'll be right as jolly old rain.'

Stew put on a fake Oxford accent for the last bit.
Couldn't resist taking the piss out of Piers sometimes.
The joke was, he was supposed to call him 'sir', being
an officer, but they'd none of them ever bothered with
that bullshit. It'd been first names all round, right
from the start.

Poor old Piers couldn't take the grog, Stew
reckoned, giving him another sideways look. Not like
himself. Christ, he'd been drinking since he was about
twelve – pinching beer out of the fridge when nobody
was looking. Smoking, too. Nicking the fags from his
parents whenever he got the chance. Even so, he had
to admit he'd felt a bit rough after the night out in
Lincoln. It'd been a pretty good party – what he could
remember of it.

'I'm afraid I must have behaved most frightfully
badly,' Piers said. 'Terribly bad form.'

He was like a cartoon Pom! 'Do us a favour, sport.
Spit the bloody plum out.'

Piers, of course, didn't have a clue what he

was talking about. 'The trouble is, Stew, I can only remember bits of the evening . . .'

'Yeah, same as the rest of us, 'cept Jock. Ask him. He'll tell you what a bad boy you were. You had that waitress on your lap. Wouldn't let her go. Tut, tut, old chap. Dashed poor behaviour.'

'Gosh, did I really? What on earth did the hotel people think?'

'Well, they weren't too thrilled, as I recall. Some bossy sheila came and told us people were complaining. Asked us to pipe down.'

'Did we?'

'Don't think so.'

'God, how dreadful.'

'Well, so what? We risk our bloody necks for them. The least they can do is let us enjoy ourselves while we're still alive and kicking.'

'Just the same, Stew, I think I ought to go and apologize. I say, you wouldn't like to come with me?'

'Me? No, thanks. Not bloody likely.'

'I'd be most awfully grateful. I'll buy you a beer. *Several* beers.'

What a mug he was. 'OK. You're on.'

They drove the twelve miles to Lincoln in Piers' Wolseley. He was the only one of the crew to possess a car and that went a long way, in Stew's book, to making up for the Pommy toff-talk that got on his wick. Buses cost money, taxis even more. A bike was OK for getting around to the local boozers, but not if you wanted to go much further afield. He wondered, and tried to remember as they spun along, how the hell they'd got back to the station after the birthday bash. Piers couldn't remember anything about the journey either but between them they came to the conclusion that it was Jock who must have driven since he'd been the only one sober. And Jock couldn't drive.

Piers parked the car outside The Angel. Privately, Stew couldn't understand why Piers wanted to go and stick his head in the noose. What was the bloody point? He supposed it had something to do with the way he'd been brought up. His nanny had probably spanked him if he didn't go and say sorry when he'd been naughty.

The revolving entrance door had a bad case of the squeaks – he remembered that from before – and there was no-one at the reception desk. A grandfather clock tick-tocked away slowly in the silence like a knell of doom, and a stuffed stag's head stared down with sightless glass eyes. Cripes, what a bloody morgue! He poked his head into the Oak Bar which was deserted too. 'OK, nobody about, let's go,' he said, keen to be out of there. They could go off down the hill to The Saracen's Head, better known as the Snake Pit, and sink a few beers. It was a bloody sight more lively than this place.

But Piers had gone over to the desk, picked up a small brass handbell and rung it firmly. At the sound, a girl came out of the office at the back. Stew remembered her too. It was all coming back to him. She was the one with the limp. The one who'd served behind the bar and sold him some matches and then come into the dining-room later and kicked up a fuss. He'd gone after her and said something – he couldn't remember what exactly, but from the icy look she sent his way, it probably hadn't been too polite.

Piers was saying his bit, stumbling through some bullshit about how *frightfully* sorry he was if they'd made a nuisance of themselves and that he hoped

91

most *awfully* that they hadn't done any damage. The girl was thawing out by degrees and by the time Piers had got to the end of his party piece, stone the bloody crows, she was smiling at him.

'Well, you did make rather a disturbance, sir, but don't worry about it. And no damage was done. It was nice of you to come by.'

That was that, then, Stew thought in relief, and headed for the door. Now they could go and have a grog. But Piers was still carrying on, asking something about the waitress . . . wanting to say sorry to her as well, for Christ's sake. The girl told him she was in the dining-room, laying tables.

'Shan't be a moment, Stew,' Piers said and, before he could stop him doing anything so bloody stupid and unnecessary, he'd gone shooting off down the hall.

He hesitated, not sure whether to stand his ground or wait outside in the car. The girl's smile had switched off like a light bulb when she glanced again in his direction and she turned her back deliberately and started rearranging some papers behind the desk. That pissed him off. There was no call for her to be so unfriendly when she'd been so nice to Piers.

He stepped forward. 'Stew Brenner's the name.'

He might not have uttered anything because she went on ignoring him completely. Her face was averted so he could only see the back of her head and the tight sausage of hair above a prim white collar.

He said, peeved, 'What's the matter? Do you want *me* to apologize, too, or something?'

No response. Not a flaming glimmer. He must have been ruder to her than he'd thought – maybe even said something obscene, though he usually tried to watch his language with sheilas, even when he'd had a skinful. 'All right . . . I'm sorry. For whatever it was. I can't remember what I did or said . . . I'd had too much to drink, see. *I'm sorry. OK?*'

At last she turned round, slowly, to look at him. 'Gentlemen usually remove their caps in the hotel.' She went off into the office behind the desk and banged the glass door shut behind her. He could see her sit down at a typewriter and hear the staccato clatter of the keys. Stew swore furiously under his breath. Some women were never bloody satisfied.

There was only one waitress in the dining-room – a girl laying a table at the far end. Piers stood by the swing doors for a moment, watching her setting out knives and forks and spoons. She was too absorbed in her task to notice him, and he watched her breathe on a knife blade and rub it carefully on the corner of her apron. He gave a small cough and she started and dropped the knife onto the carpet.

'Excuse me . . .' He hesitated, not knowing for the life of him what he was going to say, but determined that he owed her some kind of apology.

'Did you want something, sir?' She was staring at him apprehensively. 'Dinner isn't served until seven o'clock.'

'I know . . . I mean, I didn't come for dinner.' He made his way between the tables towards her. 'Actually, I came to apologize. To say how frightfully sorry I am to have behaved so badly the other evening. I'm afraid I'd had rather a lot to drink and I can't remember much about it . . . but . . . but I gather I . . . well, somebody told me I behaved specially badly – to *you*. At least, I think it must have been you.' He swallowed. 'I wanted to apologize.'

She had gone pink in the face while he was speaking – the colour starting in two small spots on each cheek and spreading like stains. She looked down at the bundle of cutlery clutched in her hands. 'That's all right, sir. It wasn't anything really . . . just a bit of skylarking. You gentlemen were just enjoying yourselves. Having a bit of fun.'

'It was my birthday, you see.'

She lifted her head and smiled at him, the sweetest smile he thought he'd ever been. 'I know it was, sir. You were twenty-one.'

He smiled back. 'Well, I suppose it's a bit of a milestone. Cause for celebration, and all that.' He wondered how old *she* was. Not more than seventeen at the most. She looked like a little waif in the starched white apron and cap and the black dress – all at least two sizes too big for her; and her eyes under the fringe of hair were the colour of, of . . . of speedwells, he thought suddenly. Those beautiful little bright blue flowers you saw dotting the grass on a summer's day.

He bent down to pick up the knife that lay between them and handed it to her. 'I say, what's your name?'

'Peggy, sir.'

'That's an awfully nice name.'

'Thank you, sir.'

Yes, the colour of speedwells, that was it. And her hair was as fair as flax. He wished he could remember her sitting on his lap. 'Well, I suppose I'd better leave you to get on . . . with the tables, and so on.'

'Yes, I must sir. I have to get everything done before the gong.'

'The gong?' Gongs were medals to him now.

'For dinner, sir. In the hall. It's my job to ring it, you see. And Mrs Mountjoy gets very cross if I'm late.'

He'd no idea who Mrs Mountjoy was. 'Yes, of course. Well, anyway, I'm jolly glad I saw you. Jolly glad.'

'Thank you, sir.' She gave him a little bob curtsey, like the maids used to at home.

He backed away awkwardly and bumped into a chair behind him, almost knocked the blessed thing over. 'Perhaps I'll see you again . . . I mean, I expect I'll be in for dinner again some time soon.'

'Yes, sir.'

'I promise to behave better.'

She smiled at him again. God, what a sweet smile!

'Well, I'll be off then . . .'

He glanced back through the glass panel as he shut the dining-room door. She was busy polishing the knife blade on her apron.

There was an overgrown vegetable patch behind the cottage. Dorothy had noticed the rhubarb first, the long sticks half hidden by nettles, and then she'd discovered a row of gooseberry bushes. There was an apple tree and a plum tree, too, so she'd be able to use the fruit to make puddings for Charlie later on. And if she cleared and dug over the patch, she could try growing a few vegetables. She'd never grown them before. When he was alive, Edward had done the garden and he hadn't liked her to touch anything. He only grew flowers – mostly dahlias that she hadn't cared for very much. She didn't like their gaudy colours or their big, flashy flowers, some of them big as saucers, but his dahlias had been Edward's pride and joy. After he'd died she'd given the tubers away to a neighbour and, instead, she'd planted roses – pale pink and creamy yellow and pure white ones. Edward would have thought them wishy-washy.

She'd been wishy-washy, too, the way she'd always deferred to him so meekly, but then that's what he'd insisted on from the first. It was up to the husband to make the decisions, he'd told her at the very start of their marriage. He knew best, with his greater experience of life, and she could trust him to look after her. It was like being the captain of a ship and he'd steer them away from any rocks. Well, what else could she have done but agree? It was his house, his money, and he was old enough to be her father.

She'd been just sixteen when she'd met Edward and he'd been close to forty and recently widowed. She'd already left school and got a job in a florist's in Bromley. She had a knack for doing nice wreaths and they'd given her the job of doing the one Edward had ordered for his wife's funeral. He'd come in afterwards to pay the bill and had complimented her on her work. Then he'd come in again to order a bouquet for his mother's birthday and asked specially for her to do it. When he'd asked her out later he'd behaved like a perfect gentleman and he'd seemed so polished and so worldly-wise that she had been flattered and over-whelmed by his attention. And when, in the course of time, he'd asked her to marry him, her parents had urged her to accept. She'd be settled for life with a good, steady man who had a nice safe job in a bank, they'd said. The age difference didn't matter – in fact, it was a positive advantage in their eyes. Even so, he'd had to ask her three times before she'd accepted him. He had spoken of the deep affection he had for her and of his great esteem and he had spoken so earnestly and so kindly that she had truly believed herself to care for him in return. It was only after they had been married for a few months that she had realized that though she might honour and obey him, as she had promised in the church, she would never be able to love him. But by then, Charlie had been on the way and she had been given someone else to love.

Absorbed in her digging and her thoughts, Dorothy didn't hear the knocking on the cottage front door, and when the old man from the farm appeared round the side path, he gave her quite a fright.

He touched his cap to her. 'Afternoon, Mrs Banks. 'Nother fine day we're havin'.'

He usually started off with the weather, and she always agreed politely with whatever he said. Somehow she felt that it was *his* weather up here in Lincolnshire and therefore his right to deliver the verdict on it.

'Doin' a spot of diggin', then?'

She leaned on the fork, her back aching. 'I thought I'd try to grow some vegetables if I can clear all these weeds.'

'You'll be stayin' a while longer, then?'

'Yes, several months.' It was always her answer.

He nodded. 'What sort of vegetables were you thinkin' of?'

'I'm not sure. Potatoes, carrots, beans . . . whatever I can find seeds for.'

He nodded again. 'Might have some of those spare. I'll take a look and come by with them.'

He'd already given her all the flower seeds for nothing.

'Only if I pay you for them.'

But he shook his head firmly. 'An apple or two off the tree'll do nicely later on. Bramleys, they are. Good cookers. Could you do with a bicycle?'

She said, surprised, 'A bicycle?'

He nodded. 'That's right. My wife's old one.

Thought to myself you might make some use of it . . . so's you could get around easier. It's a fair walk to the village, and I hear you're workin' up at the army camp. I'll lend it to you while you're here, if you like. Better'n Shanks's pony.'

'Well, thank you. It would be very handy. But won't your wife be needing it?'

He chuckled. 'Not where she is, God rest her. Gone to her grave ten years past. And I fancy she'd like you to have the use of it. How's your boy doing, then?' He nodded towards the aerodrome. 'On the Lancasters, isn't he?'

'Oh . . . he's fine, thank you.' How on earth had they found out? She hadn't said a word to anybody. Or about working at the army camp.

'Gunner, I hear.'

'Yes. Rear gunner.'

'Mrs Dane said he's a nice-looking lad.'

'Mrs Dane?'

'Runs the post office stores. He called in for sweets, or some such. Talked about you.'

So it was Charlie himself who had told them – which meant he really didn't mind if people knew.

'Worries about you, he does, all on your own here. But then I expect you worry about him.'

'I do a bit,' she said.

'More 'n a bit, I'd reckon.'

He touched his cap and told her he'd be by the next day and she went back to her digging. She did some more thinking as she worked. The bike and the vegetable seeds were the old man's way of trying to help and of showing his sympathy. But she didn't think that anyone could really understand what it was like. Unless you had a son, or a husband, or a brother –

98

someone you loved more than life itself – in terrible danger, day after day, you couldn't possibly know. There must be thousands of women all over England, and in other countries, too, who were going through just the same thing. It was a sort of comfort to think that she wasn't alone.

She worked on until the sun was going down. The patch was cleared of weeds but the earth still needed a good raking to make it fine enough for planting; her back was too stiff and sore to do any more that day.

She was putting the fork away in the shed when she heard an engine starting up over on the drome. Then another. And then two more in turn: the four engines of a Lancaster bomber. She knew the sound well enough. Her heart started its wild thumping and she waited by the shed door, listening. After a moment she could hear more engines starting and soon the sound swelled to a thunderous chorus. She thought she could feel the earth shaking beneath her feet – unless it was the trembling of her own limbs.

They'd been hanging around at dispersal for over an hour. He'd gone through the first check list – Jock crouched at his flight engineer's panel – then started the engines and run them up: starboard inner and outer, then port inner and outer. Then he'd gone through the second list. All OK. He'd signed the Form 700, accepting D-Dog as airworthy and he'd done an intercom check all round. 'Pilot to crew, can you hear me? Stew? Piers? Harry? Bert? Charlie?' 'OK, skipper,' from them all in turn. Bert and Charlie had rotated their turrets, whipping their guns up and down, while Harry and Piers checked over their stuff and Stew had fiddled around with the bomb sight down in the nose. They were all set to roll, when take-off was delayed for an hour.

It was hardly worth it, but they climbed out again and Van took yet another walk round the aircraft – no glycol leaks, tyres OK, Pitot-head cover off or he'd find himself with no airspeed on take-off. Count the engines, a Canadian instructor had once warned him, only half-joking. Make sure some jerk hasn't taken one away while you weren't looking.

The others were lying about on the grass and he joined them and stretched out flat on his back. He lit a cigarette and stared up at the pale evening sky, watching the pink seeping across from the west. Bert was telling one of his stories – this time about a chorus girl and a bishop – and then Stew told one he'd just heard round the station. After the laughter had fizzled out they started laying bets on the op being scrubbed, like the last three had been. Three times in a row they'd gone through the air testing and the briefing and the dressing-up – the whole, jittery sweat of it. They'd done the checks and the waiting around, and when they'd finally been taxiing out, ready to take off, the bastards had gone and scrubbed it. Part of you felt so bloody relieved you wanted to cheer, the other part thought what a stupid waste of effort and that it could have been another one chalked up.

He thought about Carrie, and he hadn't thought about her for quite a while, which was a big change. After the accident he'd thought about nothing else. Accident? That was the official verdict, but he'd always blame himself. To the end of his days. If he'd been going slower, not showing off, not had his arm round her, been paying attention . . . if, if, if. *If only*. People said they were the two saddest words in the English language and they were damned right.

He lit another cigarette from the end of the last one. Charlie had gone off to take another leak – the kid got real nervous before an op – and Harry was cleaning out his pipe as though his life depended on it. Stew seemed to have gone to sleep, but he knew darned well he hadn't. They were all wide awake. Waiting.

He lay back again and went on watching the sky. High above his head a flock of small dark birds headed home for the night; he could hear the faint whirring of their wings. Another, bigger bird flapped over on a solo flight. The pink was deepening to crimson, the light beginning to go fast. He shut his eyes for a while and then opened them quickly when he heard the sound of a van coming along the dispersal track. Scrubbed again? Or on? Either way it was a gut wrencher.

It was on.

They scrambled to their feet, butting the cigarettes, and had the all-together-now ritual leak on D-Dog's tail wheel before they climbed back in, each touching Sam as he passed. Van eased himself into the cockpit seat and fastened his Sutton harness.

'OK, Jock. Let's go.'

The four Merlins fired up again. More checks, then Jock gave the thumbs-up to the ground crew for the chocks to be pulled away. D-Dog trundled out of dispersal. Van gunned the outer starboard engine to turn her onto the perimeter track and gave the outer port a quick burst to straighten her up. You were meant to taxi at a walking pace but it was hard to judge so high up off the ground, and Lancs, like spirited horses, could try to run away with you. He kept his hand on the brake lever in case D-Dog got any ideas. He liked the feel of her. All aircraft had their own little foibles and gremlins but D-Dog seemed to have less than most. She'd be good company for the long haul across the North Sea to Emden.

They wound their way round the peri track to the start of the main runway where he and Jock went through the final list of checks in sequence while waiting their turn in line. Harry was standing in the astrodome, ready to watch for their green light from the control caravan. He'd be able to see the lamp as well, but two pairs of eyes were better than one.

He held the control wheel with his left hand, right hand free for the throttles, and felt the rudder pedals with the balls of his feet. *Off we go into the wide blue yonder* . . . well not blue any more, but the idea was the same. And boy, the Lanc would go down that runway like a bat out of hell. The poor old Wimpey had always lumbered, but the Lanc flew along, tail up, engines roaring like lions. He chewed on a piece of gum, waiting. The aircraft ahead of them was on its take-off run. Any moment now it would be them. He watched the bomber's dark silhouette rise slowly into the air and then saw it suddenly flop back. It veered off the concrete, tore crazily across the grass like a runaway loco and on into a field of crops where it ground-looped and burst spectacularly into flames. *Je-sus Christ.*

Fire trucks and blood wagons were racing towards the crash site when Harry spoke flatly from the astrodome.

'We've got a green, skipper. We're away.'

He'd seen the signal, too, and hardly believed it.

No pause. Press on regardless. Step over the corpses. On with the war. He took D-Dog out onto the runway and lined her up, throttles to zero boost, bouncing her gently against the brakes.

'Pilot to crew. Taking off.'

Brakes released with a great hiss, engines howling, D-Dog surged forward. The small group of people by the control tower were waving hard – harder than ever. As soon as he could, Van got the tail off the ground so it was easier to keep her straight. Jock's arm was pressed firmly against his arm, his hand ready to take over the throttles. He kicked the rudder to straighten a slight swing to port.

'Full power, Jock.'

'Full power, skipper.'

Timed to the split second, Jock's hand slid beneath his onto the throttles so he could take the control column in both his own, ready to haul her off. They were eating up the runway real fast, and out of the corner of his eye he saw the crimson pyre of fire flash past. He brought the wheel back gently. Sweat was forming under his helmet and mask. *Come on, D-Dog. Don't screw us too. Get up. Get up. Fuel, bombs, incendiaries, ammunition, men . . . the whole damn massive load. Be a good Dog and get us up, for pity's sake.* He pulled back harder on the wheel and they soared into the evening sky.

'Undercart up, please, Jock.'

'Undercart up, skipper.'

His voice and Jock's had sounded completely normal, as though nothing whatever had happened. He swung the control wheel left and looked down the long length of the port wing to the conflagration in the corn field below. Fuel and incendiary bombs were blazing away merrily, flames leaping high into the air. Except for Piers behind his curtain, they could all see it clearly: Jock beside him, Harry in the astrodome, Stew in the front turret, Bert in the mid-upper and Charlie at the rear, with the best view of all. But as they climbed on up and up above the burning bomber, nobody spoke a word.

Dorothy saw the fire from the cottage windows and ran outside into the front garden. She could hear the fierce crackling of the flames and the sound of ammunition exploding. And smell the smell of burning flesh.

The old man came down the road early in the morning. He was wheeling a lady's bike that looked as old as himself – a big black rusty thing with a large wicker basket strapped onto the handlebars. He leaned it against the post of the front gate. 'Needs a bit of a clean and some oil, but I thought your lad might see to that for you.'

If he's still alive, she wanted to say, but the words wouldn't come. She couldn't speak her anguish aloud. All night she had lain awake, certain that it would be Charlie's plane that had crashed. Hideous images of him trapped in the rear turret and being burned alive had come before her eyes, however much she had tried to stop them. She could see him struggling, hear him screaming, see the flames devouring him . . . At dawn she had gone out into the front garden again. The flames were gone and it was quiet, but she could still smell the dreadful smell.

Charlie had once told her that he'd asked the station padre to come and see her if anything happened to him. If he got taken prisoner, or anything, he'd said casually, but she'd known what he really meant. She'd get a letter, too, he'd added, but that might not be until later.

When nobody had come to the cottage first thing, she'd allowed herself to hope just a little. No news was good news. Until somebody came to tell her that Charlie was dead, he was alive. If nobody came at all then everything was all right.

The old man pointed to a sack in the basket. 'Brought a few seed potatoes for you. An' some peas an' broad beans . . . I'd plenty spare from mine, so you're more'n welcome to 'em.'

She managed to speak quite ordinarily. 'It's ever so kind of you. Thank you, Mr . . . ?'

'Stonor's the name. Ben Stonor. Bit of trouble they had at the drome last night.'

'Yes—'

'One of the Lancasters took off an' came down again with a big bump, so it seems. Poor lads. Canadians, they were.'

'*Canadians? All* of them?'

'That's right, Mrs Banks. All Canadians. So it wasn't your boy's aeroplane, that's for sure. You can rest easy.'

'How do you know, Mr Stonor?'

'Oh, the village hears everythin'. We know what's goin' on. Why, Mrs Dane at the shop, she even knows what they're bombin'. It's Essen tonight, she'll say, or Bremen, or some such, an' she's always right. Don't know how, but she always is.' He touched his cap and went on his way, walking down the road towards the farm.

The world was normal again – everything going on

105

as before. The sun was shining and it was going to be a beautiful day. She was sorry about the Canadians but Charlie was alive. *Alive!*

Dorothy wheeled the old bike through the gate and round the back, where she leaned it against the shed door. Later on, when she'd finished work, she'd give it a clean-up and maybe Charlie could get a spot of oil for the chain and the wheels. She took Mr Stonor's sack out of the basket and noticed a paper bag underneath. Inside she found six brown eggs that he'd left for her as well.

Six

However hellishly confusing it might seem from the air when you were trying to find your way around, Van acknowledged that on the ground, and in full summer, the English countryside was glorious. Pennsylvania was a pretty good-looking state, but he'd never seen anything to match this. It was partly the sheer *oldness* of it all, he reckoned – history that had been going on for a heck of a long time. Old brick and stone, thatch and tile. Ancient churches embedded in the landscape, bridges that had spanned rivers for hundreds of years, winding lanes trodden by generations of people. Fields and woods and hedges that went back to the Domesday Book. It didn't hurt either that, for once, the sun was shining.

He'd appreciated Piers' invitation to spend some of his leave at his home in Northamptonshire. On other leaves he'd gone to London, hit the theatres and the clubs and the restaurants and had a pretty good time, but staying with an English family in an English home would be a new experience.

Piers drove through yet another village. They passed an old man sitting on a bench who looked as though he'd been there since the Flood. More cottages, with front gardens like flower shows. The village pump by the village green. Another Norman church, mossy tombstones leaning at drunken angles in the shade of a gnarled yew tree.

It was obvious that Piers came from a well-off family, but, even so, Van wasn't prepared for the mansion that lay at the end of the long driveway. Piers brought the car to a halt outside the front door. He looked embarrassed. 'I ought to tell you that my parents have got a title . . . just so's you know.' He sounded as though it was something to be ashamed of.

'What do I call them?'

'Well, my father's Sir William . . . and my mother's Lady Wentworth-Young. Actually, you needn't call them anything at all, if you don't want to.'

In real life, Lady Wentworth-Young was every bit as daunting as in her photograph. He watched Piers take off his cap and peck her cheek respectfully.

'This is Pilot Officer Lewis VanOlden, Mama. Captain of our crew.'

As he shook her hand, her eyes assessed him rapidly; he saw relief in their chilly depths. That he didn't appear to be a total savage? Some hick Yank come to pollute the ancestral home? An unsavoury influence on her well-brought-up son?

The house was what he called olde-English-beautiful: panelled walls, oriental rugs, antique furniture, classy portraits, fine porcelain and flowers and gilt-framed mirrors to reflect it all. There was no shiny newness. No vulgar glitter. No ostentation. And not much affection either, he thought, observing the parents with Piers. If he was a beloved son, you'd sure never have guessed it.

Dinner was served at a table that could have seated twenty. Sir William barked at him from one end and his wife addressed him graciously from the other. Piers' older sister was home on leave from the WRNS and sat opposite, inspecting him critically during the soup course. What the hell *was* the soup, anyway? Lukewarm, thin as water and almost colourless, it gave him no clues.

The conversation limped on.

'You come from Philadelphia, I understand, Mr VanOlden?'

'That's right, Lady Wentworth-Young.'

'One of your oldest cities, of course. Have your family lived there long?'

'My great-grandparents settled there. From Holland.'

He guessed it would have been better if he could have added a couple or so more 'greats'. Better still if they'd come from England . . . preferably on the Mayflower. Lady Wentworth-Young didn't know it but she'd be right at home in Philly where blue blood was all, where old money and old families reigned supreme and everyone else stayed outside the pale.

'Well, your chaps have joined in at long last.' Sir William dabbed at his moustache with his napkin. 'We could have done with a hand sooner, but better late than never.'

'We'll try to make up for it, sir,' he said. 'Now that we're here.' He might have pointed out that he himself had given a hand sooner.

The daughter spoke up. 'We had some American Navy personnel with us for a bit recently. Rather different from our lot. Nothing like the same discipline. Pretty casual, actually . . .'

She spoke in exactly the same clipped way as her mother and she had the same ice-blue eyes. A chip off both old blocks, Pamela. How come they'd managed to produce a nice guy like Piers?

'I guess what really counts is whether they can cut it.'

'Cut it?' She looked at him blankly.

'Do the job.'

'Oh . . . Well, I suppose we'll have to wait and see.'

After the unknown soup there was some kind of fish, equally tasteless. An elderly woman in a white apron plodded about, offering dishes of soggy cabbage and gluey mashed potatoes. Sure, the rationing was tough, but he wondered what they did, or didn't do, to food that screwed it up so much. Mostly it was over-cooking, he reckoned. Vegetables boiled to pap, liver fried to leather, fish steamed to flannel.

After dinner, to his relief, Piers took him off to play billiards. The only problem he had there was winning too easily so he had to make some dumb shots on purpose to even things up. Pamela came to watch them, draped sideways in a chair, smoking a cigarette in a long ebony holder and showing off a lot of black silk-stockinged leg. He could tell that he'd passed the test and that she was interested. Only he wasn't. Not the least bit.

Stew picked the redhead up in a bar off Piccadilly. He'd checked into a small hotel in Bayswater, had a couple of grogs at the Boomerang Club in Australia House and then sank a couple more at a nearby pub where there was nothing on offer that took his fancy. He'd pushed on to try his luck elsewhere and spotted the girl as soon as he walked in the door. She was just the job: a good-looker there to pick up someone like him. She'd been giving some Pom Army bod the big brush-off and he moved smoothly into the vacuum. He never usually had much of a problem –

110

all it took was nerve and as much charm as he could muster.

Her name was Doreen and she'd taken him for a Yank at first because of his odd-coloured uniform. He guessed she'd been a mite disappointed to find out he was only an Aussie, but he didn't blame her for that: the Yanks had the loot, after all. He'd seen them cruising about with fistfuls of notes and pockets loaded with change, grabbing taxis and restaurant tables and girls. Money talked. Still, he'd saved up enough for a decent meal and plenty of booze. She wouldn't need to grumble.

He shot the usual line about what he did, tapping the side of his nose. 'Can't tell you, sweetie. Top secret.'

She peeked at him around a Veronica Lake hairdo. 'Aw, come on. I've heard that one before. You blokes think we're all born yesterday.'

'Well, I can tell you I'm on bombers.'

She leaned forward from her bar stool, showing a nice bit of cleavage, and tapped the one-winged badge on his chest with its woven 'B'. 'What's that for, then?'

'B for Bombers, like I told you.'

'So, what happened to the other wing?'

'Got shot off, darling.' He put his thumb and forefinger a quarter of an inch apart. 'It was that close.'

She laughed. 'Pull the other one.'

He knew they liked it best if you were a fighter pilot, but bombers were OK too, so long as you played your cards right. Not so glamorous maybe but by the time you'd spun a few horror stories they ended up thinking you a helluva brave hero.

He took her to the Strand Palace for dinner. He'd

been there before and the food was all right, even if the steak was horse. She was a notch above most of the girls he'd picked up on leave and good company, too. He found out that she worked as a counter assistant in the hosiery department of Swan and Edgar's and lived with her widowed mother out in the suburbs.

'She know what you get up to?'

Doreen widened her eyes. 'Get up to?'

'Going to bars on your own. Talking to strangers.'

'That's what *you* do, isn't it?'

'Different for men.'

'Why? You Aussies are the end. I met some of your Army blokes once. You treat women like muck.'

'No we don't. We're just a bit old-fashioned.'

'Must be something to do with living upside down. The blood stays in your head.'

He grinned. 'You've got that wrong, sweetheart.'

They went back to his hotel and nipped in past the receptionist when she had her back turned. Doreen was everything he'd hoped and guessed she'd be, and they both had a bloody good time. It reminded him of the old joke: Question: Have you ever slept with a redhead? Answer: Not a wink. Not that Doreen was a real one; it came out of a bottle, he could see that, but she was worth the steep price of the dinner. Too bloody right, she was.

He lit two cigarettes in his mouth and passed one to her as she lay beside him.

'What d'you say, we meet up again?'

'Mmmm. If you like, Stew.'

'Tomorrow?'

'Better not. I ought to go home and see Mum.'

'Day after, then.'

'OK.' She turned her head to smile at him. 'You're not half bad, you know . . . and I've never seen anything like what you've got.'

He took it as the considerable compliment it was intended to be. It wasn't the first time he'd been told that.

He saw her several more times during his time in London and though it cost him all his savings, he still thought she was worth it. Any amount was worth it, he thought grimly, when it could be the last time ever. They talked about meeting again next time he got leave.

'When's that?' she asked.

'In six weeks.' If I haven't copped it, he added to himself.

She laid a hand on his bare stomach, fingers playing the piano up and down, twirling the dark hairs. 'That's a long way away, Stew.'

'Well, maybe you could come up to Lincolnshire before then. I can get a night pass. I'd send you the fare.'

'Where would I stay?'

He thought for a moment. A bed and breakfast with a nosy landlady wouldn't do. There was The Saracen's Head but it always had a mob from the station. He racked his brains for somewhere a bit quieter.

'There's a place in Lincoln called The Angel.'

'What's it like?'

'Bit of a morgue. Stags' heads and potted palms, but the bedrooms're probably OK. I'll go take a dekko.'

She sighed, fingers still playing. 'It'll be a long time to wait.'

113

He rolled over towards her. 'Who said anything about waiting?'

When his mother opened the door to him, the first thing Jock noticed was the bruise at the corner of her right eye. It didn't surprise him. She'd had bruises on her ever since he could remember – usually starting on a Friday night because that was when his father got paid and drank most of his wages on the way home. Her face lit up with a pathetic gladness.

'Jock . . . oh, Jock.'

He set down his kit-bag on the step and took her in his arms. She felt thinner and frailer than ever – skin and bone under the pinafore. She was wearing a scarf tied like a turban round her head, and a few wisps of hair, the same dark red as his own, straggled free at the front. When she drew back he saw tears in her eyes. She wiped them away quickly with her hand.

'I didna expect you yet.'

'I was lucky with the trains.'

He'd stood all the way on the long journey from Lincoln to Glasgow and it was a trip he'd never have made if it hadn't been for her. She was the only reason he hadn't walked out of this slum the very first day he could and never come back.

'Come on in,' she was saying, tucking her arm through his. 'You're all wet and you'll be very tired. I'll put the kettle on.'

He closed the door on the rain and the cobbled street. His mother hurried to take down the line of washing strung across the ceiling, as though he were some sort of honoured guest.

'Leave it all be, Mother.'

She stopped, his father's patched and yellowed combinations pressed to her chest. How he'd always hated the sight of those things hanging up there. How he'd hated anything and everything to do with the brute: the very sight, sound and smell of him.

'They're dry,' she said timidly. 'I'll put them away.'

She went into the bedroom. He took off his forage cap and stood looking round at the kitchen, noting that nothing had changed, unless it was to get even more squalid. She kept it as best she could, he knew, but it was an uphill struggle against hopeless odds. Out of the corner of his eye he saw something dart along the wainscoting. The whole building was crawling with vermin of one kind or another. And that included his father.

When his mother came back she had taken off her pinafore and the turban scarf and brushed out the hair that was her one undimmed beauty. She smiled at him. 'I'd just got back from the factory. Lucky you didn't come sooner.'

'How's it going there?'

'Och, it's no so bad.'

She was slaving long hours and overtime at a bench making ships' rivets. He hated the thought of it but there was nothing to be done. Before that, she'd charred all day and taken in washing and sewing, so seeing her worn out was nothing new to him. And it wouldn't make any difference how hard she worked; most of what she earned would be drunk away by his father.

The kettle started whistling on the hob and she spooned a small and carefully measured amount of tea into the pot and poured on the boiling water.

'I saved some extra, Jock. And we've a tin of spam

115

for later. For a treat.' She fetched a cup and saucer and set it on the table. 'Sit yourself down.'

'Are you no having some?'

She shook her head. 'It's just for you. Would you like a bite to eat now? I've got some bread and a bit o' marg.'

'No. I'll wait.'

She sat down opposite him and poured the tea. Compared with the brew out of the Mess urns, it was weak as water.

'Do they feed you enough in the Air Force?'

'Aye. I reckon we do better than civilians.'

'Well, that's only right. They've got to keep the forces strong an' fit.' Her eyes searched his face. 'You're looking well, Jock. I was worried they might be working you too hard.'

'We get plenty of rest,' he said. She'd no idea that he was flying on bombing raids and he'd no intention of telling her.

'Well, drink up your tea, then.'

He drank a mouthful to please her and then fished in his breast pocket. 'I've brought something for you.'

'For me?'

He slid the little brown paper package across the table towards her. 'Aye, Mother. A present.'

She took it as wonderingly as a child.

'Go on, then. Open it.' He watched her unwrap the paper and stare at the shiny tube. 'It's a lipstick,' he said when she made no move to touch it. 'I hope the colour's right.'

There hadn't been much of a choice. The spiv in the Lincoln pub had fanned out a palmful of them and he'd tried to pick out a colour that seemed right for her. *Calypso Coral.* It had been a shot in the

116

dark, since he could never remember her ever wearing any.

'A lipstick,' she repeated. 'I've never had one.'

'Well you've got one now.'

'Wherever did you get it? It must have cost a fortune.'

He could tell by the tremor in her voice and the way she was blinking that she was fighting back tears.

'Och no. Look, you take the top off and twist the end so it comes up . . .' He showed her. 'Do you like the colour?'

'It's beautiful, Jock. But whenever will I wear it?'

'What's wrong with now, this minute?'

She bit her lip. 'Your father'll be back any moment. I don't know what he'd say—'

'What does it matter what *he* says? Who cares?'

To his shame, she flinched at his outburst. 'Well, you know how he is, Jock.'

'Aye,' he said dourly. 'I know how he is.'

How could he not know? His earliest memories were of his father coming home blind drunk and taking his belt to him for no reason at all. Of his mother's terrified pleadings as she tried to shield him with her own body, and the blows that then rained on her as well. Of lying on his mattress bed in his dark corner behind the plywood partition, shivering and shaking beneath the ragged blanket and listening to more blows falling, more piteous cries, mingled with the foul-mouthed abuse and threats that froze his blood.

It had gone on until the day when he had grown big enough and brave enough to stand up to his father – the day when he had gone for him and knocked him to the floor where he'd stayed, unconscious. It was the last time his father had thrashed him and so long as he was around, his mother was safe, too, but when he'd got his apprenticeship with the RAF and gone away he'd known that it would all start again. He'd begged her to leave, to walk out and find somewhere to live near him at Holton. And he'd gone on begging for years. As soon as he earned he would have supported her, taken care of her, given her a new life, but she'd refused to do it. 'I canna leave him, Jock,' she'd kept repeating stubbornly. 'He's my husband.' In the end, he'd given up, but he'd never understood. He felt bitter towards her; blamed her for what she had let him suffer, and for allowing herself to go on suffering so stupidly and so pointlessly. It made no sense to him at all.

She got up and went to the mirror hanging on the wall by its rusty chain. He watched as she applied the lipstick, following the line of her lips very slowly and carefully. Then she turned round. It was a shock, at first, to see her like that – the red so vivid in her white face, so unaccustomed – but when she smiled at him hesitantly, he caught a sudden glimpse of the bonny woman she might have been.

He smiled back. 'Aye, it suits you fine, Mother. Just fine.'

She opened her mouth to say something but the sound of the outside door opening stopped her. He knew it was his father by the crash of it shutting again and by the lurching tread. He rose to his feet and waited.

His father flung open the door and leaned unsteadily against the post. He looked even worse than Jock remembered – older, meaner, dirtier and drunker.

'Och, look who's turned up like a bad penny, then . . .'

'Hallo, Father.'

'What're you doing here? Thought we weren't guid enough for you.'

'I came to see Mother.'

'Did you now . . . where is the woman?' The bloodshot eyes swivelled and re-focussed. 'There she is. Come here, Jessie. Come here where I can see you.'

His mother crept forward, cringing, the back of one hand held across her mouth.

'What's the matter wi' you, for God's sake?' His father lunged and grabbed at the hand. 'What's that muck on your face? What've you done wi' yourself?'

'It's only lipstick, Donald.'

'*Lipstick!* That's for trollops. Trollops 'n tarts.'

Jock stepped forward. 'I gave it to her. It was a present. There's nothing wrong in it. The Queen wears lipstick.'

'Shut yer mouth! Coming here telling me what's wrong and what's right. I'm not having any woman of mine painting her face like a whore—'

'Don't mind him, Mother.'

But she was already scrubbing at her lips with a handkerchief and he knew there was nothing he could do. He picked up his kit-bag and made for the door. She called after him in a pleading voice. 'You're no leaving, Jock?'

'I'll be back later,' he muttered. 'When I've found somewhere to stay.'

It was raining hard as he walked from his old home, kit-bag slung across his shoulder. He got a room in a boarding-house a few streets away; it was a grim place, but cheap. He sat down on the edge of the bed and stared at the rain streaming down the dirty window panes.

119

'God damn him,' he said aloud. 'Damn him to everlasting hell.'

'I always said she wasn't good enough for you, Harry. Why you ever went and married her I'll never know. Anyone could see she was just a fortune hunter. Spent all your money and then looked for someone else to bleed dry.'

He'd heard it many times before and, although he knew it was probably true enough, it didn't help to hear his mother say it all over again. He wished he'd gone somewhere else after he'd been down south to try and see Paulette. Anywhere.

And what a waste of time that had been. When he'd got to the house in the avenue, Rita had answered the door and told him that Paulette was in bed with a temperature and couldn't come out. There was something about the way she'd said it that had made him sure she was lying, but he couldn't argue. He hadn't even got past the doorstep, let alone seen the child. She was feverish, Rita had said, too poorly to be disturbed. And besides, she'd added cruelly, seeing him always got her all upset. He wouldn't want to do that, would he, when she wasn't well? So, he'd given up and gone away meekly, leaving his present – a jigsaw of farm animals that he'd bought in Lincoln. He doubted Rita would ever give it to Jennifer; most likely, it would be thrown straight into the dustbin.

His mother was still going on about Rita, knitting needles clicking away at top speed. Harry stood at the window, hands thrust in trouser pockets, watching the rain and hardly listening. His father had given up listening years ago and was asleep in his armchair – or pretending to be. He wondered what the rest of the crew were up to. Jock was in Scotland, Stew in London on one of his jaunts, Van staying with Piers, Charlie with his mum, and Bert had pranced off, all smiles and winks, which most probably had something to do with that tarty parachute WAAF. He wasn't sure if he approved of it, but then he knew he was old-fashioned. He'd never go with a woman unless his intentions were honourable, and Bert's certainly weren't that.

'. . . never brings our granddaughter to see us, and never a word of thanks for anything. Did you ask if she got that last birthday present we sent Paulette?'

'I forgot.'

'Well, you'd think she'd write at least. What's the point of bothering, I say? I don't know why *you* do, Harry.'

Because I have to, he thought. Paulette's my daughter and I'm not going to give up on her. I'll never do that.

'Is that deep enough, Mum?'

She looked uncertainly at the long trench he'd dug at one end of the vegetable patch. 'I'm not sure, Charlie. I should think it'd be about right for the potatoes. I don't think the peas and beans will need to be as deep.'

He smiled at her. 'Digging for Victory, aren't we? Just like the poster.'

She laughed. 'Well, I hope the vegetables grow like in the picture.'

They laid the seed potatoes along the bottom of the trench, the way Mr Stonor had told her, and Charlie covered them with the soil again, raking it up into a ridge which the old man had said to do as well. It had been raining the night before and the earth was heavy and hard to work, but he managed to make a reasonable job of it. When that was done he started work on making shallow drills for the peas and broad beans. By the time he'd finished he was hot and thirsty and his mother went indoors to fetch some lemonade.

While he drank it and rested a bit she planted the peas and beans. He watched, leaning on the rake handle, and wondered if he'd live long enough to see them come up. They'd lost three more crews on the last op – not that he'd told her that, of course. Nor did she ever ask, but he knew that it was always in her mind.

> *If I should die, think only this of me:*
> *That there's some corner of a foreign field*
> *That is for ever England . . .*

He'd learned that poem by heart and it was one of his favourites. It didn't matter that it was all about a soldier. It wasn't any different for airmen, after all. The bombers' crews would lie in foreign fields – if there was anything left to bury. That's if the Germans would give a decent burial to people who'd been dropping bombs on them.

All he asked was that if it happened it would be quick. Over and done with before he knew what had happened. Like it must have been with Micky O'Rourke, Tail-End Charlie on Q-Queenie. His Lanc had got back from Hamburg badly shot up and word had got round the station that Micky had taken a cannon shell full in the chest and been spattered all over the turret. Charlie couldn't stop himself going over to take a look at poor old Queenie, who'd had more holes in her than a sieve. He'd walked round to the rear turret – couldn't stop himself doing that either – and some erks had been working away with scrubbing brushes and hoses, trying to clean it out. There'd been blood and stuff smeared everywhere, sticking to the Perspex . . .

First time he'd ever seen anything like that. The funny part about the RAF was that, although men were getting killed day after day, you never saw any dead or wounded. Either it happened on ops or, if they made it back, they were rushed out of sight in a flash, and all their belongings, too – as though they'd never existed.

There'd been three different crews sharing the sergeants' hut with them so far and all of them had bought it. First time, it'd been a bit of a nasty shock. He'd gone into the hut and found a couple of officers emptying lockers and piling stuff onto beds. They were the Committee of Adjustment, they'd told him, busily sorting through socks and shirts, letters and photographs. Taking care of the deceased's belongings. He'd stood there in silence watching them, unable to believe that the blokes he'd been having a joke with only a few hours before were dead. Would never be coming back. Len, Chalkey, Badger, Kiwi, Bill. All gone for ever.

The next time it happened after that, it wasn't quite such a shock. And when the third crew got the chop, he was almost getting used to it.

Mum finished the planting and he raked the soil back carefully over the drills. He was glad he'd had the chance to help her with things on his leave. They'd done a whole lot of weeding together, and now the vegetable planting, and he'd cleaned and oiled the old bike she'd been lent and got most of the rust off the handlebars. He couldn't make the bell work, though, and the chain kept coming off. Maybe he'd ask Jock to take a look at it some time – he was good with things like that.

He cleaned the tools and put them away in the garden shed, then he stood for a moment in the open doorway looking towards the drome. They'd been doing air tests all that morning, so he knew they'd be going tonight. By now they'd have bombed up, armed and fuelled, and the ground crews would be fussing around the Lancs. Briefing would be about twenty-hundred, take-off around twenty-two or so – timed to cross the enemy coast in darkness. He wondered which target it would be. Essen? Emden? Stuttgart? Bremen? Strange to hear them take off and not be going with them. The night before last he'd lain in bed, listening to them roaring over the cottage, making the windows shake and rattle. When they'd gone, he'd stayed awake for a long time, flying with them in his mind.

His mother called out from the cottage, 'Supper's ready, Charlie.' She sounded lighthearted and happy. Still three more days of his leave left.

'Coming, Mum.' He shut up the shed, wedging the stick of wood through the hasp, and went indoors.

PART II

Seven

They were fifteen minutes late reaching the target and when they finally got there, the Duisburg reception committee had hotted up.

Things had gone wrong from the start. Van had had a hell of a job getting S-Sugar to climb to twenty thousand: she'd struggled up, groaning and moaning all the way. It could have been to do with the warm night and some obscure law of physics, or maybe she was just a bitch. Personally, he went for the latter. Unlike friendly, steadfast D-Dog who was home having an engine change, S-Sugar was determined to make life tough for you. She didn't want to stay on course, kept dropping one wing and he had his work cut out to maintain the hard-won height.

Approaching the enemy coast, they'd presented a nice target for a flak ship lying unexpectedly in wait off-shore. They'd flown into its web like a careless fly, and the first salvo of shells had bracketed them neatly. He'd dropped the nose in a steep dive and S-Sugar went down a lot faster than she went up. The next shells exploded harmlessly above them and they were out of range before the gunners could have another go.

He'd started the long haul of clawing back the height lost and then he and Piers had gone and got their wires crossed over a course change and he'd

127

ended up way off-track before he'd realized the mistake. Back on the right course, they'd flown into a violent electrical storm that had S-Sugar plunging around like a bucking bronco and he'd damn near lost control of her.

Latecomers over the target, and getting all the attention, they staggered on through the flak and flame and searchlights. Stew did his stuff up front. 'Left, left. Right a bit. Steady . . . steady . . . steady . . . Bombs gone, skipper . . . Bomb doors closed.'

He grabbed the lever beside him. 'Doors closed. Let's get the hell out of here.' He hurled the bomber away to port as a searchlight beam fingered the tip of the starboard wing.

Relieved of her massive load, S-Sugar skipped homewards and he made the mistake of imagining that their troubles were over. Far from it. First, Bert sighted a non-existent enemy fighter and had them corkscrewing all over the skies to avoid it, then Charlie spotted a real one and he had to do it all again. When they'd managed to shake off the lone Me110 and he'd levelled out, his arms ached and trembled from the strain of throwing a heavy bomber about and he was drenched in sweat. It was an effort to flip on the mike switch.

'OK, intercom check. Bomb aimer? All right down there, Stew?'

'OK, skip.'

Nothing wrong with tough digger Stew. The rest of them answered quick enough, though he thought Charlie sounded kind of shaky. Christ knows what it had all been like in the tail. Well, at least they were alive and kicking and on oxygen. Without it you died in around ten minutes – easy enough to happen if he

128

didn't keep checking on them. Oxygen tubes could freeze up, get shot up, or just go u/s and you could lose consciousness before you even realized what was happening.

S-Sugar trundled on docilely towards England, and Van allowed himself to relax a bit. His arms had stopped their involuntary trembling, if not their aching. When they got below ten thousand and off-oxygen, he'd have a cigarette. It was against regs and Jock didn't like it, but the hell with Jock. He'd earned it on this one, he reckoned.

When Jock suddenly tapped him sharply on the shoulder he thought the guy must have read his thoughts until he saw with a shock that the starboard outer was on fire, flames licking merrily round the nacelle. The next second Jock had closed the throttle, hit the feathering button and shut the fuel cock. The propeller windmilled to a stop and the flight engineer zapped the fire-extinguisher button. They both watched the flames flicker and die and Van's heart went back to normal. Jeez, for a while it'd looked like it was going to spread . . . as though the fuel tanks would catch, same as he'd seen happen with other guys. Woomph and up she'd go and they be dead ducks. He trimmed the Lanc and called up Piers for a course. They'd be slower with the dead engine but who cared, so long as they got there in the end.

He might have known he'd counted his chickens too soon.

They were nearing the English coast at two thousand feet, dawn coming up, when a Royal Navy warship opened fire on them. His first reaction was one of blind fury – the assholes couldn't even tell a Lanc from a Heinkel! The second, to do something about it as fast as possible before they were hit. S-Sugar, shaken out of her trundle, was stampeding about again as shells burst unpleasantly close. The cockpit stank of cordite.

'Pilot to wireless operator. Sure the IFF's on?'

Harry came back at once. 'Dead sure, skipper. I'll fire the Very.'

Two stars blazed brilliantly above them in what Van fervently hoped were the right colours of the day. *Stop shooting you fucking maniacs, we're on your side.* The firing stopped, but his fury stayed. To be shot at by your own people, by some stupid, trigger-happy jerks . . .

Coming down to land at Beningby on three engines, he made the normal left-hand circuit turning away from the dud engine, like the drill said. His arms still ached and the wakey-wakey pill had worn off so that he was finding it hard to concentrate for tiredness. And S-Sugar was acting as though she was taking her latest scare out on him, fighting him all the way down. The old bucket shimmied in over the boundary hedge and floated stubbornly along, several feet above the runway. He heaved the wheel back, sweating. They were running out of concrete before she finally touched down as demurely as a debutante curtseying at the Philadelphia Assemblies Ball; light as the proverbial feather; innocent as a newborn babe; sweet as her name. What a bitch!

At de-briefing, the WAAF intelligence officer's ice-cool voice grated on his buzzing ears and refuelled his anger. His crew were dead on their feet: Charlie reeking of spew, Piers the colour of chalk, Bert with a lump on his forehead the size of an orange, all of them back from staring death in the face, and she sat there as calmly as if they'd been off on some sort of joy ride. He cut brusquely across one of her interminable questions.

'Your Royal Navy opened fire on us over the coast. Damn near got us.'

She looked at him as though he were the bad boy in class. 'Not *mine*, exactly—'

'They were British. *Your* people.'

'Was your IFF on?'

'Of course it damn well was. Might as well not have bothered for all the notice they took. We had to fire the Very to stop them shooting us down.'

'I'm sorry. Mistakes do happen, I'm afraid.'

She was *sorry*, for pity's sake! Frightfully, terribly Englishly sorry. He squashed out his cigarette with his thumb, grinding it savagely into the ashtray. 'Can't they tell a Lanc from a Kraut bomber? Doesn't anybody teach them? Or is that asking too much? Doesn't anybody on this godforsaken island *care* if they shoot down their own side? Jesus *Christ* . . .' He was sorry as he spoke, but he couldn't help himself. It enraged him to see her sitting there, so neat, so smug, so composed. What the hell did *she* know about any of it, anyway? He'd like to take her along on an op and see what it did to her. See how fucking cool and calm she kept then. He was gratified to see her flush deeply.

'Brought somethin' for you, Mrs Banks.'

'You shouldn't have, Mr Stonor . . . you've been kind enough already.'

'Wait till you see what it is. You mightn't be so pleased.' The old man was carrying a sack in one hand and set it down inside the front garden gate.

Dorothy jumped back as it moved. 'What on earth is it?'

131

Instead of answering, he tipped the sack upside down, shaking it by its corners. With an indignant squawking and a flapping of wings, a brown hen fell out onto the brick path. Feathers drifted about.

'They don't want her no more at the farm . . . only fit for the pot, see. Gettin' on, so she don't lay so much. Still, she's a few eggs left in her yet, so I said as how *you* might like her. You can cook her later on. Make you and the lad a good supper.'

She stared at the hen, who had started to peck about at the path's edge. It was a scrawny old thing, with bedraggled feathers and a tatty-looking comb. 'I don't really want her either.'

'Don't fret. I'll take her back.' The old man swung the hen up by her legs and the wings flapped frantically again.

'Will they – will she go in the pot?'

He nodded. 'Bit tough, I reckon, but she'll stew up all right.' The wings beat the air wildly, upside-down, as though the hen had heard and understood. 'Poor old girl, been pecked at by the rest. Hens're like that . . . nasty ways sometimes. All take against one. I've seen one pecked to death. She'll be well out of it.' He picked up the sack and started to stuff the hen back inside.

'Oh, no, don't do that, Mr Stonor. I'll keep her.' What was she saying? She didn't want her in the least. 'Only I don't know how to look after her.'

'Nothin' to it. I'll fetch you a bit of corn to feed her now'n again, an' you can mash up any old scraps you can spare – stale bread crusts, vegetable peelins . . .'.

'But where would she live?'

'I'll bring some wire netting and that lad of yours c'n make a run, else she'll be layin' any old place an'

132

scratchin' up your plants. You could make a house for her out'f an apple box or two. She won't need much. Somewhere to lay an' be safe at night.'

'There are some wooden boxes in the shed.'

'There you are, then. Easy.' He was still holding on to the hen's legs who was hanging limply now, wings quiet, as though resigned to her fate.

'Would you put her down, Mr Stonor? She couldn't be very comfortable like that.'

He chuckled and let the hen go. 'Don't do to have too tender a heart, Mrs Banks. Not where farm animals're concerned. If she don't lay for you, you tell me an' I'll wring her neck so's you can make a meal of her. No point keepin' her otherwise.'

They both watched the hen fluffing out her red-brown feathers. She stalked away from them up the path towards the cottage door, pecking here and there at the bricks as she went.

'What kind is she?'

'Rhode Island Red. Nice lookin' birds when they're in their prime. She's past hers.'

The hen was heading straight for the open door and presently disappeared inside. Mr Stonor gave another chuckle.

'Bit of a character that one . . . bit cheeky.'

'Charlie won't be here again for a day or two,' she said. 'What'll I do with her till we can get a run made?'

'Let her range free in the daytime – she won't do too much harm. You'd best shut her up in the shed at night, though, or the foxes'll get her.'

'Won't she wander off?'

He shook his head. 'Not if you feed her. Not that one. She'll know she's lucky. Be in clover here, she will.'

'Has she got a name?'

He looked even more amused. 'Bless you, no . . . there's thirty or more at the farm. No time to give 'em all names. You can give her one, if you want, though. Call her anythin' you like. She's yours now.'

He went away with the empty sack, and Dorothy hurried into the cottage where she found the hen pecking round the floor under the table. 'You can't stay in here,' she told her. 'You'll have to go outside.'

The hen took no notice whatsoever, so in the end Dorothy had to shoo her out, chasing her round and round the table and out of the doorway down the path. She stopped by the gate and started scratching away again and pecking about, making herself quite at home. From time to time, she looked at Dorothy sideways out of one eye. The name came from out of nowhere: Marigold. That's what she'd call her. Marigold.

Peter wasn't in his usual place at the bar of The White Hind. Catherine found a seat in a corner where she could wait, and got out her cigarettes.

'Light?' The American skipper was standing over her, Zippo at the ready.

'Thank you.' She leaned towards the flame, wondering why he was suddenly being so friendly. She'd had the distinct impression that he couldn't stand her.

'I'd like to apologize.'

God, she hadn't expected *that.*

'I was pretty rude to you at de-briefing last time. I'm sorry.'

He had been, but she hadn't blamed him. 'That's perfectly all right. You were very tired. It was quite understandable.'

'No excuse, though. You're only doing your job.'

'We both are. But yours happens to be a great deal tougher than mine.' She smiled up at him wryly. 'It's easy for me. All I have to do is sit there and ask a whole lot of questions and write down the answers. It must be very irritating for crews when they've just been through hell and need to sleep. I think I'd probably blow my top myself sometimes.'

He looked down at her for a moment. 'I guess I got you figured all wrong.'

Out of curiosity, she might have asked what he meant exactly but at that moment she saw Peter come in. She stood up. 'Excuse me, I'm meeting someone and he's just arrived.'

'Sure.' He moved back to let her pass and she made her way through the crush to Peter's side.

He stared at her suspiciously. 'What were you doing talking to that Yank?'

'He wanted to apologize.'

'What for?'

'Nothing really. He thought he'd been rude to me at a de-briefing.'

'Bloody Yanks . . . I wish they'd stay in their own bloody Air Force.'

He was in a dark mood, and she knew that the evening was spoiled before it had begun.

'Can I ask a favour, Jock?'

'Aye, Charlie – so long as it's not money you're after, because I'm skint.'

'Nothing like that,' Charlie said hastily. 'I wondered if you'd take a look at an old bike my mum's been lent. The chain keeps coming off. I thought you might be able to fix it.'

'I'll have a go. Should be able to manage something. When did you want me to?'

'Well, today, if that's OK, as we're on stand-down. She's on the early shift at her work this week so she'll be back by now. I thought I'd go over and see her this afternoon.'

Jock put down his book and got up. 'No time like the present, then. I'll fetch some tools.'

Harry had listened to the exchange from where he was sitting on his bed at the end of the hut. He was trying to sew on a button that had come off one of his shirts, but the thread had got all knotted up. The button was hanging away from the cloth instead of tight in like it ought to be. He stabbed at it again, pricked his finger badly and chucked the shirt down in disgust. No good getting blood all over it. He sucked at the finger. It was hot and stuffy in the hut and he could do with a breath of air. Maybe he could give Jock a hand with the bike? It would be something to do and he could have another go at the button later on. Start all over again.

He caught up with Jock and Charlie as they were setting off on their bikes, and the three of them rode out of the station gates and round the boundary road to the far side of the drome. It was the first time he'd seen Charlie's mum's cottage. Bit run-down, he thought. Could do with a lick of paint round the windows and on the front door, but then so could most places these days. You couldn't get the paint, so that was that. There were some tiles missing from the roof, too, and a broken gutter that needed mending before the wet did some serious damage. The garden was in good order, though. That must be her work; the owners wouldn't have bothered, judging by all the rest.

Charlie had hopped off his bike and leaned it against the front hedge. He and Jock followed suit and they went up the pathway to the blue door. There was a chicken scratching around in the flower bed. It stopped to look at them and then went on with its scratching and its pecking.

The door opened and a young woman appeared. Her face broke into a smile as she saw Charlie and she put out her arms and gave him a hug. This couldn't be the mother, it must be a sister that he didn't know about. To Harry, all mothers were presumed to be something like his own who'd been old and grey for as long as he could remember. He hung back behind Jock, and to his astonishment heard Charlie call her 'Mum'. She didn't look anything like old enough – scarcely more than a girl herself, dressed in a cotton frock with her bare arms tanned by the sun. He waited while Charlie introduced Jock, still uncertain that he'd heard right.

'And this is Harry, Mum.'

No, there'd been no mistake. He stepped forward. Her hand felt small and cool in his sweaty palm and he wished he'd wiped his own first. She was even littler than Charlie – only up to his chest, so that he found himself looking down into her upturned face. He went on staring at her while Charlie was asking about the chicken and his mother was explaining that someone had given it to her.

'He brought me some wire netting and posts as well this morning, Charlie. I was wondering if you could put up a run to keep her in? Would it be a lot of trouble?'

'Nay, we could do that easy,' he heard himself saying quickly. 'Just show us where you want it.'

While Jock went to see to the bike, he and Charlie took their battledress jackets off, turned up their sleeves and got going on the chicken run in a corner of the back garden. They were unrolling the netting when she came over and asked shyly if they could make a house for the hen, too, out of some old wooden boxes. He assured her that that wouldn't be any trouble either, though he wasn't quite sure how it could be done; he only knew that somehow he would do it.

She showed him the apple boxes in the garden shed and he found a rusty saw, a hammer, some wire and an old tobacco tin full of odd nails and screws. He'd never made anything like a henhouse before but in the end he managed a pretty good job. He made a guillotine door for the front which slid up and down between two runners, and fashioned a good strong catch for it out of wire and two pieces of wood. He knew chickens had to be shut up at night or foxes would get them and that foxes were cunning devils who could open things if they weren't secure.

When he'd finished the house, he set it down at the end of the run, propped up on some bricks to keep out the damp, and, as a finishing touch, he made a little gangplank for the hen to walk up.

Charlie's mother came out of the cottage and admired everything. He showed her how to pull the door up and down and how to fasten it safely.

'I think it's wonderful,' she told him. 'I don't know how you managed it. Thank you ever so much, Harry.' She fetched some straw to put inside the henhouse, which made it look all nice and cosy.

He and Charlie had made a gate in the wire-netting run and he held it open while she went to get the hen.

She had a spot of bother making it go into the run, though, and in the end the four of them had to chase it all round the garden and herd it in through the open gap. He shut the gate quickly and the hen strutted up and down looking for a way out, none too pleased with her new home. He'd left the guillotine door open and presently she went close by the little house and stopped, head on one side. He held his breath. Somehow it was very important to him that she should like the house he'd built. After a moment she stalked on and his heart sank. And then, quite suddenly, she stopped and turned back to take another look. He watched as she paused again with her head cocked and one scaly foot lifted. She put the foot down on the bottom of the gangplank, hesitated some more and then started upwards. As she went inside he let out his breath in relief. The others had been laughing because she'd looked so comical; now he could laugh too.

'I've called her Marigold,' Charlie's mother said, standing beside him in the warm sunshine. 'Silly isn't it?'

He thought she looked even younger when she laughed. Like a girl. 'I think it's a grand name,' he said. 'It suits her.'

'She hasn't even laid a single egg yet – at least I haven't found one.'

'She will,' he told her. 'For you.'

They had a cup of tea and some home-made biscuits in the cottage. The inside was a lot better than he'd expected, but he could see that was because of her. Everything was clean and bright, and there were little homely touches – flowers put round in jam jars, a pretty cloth on the table, the smell of fresh baking.

139

As she poured the tea, she asked Jock what he did in the crew. It was funny to see Jock, usually so curt, explaining it all to her nicely so's she could understand. He felt a bit left out, though, until she turned to him and asked what *he* did.

'I'm the wireless operator,' he told her. But when he talked about fixes and codes and signal strengths it sounded right dull compared with Jock. The fact was that he was jack-of-all-trades in the aircraft, not just the W/Op. He was look-out in the astrodome and in charge of the Very pistol and knowing the colours of the day. He was the one who had to check for hang-ups in the bomb bay and inspect the flare chute to make sure the photo-flash had gone all right, and the one who had to remember to switch on the Identification Friend or Foe going out and coming home to show they weren't Jerries, and to wind out and wind in the trailing aerial by hand, which meant crawling on his stomach to reach it. He was supposed to understand the intercom system and how the navigator's equipment worked and to help him with the Gee fixes. And it was his job to look after the bloody carrier pigeon. On top of all that, they expected him to be able to give first aid.

He'd like to have told her about all that, and about how hard he had to concentrate to hear the signals with all the engine noise and the interference and the static, and how his station was called the sweatshop because it was the hottest place in the Lanc, right beside the warm air outlet, and how everyone else always wanted the heat turned full on, so he always roasted. And how he'd done six weeks at gunnery school as well as his wireless op training, so he was a gunner too, not just a knob twiddler. He didn't tell her any of this, though. Instead he went on drinking his tea in silence while the others talked.

Jock had finished work on the bike and Charlie's mother rode it up and down the road to make sure the chain was working properly. Then Jock adjusted the saddle height and the handlebars so that they were more comfortable for her. Harry watched, wishing there was something else he could do to help. Before they left, he asked her if there was.

She hesitated. 'Well, there *is* one thing . . . but you've already done so much.'

'I meant what I said, Mrs Banks.' He waited hopefully.

'Well, the wireless here doesn't work,' she said at last. 'But I don't suppose anything can be done with it. It's just that it'd be nice having something to listen to in the evenings . . . and maybe with you being what you are, you might know what's wrong.'

'I'll take a look,' he told her, 'but I'm not a wireless mechanic. That's a different thing.'

'I'm sorry.' She blushed. 'How stupid of me!'

He cursed his own stupidity. 'Why don't I take it with me? If *I* can't make it work I can get one of our lads to see to it. I'll bring it back soon as it's done.'

It was a heavy old thing, all dark brown varnish and brass trim. He had to walk all the way back to the station, balancing it on the handlebars of his bike while Jock and Charlie zoomed on ahead. But he didn't mind a scrap.

Stew had cadged a lift with Piers into Lincoln, though he got the feeling Piers wasn't that keen on taking him. Probably had some sheila lined up and didn't

141

want him around. Fair enough. He'd make himself scarce once they got into town. He wondered what she was like. Some snooty English rose, most likely. He couldn't see Piers with anything else. Personally, he couldn't stand the type, though he'd heard some of them weren't half so goody-goody as they pretended, not once you got past the thorns. Only he didn't have the patience.

'Drop me off at The Angel, would you, old boy? If it's on your jolly old way.'

'Actually, I'm going there myself.'

Are you now, Stew thought. Maybe I'll get a squint at her.

They drove into the city through the old gateway. It slayed Stew to think that the Romans would have gone under the very same arch in their chariots, or whatever they nipped about in. He looked up at the cathedral as they went past. He usually got a bird's-eye view of it, the other way round, looking down through the bomb aimer's window.

Piers said casually – too bloody casually, 'I thought I'd have some dinner there.'

'Frightfully good idea, old chap.'

'I suppose you wouldn't like to join me?'

Now that was a surprise. Three's a bloody crowd. Perhaps he'd got the whole thing wrong, after all. 'Can't afford it, sport.'

Piers went a bit red round the gills. 'I could lend you some money.'

Stew hesitated. He wouldn't have said no to a free meal but it went against the grain with him to borrow. Never did unless he was in a real jam. Besides, Piers had probably only offered because he was too polite to tell him to piss off. No, he'd nip into the hotel and find out about the room, then he'd toddle on down to The Saracen's Head for a couple of beers.

He shook his head. 'Thanks all the same. I'm only going in to ask about their rooms – for someone I know.' No point explaining Doreen to Piers.

They parked the car and went through the squeaky revolving door into the hotel foyer. Piers went off to the dining-room and Stew sauntered over to the reception desk. He could hear the typewriter clattering away and see through the glass door into the inner office. The same girl was sitting at the desk, pounding at the keys. She went on typing without looking round, so he picked up the brass bell on the counter and shook it. No response. No sign that she'd heard or noticed and yet he had a feeling she knew damn well that he was there. He picked up the bell again and rang it louder and longer. She stopped typing then and came out to the desk, but she didn't hurry or look like she was overjoyed to see him. He kept his cap on.

'Did you want something?'

No 'sir' like with Piers, he noted. 'Yeah. If you can spare the time.' He injected a dose of sarcasm into it. 'I'd like to know the price of your rooms.'

'Double or single?'

'Single.' He leaned an arm on the counter and she moved further along, well away from him.

'That would be fifteen shillings per night, breakfast included.'

'Bit steep, isn't it?'

'Perhaps you'd prefer to look elsewhere.'

'Before I make up my mind about that, I'd like to see some rooms.'

She frowned. 'Only one of the singles is unoccupied at the moment.'

'I'll see that, then.'

'It might not be available for you.'

'Doesn't matter. It'll give me a clue what the rest're like, won't it?'

She shrugged and took down a key from the row of hooks on the wall behind her. 'If you'll come this way, then.'

He followed her up the stairs. She had quite a bit of trouble getting up them with that foot of hers, he noticed, though she tried hard not to show it. Too bad. The legs were pretty good otherwise. Better than he remembered.

They went along a corridor. Good grief, it was gloomy! Dried blood carpet, porridge wallpaper, more pictures of cattle in fog and a couple of stuffed foxes' heads snarling down. The room, though, was a lot nicer than he had expected. It overlooked a garden at the back of the hotel, and the evening sun was coming in through the window, cheering things up no end. And the bed looked comfortable. He went and sat on the edge of it and bounced up and down.

She was standing over by the wardrobe, as far away as possible, acting as though there was a bad smell in the room. Just to annoy her, he swung his feet up onto the bed and lay there at ease, hands linked behind his head.

'Would you mind not putting your shoes on the counterpane.'

He turned his head to look at her. Yes, she was annoyed, all right. Good.

'Have to test it properly, don't I? Where's that door in the wall go?'

'It connects to the next room.'

'Another single?'

'Yes. Occupied.' She jangled the key in her hand. 'Did you wish to book this one, then?'

'I'll let you know.'

His next leave was still four weeks away and first he'd need to find out from Doreen for sure if she could get away. If she could, he'd book the two connecting singles, if possible. No chance of getting away with a double and the Mr and Mrs Smith routine here. He put his feet to the floor and stood up, the springs twanging.

'I suggest you do so as soon as possible. We get very booked up, especially at weekends.'

She moved towards the door but he was nearer to it and he blocked her way, standing close – just to annoy her some more. She'd got a beautiful skin: he'd never seen one as good. On second thoughts, maybe she didn't need a load of make-up like most girls. 'What's your name?'

'I don't see—'

'I might want to ring about the booking. You're in charge, aren't you?'

'It's Miss Frost.' She hissed it at him.

'I already told you mine.'

'I'm afraid I don't remember.'

'Stewart Brenner. Everyone calls me Stew.'

'Really? Well, if you'll excuse me, Mr Brenner, I've got a lot of work to do.'

'Sergeant.' He tapped the stripes on his arm.

'If you'll excuse me, *Sergeant* Brenner . . .'

He moved away from the door and she limped past him as fast as she could. After you, Miss Iceberg, he muttered under his breath. He followed her downstairs, determined not to let it rest there, but there was some doddery old codger waiting at the reception desk and she started fussing all over him, sweet as pie.

'Yes, of *course*, Colonel. Don't worry, Colonel, I'll see to it right away.'

He decided to go and take a gander at what Piers was up to in the dining-room, and she called after him, 'That's not the way out, Sergeant.'

'I'm not leaving yet.'

He peered through the glass panels in the doors and caught sight of Piers sitting at a table, drinking his soup, all alone. No sheila in sight. Bloody odd.

'I say, do you think I could possibly have some more water, Peggy?'

'Certainly, sir.' She smiled at him as she stopped by his table, and Piers watched her go off towards the kitchens, carrying the empty jug. After a while she came back with it refilled.

'Shall I put some in your glass for you, sir?'

'Oh, thanks awfully.'

'Are you finished with your soup, then?'

'Gosh, yes, thanks.'

'Was it all right, sir?'

'Oh yes, frightfully good.' He couldn't even remember what it had been supposed to be . . . some kind of vegetable thing.

She smiled at him again – but then he'd noticed that she smiled at everybody as she went round the tables, even at that appalling old woman in the corner who kept grumbling in a loud voice. 'I'll bring you your chicken, then, sir. If you're ready.'

'Jolly good.'

She bent a little closer and whispered. 'It's rabbit

really, sir . . . but don't say I said so or I'll get into trouble.'

'Oh, I won't,' he promised. Wild horses couldn't have dragged it out of him.

He followed her with his eyes as she went off again. After the chicken there'd be the pudding and she'd have to come and see what he'd decided to have. That was going to be his chance. He could ask her then – if he could get up the courage. He'd rehearsed what he was going to say. *I was wondering if you'd care to come out with me, one evening, Peggy? I thought perhaps we might go to the cinema, or to the theatre?* There was actually quite a decent little theatre in Lincoln. Or dinner somewhere? Whatever she wanted. *If* she wanted at all. She'd probably turn him down flat. Probably had lots of boyfriends taking her out all the time. Bound to.

Driving in, he'd felt so nervous about asking her that he'd gone and asked Stew to join him so he'd have the excuse of putting it off till another time. But Stew was up to something else so there was nothing to stop him jolly well speaking up.

She was back with the chicken – or rabbit, rather. It was smothered in a white sauce so he couldn't see it properly, anyway. Well-disguised. She winked at him as she set the plate before him, together with a dish of carrots and boiled potatoes. 'There's your *chicken*, sir.'

He wasn't very hungry, but he ate his way through it doggedly. In spite of the sauce, he would have known it wasn't chicken; they'd had rabbit enough times in the Mess to be able to recognize the taste. When he'd finished he had to wait for a while before she came back to his table. The dining-room was full and she was scurrying here and there, attending to everybody. The old waiter didn't seem to do anything – just stand around, snapping his fingers at her. At last she came over, looking hot and bothered.

'I'm very sorry to be so long, sir. We're ever so busy this evening. I've been rushed off my feet.'

'It doesn't matter at all,' he said quickly. 'I'm not in any hurry.'

'Thank goodness for that.' She took the pencil from behind her ear and held up the little notepad that hung on the end of a chain from her waist. 'What would you like for sweet, then, sir?'

It was stewed apples and custard, or sultana roll and custard, or gooseberry tart and custard.

'Gosh, which do you recommend?'

'The gooseberry tart,' she said, without hesitation. 'They're from the garden here.'

'Right . . .' He took a gulp of water.

'One gooseberry, then, sir.' She began writing with her pencil.

In a moment she'd be off again. He cleared his throat. 'I say, do you think—'

'Sorry, sir?' She stuck the pencil back behind her ear.

'I was going to say . . . would you come out with me one evening? To the cinema, or something?' The words tumbled out in a rush. He smiled at her hopefully.

Her mouth had fallen open in astonishment. 'Beg pardon, sir?'

'I asked if you'd like to come out with me one evening, actually.' His heart was racing away. Was she going to feel insulted and call the head waiter over? Or, worse, laugh at him?

Instead, she looked bewildered. 'Is it a joke, sir?'

'No, of course not.' He was dismayed she should think such a thing. 'I meant it. Would you? I mean, on your evening off . . . if you have one. Do you? You must have.'

Her cheeks were turning bright pink. 'Well, yes, sir. Wednesdays.'

'Would you, then?'

'Oh, I couldn't do that, sir.'

'Why not?'

'Well, sir . . . it wouldn't be right, would it?' She started to back away from the table. 'Thank you just the same, sir.'

He said desperately, 'Will you think about it? Please?'

'There wouldn't be much point, would there, sir? So, if you'll excuse me . . . I have to go and give your order now.'

She fled through the swing doors into the kitchens and he sat there miserably, knowing that somehow he must have made a complete hash of it.

Eight

Bert had caught the grass snake out on dispersal. He'd spotted it slithering off into the undergrowth when they were all lounging around on the grass, waiting for the ground crew to fix some dud wiring in D-Dog.

At first he kept the snake in an old shoe box and fed it on dead insects and milk. It was a friendly little chap and after a while he started taking it around the station in the breast pocket of his battledress jacket. He taught it to poke its head out when he whistled, and it grew rather fond of having a spot of beer in the Mess. He named it Victor because he thought that was rather appropriate.

The only trouble was that Emerald didn't like Victor one bit. First time Victor had poked his head out of his top pocket when he'd whistled, she'd screamed the place down. So had other WAAFS, come to that, and he had to admit he'd done it on purpose just to give them a fright. So, when he went out with Emerald, Victor had to stay home in the hut, shut in his shoe box. He kept him out of sight of the new Flight Commander, too. It would have been OK with the old one, who'd been a good sort of bloke, but he'd got the chop over Bremen and the replacement was a bastard: morning parades, hut inspections, a whole lot of daft bloody bull. What did any of that matter when blokes were being written off before they could even unpack their kit? What was the point of polishing your buttons and shining your shoes if you were going to be burned to a bloody cinder?

Mostly, he didn't let the constant disappearing acts on the station get to him too much. Best way was to keep saying to yourself that it wasn't going to happen to you – only to the other blokes. Old Titch, for instance, who'd been a regular drinking mate till he'd copped it on his last trip. The shell had taken his head off clean as a whistle, he'd heard. Just like all those horror stories about mid-uppers. They'd had to put him back together again when they'd got him out of the turret. Poor old Titch.

What really bothered Bert was knowing he was no great shakes as a gunner. It seemed to him that he was the only one of the crew who hadn't got any better, and he was scared stiff of cocking it up for the rest of them. He could've sworn he'd seen a 110 that last time and felt a real muggins when they'd gone corkscrewing all over the sky for nothing. The skipper had told him he'd much sooner it that way than the other but, even so, next time he fancied he saw something he was going to make sure of it before he opened his cake-hole. Bloody sure.

The last rays of the setting sun glowed like gold across the corn as they took off. Stew, lying prone in the nose turret, got his usual kick out of the sensation. He stared down through the Perspex blister at the panorama of fields and woods spread out below him in the evening light. Not a bad-looking country some-times, it had to be said, though you could keep it in winter.

They headed east and towards the night. He

151

re-settled himself in the compartment and went over the flak positions on his map again. There wasn't much else for him to do for the moment, except keep a sharp look-out. He'd checked everything while the skipper was running up the engines before take-off – gone over his box of tricks. His eye ran across the panel once more: selector switches, timing device, selector box for order of dropping, master switch and camera controls, photo-flare releases, bomb release tit . . .

It always amused him to have to sign a receipt for the bombs when he'd checked the load. As though he might go and flog them, or something. This time they had a lot of bumf packed in among the bombs: bloody stupid leaflets for the Krauts, telling them to blame their leaders for their homes being smashed to rubble and not the nice kind RAF. They might as well load up with a few hundred boxes of Bronco and drop those instead.

He hated things that got in the way of the real job, and that included the load of bullshit dreamed up by that wanker of a Flight Commander. Polishing buttons and shaving, saluting and parading about like a lot of nancies. Not that it had lasted long – no longer than the bloke himself, which hadn't been more than a week. Soon as he'd bought it, they'd all gone back to the good old bad old ways, and Victor, Bert's snake, had come out of hiding. The new Flight Commander didn't have any flaming stupid ideas like that, thank Christ, and it wasn't his fault about the bloody leaflets. Some arsehole pen-pusher at HQ had thought that one up.

The noise of the four Merlin engines throbbed loudly in Stew's ears. Sometimes he fancied he could hear music when he listened to them. It was always the same tune: *The Warsaw Concerto* from that film about Poland where the bloke had sat playing the piano in the moonlight while the place was being bombed flat. He'd never told anyone that he heard music, though; they'd think he was going off his bloody rocker, or trying to work his ticket.

There'd been a wireless op in one of the other crews who'd gone crackers towards the end of his tour. Not hearing things but seeing them. Been sent aft to find out why their Tail-End Charlie wasn't answering and found him turned to strawberry jam. He'd seemed OK for a while till he'd suddenly flipped one evening in the Sergeants' Mess, rocking to and fro and gibbering and crying like a lunatic. Strewth, it'd given them all the willies! He'd been carted off and sent away, labelled LMF, poor sod. Lack of moral fibre. Stripped of his rank, put to cleaning bogs and marked down on his service record as a coward for ever. If he'd been a bloody officer, they couldn't have done it to him. That was RAF justice for you.

Stew shifted his position again. They were over the North Sea now and it was almost dark, but he could make out the white horses galloping about. Must be bloody rough down there. No chance if you came down in that lot. He listened to Piers giving a course alteration to the skipper. Funny about that business with Piers at The Angel. No sheila after all, unless she'd stood him up, and he didn't think that likely. Not with the posh family and all the cash. Most women knew bloody well when they were on to a good thing, in his experience.

Not long now and Doreen'd be coming up. That'd be something to look forward to, all right. Which reminded him. He reached for the steel helmet he always brought on ops. When he was lying face-down in the turret, trying to get the target in his sight and with all the Kraut crud flying up, the most vital and delicate part of him needed protecting. Next stop Düsseldorf. They'd never been there before and he wouldn't mind betting it was going to be a bastard. Nothing to be done but get on with it. At the start, he'd shit bricks on every op until he'd stopped worrying about getting the chop and simply thought of himself as already dead. The odds were he would be soon enough. Once you did that it was a whole lot easier.

He could swear he could hear that music again . . . *da daaa, da-da-da-daaa da da* . . . Strewth, maybe he really *was* going nuts.

Charlie pointed his guns at the stars. The night sky above was full of them, twinkling away. He found them a huge comfort. There was usually something to look at in the darkness: the changing light and shade of the sky, the passing clouds, the detail on the ground far below. It was when he could see *nothing* – just total blackness all around the turret – that he felt most alone. The stars were like friends, cheering him on. He knew there were billions of them and that their light took years and years to reach Earth so that what he was seeing wasn't really there any more, but that didn't worry him. And he knew there were other galaxies you couldn't see at all because they were even further away. Other worlds maybe.

> *My soul, there is a country*
> *Far beyond the stars,*
> *Where stands a winged sentry*

> *All skilful in the wars.*
> *There above noise and danger*
> *Sweet Peace sits crowned with smiles*
> *And one born in the manger*
> *Commands the beauteous files.*

He liked the words a lot. *Far beyond the stars . . . a winged sentry . . .* Of course, it really meant heaven, but if there *was* another country beyond the stars, he certainly hoped it would be a better place, without wars and killing and suffering. He swung the turret, searching and searching. They'd be over the enemy coast soon and the fun would begin. The butterflies were already fluttering about in his stomach.

'Pilot to crew. Intercom check.'

He listened to their answering crackles, in turn.

'OK Charlie?'

'OK, skip.' His flying suit was uncomfortably hot but there was nothing much he could do about it. It was either on or it was off, and if he left it switched off he'd freeze. The cushion helped, though. When he'd tried to give it back to Two-Ton-Tessie she'd made him keep it. The others had taken the mickey out of him, of course, but he didn't mind too much because it was a lot better than just having the padded seat. There wasn't room to stretch his legs – he could hardly even move them – and sometimes on a long trip the cramp got really bad.

No flak to worry about yet. Piers must have kept them right on track, so they'd stayed well away from it. Funny to think how he always used to get them lost. Thirteenth op now, so they were nearly half-way through the tour. *Thirteenth*. He'd touched Sam's ear twice for an extra bit of luck.

Stew's voice said suddenly, 'Christ, look at all that bloody flak!'

His stomach somersaulted. It was going to be a dicey one. The tail began bumping about as they ran into the barrage and the Lanc was hurled sideways by a shell bursting very close. For a heart-stopping moment he was sure they'd been hit, but after a bit she steadied. A searchlight beam flicked over the rear turret and he held his breath until it swept on to fix on another Lanc to starboard of them. Other beams hurried over to join it, locking together in one great white tower of light. He saw the bomber pinned helplessly in the glare, saw it burst into flames, saw it going down, saw a parachute mushrooming out behind. Just the one. *Only one.*

He heard Stew's 'Bombs gone!' and felt the aircraft lift. Twenty more ever-lasting seconds for the camera to take the photos of the fires raging in the city below then the skipper went into a fast, diving turn, taking them away from the noise and the stink and the flames and the terror.

The stars were there again, still twinkling away quietly above. *If thou canst get but thither, there grows the flower of peace* . . . If only there was a world like that. Somewhere.

'Pilot to navigator. What's up with you, Piers? Where the hell am I supposed to be heading?'

'Hall-o there, Van! How are you? Jolly good. Absolutely super. It's a long way to Tipperary, it's a long way to go . . . Never mind. Nothing to worry about.'

'Pilot to navigator. Check your oxygen.'

Piers giggled. 'Masses of time . . . I'm putting the rabbit in the sock . . . counting the chickens . . . jolly good . . . absolutely wizard . . .'

156

'Take a look, Jock, will you? Sounds like he's lost oxygen.'

Christ, no oxygen at twenty-one thousand! Thank God, he'd called him up.

Jock returned. 'He's OK now, skipper. A chunk of shrapnel took a bite out of his oxygen tube. Luckily it missed him. I've fixed it and he'll be all right in a tick.'

Piers' voice came on after a few minutes, back to normal. The same old earnest, anxious Piers. 'I'm most frightfully sorry, skipper. Would you please turn onto two nine six.'

If it hadn't been such a hell of a close call it would have been funny.

Honor Frost was awake when the bombers came back at dawn. She lay listening to the distant rumble of their engines for a while before she got out of bed and raised the blackout blind at the window. Her home was on the east side of the city, up on the hill, and she could see one of the bombers – a long, dark shape sliding in and out of low cloud. Maybe it was the crew who'd come to the hotel – with that boorish Australian sergeant. She watched the bomber descending gradually. Whoever they were, they'd got back safely.

'One Lanc went down over the target area,' the American skipper offered. 'Charlie saw a 'chute.' Since the apology he'd been quite different.

His rear gunner said, 'Just the one, that's all.'

Catherine wrote it down. Her hand was steady, her voice as calm as usual. 'It was definitely a Lanc?'

'Oh, yes. Definitely. I could see it clearly in the

157

searchlights. They'd coned it. Then I saw it burst into flames.'

'You're sure it went down?'

'That's right. It went down fast.'

'But you only saw *one* parachute?'

'There might have been more later,' the rear gunner said. 'But I couldn't keep watching. Sorry.' He looked upset.

'No, of course you couldn't.' She bent her head over the form and went on with the questions. They'd bombed right on target – the Aussie bomb aimer gave her his customarily fierce look for that one – the flak had been heavy and a chunk of shrapnel had sliced through the fuselage and severed the navigator's oxygen supply, but they hadn't encountered any enemy night fighters. She let them go as soon as humanly possible and stayed at her table, watching the clock on the wall and waiting, even though she knew it was pointless. *They'd coned it . . . I saw it burst into flames.*

O-Orange was the only Lanc that hadn't yet returned from Düsseldorf: Peter's.

Nine

Whenever they had a stand-down, Jock got off camp and rode around the countryside on his bike. He'd got used to living cheek by jowl with a crowd of others since the day he'd left home at fifteen, but, given the chance, he liked some time on his own. He did the circuit of the drome boundary, past Charlie's mother's cottage. Charlie's bike was propped against the hedge by the gate, and the front door was open, but he'd no intention of intruding. She'd want Charlie to herself as much as possible. Every moment would be precious when time might be running out. He felt very sorry for her, seeing how close she and Charlie were, but he also envied them. They understood and cared about each other – he'd seen that with his own two eyes. That's how a family should be. Charlie was a lucky lad.

Farther on, by the farm on the northern side of the drome, he heard the sound of a tractor working in the field on the other side of the hedge. He slowed to a stop by a gateway, balancing the bike with one foot on the ground, and watched the tractor chugging to and fro in the distance, towing a reaper-binder. It was a fine sight to see a good crop being harvested, going down cleanly before the knives, falling in neat, golden swathes. He admired the tractor going up and down a few more times, gradually working its way closer to him. And frowned. His eyes approved the sight, but his ears told him that there was something wrong with the tractor's engine. It had started to miss badly and the sound offended him. What sort of a farmhand could go on driving it like that? He followed the machine's jerky progress and wasn't a bit surprised when the engine finally petered out and stopped. The figure in the driver's seat climbed down and stood, hands on hips, staring at the engine. He waited for a while longer, watching the man poking and prodding about and he could tell he hadn't a clue. When he could stand it no more, he leaned the bike against the hedge, padlocked it and climbed over the gate.

He strode round the edge of the standing corn and, as he drew near, he shouted out. 'D'you need some help, mebbe?'

The figure turned round and, with a shock, he realized that it wasn't a man at all. It was a girl. The clothes had had him fooled at a distance. Women shouldn't wear those sort of things, he thought. It wasn't . . . well, *womanly*. Breeches like a man's and a flat tweed cap. No wonder he'd been mistaken.

'Where did *you* spring from?'

'I was passing – on my bike.' He jerked a thumb towards the road. 'I could see you were in trouble.'

She took off the cap and scratched her head; her hair was almost as short as a man's and looked as though it had been cut with sheep shears. It stuck out raggedly round a thin face burned brown by the sun. He'd never seen a lass look so unfeminine.

'It just stopped. I don't know what's the matter with it.'

'It's missing. Couldna you tell?'

'Well, I could tell *something* was wrong by the sound of it, that's all. Can you mend it?'

'Aye, I should think so. Probably dirt in the fuel. I'll take a look.' He took off his battledress jacket and rolled up his shirt sleeves. They shouldn't let females drive the things anyway. Tractors were dangerous. You could tip them over and get crushed, easy as anything.

There was a tool box on the tractor, but half of what should have been in it was missing, which didn't help the job. He found he was right about the dirt. Most likely muck from the bottom of a rusty fuel tank. She'd let it run too low and that had done the damage. He soon had it cleared and while he was at it, he checked over the rest of the engine, making adjustments here and there. He wouldn't have been surprised to find a bird's nest; it didn't look as though anyone had touched it for months. The girl watched him in silence, thumbs stuck in her breeches' front pockets, chewing on a piece of straw. He went round to the front of the tractor to swing the handle. The engine started up on the third swing, running smooth and true.

'She'll be all right now.'

'Thanks a lot.' She raised her voice above the din. 'What was wrong?'

'Dirt in the fuel, just like I said. Rust particles on the bottom of the tank. Don't let her run low or she could do it again.'

She peered out at him from under the peak of her cap. 'You look as though you know about engines. Are you a mechanic or something?'

'I'm a flight engineer,' he said stiffly. 'On Lancasters.'

'I'm a land-girl.'

161

'Aye, I thought you must be something like that — by the clothes.'

She laughed. 'The cap's the farmer's. I like it better than the uniform one we're supposed to wear. Well, I'd better get back to work. Thanks again.' She hopped up into the driver's seat and looked down at him. 'I could do with a hand stooking, if you've nothing better to do.'

He glanced towards the long trail of sheaves left lying in the stubble. 'All that?'

She grinned. 'And the rest. Don't blame you if you don't fancy the job. If it's too much for you.'

He yanked his tie undone. 'Get going, then.'

He toiled under the hot sun for the rest of the afternoon, propping the sheaves of corn up against each other in rows of stooks across the field. As soon as she had finished the reaping, the girl stopped the tractor and came to help him and they worked together. She was strong, he saw, in spite of being thin, and she could almost match him for speed. It was a while since he'd done any PT and it showed. Getting soft, he thought ruefully, wiping his forehead. Too much sitting on his backside in a bomber.

With the last stook done, she took off her tweed cap and fanned herself. 'Tea-time. Come back to the house for a bite. They'd want you to. They're nice.'

He hesitated but she was already walking away from him and, after a moment, he collected his battledress jacket and tie and followed. He rode down to the farmhouse, standing behind her on the tractor and she took him into the kitchen where the table was loaded with the kind of spread he'd never seen before in his life: home-baked scones, butter, jam, cream, honey, cake, ham, eggs . . . The farmer's wife, wielding a huge brown teapot, refilled his cup again and again and pressed him to eat until he could eat no more. He noticed that the girl ate plenty, too. No dainty picking at her food.

'Come over again for tea, whenever you want, Jock,' Mrs Gibbs told him. 'And bring some of the other lads from the station. We'd like to have you.'

As he was leaving she pressed a clutch of warm eggs into his hands. 'Wages – for all that work in the five-acre. Helping Ruth.'

The land-girl came to see him off. 'She meant that, you know – about coming again. For tea.'

'Och, well—'

'They could do with a hand with the harvest – if you get any time spare. There's only me and an old man.'

'I'll try,' he said. 'But we never know.'

She looked at him from under the cap brim, arms folded across her thin chest and nodded. 'If you can.'

He walked back to where he'd left his bike, the eggs tucked carefully in his battledress jacket pockets.

The faint memory of a bible story came back to him from a school scripture class of long ago – something about Ruth in a corn field.

'I've brought it back.'

When Dorothy opened the front door she found Harry standing on the path in the evening sunshine. He was cradling the old wireless in his arms.

'I got it going,' he went on. 'Well, with a bit of help from one of our mechanics. It needed some parts.'

'I'm ever so grateful.'

'Will I bring it in?'

'Thank you.' She stood back to let him enter and he carried the wireless through to the sitting-room

163

and set it down on its shelf. 'Shall I turn it on – just to make sure it's all right?'

She nodded. 'If you've got a moment.'

He switched on the knob and the yellow light glowed on the dial. 'Give it a moment to warm up, then we'll try it,' he said. 'What would you like? Home or Light?'

'The Light, please.'

He turned the tuning knob and there was a lot of crackling until, suddenly, clear as a bell, Mrs Mopp shrieked out in her corncrake voice, 'Can I do you now, sir?'

She clasped her hands, delighted. 'Oh, I love ITMA. It's my favourite programme.'

'Mine, too,' Harry said.

'Would you like to stay and listen to it?'

'Only if you don't mind?'

'Of course I don't.'

He took off his cap and they sat down in the easy chairs. Mrs Mopp was giving His Washout the Mayor, Tommy Handley, a jar of carrot jelly . . . 'strained through me own jumper' she told him proudly, and the audience in the studio roared with laughter. So did Dorothy, and Harry joined in. They laughed at Ali Oop, the pedlar: 'I go – I come back', Claud and Cecil, the brokers' men: 'After you Claud. No, after *you*, Cecil.' Funf, the German spy with his sauerkraut feet: 'This is Funf speaking.' And the Diver, who always said, 'Don't forget the diver, gents. Don't forget the diver. I'm going down now.'

At the end of the programme Harry stood up – a bit reluctantly, she thought. 'Well, I'd best be off, Mrs Banks. Thank you for letting me listen.'

'Goodness, it's me should be thanking *you*, Harry.

You've been so kind. It'll be lovely having the wireless to listen to.'

'Must get a bit lonely here sometimes. All on your own.'

'Not really. Not with Charlie so near. And then I've got my work at the army camp. That keeps me busy.' She didn't enjoy it much. It was mostly washing-up and peeling vegetables and not really cooking at all, like they'd made out. Just skivvying, really. Still it was doing something useful. Her bit. She turned off the wireless. 'Would you like a cup of tea before you go?'

'If it's not a bother.' He was all consideration. So polite and never pushing himself forward. He came to stand in the kitchen doorway and watched her setting the cups out on the tray, seeming to fill the space, with his head nearly touching the lintel – such a big man compared with Charlie.

'If you don't mind my sayin' so, Mrs Banks, you must've been married very young.'

He said 'moost', not 'must' and she thought how the Yorkshire accent suited him. He spoke as he looked: not a man to rush anything – deliberate and dependable.

'I was sixteen. Charlie was born a year later.' She could see him doing sums in his head. 'Charlie lied about his age at the recruiting office, but I expect you know that.'

He smiled slowly. 'Matter of fact, I lied about mine, too. Only t'other way round. Said I was much younger, so they'd take me. I'm really thirty-four.'

'Then we're exactly the same age.'

He nodded. 'So we are.'

She made the tea and he carried the tray through to the sitting-room for her. When they were sitting down, drinking it, he said awkwardly, 'You mustn't worry about Charlie.'

'I try not to.'

'We'll take good care of him.'

'I know you'll do your best. Thank you.'

'Sam comes with us on every op, did you know?'

'Charlie told me. When I watch the bombers take off I think of Sam, up there, going with you. Bringing you luck.' She put her cup down in the saucer carefully. 'The rear turret – where Charlie sits – it looks a very dangerous place to be.'

'Nay, no more than anywhere else,' he said. 'And he's got the guns. He's very good with the guns, is Charlie.'

But she went on, unable to stop herself, 'When I went into the village shop the other day, they were talking about a rear gunner at Beningby who'd been killed on a raid. Hit by a shell. They said he'd had to be hosed out of the turret. Those were their very words. It's been on my mind ever since. I can't stop thinking about it.'

Two women, hair curlers under their headscarves, shopping baskets hooked over their arms, had been gossiping at the post office counter in the corner. They hadn't noticed her come in, and when Mrs Dane had caught sight of her standing by the door, she'd shushed the other two at once.

'You don't want to take no notice of them,' she'd said to her later, snipping the sugar coupons out of her ration book with the points of her big scissors. Snip, snip, snip. 'It's all made up.'

Of course, she *had* taken notice, had pictured it very clearly. *Hosed out.* She could see the swooshing jet of water, the red blood swirling, shreds of mangled flesh, splintered white bone, bits of blue uniform . . . If that ever happened to Charlie she'd want to die herself.

The wireless operator was looking red in the face and angry. 'That's a load of rubbish. Some folks like nothing better than to spread gory tales like that. It's just a pack of lies.'

But she'd seen how the rear turret was all clear Perspex, like a small greenhouse stuck on the end of the bomber's tail. There'd be nothing to stop the shells and bullets. Nothing to protect Charlie at all.

'Where do *you* sit in the Lancaster exactly, Harry?'

'Forward,' he said. 'Towards the front, just behind the navigator.'

'In front of the wings?'

'Aye. Me and the navigator, the pilot and flight engineer and the bomb aimer, we're all forward of the main spar. The mid-upper gunner's up in a turret on top, between the wings and the tail.'

'So Charlie's on his own at the back? There's nobody near him? None of you?'

He shifted uneasily in his chair. 'It's not like it sounds. We talk to each other all the time. And I go aft for things. I'm the fetch and carry one.'

'Would you know if anything had happened to Charlie?'

He nodded. 'The skipper calls us all up regular. We'd know. Don't you worry. I'll keep an eye on him, I promise.'

She changed the subject and asked him about himself. He muttered something about a wife who'd left him and he mentioned a daughter.

'Then you know what it's like,' she told him. 'To worry about a child.'

'I don't see her much. Hardly know her. It's not the same as you and Charlie.'

'I oughtn't to have come here, though, did I? Fussing over him? You must all think so.'

'We don't think that at all,' he said. 'We think Charlie's right lucky.'

He stood up to go as soon as he'd finished his tea, and she saw him to the door. With the double summer time, it was still light and so quiet there might not have been a bomber station there at all.

The wireless operator turned to look up at the cottage roof. 'That gutter needs fixing. Ought to be put right before winter comes. I'll come by and see to it, if you like.'

'You've done enough for me, Harry. I wouldn't want you to trouble.'

'It's no trouble, Mrs Banks. It'll give me something to do when we're on stand-down.'

'Please call me Dorothy.'

He put on his cap. 'Goodnight, then – Dorothy. And thank you for the tea.'

He was unpadlocking his bike by the gate when she suddenly remembered something.

'Wait a moment, Harry.' She ran indoors and came back to the gate. 'Marigold suddenly started laying, like you said she would. These are for you – for making the run and mending the wireless.'

He stared down at the two eggs in her hands and then closed her fingers over them gently with his own. 'Nay, you keep them, Dorothy. Keep them for you and Charlie.'

When he had ridden off up the road, she put the precious eggs back in the bowl in the kitchen and went to shut Marigold up for the night. The hen was still outside, pecking about the run, and she had to chase her, as usual, until she stalked up the gangplank into her house. Dorothy wired up the guillotine door tightly and went back indoors to wash up the teacups and set them on the rack to drain. After that she switched on the wireless again. Lovely dance music filled the room and she held out her arms to a pretend partner and did a few steps to and fro and then round the room. Years ago – before she married Edward – she used to go dancing at the local hall. There'd been a band, of sorts, but nothing like this one. This was one of those big London ones, smooth as silk. It made you want to dance and dance . . . only, of course, her dancing days were over.

She didn't bother with the blackout yet; instead she curled up in one of the easy chairs and stayed there for a long while, head pillowed on her arms, listening to the music. Gradually the room grew darker around her until the only light came from the little oblong yellow glow on the wireless dial.

'Can I buy you a drink?'

She looked as astonished as when he'd offered her a light in the pub. 'Well, I was just going, actually.' She'd been sitting in a corner of the Officers' Mess in one of the sagging armchairs that must all have been collected off the local dump. She'd been talking to another WAAF officer and he'd been observing her from behind his newspaper. When the other WAAF had left he'd put down the paper and strolled over.

'Have one for the road.'

She smiled. 'I wasn't planning on leaving camp. Just the room.'

'Figure of speech.'

'Well, all right. Thank you. A shandy.'

'Shandy?'

'Beer and lemonade.'

'Ow! Some mix! You sure?'

'Quite sure. I like it.'

'It's Van, isn't it?' she said when he'd fetched the drinks from the bar and sat down in another sagging armchair with broken springs. 'That's what they all call you?'

'Except my parents. They call me Lewis – the name they tried to give me in the first place.' He lit her cigarette. 'And people call you Catherine. Mind if I do the same?'

'Not at all.'

'I'm sorry about Pete.' He'd never liked the guy, but that had nothing to do with it. Jerks or nice guys, you were sorry when they went missing. As sorry as you could afford to be. Along with being sorry, there was always that nasty little gladness that it was someone else, not you. 'Any news?'

She shook her head. 'Nothing, so far. It can take a long time to hear through the Red Cross. He could have evaded capture and be hiding up somewhere.' She drew on her cigarette. 'Or, of course, he could have been killed.'

'My rear gunner definitely saw a 'chute. He's got exceptional vision and he's a reliable kid. He wouldn't have made a mistake about it.'

'One. Out of seven.'

'Charlie couldn't keep on looking. There may well have been more. They were at twenty thousand. There was time.'

She tapped the end of her cigarette against the ashtray – unnecessarily. 'I wouldn't think it was

170

particularly easy to get out of a Lanc going down fast, in flames.'

You've got that right, sister, he thought. Only for that glorious piece of British understatement, substitute fucking impossible. First, find your parachute. Unlike the rest of the crew, Pete would have been sitting on his, so that was a point in his favour. Get it clipped on right. Crawl through the fuselage to one of the escape hatches, down in the nose preferably so the tail plane didn't mash you to pulp when you jumped out, or up in the roof, mid-ships – too bad for you if you had to clamber over the main spar to make either of them. Once there, get the damn hatch open. Turn the handle, lift it inwards and throw it out – always supposing it hasn't jammed – and then launch yourself into the roaring slipstream and pray you miss the rest of the bomber as it goes by.

And all this upside down in the dark, maybe with a little touch of centrifugal force from a spin trying hard to keep you inside, not to mention the flames trying even harder to get you and your parachute. Oh, and the small matter of your parachute opening before you hit the ground around twenty thousand feet below. Or the Jerries not taking pot shots at you on the way, if they felt in the mood.

'We practise the escape drill pretty often,' he lied. 'And Pete had a quick-release panel in the cockpit roof he could have used.'

Don't tell her about the chances of smashing into the mid-upper turret or getting cut in half by the tail plane or rudders if he was desperate enough to try that.

She looked him straight in the eyes. 'It's nice of you

to be so encouraging, Van, but I do know the odds. Only too well.'

'Yeah. Well, I guess you do in your job.' He sipped his beer. 'You see them come and you see them go. Must get kind of depressing.'

'I'm so sorry – I should never have said that to you. It was inexcusable.'

'In case you depress me as well, you mean?' He smiled. 'Don't give it another thought. I know the odds, too.'

'But you're doing awfully well with your tour,' she said brightly. 'How many is it now?'

'Fifteen.'

'Half-way through. Veterans.'

'Yep.' The sprog crews watched *them* now – copied them and hung on their nonchalant words.

'I overheard Squadron Leader Lowell say he'd thought you'd make it all right. He doesn't say that about many crews.'

The Squadron CO was a demanding sort of guy, to put it mildly. He wondered if she was telling him a little white lie – if she fed that sort of bull to everybody. 'That's not exactly what they were saying about us when we started. We were odds-on for the chop.'

'So are most sprog crews. Sadly. But you're well past that stage, and you've got a good crew, haven't you?'

'Yeah . . .' He smiled again. '*I* think so, but then I guess you could say I'm prejudiced in their favour. For one thing, they put up with me driving them around.'

'Your aiming-point photographs are pretty good. Often the best.'

'I've a very competitive bomb aimer.'

'Oh yes, the Australian. There are so many of them

172

from the colonies. It's wonderful the way they've come over here.'

'Tell that to Stew. He'd be delighted.'

'He usually looks anything but delighted at de-briefings.'

'That's if he thinks you're questioning his accuracy.'

She said defensively, 'Really, I'm not. It's just that I'm supposed to get it as exact as possible. It's important when they analyse all the information . . . I know the crews often hate it, though – Peter always said so. Having to sit there for ages, dog-tired, being interrogated by somebody who's been safe and sound on the ground. I'm afraid I must sound very bossy sometimes but I'm trying to make sure I get all the details. That nothing vital's left out. Inside, I feel awful at keeping crews from their rest.'

'You always look pretty calm.'

She tapped her cigarette end again. 'A navigator in one of the crews once told me that seeing me sitting there every time he got back, acting as though everything was perfectly normal, was the only thing that kept him going. He found it a great comfort. I've always remembered that.'

He could see the point. 'Did he make it?'

'He was killed on his last op.'

'Tough luck.'

'Yes . . . very tough luck.' She drank some of the shandy. Lousy-looking stuff, he thought – like fizzy bathwater. Tepid fizzy bathwater. What had the British got against ice? He didn't get it. Also, he thought, how the hell could I have got her *so* wrong?

'Of course,' she went on quite seriously, '*you're* not from the colonies—'

173

'Not since seventeen seventy-six.' He smiled.

'So what on earth made you join up? Long before your country came into the war?'

'That's another story,' he said. 'Maybe I'll tell you some day.'

As soon as he saw the girl on the tractor, Stew twigged why Jock hadn't wanted them to come a-harvesting with him. No chance of stopping them, though – not once they'd spied the cackleberries and heard about the beano tea. If he'd wanted to keep her to himself, Jock should've hidden the booty and kept his trap shut. The minute they'd got wind he was going again, they'd tagged along, harder to get rid of than a dose of clap: him, Bert and Charlie. Harry was off mending gutters at Charlie's mum's cottage, or he'd have come along too.

Stew didn't mind the hard work part of the deal. He was strong as a bloody ox and he enjoyed heaving sheaves of corn around. He knew he looked good stripped to the waist and still with a bit of his Bondi tan – a lot better than old Jock, lobster-red from the sun, let alone skinny white Bert and Charlie. And he knew the girl had noticed.

She stopped the tractor by him as they were finishing off the stooking in one field. 'When this lot's done, we can start the next. If you're up to it.'

He grinned up at her. 'I'm always up to it.' He liked the tweed cap and the weird hair-do and the big brown eyes. And he'd liked the way she hadn't batted an eyelid when Bert had pulled his Victor trick, whistling to the snake so he poked his head out of his breast pocket and looked around. Most women screamed the place down whenever he did that, but she'd just

174

laughed. She was on the thin side – all bones and not much meat – but the rest was bonza.

She was giving him a straight look from under the cap that told him she'd got his number pretty well. And she wasn't playing. That didn't worry him. He was used to sheilas who put up a red flag and then hauled it down when they'd got tired of playing hard-to-get. And he could tell she'd been around.

'Can you shoot? The rabbits'll come out when I start with the reaper.'

'Too right I can.' Well, he was a dab hand with the Brownings, if not the sort of gun she meant. The Poms seemed to think Aussies spent their time shooting kangaroos.

'How about the others? Can they?'

'Bert and Charlie are gunners – not that that means a thing. Don't know about Jock.'

'OK, I'll fetch the guns.'

He watched her go off, following the tractor's bumpy progress across the stubble. She handled it pretty well – for a woman. He was looking forward to a shoot-out – see who could get the most rabbits and impress the lady at the same time. Like one of those olden day tournaments with knights charging up and down, knocking each other off their horses. The best bloke got the classy sheila in the wimple waving her lace hanky.

But when it came to it, and the girl was handing out the twelve-bore shotguns, Jock and Charlie both chickened out. Jock said he'd never handled one before and Charlie said he didn't like the idea of shooting animals. Just as well he didn't feel the same about Jerries. So it was between him and Bert, and with Bert's eyesight being what it was, he didn't reckon it would be too much of a contest.

The minute the girl started off with the tractor on the far side of the field, working round in a big circle, he positioned himself, lying down at the edge in what he judged would be a prime spot. At first, nothing happened. Not a dicky-bird showed up. Not even a field mouse. He'd begun to think maybe she'd got it all wrong about the bunnies until she was on the fifth or sixth circuit and a rabbit suddenly came streaking out of the corn, heading right towards him. No time to take aim properly before it was into the hedge and out of sight. Then another appeared and the same thing happened. And another. On the far side of the field, Bert's gun was blasting away. Stew swore violently. The little buggers were craftier than a bunch of Messerschmitts, split-arse-turning in all directions, and he was firing away like a loonie and not hitting a flaming thing except clods of earth.

The girl finally got down to a small circle of standing corn and a rabbit came out much slower than the rest. Stew raised the shotgun yet again, fired as it loped past and saw it fall to the ground. He went over and picked it up by the hind legs. There was a grizzled look to the fur, a rheumy look to the open eyes. Poor old grandad, left behind when the rest were deserting the sinking ship.

He met Bert half way across the field and, stone the crows, he was carrying several of the little sods, dangling from each hand. Six, when he counted them – *six* to his one. And Bert was grinning all over his face, pleased as bloody punch with himself. Well, he knew when it was the time to be gracious, give credit

176

where credit was due. Besides, it was nice to know their mid-upper could hit *something*.

At the farmhouse spread – and Jock hadn't lied about that – he made sure he sat next to the girl. Beat Jock to the empty chair by a short head. With the cap off, he thought she looked even cuter.

'When do land-girls get time off?'

'We don't during the harvest.'

'How about after?'

'We get a week's holiday a year, Sundays and a half day. Sometimes we get a long weekend, but not often. There's too much to do.'

'Sounds like slave labour.'

'It may be for some,' she said. 'But I like the work. And they treat me like family.'

'Where's your real family?'

'I don't have one,' she said. 'I come from an orphanage. And, by the way, Aussie, you're wasting your time. Just thought I'd tell you that now, so's you'd know.' She picked up a plate and shoved it under his nose. 'Have another scone.'

It wasn't his day, Stew decided. You win some, you lose some. Rabbits, sheilas . . . what the hell!

The tea had been a real blow-out, and the old girl gave them each half a dozen eggs when they were leaving. Like the others, he tucked his into his jacket breast pockets. It might have been an accident, though he bloody well doubted it, when Jock ran into his rear wheel, biking back to the station. Tipped him off so that he smashed every single flaming one.

It didn't finish there, though. There was a letter from Doreen waiting for him.

Dear Stew, Sorry I won't be able to come next weekend after all. My mum's not well and I have to take care of her . . .

For mum, read Yank, he thought sourly. Or anybody with enough bait on the line. He went to phone The Angel and Miss Iceberg answered.

'Sergeant Brenner speaking. About those two single rooms I booked – I've got to cancel.'

'Sergeant who?'

'Stew Brenner.' She knew bloody well who it was. 'Miss Roberts can't make it.'

'That doesn't give us much notice.'

'Well, she can't get here. Someone's ill.' His temper was short after everything, and she'd no call to sound so flaming disapproving. Miss Roberts could be his maiden aunt for all she knew. Unlikely, it was true, but possible.

'I suppose you'll be wanting to cancel both rooms, then?'

'Not necessarily.'

'Well, yes or no, Sergeant? I can't keep the booking open.'

He considered the situation. What the hell was he going to do with his leave, anyway? There was nowhere to go except London and he was getting tired of it on his own. Besides, you could spend a bloody fortune down there, if you weren't careful. Maybe he could stay at The Angel for the weekend – take it easy for a bit, be waited on hand and foot, and see what he could find in Lincoln? That still left time to head off to London if he felt like it.

'Sergeant? I haven't got all day . . .'

'I'll keep one room,' he said.

'For *you*?'

'That's right, sweetheart. For me. See you soon.' He hooked the receiver back and grinned.

Mrs Mountjoy was making a big to-do over the soup again. She'd pushed it away from her, hardly touched, spoon plonked down in the middle.

'This is *exactly* the same soup that I complained about yesterday, Peggy.'

'I don't think so, madam. Yesterday's was pea soup. It's *potage au jardin* today.'

'There you are! All that man has done is add some tinned carrots and given it a different name. Never been *near* the garden. It was uneatable yesterday and it's even more so today. It's scandalous with the prices they charge here.'

'Yes, madam.'

Mrs Mountjoy flapped her napkin at her as though she was scaring crows. 'Well, take it away, girl. Take it away. And tell him I *refuse* to eat it. He'll have to produce something else.'

Peggy carried the plate into the kitchens. 'I'm very sorry, but Mrs Mountjoy says she doesn't like the soup. And could she please have something else?'

For a moment she thought the chef was going to hit her with his wooden spoon. He shook it at her ever so angrily. 'Tell her she can go without. If that woman won't eat what I've prepared then she can starve for all I care. I trained in Paris, I'll have her know. Cooked at the best restaurants in London . . .' On he went about how he'd cooked for kings and princes and dukes and duchesses and how Mr Churchill had once complimented him on his steak and kidney. Peggy had heard it all before, many times. There'd be no stopping him, so she put down the soup plate and waited politely till he'd finished, before she slipped out of the kitchens. The only thing to do was to go in search of Miss Frost. It took Miss Frost to calm the chef down and butter up old Mrs Mountjoy. To sort out any trouble. She found her in her office, sitting at her desk. She'd just put down the telephone and was looking rather cross, too, but when she told her what had happened, she got up at once.

Peggy carried on waiting on the other guests, keeping half an eye on Miss Frost. There was a lot of table thumping from Mrs Mountjoy and she could hear her going on about tinned carrots and the garden and the prices. Miss Frost was speaking so softly she couldn't hear what *she* was saying, but whatever it was, it must have done the trick because Mrs Mountjoy stopped complaining and started looking all right. Or as all right as she ever could. And when Peggy went into the kitchen later with a trayload of dirty plates, she found the chef opening a tin of cream of mushroom. After he'd heated it up, she carried the fresh soup plate back into the dining-room.

'The chef says he hopes you'll care for his *crème de champignons*, madam.' She had a bit of difficulty getting her tongue round the French words, especially the last one, but she did her best, and Mrs Mountjoy grunted to show she was graciously prepared to try.

What with Mrs Mountjoy and old Colonel Millis, who had lost his spectacles yet again – they were in his top pocket all the time – and an old RAF officer who kept calling her over and then pinching her bottom whenever he got the chance, Peggy was glad when the dinners were over at last.

She gave Mavis, the kitchen help, a hand with the washing-up and with mopping the floor and doing the stoves and when everything was clean and tidy she went to take off her cap and apron and put on her cardigan and headscarf. She let herself out of the side door and made her way to her bike against the back yard wall. It was almost dark, even with the double summer time, and when someone spoke suddenly behind her, she nearly jumped out of her skin.

'It's only me, Peggy. Pilot Officer Wentworth-Young. Piers. I'm most terribly sorry if I startled you.'

Startled her! He'd frightened the living daylights out of her. She'd thought it was Jack the Ripper at least. She leant against the wall, hand clasped to her racing heart. 'Oh, you, sir . . .' For a moment that's all she could find the breath to say. 'Whatever are you doing here?'

'Well, waiting for you, actually. I wondered if you'd like a lift home.'

'I've got my bike, sir. Thank you all the same.'

'Yes, but it'd be much quicker in the car – and we could put the bike in the boot.'

It was the sort of thing Mum was always warning her against. *Don't take lifts from strangers.* Only he wasn't a stranger. And he was an officer in the RAF.

'I'll be quite all right, sir. I always go home on the bike.'

'Is it far?'

'Not very. A mile or two.' It was six miles, in fact, but she didn't want him to know that.

He stepped forward closer, all serious. 'Please let me take you, Peggy. You've nothing to fear from me, I swear it.'

'I never thought so, sir. But it'd be an awful bother for you . . .' She was weakening, though. It was late, and the ride alone along the lanes would be a bit scary, and she was that tired.

'No, it wouldn't. And I'll get you there in no time.'

Well, what harm could there be? And it was ever so kind of him.

'All right, then. If it's really no trouble.'

Somehow he managed to get the bike into the boot of his car. One wheel was left sticking out, but he made it safe with some rope. Then he opened the door for her very politely so that she could get into the front seat. Nobody had ever opened any kind of door for her before, and she'd never been in a proper car – only in an old van and once on a charabanc trip to Skegness. It felt as comfortable as sitting in an easy chair.

'You'll have to tell me the way, Peggy,' he said when he'd got in beside her. 'Say where to turn, and so on.'

'Yes, sir.'

He started up the engine and switched on the covered-up headlamps. They drove down Steep Hill and out of the city onto the Skellingthorpe road.

'Could you turn left at the next, please, sir?'

'Roger.'

'Who, sir?'

He laughed. 'It just means understood.'

She guided him through the darkening lanes. The car headlights weren't much better to see by than her bicycle lamp, but then you had to be very careful because the German bombers could see lights from high up; they could even see people striking matches. He'd know all about that most probably.

'Are you in the bombers, sir? Is that what you do?'

'Yes, I'm a navigator.'

'What's that?'

'Well, I have to tell the pilot which way to go. Just

182

like you're doing for me tonight. Only it's a bit more complicated, of course.'

'To Germany, and places like that? To drop the bombs?'

'That sort of thing.'

She'd overheard the RAF officers talking to each other at the dinner tables in The Angel while she was serving. *Bad luck about so-and-so . . . went down in flames . . . not a hope . . . half the kites didn't get back . . . one in three get the chop, you know . . .*

'It sounds ever so dangerous, sir.'

'Gosh, not really. Piece of cake mostly.'

She'd heard them saying that, too, and knew it meant easy, but she didn't believe him. How could it be easy to fly all the way to Germany and back in the pitch dark, and with the Germans shooting at them as well? Still, he probably didn't want to talk about it and answer silly questions. She sat silent beside him, except to say when to turn.

'I live on the right down here, sir. The last one of those cottages.'

He stopped the car outside her gate and came round to open the door for her again.

'Thank you, sir,' she said to what she could see of him, as it was quite dark now. 'It's been very kind of you.'

'I'll see you again . . . at The Angel.'

'I expect so, sir.'

'The thing is, I'm going on leave soon.' He didn't sound all that happy about it. 'I have to go home to see my parents. But it's only for a week. I was wondering . . . well, if you'd changed your mind about coming out with me some time – when I get back? To the cinema one evening?'

'I haven't thought about it, sir.' That was a lie – she had, a lot.

'So you might change it? Your mind?'

'But, it wouldn't be right, would it?'

'I honestly don't see why not. Unless you really *hate* the whole idea. That'd be different, of course. I say, *do* you hate it?'

'No, of course not, sir. It's not that at all.'

'So there'd really be nothing against it. If you didn't mind.'

She was getting a bit muddled. There couldn't be anything wrong in just going to the pictures, could there? He must be lonely. Away from his home and fighting this horrible war for people like herself. Doing those terrible, dangerous journeys. *One in three get the chop.*

'Well . . . if you'd like it, sir.'

'*Like* it? I should say so. Gosh, Peggy. Do you really mean it? That's absolutely wizard!'

He sounded thrilled to pieces. It didn't make any sense to her, him being what he was.

'I ought to go in now.'

'Yes, yes, of course.'

'My bike . . .'

'Golly, I almost forgot. Frightfully sorry.' He untied the rope and lifted the bike out for her.

'See you when I get back from leave, then?'

'All right.'

'Super. I'll come here and fetch you on your day off. Wednesdays, isn't it? That's if I'm not flying.'

'However will you find the way back now, sir?'

He laughed in the darkness. 'I'm a navigator, remember.'

She waited until he had driven away and then

wheeled the bike round to the shed at the back. Mum had gone to bed but Dad was still up, though he'd fallen sound asleep in his armchair. She knew he'd been waiting for her to get safe home. She touched his shoulder.

'I'm back, Dad.'

He opened his eyes and smiled up at her. 'Hallo there, Peggy, lass. Good day?'

'Not so bad.'

He wouldn't have heard the car and she didn't tell him anything about the lift. He might not have understood that it was quite all right with someone like Pilot Officer Wentworth-Young.

Lying in bed later, she remembered his other name. Piers. That's what he'd said. She'd never heard the name before, and it suited him. *Piers.* A real gentleman's name. Fancy him wanting to take her out.

They were half-way to Munich when Bert realized he'd brought Victor by mistake. He'd clean forgotten he was still in his left-hand breast pocket. Emerald's bra and knickers were stuffed in the right-hand one – her latest good-luck present to go with the silk stocking round his neck. What with Victor on one side and those on the other, he must look like Mae West even without his Mae West. He groped beneath the life jacket and his flying suit, and felt for the snake. He seemed OK, though he wasn't too lively. Probably a bit woozy from lack of oxygen. Harry's carrier pigeon spent the time on ops with its head under its wing, fast asleep. Lucky sods, both of them. Wake up when it was all over. That would be just the ticket. Suit him no end.

'Skipper to mid-upper. OK, Bert?'

185

He clicked his mike switch on. 'OK, skipper.'

No chance of a kip for him. No peace for the wicked. Got to keep lively and looking round the whole bloody time. He rotated the turret slowly, scanning the night sky. The moon would make it easier for the Jerries to spot them. On the other hand, he'd be able to see *them* easier too. Since getting those six rabbits, he'd been feeling a whole lot better about himself. Nice neat deflection shots, just like he'd been taught in gunnery training. Same as if they'd been Jerry fighters zipping past his turret. Stew had been flabbergasted. Mouth wide open when he'd seen them all. Well, he'd flabbered his own gast, to tell the truth. Though he hadn't told it. Acted like it was nothing special to him at all.

The Lanc droned on through the darkness. On and on and on. Drone, drone, drone. Bloody miles to go to the target. Bloody miles back again. Still, shouldn't be too dicey by the sound of it, and the Pathfinder blokes would be marking it with flares before they got there. Not half the pissing around since *they'd* got in on the act. Piece of cake for Stew. They'd be in and out like a dose of bloody salts.

Speaking of doses of salts, maybe he should have taken one. Must've eaten something that'd given him the collywobbles. His guts were bloody killing him. He pressed the mike switch on again.

'Mid-upper to skipper.'

'What is it, Bert?'

'Permission to leave the turret?'

'What for?'

'Elsan, skipper.'

'Sorry, mid-upper. Not now. Too many night fighters around looking for us.'

'Put a cork in it, Bert.' That was from Stew, of course.

Bert sat and suffered. Well, it was the last op before they went on leave. Six days with Emerald in a nice little place in Cleethorpes. Forget about the bloody war. Forget about everything but him and Emerald. He couldn't wait. He patted the right side of his chest directly over the pocket that held the bra and knickers, and then the other side too, just in case Victor was feeling left out of things. Not that he'd take him, of course. Emerald wouldn't put up with that. Poor old Victor would have to stay behind in his shoe box.

Six whole wonderful bloody days.

'You're going to London, then, Van?'

'That's what I figured. Take in a show or two. See the sights. Why?'

'It seems a bit lonely. Of course, you haven't got a home to go to over here, like us. That's so sad.'

'What do you suggest then, Catherine?'

'Well . . . I've got a few days leave due, too. As it so happens.'

'No kidding?' he said politely, hiding his amazement.

'And I live in York. Or rather, my mother does. It's not too far away. Easy by train. And it's rather a beautiful old city.'

'We have the new version.'

'So you do. I'd never thought of that.'

'I'd sure like to see the old one.'

'I think you'd enjoy it. And my mother's always been fascinated by America. I know she'd love to meet you.'

'I'd love to meet her. How about your father?'

'He was killed in France, serving in the army. At Dunkirk.'

'Hell, I'm sorry . . .'

'Thank you.'

She spoke calmly but he saw the sadness in her eyes. She wasn't going to talk about it, though. Nobody over here did. He'd never seen open grief.

'Would you like me to ask my mother, then?'

'I guess that rather depends on you.'

'On me?'

'Whether *you* want me there.'

A pause. Rather too long for his liking. 'It's the very least we can do. Unless, of course, you'd rather go to London . . .'

'No,' he said. 'I'd much rather go to York.'

Ten

'I've brought you some chocolate, Mum.'

'Oh, Charlie, you shouldn't have.'

He swung his kit-bag off his shoulder, set it down and took the paper bag out of the top. 'There's some boiled sweets, too.'

She peered into the paper bag. 'Wherever did you get all this?'

'We're given it when we go on ops.'

'But why don't you eat them?'

'I forget.' He'd saved them all up for her specially, but he wasn't going to tell her that.

'Charlie, I don't want them – really I don't. I've got my ration if I want any sweets.'

'Not much is it, though? Half-a-pound a month. I just thought you'd like some extra.' He could tell she was ready to give it all back and added quickly, 'I'll help you eat them, if you like. Seeing as I'm here for a while.'

She smiled at him. 'All right then. We'll share them. But don't you dare bring me any more. In future, I want you to eat them yourself, like they're meant for.'

She'd done a good bit more to the garden, he saw, when he went out and wandered around. There were lots of flowers blooming in the front, all different kinds and colours jumbled up together and looking

189

as pretty as a picture postcard. He told her so when she came out to join him.

'I've picked some of the beans for your supper. And dug up some potatoes. There're hardly any peas though. Something ate most of the plants. Mr Stonor says it was probably slugs.'

'How's Marigold?'

'Blooming. She's been laying every day. I've saved the eggs for your leave.'

'You oughtn't to have done that, Mum.'

'Oh, I didn't need them.'

We've both been saving things up, he thought, and going without. And neither of us would want the other to do it. Funny, really . . .

'Harry came and mended the gutter for me,' she said, pointing up at the roof. 'It doesn't leak any more. It was very good of him.'

People often did things for Mum – he'd noticed that. They liked her and wanted to help, with her being all on her own. He had a feeling, though, that Harry liked Mum more than the usual amount, though he'd never said a word and wasn't going to.

'Does the wireless still work OK?'

'Oh yes, and it's wonderful. I sit and listen to it in the evenings. It's lovely.'

He was glad of that. Glad of anything that made it less lonely for her and stopped her worrying. 'I almost forgot – I brought someone with me. Someone you know well.'

'Whatever do you mean, Charlie?'

He fetched Sam from the kit-bag and handed him over. 'He's come home on leave too.'

*   *   *

Harry stood in the train corridor, feet planted wide apart, back pressed up against the compartment behind him. No empty seats in third-class, as usual, so he'd probably be standing all the way to London. His present for Paulette lay in the kit-bag propped beside him, wrapped up ready to give her: a luminous china rabbit that he'd found in a shop in Lincoln. He'd seen it in the window and thought it looked the sort of thing a little girl might like, with its one ear up and one ear down. And she'd be able to see it in the dark when she was in bed.

He was longing to see her, though he dreaded the sort of greeting he'd probably get. And maybe she wouldn't even remember him, after all this time. Maybe she wouldn't even be there. It didn't mean a thing that he'd written ahead. Rita would suit herself. They might go out for the day on purpose to avoid him. He wouldn't put anything past her. He didn't hate her – he didn't hate anybody – but if it hadn't been for Paulette, he'd never have wanted to set eyes on Rita again.

When the war was over he'd got to find himself a place of his own so Paulette could come and stay with him when she was older, and they could get to know each other. Rita wouldn't be able to stop that; the court had given him the right. He'd look for a small flat, same as he'd had before – with two bedrooms, if possible, or he could sleep on the settee when Paulette came to stay. What he'd really like, though, would be a cottage like the one Charlie's mother was renting. All the better if it needed some work doing to it. He'd enjoy that. He was good with his hands. He could mend things and put up shelves and paint walls, do pretty well anything round a house. He pictured it in his mind's eye: a little house with a blue door and a front garden full of flowers. He was standing at the gate, looking at it and, as he did so, the door opened and Dorothy was there, smiling at him.

The train jolted him out of his dream. They were coming into a station and a five-deep crowd of army blokes, kit-bags on shoulders, elbows up at the ready like battering rams, lined the platform. He braced himself for the scrum.

In London he took the tube out to Rickmansworth and walked from the station to Sycamore Avenue. As he opened the gate to number sixteen, he caught a glimpse of a child's face at one of the upstairs windows. It was gone in a flash but it must have been Paulette. He went up the crazy-paving path and rang the bell. He felt hot and grubby after the long journey and knew he must look it. When Rita opened the door he could tell she was pretending to be surprised to see him.

'Harry! We weren't expecting you.'

'I wrote I'd be coming. I'm on leave.'

She was still pretty, he thought. Still all dolled-up in smart clothes and make-up in spite of the coupons and the prices and the shortages. He wondered how she managed it.

'Well, we didn't get the letter.'

He knew she was lying but there was no point arguing. 'Anyway, I'm here. To see Paulette.'

'She's out for the day, I'm afraid. She's gone to a friend's.'

He looked at her steadily, at her hard, painted face. 'No, she's not, Rita. I saw her just now at an upstairs window.' She opened her mouth to deny it, but he cut her short. 'I'd like to see her, please – just for a while.

And I'll remind you that I'm her father and the law says I've a right to do so. It was agreed in the court.'

'It always upsets her. She's a very sensitive child.'

'She's my daughter, Rita, as well as yours. And I've come a long way to see her.'

She shrugged. 'All right, if you must. I suppose you'd better come inside. I don't want you taking her off somewhere – it only tires her.'

He'd never been into the house before, always collected Paulette from the front door. It hadn't been built that long, he guessed, probably only a few years before the war had started. The hall floor was made of varnished wood blocks, fitted together in a herring-bone pattern, and there was a solid oak staircase and nicely moulded doors. Must have cost a bob or two, he reckoned, looking around.

'I'll go and fetch her,' Rita said. 'You can wait in the lounge.' She opened one of the doors. 'Len's in there.'

He stepped into a long room with french windows facing onto a back garden. More wood-block flooring and a patterned rug, and pictures on the walls with lights over them. The furniture must have cost a bit, too: a blue moquette three-piece suite, a swanky standard lamp, a set of side tables that fitted inside each other, and some sort of big cabinet in the corner with mirrors all over the front.

The man sitting in one of the armchairs got to his feet, newspaper in one hand, cigar in the other.

'You must be Harry. I'm Len.'

He'd never met Rita's second husband before and now that he saw him he could understand why she'd gone for him. He was good-looking, no doubt about it, in his flash civvy suit with smooth black hair no

193

Service barber had ever got his hands on and a little moustache like Ronald Coleman.

'Have a drink, old boy?'

'No, thanks.'

'Think I will, if you don't mind.'

The mirrored thing in the corner turned out to be a cocktail cabinet. A light went on when the doors were opened to show more mirrors inside and a dozen or more bottles of spirits – unless he was seeing double with the reflection.

Len held up a dimple bottle of Haig. 'Sure you won't join me?'

He refused again, though he could have done with it. He'd never fancied drinking with people he didn't like, and he didn't like Len. Never mind about him and Rita; he wouldn't have liked him anyway.

'Busy lot, you Raff, bombing the Jerries night after night,' Len was saying through his cigar, pouring himself a stiff one.

'Aye.' He wasn't seeing double with the bottles – there were at least twenty. Must be black market.

'Give 'em hell, that's what I say. That's the ticket. Smash 'em to smithereens.' Len waved the big cigar. 'Wish I could do the same myself. Failed the medical though. Believe me, I envy you, Harry.'

He didn't believe him. He'd heard that before from other men like Len, and from men that really meant it. And he knew the difference. Len looked as though he'd done very nicely, thank you, safe out of it all. Doing whatever business he did.

'Here she is, then.'

Rita was standing in the doorway, holding Paulette by the hand. He hardly recognized his daughter, she'd grown so much. And changed. He could see now what she was going to look like when she was grown up – just like Rita. There wasn't a trace of him, or of his side of the family, not that he'd've wished that on her. The frock she was wearing looked like a party frock to him, made of some shiny pink material with puffed sleeves and bows and a ribbon in her hair to match. All dressed up, just like her mother.

He took a step forward. 'Hallo, Paulette. Remember me?'

His daughter didn't answer. She went on staring up at him as though he were a total stranger.

Rita gave her a push. 'Go on, then. Say hello.'

'Do I have to, Mummy?'

'I *told* you—'

Paulette stayed where she'd been pushed, staring down at the floor instead, not speaking and refusing to look at him now.

'I've brought you a present, love,' he said desperately and then remembered that it was still in his kit-bag in the hall. 'I'll just go and get it.'

When he'd come back Paulette was sitting on the sofa with Rita beside her. Len was back in the armchair drinking his whisky and smoking his cigar. They all stared at him.

Harry cleared his throat. 'Here you are, Paulette. Hope you like it.'

She turned to her mother.

'Go on, take it,' Rita said in a let's-get-this-over-with tone.

He stood waiting anxiously as his daughter unwrapped his gift. When the luminous rabbit appeared he said, 'It's got special paint that shines in the dark, love. If you keep it by your bed you'll be able to see it when you turn out the light.'

But now that he looked at the rabbit again it didn't seem nearly so nice as it had in the shop: rather cheap and ordinary – like something you got at a fairground.

'I don't like it. *It's ugly!* I don't want it.' Paulette threw down the present, jumped up and ran out of the room. He could hear her sobbing as she pounded up the stairs.

Rita bent to pick up the rabbit. One ear – the upright one – had broken off as it hit the floor. 'What a thing to get her!'

'I'm sorry.' He stood there, dismayed. 'I thought she'd like it.'

'Paulette likes *pretty* things – you should know that, Harry. I told you, you always manage to upset her.'

'I'm sorry,' he said again miserably. 'I didn't mean to.'

'I'll have to go and see to her. You'd better leave. She won't want to come down again.'

Rita dumped the broken rabbit in his hands and went out of the room.

'Bad luck, old boy,' Len said. 'Tricky things, females.' He drained his glass and put it down. 'I'll show you out.'

At the front door he clapped him hard on the back. 'Give the Huns hell, Harry. That's the ticket.'

'Will you be all right in here, Jock? Sorry it's not better, but we haven't used the attics for years.'

He looked round the spotless room: at the white-painted iron bed and chest of drawers, at the nice old washstand with its rose-patterned china jug and basin, at the rag rug on the floor and the starched cotton curtains. Compared with the Nissen hut, it was a palace.

'Och, it's grand, Mrs Gibbs. I like it just fine. Thank you.'

The farmer's wife smiled at him. 'I ought to be thanking *you*, Jock. We're glad to have you. Grateful for the extra help.' She went to the door. 'I'll leave you to get yourself unpacked and settled. When you're ready, come down and have something to eat.'

He put his kit-bag down and opened the attic window to chase out a wasp buzzing against the glass. The hens were scratching about in the farmyard below – some white, some black and some red-brown like the one Charlie's mother had been given.

Ruth came out of the barn with a bowl of feed and he watched her scattering it and the hens scrambling about. He could hear her talking to them, ticking them off for being so greedy and bad-mannered. She stayed out in the yard for a while, going about, doing odd jobs, and he drew back from the window so he could go on watching her, unseen.

'I've got some leave coming up,' he'd said to her when there'd last been a stand-down and he'd gone over to give them a hand and do a bit of maintenance on the tractor engine. 'I could spend it working here if you think they could do with the help.'

'I'd've thought you'd want to get away, Jock. Go home, or something. That's what they all do, isn't it? Get as far away as possible?'

'I went home last leave.'

'Well, there's plenty to do. Why don't you ask them?'

He hadn't wanted payment, he'd explained to Mr and Mrs Gibbs, he wouldn't take it. That had caused a spot of bother because they didn't like the idea of him working for nothing. In the end they'd settled

197

that it would be in exchange for all his food and that he was to live in with them, like Ruth did.

'One of the family,' Mrs Gibbs had said. 'We won't have it any other way.'

Ruth had been right about there being plenty to do – he soon found that out. He was up early the first day, cleaning out, feeding and watering the livestock and then working with the thresher until evening. Ruth fed the monster with sheaves from the top while he heaved away the full sacks of grain, and the old man, Ben Stonor, made a rick out of the straw left over. In between hauling the heavy sacks he had to keep clearing out the chaff at the bottom before it gummed up the whole works. It was filthy, dusty, noisy, hot work but he'd never felt more content in his life.

'You're a bit of a mystery, Jock,' Ruth said to him when they were taking a midday break, sitting on a stone wall in the yard. 'You never talk about yourself and you shut up like a clam if anyone asks anything.'

'There's nothing to say.' He took a bite of Mrs Gibbs's home-made pork pie and chewed on it.

'I've told you all about me.' She'd told him quite matter-of-factly about the orphanage. Her mother had handed her over when she was a baby, she'd said, and gone away. She didn't know any more than that. Sometimes she wondered about her, but mostly she didn't because what was the point? As soon as she was old enough she'd left the orphanage, gone to London and got a job in Bourne and Hollingsworth in Oxford Street, and lived in a hostel. She'd joined the Land Army because she'd seen a recruiting poster showing a smiling girl carrying a bucket to feed two little calves frolicking about in a daisy-covered field. It had been

198

a bit of a shock when she'd found out it was nothing like that, but she'd soon got used to everything.

'So, it's your turn, Jock. No getting out of it. Spill the beans.'

He said slowly, 'Well, I was born in Glasgow. And my mother and father still live in the same place. I went to school there until I got an apprenticeship with the RAF, at Holton. I was a fitter before I remustered as a flight engineer after the war broke out. That's about it.'

'Is that all? It's not much.'

'I warned you. I'm no a very interesting person.'

'You interest me.' She flapped away a fly with her hand. 'Why did you become a flight engineer, for instance?'

'I wanted to serve in bombers, rather than on the ground.'

'So what does a flight engineer do?'

'Pilot's mate. There're four engines and they've got to be monitored all the time. The skipper can't do it all on his own. And I'm Mr Fixit if anything goes wrong when we're in the air.'

'Could you fly the plane yourself?'

'I've done some link training, so I could keep her straight and level at least. Mebbe land, if anything happened to the skipper. We all have to know something about each other's jobs.'

She said through a mouthful of the pie, 'That Aussie who came here with you that day . . . Stew. What does he do?'

'He's our bomb aimer,' he said shortly. 'He aims and drops the bombs when we're over the target.'

'I bet he's good at that.'

'He's no so bad.'

'You're not much like him, are you? Or like a lot of the others.'

'How do you mean?'

'Well, for one thing you never swear and for another you don't drink. You wouldn't touch a drop of Mrs Gibbs's potato wine. That's unusual.'

'I've got my reasons.'

'You're supposed to be telling all, Jock. Come on.'

He hesitated. 'Well, I don't swear and I don't drink because my father does far too much of both. He's a foul-mouthed drunkard who beats my mother – if you must know.' As soon as he'd said the words he regretted it. Family troubles were nobody else's concern.

'Sorry, Jock. Shouldn't have asked.'

'It's all right. I shouldna've answered.'

In his attic room that evening he stood by the open window with the light turned off, gazing out. If he survived the war, which seemed very unlikely, he knew he'd never again be able to look up at a night sky without seeing it in bombing terms. Hardly any cloud tonight, probably nice and clear over the target, only a fingernail moon. People talked about a full moon as a bombers' moon, but that was in the old days before the modern navigation aids. *Fighter's* moon, more like now.

He could hear the mounting activity in the distance at the drome: the snarling progression round the peri track to line up for take-off.

'Jock . . .'

He turned to see Ruth standing in the doorway.

'They're going tonight, then?'

'Aye.'

She shut the door and came to stand beside him at

the window. They listened together to the bombers taking off – engines crescendoing to maximum power and then fading away into the night. He was with each one as though his own hand had been on the throttles.

She said, 'I hate hearing them go. Imagining what they've got to face.'

'They know it has to be done.'

'Don't you get afraid?'

'We all do. We'd be fools if we weren't. But it doesna stop us.'

'Brave men.'

'Just men getting on with the job of fighting a war that's got to be won. That's all.'

'Do you think we *will* win? In the end?'

'Aye, I think so. Now we've the Americans with us. I wasna so sure before.'

'Hope you're right, Jock.'

'So do I. I'd better be.'

'Yes, you had.' She leaned her elbows on the window-sill. 'What's that bright star up there?'

'Venus. It's a planet.'

'Do you have to know about the stars – or is that just the navigator?'

'I've a pretty fair idea. It could come in handy.'

She was silent for a while, standing close to him, leaning on the sill. He didn't speak or move. Didn't dare.

'I haven't told you everything about myself, Jock.'

'You don't need to.'

'I want to. It's not fair otherwise. I made *you* tell me.' She looked upwards, speaking to the stars. 'The people in charge at the orphanage were a husband and wife. When I was about fifteen they gave me a room of my own and the husband came and got into

201

bed with me one night. I couldn't stop him . . . it was revolting. Made me physically *sick*. I told him if he tried it again I'd tell his wife.'

'Ruth—'

'I *want* to tell you. All of it. After I'd gone to London to live in the hostel I picked up a man in a cinema one evening and I went to bed with him as well. I wanted to see if it would be any better. Only it was worse. *Much* worse. Even more disgusting. He was like an animal . . . I thought I'd never ever feel clean again. I cut off my hair. Dressed in men's clothes. I didn't want to look like a woman and I never wanted a man to touch me again.'

He waited, not knowing what to say, and presently she went on. 'But lately I've been thinking that maybe it could be quite different with someone else. If I liked them, and they liked me? I just wish I knew. What do *you* think?'

He thought of his own one joyless experience on leave in Glasgow. And how it must be with his parents. And how Ruth must feel. And how he felt about her. 'I think it could be.'

'Do you think it'd be worth a try?'

He said quietly. 'Aye. I do.'

'So do I, Jock.' She turned her head towards him in the darkness. 'So do I.'

Stew got out his best blue and cleaned the buttons. He hadn't bothered with them for months, but he thought he'd smarten up a bit for The Angel. Show that girl he hadn't come straight from the outback, like she seemed to think. He even borrowed a decent suitcase from someone. Walking along the Wragby road, he cadged a lift from a doctor going on his rounds, and entertained him with a lively and totally false account of an op in which they'd come back on one engine, tail shot off and with a jammed undercart. Well, who wanted to hear about easy ones?

The doctor set him down on the outskirts of the city and he walked the rest of the way to The Angel, noting any local talent that he passed. There wasn't much worth looking at, and he was already wishing he'd gone to London instead of doing this bloody stupid caper. Still, a couple of days rest and he'd be fighting fit to move on for some proper fun.

No doubt about it, he was tired. Shagged out. The last op hadn't been as bad as he'd told the doctor, but it hadn't been much of a picnic either. They'd slogged all the way to Munich, lost a dirty great chunk of one wing over the target, and Van had had to fly back without starboard aileron control and bang D-Dog down in mid-roll when they came in. They'd pulled up with their nose hanging off the end of the runway. To celebrate being alive and in one piece, he'd had a real skinful in the bar and given himself a beaut of a hangover that was going to take some getting rid of.

He swanned into the hotel through the squeaky door and set his borrowed suitcase down near the reception desk. Some old hag was at the counter giving Miss Iceberg hell. He listened with interest.

'. . . absolute disgrace. Nobody's been near my room today. Bed still unmade . . . dust an inch thick . . . I demand to see Miss Hargreaves this instant.' Rap, rap, rap with a stick on the edge of the counter.

'I'm so sorry, Mrs Mountjoy, but Miss Hargreaves is out at the moment.'

'She's *always* out. She leaves the hotel to be run by

incompetents. I shall demand a reduction in my bill if this sort of thing continues.'

More raps and Miss Iceberg, who had caught sight of him standing there, went all pink in the face.

'We're very short-staffed at the moment, Mrs Mountjoy, but I'll make sure that your room is done at once.'

'And tell them to clean it *properly*, not that flick round they usually do.'

'Yes, Mrs Mountjoy.'

'And furthermore, Peggy was late ringing the gong for luncheon again today. That girl is useless. You ought to get rid of her.'

'Peggy does her best, Mrs Mountjoy. She's still quite new to the job. If you would like to sit in the Residents' Lounge, I'll let you know the minute your room is ready.'

The old bitch stumped off, muttering and grumbling. He stepped up to the desk.

'Strikes me *she's* the one you ought to get rid of. Why do you put up with all that baloney?'

'She happens to be an old and valued customer.'

'She's old all right, but not much value to anyone, if you ask me.'

'I didn't ask you, Sergeant.' She whipped the registration book round towards him. 'If you'd like to sign in, please.'

He dipped the pen in the inkstand and scrawled his name while she unhooked a key.

'Number sixteen. It's the one I showed you before. Up the stairs, turn right.'

'What time's tea?'

'Four o'clock. It's served in the lounge.'

He shook his head. 'Not that. The evening meal.'

204

'You mean *dinner*?'

'That's what you Poms call it. Not me.'

'*Dinner's* at half past seven. You'll hear the gong.'

He picked up his suitcase. 'That revolving door needs oiling, by the way. It squeaks like hell.'

'I'm aware of that, thank you.'

'Just thought you might want to do something about it.'

He found the room and lay down on the bed on top of the counterpane, shoes on. Too bloody bad if they didn't like it. Christ, he felt really crook now. There were hammer blows going on inside his skull, his throat hurt and his legs were aching. He closed his eyes and slept.

The sound of the door opening woke him suddenly. He braced himself for the: *Wakey, wakey, rise and shine! Ops tonight!* before he remembered where he was. Not in the hut ready to go on ops but safe in a hotel room. Miss Iceberg was over by the window, fiddling with the blackout blind. He grinned to himself. She hadn't spotted him yet.

'Evening.'

She spun round like a top, letting go of the blind so that it rattled all the way up again. 'I'd no idea you were there, Sergeant.' More than a mite flustered, she was.

'Having a kip. What time is it?'

'Quarter past nine. I just came to do the blackout. I'm afraid you've missed dinner, if you wanted some.' She pulled the blind down again, drew the curtains across briskly and switched on a lamp.

He rubbed his forehead. 'Don't think I could eat it anyway. I'm crook.'

'Crook?' Her voice softened a fraction, unless

205

he was dreaming. 'You mean you don't feel well?'

'Too right.' He put his hand over his eyes. 'Thought it was just a hangover, but I reckon it's more than that.'

She came closer to the bed and when he peered between his fingers he was pleased to see that she was looking quite worried.

'Should I get a doctor?'

'Strewth, no—'

'You ought to undress and get into bed properly.'

'Yes, nurse.' He started undoing his tie and she backed away towards the door.

'I'll send someone in to see how you are in the morning.'

The door clicked shut. He dragged off his clothes and threw them anyhow onto a chair and then fell into bed. The room was spinning round him. Christ, he didn't know when he'd felt so flaming ill in his whole life.

'Oh, there you are, Piers. I've been looking for you.'

The ball missed its target and ricocheted uselessly round the billiard table. Piers straightened up. 'Just practising a bit.'

His father took down a cue and chalked the end. 'What about a game?'

'Fine.' He knew he'd lose. He'd only beaten him once in his life and that had been more by fluke shots than anything else.

'Matter of fact, Piers, I've been wanting a word with you . . .' His father took careful aim. Click and the ball rolled smoothly across the baize. 'Your mother thinks you're moping. Women always notice that sort of thing. Or think they do.'

'I don't quite—'

More clicks and a ball glided into a pocket. 'Got it into her head there must be some girl. Someone you're rather keen on.' Click. 'Your go.'

Piers moved round the table and tried to concentrate on his shot.

'She's worried about the kind of girl you might be meeting in the RAF. New Service. No tradition. Not like the Army. Pity you wouldn't join the regiment, as we wanted. Hmmm. You want to take a bit more time. You rushed that shot. Watch me . . .'

They played on. His father was winning easily.

'I don't need to remind you that you have a duty to the family name, Piers. Make sure it's the *right* type of girl. Same background and all that. Know what I mean? You can fool around with the other sort if you must, and no harm done, but leave it at that. Understand?'

'Actually I—'

'Of course you do. I can tell your mother she's got nothing to worry about. Enough said. Your go. And don't be in such a rush over it this time.'

'How're you feeling this morning, sir?' The little waitress from the dining-room was standing at the end of his bed, holding a tray. 'Miss Frost said to bring you up a bit of breakfast today. See if you could manage it.'

Stew closed his eyes again. 'Thanks. Leave it on the side, will you?'

'It'll get cold, sir. Wouldn't you like a nice hot cup of tea now and a bit of toast? It'd do you good.'

He opened his eyes slowly. 'All right.'

She helped him sit up, plumped up his pillows and then set the tray before him. White cloth and napkin, silver toast rack, silver teapot and milk jug, silver cutlery, a boiled egg, butter curled up in a fancy roll, little pot of marmalade . . . oh, my word! He'd never had breakfast in bed in his life, and now all this.

'You're Peggy, aren't you?' Pretty kid. Bright blue eyes. The sweet innocent. With his four-day beard he felt like the wolf dressed up as Red Riding Hood's grandmother.

'That's right, sir.'

'Well, thanks for everything you've done.'

She'd been tiptoeing in with jugs of barley water and those bloody stone hot water bottles he'd kept stubbing his toe on.

'Miss Frost said we must look after you, sir. As you were so far from home.'

That didn't sound at all like the Iceberg talking – more like Peggy herself. She fussed over the tray, turning the cup the right way up and putting everything so he could reach it easily. 'You've been very poorly, sir. But the doctor said you'd be all right with a few more days in bed. He said it was the influenza. I thought you could only get that in winter. Shall I pour your tea for you, sir?'

'OK.'

'Aren't you going to eat your egg and toast, then?'

He lopped off the top of the shell and spread the curly butter onto a dainty triangle. 'I've got to get up and get out of here today, Peggy.'

'Oh, you mustn't do that, sir. You're not well enough.'

'Can't afford to stay any longer.' He waved the knife over the tray. 'Paying for this lot. Can you tell them downstairs that I'm leaving and I'll need the bill.'

'Very well, sir, but I think you should stay in bed. Really I do.'

She went away, looking worried, and he lay back on the pillows and ate the toast and drank the tea. Well, he didn't feel like getting up yet, either, but there wasn't much choice. The best thing would be to find a cheaper room – somewhere like the Great Northern – and hole up there.

He still felt pretty crook when he got out of bed, but a bath and shave helped. He dressed – cripes, they'd even gone and laundered his shirt and underclothes, and it looked like they'd polished his shoes – and went downstairs. The same old woman was at the reception desk again, banging away with her stick and complaining, this time about the sausage at breakfast.

'. . . all gristle. *Uneatable*. That chef of yours should be sacked.'

He leaned across. 'You should be sacked too, lady, while they're at it. Don't you know there's a war on?'

After she'd stopped squawking and been carted off to the Residents' Lounge, Miss Iceberg came back.

'That wasn't very helpful of you, Sergeant.'

'Sorry. I reckon she deserved it.'

'She'll be difficult for days now.'

'I'll bet she is always. You should kick her out, like I said.'

'It's not my hotel so I couldn't possibly do anything of the kind. I've got your bill ready.'

He looked at it. 'This is only for two nights. I've been here four.'

'I'm going by what I've got down in the bookings. It says, Sergeant Brenner: Room sixteen for two nights. That's what you booked, isn't it?'

'Yeah, but—'

'As you pointed out to Mrs Mountjoy, there's a war on. You've come a very long way to fight in it, Sergeant and you've been ill. Your bill is for two nights. Please, let's just leave it at that.'

'Well . . . OK, thanks. That's nice of you.'

The wind had been taken clean out of his sails. He paid the bill and picked up his suitcase. 'By the way, the name's Stew.'

'You did tell me.'

'How about yours?'

She was busy with something at the counter. 'It's Honor.'

'Strewth,' he muttered under his breath. 'Well, thanks again, Honor.' He put his cap on and tipped his hand to it. 'Be seeing you.'

When it came to gardens, the English had got it made, Van thought. They didn't get plumbing, or ice, or showers, or coffee, but gardens they understood. Like nobody else. He followed Catherine's mother as she led the way round the walled garden behind her house in York, admiring the way everything looked so natural – as though plants had planted themselves and grown the way they wanted, rambling and cascading and creeping all over the place.

'Actually, it's past its best,' she told him. 'With autumn around the corner. Looking a bit blowsy.'

'Not to me. And I've never seen grass so green and smooth.'

'Yes, it's not a bad lawn.'

'How does it get so "not bad"?'

'Oh, over the years, you know. Rolling and mowing and feeding. It used to go right to the wall at the far end, but we turned some of it into a vegetable garden

210

when the war started. Tom, my husband, dug it up on one of his leaves. He was killed in France later, on the beaches at Dunkirk. I don't know if Catherine mentioned that.'

'Yes, she did. I'm real sorry.'

'So many of them got away, but Tom was one of the unlucky ones. They told me he was seeing his men onto one of the boats – waiting until they were all on board – and the Germans came over and strafed the beach.'

'I'm sorry,' he said again. It seemed totally inadequate.

'Yes . . . He was a wonderful man. I was devastated. So was Catherine, but one just has to keep going, somehow. Of course, I rattle around in this house now, with Catherine away so much.'

'I guess you miss her.'

'I do – terribly. But I'm very proud of what she's doing. I only wish I was young enough to join up, too. I drive one of the YMCA tea vans around, trying to do my bit. Actually, I quite often go out to some of the RAF bomber stations and go round dispersals, handing out cuppas. So, I've seen a bit of your world. Look, this is my favourite rose, *The White Rose of York* . . . gorgeous, isn't she?'

The mother was very different from his expectations, as natural as her garden and dressed casually in slacks and a sweater. He liked her a lot. As much as he had disliked Piers' mother. The two of them strolled on. She showed him the rows of cabbages and carrots and onions and beans. 'I'm rather proud of them. You'll have some of the runner beans for dinner tonight. I hope you like them.'

He'd never seen the kind before so he didn't know

the answer to that one, but he'd have laid a bet they'd be better cooked than any he'd eaten in England so far.

'And I hope you didn't mind my asking you all those questions about America at lunch Van.'

'Wish I'd known more of the answers. I haven't seen much of it myself.'

'Tom and I always planned to visit your country one day. I'm not sure that I ever will now – not without him.' She stopped as they reached the far end of the garden and turned to face him. 'Actually, I've got another question I wanted to ask you, but I'm afraid it's a terrible cheek and none of my business.'

'Fire away.'

'Are you by any chance in love with Catherine?'

He smiled. 'Does it show?'

'It was just that I caught you looking at her . . . And I so hoped you might be. She doesn't know, does she? You haven't said anything to her?'

'Well, it sure didn't seem the right time, with Peter posted missing. Besides, I don't think she'd want to hear it.'

'Oh, I think she might. I've seen her look at you, too. She's feeling guilty about Peter, of course. That's always been the trouble. He made a bee-line for her at Beningby and she thought she was in love with him. She's not so certain now.'

'It didn't seem that way. They were always together.'

'Oh, they would have been. He'd scarcely let her out of his sight, if he could help it. Peter was in-sufferably possessive – *is* I suppose I should say. Insanely jealous of anything and everything he saw as coming between him and Catherine. When she brought him home here and I saw how it was, I started

212

saying my prayers that she'd never be crazy enough to marry him. He'd asked her several times, you know. So far she's had the sense to say no. Or at least, that they should wait.'

'Well, I guess that's what they're going to have to do now, anyway.'

She nodded. 'When I heard Peter was missing, I'm ashamed to say I was almost glad. That's a dreadful confession, I know. But I've been so convinced that he'd make Catherine unhappy – was *already* making her unhappy – and that was something I couldn't bear. And then you came along . . . like the answer to my prayers. So different. So right for her.' She touched his arm. 'I'm so sorry, Van. I shouldn't have said any of this to you. Please forget I ever did. Let's go back inside. Catherine will be wondering why we're taking so long.'

They turned back towards the house, and when they were half-way across the lawn, Catherine came running out. From the look on her face he knew exactly what had happened.

'Peter's mother 'phoned. They've just heard – he's a prisoner-of-war with the Germans. Thank God! He's *alive*.'

PART III

Eleven

Harry stood in the cold drizzle, waiting with nearly a hundred other men for the trucks to take them out to dispersal. They were dressed in heavy flying clothes, wearing life jackets and parachute harnesses with the rest of their clobber strewn around their feet – parachute packs, navigation bags, ration boxes – so that the place looked a bit like a refugee camp. Sam was tucked inside Harry's battledress jacket under his Mae West, safe out of the wet, the carrier pigeon snug in its box. He wished he was so lucky.

Their seventeenth op, and he still got the jim-jams every time. He was OK for most of the day until after the briefing and the flying supper. It always started in the locker room while he was getting togged up, and got worse with every stage: the hanging around for transport, the ride out to dispersal, the final look round before he climbed the ladder . . . all the time hoping up till the very last minute that they'd scrub it. Once he got down to the job, it wasn't so bad – mainly because there wasn't much time to think about anything else. He was all right until they were approaching the target when the jim-jams got going again and stayed with him until they'd dropped the bombs and were safely away. He didn't know how it was with the others, but that was the way it always was with him. He groped in his top pocket for his pipe;

he wouldn't smoke it but it gave him a bit of comfort just to clench it in his teeth.

All the other blokes standing around looked so calm, when he was bloody sure they weren't inside. The jawing and joking going on was to cover up what they were really feeling underneath – bloody scared, like him. But what they were all saying to themselves, same as him, was that it wouldn't happen to *them*. It'd be the other bloke who bought it. Always the other bloke.

Stew came over for a match – as usual his lighter had gone u/s. His Irvin jacket collar was turned up round his ears and under it he wore a heavy wool sweater up to his chin; thick white seamen's socks showed above his flying boots. His face was wet with rain, the cigarette in his mouth soggy.

'Sodding weather! If they cut the barrage balloon cables, the whole bloody country'd sink. Jesus, I don't know why I ever came here.'

Harry sucked at his empty pipe. 'To show us you could stand the right way up.'

'Yeah . . . that was it.'

It took three matches to get Stew's cigarette alight. Unlucky, that, Harry thought uneasily.

The lorries were arriving, the crews starting to collect up their gear and make their way over towards them. He picked up his 'chute pack and the pigeon's box. His stomach felt like a cement-mixer as he waited his turn to clamber up into the back of a lorry, giving Charlie a hand-up ahead of him, passing up his stuff. Not much chance of a scrub now.

Tubby Green's crew were in there and it was their last op. They were swapping a few jokes about it and what they'd do when it was over, but he could tell they were afraid of tempting fate. He caught the eye of their wireless op and gave him a nod and a thumbs-up. If all went well they'd be finished and done in a few hours. Lucky devils.

He looked further down the bench to where Charlie was sitting, twice his real size in his padded suit. The lad had got a bad cold and shouldn't really be flying. He'd tried to talk him into seeing the MO for a chit, but he wouldn't hear of being left behind. He ought to have got the skipper to stop him. He'd promised Dorothy he'd look after him, and a fat lot of good he was proving to be at it.

They were the third lot to get off round the peri track. U-Uncle loomed up at them out of grey mist and drizzle, and Harry's hopes of a scrub rose again. Ops had been cancelled in much better weather.

He went up the ladder first, as always, so he could hang Sam up in his place for the rest to touch. Charlie was last and he waited to help him with his 'chute pack over the tail spar. 'There you go, lad. All right?'

Charlie croaked an answer; he sounded proper poorly.

While the skipper and Jock warmed up the engines he sorted himself out in his compartment so everything was neat and tidy. He liked it all just so: log book in place, sharpened pencils lined up, Thermos flask and sandwiches out of the way – he wouldn't touch those until they were well on the way home. Never did. With all the activity, he was already forgetting about the jim-jams when a message came through from control that take-off had been delayed for one hour. They were to stand by.

Out they got again, lumbering along like polar bears in all their heavy gear. They took shelter in the ground crew's hut where there was a good old fug-up from the coke stove. They were warm and dry, but the jitters had come back again.

Harry got out his pipe and started to fill it for something to do. Stew had joined the ground crew, playing cards on an upturned tool box; Van and Jock were talking engines; Piers was staring out of the window; Bert had his nose to some pin-up girl picture on the wall; Charlie was coughing away in the corner.

'Here, Charlie, there's room over here.' Harry urged him closer to the stove.

'Thanks, Harry, but I'm too hot already.'

There were beads of sweat on the lad's forehead. Running a temperature, he thought worriedly. He ought to be back in bed in the hut. He'd go and get pneumonia, or something. Come to that, he shouldn't be doing this at all. It was a job for men, not boys.

Stew had won a pile of cigarettes by the time a sergeant came into the hut with another message from Control to taxi out for take-off. Harry watched the fitters managing grins as he scooped them all up. Probably because they weren't going too.

It was dark when they moved out of dispersal. Stew was lying in the nose, shining the Aldis lamp down on the skipper's side of the peri track, guiding him along, and Harry stood in the astrodome, keeping a good look-out. When they got to the take-off marshalling point he was ready to flash their aircraft number. He could hear Van and Jock going through their final checks and kept his eye on the control cabin, waiting for the signal back.

'It's green, skipper.'

'Roger, Harry.'

U-Uncle surged forward down a runway that looked

like a black river. They took off and climbed upwards through the clouds. As soon as the skipper gave him the OK, he left the astrodome. When he'd wound out the trailing aerial and tuned the W/T receiver, he switched on the IFF and began his listening watch. The frequency kept drifting and he had to keep re-tuning the receiver, concentrating hard. The route could be changed, or they could be recalled and one of his worst nightmares was of missing a vital message.

Twice, Piers asked him to check the DR Compass and twice he clambered aft over the main spar, shining his torch ahead as he ducked and crouched his way down the fuselage to the compass housing forward of the entrance door. He wondered how Charlie was doing behind the turret doors.

On the way back he had to grab at handholds to steady himself against a lot of turbulence. U-Uncle was doing a right fandango. He wished it was D-Dog; he always felt better when they flew in her. U-Uncle was brand new, straight out of the factory, and maybe with teething troubles.

They cleared the cloud soon after crossing the enemy coast, and the constant flickering of gun muzzle flashes lit the sky ahead as they approached the target. The Jerries were ready for them. This was the time he dreaded most. The time when the jim-jams were worst: when they were weaving and dodging and dicing with death. No matter how hard he tried to control himself, his insides turned to jelly. He'd seen exactly what happened to a bomber copped by flak and it wasn't a pleasant way to go. And if they escaped that fate, there was another possibility just as horrible: of colliding with another bomber converging on the target. He'd seen that, too.

He flinched and ducked as another burst of shellfire rocked U-Uncle, and shrapnel struck the fuselage above him. Good job nobody else could see him. The skipper had stopped the jinking to port and starboard. Now they had to fly straight and level on their bombing run. Into the open jaws of death – that's how he thought of it. Jaws that could snap shut any moment.

The only voices on the intercom were Stew's and the skipper's; everybody else kept their mouths tightly closed.

'Open bomb doors, skip.' Stew, cool as ice.

'Bomb doors open.'

'Bombs fused and selected.'

Harry clenched his fists and held his breath. Five tons of high explosive and incendiary bombs exposed to a hail of red-hot metal from below.

'Right – right. Steady, steady . . .'

Harry wiped his forehead.

'Left, left. Steady . . . steady . . .'

He wiped it once more.

'Bombs gone, skip. Bomb doors closed.'

'Bomb doors closed.'

He unclenched his hands slowly and breathed again. U-Uncle's nose was hard down, diving away from the target. Going home.

Then Stew's voice came on again suddenly. 'Shit! We've got a hang-up, skip. The cookie. Must've got bloody stuck somehow.'

'Pilot to wireless operator. Check it out, Harry, will you?'

Harry grabbed his portable oxygen bottle, torch and screwdriver, climbed back over the main spar once again and unscrewed the inspection panel above the

222

bomb bay. He aimed the torch downwards. Christ, there it was! The cylinder-shaped casing of the four-thousand pounder glinted as he played the beam. He shone the torch round the rest of the bomb bay.

'Wireless operator to skipper. All the five-hundred pounders have gone but it looks like the cookie's got itself caught up.'

'I'll open the doors again and try the manual. Let me know if that works, Harry.'

The skipper had a jettison control on the starboard side of his instrument panel. That might do the trick. As the bomb doors swung open a blast of freezing air rushed in. Harry kept his torch trained on the cookie.

'Still there, skipper.'

'OK, Harry. Stand by, crew. I'm going to see if we can shake her loose.'

Harry clung on as the Lanc started see-sawing from side to side and then plunging up and down. The bomb was fused, but he knew bombs were quite safe until the fall from the aircraft automatically armed them. He also knew they tended to go off on impact or with any heavy deceleration.

Van levelled out.

'How're we doing, Harry?'

He collected himself and shone the torch. 'Still there. Hasn't budged at all.'

'I'll give it another go.'

He staggered and lost his balance as the bomber leaped about again. The torch flew out of his hand.

'Any luck this time, Harry?'

He fumbled for his mike switch as he crawled about the roof of the bomb bay. 'Sorry, skipper, I dropped the torch. Just a moment.' Clumsy fool, he thought, scrabbling desperately about in the darkness.

Letting them all down. If they didn't get rid of the bomb somehow it'd mean landing with it on board. If the skipper did a smooth landing it could be OK, but if he didn't . . . or if something went wrong with the undercarriage and they had to belly land . . . Don't be so pathetic, he told himself. No point starting to think about things like that. Looking for more trouble. Just find the bloody torch. His groping fingers finally located it where it had rolled away aft. Thank God, it was working. He hauled himself back to the inspection panel.

'It's still there, skipper.'

'Can you try releasing it manually, Harry?'

He went back to get the stick kept in his tool kit. He'd never used the blessed thing before – had no occasion to – but the hooked wire at its end was supposed to be able to release the shackle holding a bomb, if you could reach it. He shoved his arm down into the bay, stretching as far as he could towards the cookie, probing desperately with the stick.

'Sorry, skipper – can't seem to do it.'

Jock's voice came over. 'If we have to carry that lot back, we'll have dry tanks before we cross the English coast. An' I wouldna fancy ditching with the extra weight.'

Nor would Harry. The cookie would take them straight down. He angled the torch along the underside of the bomb-bay roof.

'Wireless operator to pilot. How about if I try making another hole nearer with the fire axe? It might be easier.'

Stew clicked on his mike switch. 'I'll give him a hand, skip. Reckon two of us'd have a better chance.'

'OK, Stew. Mid-upper and rear gunner, keep watching out for enemy fighters. They'll be around.'

That'd be all they needed. Harry started hacking at the aluminium roofing over the bay and then Stew appeared carrying another fire axe. Together they chopped away furiously until they'd opened up a hole large enough for a man to lean down into the bomb bay. With the doors wide open, the slipstream was a howling gale, the cold bitter.

Stew motioned that he'd be the one to have a go. Well, fair enough, it was his bomb, so to speak. He knew all about them. Harry handed him the hooked stick. He grabbed hold of Stew's parachute harness as he lowered his head and shoulders through the jagged hole and hoped to God his hands wouldn't be too numb to hold on if Stew fell through the whole way. The harness wouldn't do him much good without the parachute.

'How're you guys doing back there?'

Harry dared not let go to turn on his mike switch and answer the skipper. Stew had inched even further through – almost as far as his waist.

'Pilot to navigator. Go take a look, Piers.'

'Right, skipper.'

Harry turned his head as Piers came crouching across the bomb bay roofing towards him, eyes widening above his mask at all that was visible of Stew. He nodded back as though everything was going all right. Piers disappeared again and a moment later he heard his report.

'Navigator to pilot. I think Stew's reached it through the hole. Harry couldn't answer you because he's holding on to him.'

'Thanks, Piers. Harry, let me know what's

happening soon as you can. Gunners keep a good look-out.'

He went on kneeling there, gripping the straps with his frozen fingers, unable to see what *was* happening. If an enemy fighter turned up the skipper would have to corkscrew fast, and he couldn't see how Stew'd get back out of the hole quick enough, or how he'd be able to go on holding on to him when they dived. Stew would have had it – if he wasn't already dead from the cold.

Then U-Uncle gave a sudden lurch and Stew started to wriggle backwards out of the hole. He stuck up his thumb and flicked his mike switch.

'She's gone, skip. Managed to free her. You can close the doors.'

'Well done, bomb aimer. They ought to give you a gong for that.'

A few moments later Charlie spoke up croakily from the tail. 'Rear gunner to skipper. Big explosion directly below. Must've been our cookie. Hope it hit something.'

'I felt bad about that hang-up,' Stew told Harry afterwards. 'Thought at first it could've been all my fault. But the bomb blokes told me it was a ball-bearing got gummed up with paint in the factory. Got stuck in its socket and cocked up the circuit. The bastard that did that could've got us all killed.'

It wasn't that he begrudged Stew the glory. It'd been right brave of him to do what he did, but Harry couldn't help wishing he'd had the chance of being the hero. Charlie might have told his mother about it and, well, she might've seen him in a different sort of light. When it came down to it, though – down to the nuts and bolts, as you might say – it was Stew who'd looked after Charlie, and not him at all.

226

'Looks proper dodgy this morning, sir. I don't think you'll be bothered tonight.'

The WAAF batwoman handed Piers his cup of tea and went over to take down the blackout from the window. 'Nice 'n nasty it is. Heavy rain and low cloud – set in till tomorrow at least, I'd say.' She turned round and beamed at him. 'Just what the doctor ordered.'

She had spoken in a loud whisper. Van groaned in the other bed and dragged the covers over his head.

'He won't be wanting a cup, will he, sir?'

'No, he won't, thanks all the same.'

She was always hoping against hope that Van would change his mind. 'He ought to have something hot first thing, but still, I suppose they're different Over There. Takes all sorts to make the world go round, that's what I say. Live and let live. Except the Germans, of course, and those Japanese.'

Her name was Mabel and she came from Huddersfield. She was older than most of the WAAFs and fussed like a mother hen. He'd seen her crying when chaps bought it. Van wouldn't let her fuss over him too much but Piers rather enjoyed it. She reminded him of Matron at prep school who used to bring them cocoa at bedtime and tuck them in and be decent to new boys when they were homesick.

Mabel stopped by the end of his bed and made a hospital corner with the covers. She patted the blanket. 'You get a nice bit of rest, sir. Take my word for it, nobody's going flying anywhere today.'

She was usually right about the weather. In fact, she was a better forecaster than most of the met lot.

Sometimes he thought they ought to get Mabel to do the ops briefings.

She watched him drink his tea. 'I put an extra bit of sugar in for you this morning, sir.'

'Oh, thanks awfully.'

'Well, it gives you energy, doesn't it? You young gentlemen ought to have as much as you like.' She gave a final pat to the blanket and tiptoed out of the room on the toes of her heavy lace-ups, making more noise than if she'd walked normally.

Van groaned again.

When he'd finished the tea, Piers lay back and shut his eyes, listening happily to the rain drumming on the hut roof. Bliss to think of not having to worry about ops. No sinking feeling as he biked over to see if they were on the Battle Order pinned up in the Flight Commander's office. No flying test. No ghastly jitters hanging around. No worrying about which target. And today was Wednesday – Peggy's day off. Since he'd been back from leave there hadn't been a Wednesday when he'd been able to get away from the station, but it looked as though he might manage it today. He could drive over and take her out. Hang on, supposing she'd changed her mind? No, she wouldn't do that. Not when she'd pretty well promised.

He'd thought about her all the time during his leave – could hardly think of anything else. Mama had noticed, of course, and told Papa to give him that lecture. God, as though that sort of thing mattered any more! Everything was different now. The war was changing all that class rot, and a good thing too. Everybody mixed with everybody. He'd jolly nearly said so, only he hadn't really had the chance.

It wasn't easy standing up to the parents but he'd

somehow stuck to his guns over joining the RAF. Made a bit of a stand over it, for once. Just as well. If he'd gone into the Army he'd probably have been killed already in France, or a POW at least. Not that he'd got much chance of surviving his tour. Chaps were going down like ninepins. You got hardened to it. Jolly well had to. *Did you hear old Dusty went for a Burton over Cologne? Bad show. Can you pass the marmalade, please?*

He wondered if Mama would cry, like Mabel. He'd never seen her cry and couldn't imagine it. He could imagine Peggy crying, though. See her blue eyes filling with tears if she were very sad about something. He pictured her hearing the news of him getting the old chop and weeping buckets.

Mabel was quite right about the weather and the stand-down. In the afternoon Piers gave Stew and five chaps from another crew a lift into Lincoln, all squashed into the Wolseley, and when he'd dropped them off he drove out on the Skellingthorpe road, following the route he remembered to Peggy's home. It was still pouring buckets and the windscreen wiper wasn't doing too good a job, so he almost missed the row of cottages. He hadn't seen them properly in the dark last time and in the light of day, he was dismayed that Peggy should have to live in such a rundown place. The tenants' cottages at home were much better kept.

Someone was watching him from next door as he walked up to the end cottage. He could see a face pressed close to the window glass, peering out. There was no doorbell or knocker, so he rapped timidly with his knuckles. Nobody came and after a moment he knocked again, a little louder. Perhaps he ought to have asked Peggy's parents first for permission to take her out? They might slam the door in his face. He fingered his tie nervously.

The door was opened by a woman wearing an apron and carrying a small boy on her hip. She looked astonished to see him standing there. 'Are you lost, sir? Looking for one of the aerodromes?'

Another child, a larger boy, squeezed into the gap between the woman and the door-post and fixed him with an unwinking stare.

Piers cleared his throat. 'Actually, I was looking for Peggy.'

'Peggy?' She still seemed surprised.

'Gosh, I'm most awfully sorry, I must have got the house wrong. I thought this was where she lived.'

'It is, sir.'

He could feel himself blushing. 'Oh, jolly good. Actually, I'm a friend of hers – Piers Wentworth-Young. I wonder if I could possibly see her?'

The woman hesitated and then stood back from the doorway. 'You'd better come in, sir. Mind out of the gentleman's way, Billy.'

The boy moved aside reluctantly and Piers took off his cap and stepped over the threshold into a tiny front room. The furniture was frightfully shabby, the floor covered with brown linoleum. There was a cut-out colour photograph of the King and Queen pinned to one wall and a framed picture of Lincoln Cathedral hanging on another. A china plate over the fireplace said *Bless this House*.

'Peggy's out in the shed, if you'll wait a moment, sir.'

She left the room carrying the child. Billy stayed behind, still staring hard. The eyes, Piers realized, were exactly the same blue as Peggy's.

230

'You must be Peggy's brother?' he said awkwardly, wishing he had some chocolate or chewing gum to offer.

The boy nodded. 'You a pilot, mister?'

'No. I'm a navigator, actually.'

His face fell. 'Oh.'

He tried to explain. 'I sort of map read for the pilot.'

He looked even more disappointed. 'Is that all?'

'I'm afraid so. Sorry.'

'That's *boring*.'

'Billy, don't be so rude! Say you're sorry to the gentleman.'

He turned to see Peggy standing in the doorway.

'He doesn't understand about crews, sir. He thinks everyone in the RAF is a pilot. *Billy*. Go on.'

The boy muttered something and ran out of the room.

'He said he was sorry.'

'Honestly, I don't mind. Not a bit.' He couldn't help staring at her. She looked even prettier than he remembered. 'I would have come sooner but I couldn't get away before. We're on stand-down today and . . . well, Wednesday's your day off, isn't it? I thought we might go to the cinema. If you'd still like to, that is.'

'I've been cleaning the bike,' she said, holding out her hands. There was an oily smudge on one cheek. 'I'm all dirty.'

'Heavens, that doesn't matter.' Was she going to refuse, after all? Make excuses.

'I'd have to get tidy. I couldn't go like this.'

He smiled at her. 'I'll wait in the car.'

*　　　*　　　*

231

'You'll be stood-down with the bad weather, then, Jock?'

'Aye, Mrs Gibbs. Thought I'd come over and give the Fordson's engine a bit of a going-over – if you'd like?'

'That'd be kind. It's gone so well since you've been looking after it.'

'Right.'

She looked at him sideways. 'Ruth's out in the barn. I expect you'll want to say hallo to her.'

He squelched across the muddy yard and stepped in through the small door at the end of the barn. She was dragging a sack of grain across the floor.

'Ruth . . .'

She whirled round. 'What're you doing here, Jock?'

'We're stood-down. I came to do a bit of work on the Fordson.' And to see you, he added to himself, looking at her. As well you know.

The couple of times he'd been over since his last leave, he'd never got to see her alone. Somehow she'd contrived things so it never happened. He couldn't understand why.

'Let me give you a hand.'

'I can manage.'

He took hold of the sack firmly. 'Just tell me where you want it to go.'

'There.' She pointed. 'It's the hen feed. I can get at it easily then.'

He hefted it over. 'Any more to move?'

'No, thanks.' She tugged her cap brim down still further. She was wearing some kind of cast-off man's jacket over her Land Army sweater and an old plaid scarf wrapped round her neck. Her hair looked as though she'd been at it again with the shears.

232

'The Fordson's in the shed.'

'I know where it is. What I want to know is what's the matter with you?'

'I don't know what you mean.'

'Aye, you know, all right. You weren't like this before.'

'Before what?'

'Don't play games with me, Ruth.'

'Games?'

He looked hard at what he could see of her face. 'I thought it was different – with us. Like you wanted. Like you hoped.'

She moved away and started dumping things into a wheelbarrow. 'I wish I hadn't told you about that.'

'I'm glad you did. So there wouldna be anything between us.'

She swung round again suddenly. 'You're a fool, Jock. You don't know me at all. I'm not your sort of woman. I'd never live up to your standards.'

'What do you mean, *my* standards?'

'I know what you'd expect. The kind of man you are. And I didn't tell you the half of it. About me. Oh, the first part was true, but it wasn't the *whole* truth, see. There were other men – after that one in London. I was just leading you on for fun, like I did with them. I've done it lots of times. Men always fall for it. They can't wait to show you they're God's gift. How different they are from all the rest. Only they're not. You're all the same.'

He stared at her. 'What in God's name are you saying? That it was all play-acting with you, then? Some sort of trick?'

'That's it. It was a trick. A joke. On you.'

'I don't believe you,' he said slowly. 'I don't believe any woman could pretend like that.'

'Then you've got a lot to learn about women. It's easy to pretend.'

'You weren't pretending.'

'I'm busy, Jock. I haven't the time to argue with you.'

She turned her back on him and after a moment he went away to work on the tractor. There was a terrible bitterness in his heart.

It had been a disastrous morning. The rain was coming in through one of the ceilings, the chambermaid was off sick, the boiler had broken down, Cedric had found an old bottle of sherry in a cupboard and was dead drunk. A guest had complained about the lunch and refused to pay his bill, the chef had taken umbrage and threatened to leave, the colonel had lost his spectacles yet again, and, on top of it all, Mrs Mountjoy had sent for her after lunch to look at the blackout blind in her room.

'It's torn. A great big hole there . . .' She jabbed upwards with her walking stick. 'Surely you noticed? The whole thing is falling to pieces. It must be mended at once, Miss Frost.'

'I'll see to it before it gets dark, Mrs Mountjoy.'

'I should hope so unless you want every enemy bomber dropping their bombs on this hotel.'

It didn't seem such a bad idea, Honor thought, if they aimed at Mrs Mountjoy's bedroom. She left the old woman to her afternoon rest and, as she crossed the upstairs landing, heard the reception desk bell being rung loudly below. She started down the stairs and then stopped. The Australian sergeant was standing in the hall below.

'My word, I thought everyone in this place must've dropped dead.'

'I was busy upstairs.' She went down a step or two and stopped again. 'Did you want something?'

'Yeah. You to come down here.'

'What is it?'

'Come on and you'll find out.'

She limped slowly down the rest of the stairs. 'Well?'

He held out a brown paper parcel. 'Something for you, Honor.'

'What is it?'

'Strewth, you don't need to look so worried. It's not a bomb.' He had taken off his forage cap and was slapping it to and fro against his greatcoat sleeve. Droplets of rainwater flew about. 'Open it and you'll find out.'

She carried the parcel over to the reception desk. The paper was tied up roughly with knotted string.

'Sorry,' he said. 'Didn't make too good a job of it.'

She undid the string. 'Do you want this back?'

'Cripes, no. You keep it.'

She saved everything like that – string, paper bags, brown paper – everybody did. Her mother had a big hoard kept neatly wound or folded in separate piles in the bottom drawer of the kitchen dresser.

When she opened up the brown paper she found four large tins of food: ham, chicken, condensed milk and pineapples.

'It's part of a thank you,' he said off-handedly. 'For looking after me when I was crook. Letting me stay the extra days for free.'

'How on earth did you get these?'

'Didn't pinch them, if that's what you're thinking. My family send stuff from home. I would've given you

235

more but I always share things around with the other blokes too.'

'I couldn't possibly take them.'

'Well, I'm not carrying them all the way back, that's for sure.'

It would be useless to argue with him, she could see. 'I'll take them home to my mother. Thank you.'

'So long as you get to eat some.'

'Do you want the paper back?'

'No thanks. Give it to your mother too.'

The telephone shrilled suddenly in the office and she went to answer it. When she came out he was still there, leaning against the reception desk.

'What time d'you finish today?'

'It depends.'

'On what?'

'On how much there is to do. If I'm needed.'

'Don't you have hours? You know, a set time to start and stop?'

'It never works like that.'

'Oh, my word, that's not right. All work and no play. What time're you *meant* to get off tonight, then?'

'Six o'clock. But—'

He levered himself away from the desk, heading for the door. 'Right. I'll come back at six and take you for a grog. The other part of the "thank you". See you later.'

He was gone before she could tell him that it was quite impossible, and she was left staring at the revolving door squeaking round and round.

She mended Mrs Mountjoy's blackout blind with sticky tape, found Colonel Millis's spectacles down the side of his armchair and dealt with table reservations for dinner. Ron had just arrived to open up the Oak

Bar – on time for once – when the Australian returned. He came into the hall, slapping the rain off his cap again.

'You ready?'

'I can't leave now. There'd be nobody on the desk.'

The grandfather clock started striking in its corner as she spoke. He leaned both forearms on the desk. Looked at her. 'You said six o'clock's your knocking-off time, right? That's what it is now. The old tick-tock just told us.' He pushed back his sleeve. 'And my watch agrees. So, how about getting your coat?'

She said lamely, 'I'd have to ask Miss Hargreaves.'

'Fair enough. Ask her, whoever she is. I'll wait.'

Miss Hargreaves was listening to the wireless in her upstairs sitting-room. 'Go? *Now?*'

'It's six o'clock, Miss Hargreaves. That's the time I'm supposed to leave.'

'But there will be nobody on Reception.'

'Ron will keep an eye on the desk if I ask him.'

'That won't do at all, Miss Frost. Why must you go so early all of a sudden?'

'I'm extremely tired,' she said. 'I've been working overtime every single evening since I started here. I stay *hours* late sometimes – without any extra pay. I think I'm more than entitled to leave on time tonight.'

Miss Hargreaves looked at her as though she'd gone mad. Perhaps she had. 'Oh well, if you insist, I suppose I shall have to come down and take over myself.'

She found the sergeant waiting at the bottom of the stairs. 'I'll just get my coat.'

He grinned. 'Easy, wasn't it?'

*   *   *

237

Piers had parked the car near the cinema. It was still pouring with rain but luckily he'd got an old umbrella in the car and he held it over Peggy while they waited in the queue. He was left half-out in the wet, himself, with cold drops dripping down the back of his neck, but he didn't care. Nor did he care what the film was, though Peggy seemed to know all about it.

'Mavis told me. She went on Monday.'

He tugged up the collar of his greatcoat with his free hand. 'Mavis?'

'She does the washing-up at The Angel. She said it was ever so good, but then she likes anything with Errol Flynn in it. Anything American, really. She talks with an American accent sometimes – just like them. She copies it from the films, see. She's never met a real American. Nor've I.'

'Our pilot's American, actually, so you have. He came to my birthday dinner, remember? The tall one with the wings on his chest.'

'Oh, I thought he was Canadian. We get quite a lot of Canadians in the hotel and they sound like that. Mavis likes them too, but not as much as Americans.'

The cinema doors opened and they started to shuffle forward with the queue. When it came to their turn at the kiosk, Peggy tugged a little brown purse out of her coat pocket and tried to pay for her own ticket. He stopped her, of course.

'I've never sat up here,' she said as they took their places in the circle. 'I always sit downstairs. It's much cheaper there.'

He'd never sat in the pit. 'But you can see better from up here.'

'Yes, you can,' she agreed. 'People's heads don't get

in the way. But I didn't want you to spend all that money on me.'

The lights went down and the 'B' feature started, followed by a cartoon and the Gaumont British News. There was a film of grinning Tommies advancing in Africa, thrusting thumbs up at the camera, and of pack-laden American soldiers disembarking down a gangplank at some port in England, not looking quite so happy. Piers scarcely saw any of it. He kept sneaking looks at Peggy, sitting close beside him with her eyes fixed on the screen. He didn't think much of the Errol Flynn picture about spies in occupied Europe. It was pretty far-fetched, but Peggy seemed to enjoy it. He went on watching her surreptitiously.

When they left the cinema it was dark and still raining hard. He found his torch in his greatcoat pocket and took her arm quite firmly. 'We'll go and get something to eat.'

'Oh no, if you'd just take me home, sir.'

'Aren't you hungry? I jolly well am. I could eat a horse.'

She giggled. 'You probably would at The Angel, sir.'

'Well, we won't go there.'

He took her to The Saracen's Head. It was still early and there were plenty of empty tables in the dining-room. Peggy seemed awfully nervous.

'Is anything the matter, Peggy? Don't you like it here? We could go somewhere else.'

'It's just that I'm not used to this, sir. I've only ever done the waitressing.'

'Gosh, well it's your turn to be sitting down now.' He picked up the menu quickly. 'What would you like to eat? It says there's chicken fricassée, or do you think that's really rabbit?'

It was a feeble joke but it made her smile a bit. 'I expect so, sir. It usually is.'

'I say, do you think you could possibly call me Piers?'

'Not really, sir.' She was looking quite upset. Perched on the very edge of her chair as though she'd make a bolt for it if he wasn't very careful.

He racked his brains for a safe topic of conversation. 'How old is your brother, Billy?'

'He's five. And I'm sorry he was so rude to you. He's a good boy really.'

'I'm sure he is,' he said hurriedly. 'And your other brother? The smaller one?'

'He's only two. Well, nearly two-and-a-half.'

'Do you have any other brothers, or sisters?' He couldn't imagine there could be room for more in that tiny cottage.

'I did have another brother – Eddie. He was two years younger than me but he died when he was seven. From the measles.'

'I'm terribly sorry.' Just his rotten luck to go and ask that.

'Oh, it's all right,' she said. 'I don't mind talking about it. Not now. What about you?'

'I've got one sister, Pamela.'

'That's a beautiful name.'

'She's in the WRNS. The women's navy, you know.'

'I expect she's an officer. Like you.'

'Yes, as a matter of fact she is.'

She was still sitting on the edge of her chair, bolt upright, hands clasped tightly in her lap. He tried again.

'I'm jolly glad you enjoyed the film.'

'It was lovely. I like Errol Flynn. Not as much as Mavis, though. I really like Lesley Howard better.'

That sounded promising. Lesley Howard was fair, like himself. Not that he could compete with a film star.

'I hope you'll come out with me again? We could go and see another film. As soon as I can manage to get away again. They keep us pretty busy, that's the trouble.'

She looked at him. 'Don't your mum and dad worry about you a lot, being in the bombers?'

'I'm not sure,' he said honestly. 'They don't say anything, but I suppose they do.'

'I bet they do. Bound to. Mum and Dad worry about me going to Lincoln and back on the bike, and you go all the way to Germany and get shot at. Yours must worry a lot.'

'Anyway,' he said, 'we're not on ops for ever. They only make us do thirty.'

She was watching him, blue eyes clouded. 'How many've you done so far?'

'Nineteen. Eleven to go. Of course, with the winter it'll probably take a while. We don't go unless the weather's all right.'

'I don't know how you ever manage it,' she said. 'All that way there and back and all in the dark. It's wonderful.'

He blushed. 'Oh, it's not so difficult, really. Actually, I was always getting us lost when we first started but I've got the hang of it now.'

'I'd be ever so frightened if it was me.'

'There's not much time to be,' he lied. 'We're kept pretty busy.'

The chicken turned out to be rabbit, of course, but they had a laugh about that and everything was going rather well when Peggy suddenly stopped eating, fork half way to her mouth.

'What's the matter?'

'The gentleman over there – the officer at the table in the corner . . .'

'What about him?'

'He comes into The Angel a lot. I've often waited on him. He knows me.'

'That doesn't matter, Peggy.'

'Yes, it does.' She dropped the fork with a clatter. 'He's *staring* at me. He knows I oughtn't to be here. Oughtn't to be with you.'

Piers glanced over his shoulder and saw a middle-aged RAF squadron leader glaring in their direction. Obviously one of the old pre-war lot that hadn't moved with the times.

'It's absolutely none of his business. Don't take any notice of him. There's nothing to worry about.'

'I want to go,' she said, getting up. 'Please take me home *now*.'

In the car she gave a stifled sob. 'I'm very sorry, sir. I spoiled your dinner. You never even finished it.'

'I don't care about the dinner. Honestly.' God, he'd made a complete mess of everything. He should never have taken her somewhere like that. He'd been a thoughtless bloody idiot.

He stopped the car outside the cottage. 'Look, I'm terribly sorry you were upset, Peggy. I honestly had no idea—'

She gulped. 'It wasn't your fault, sir. You couldn't help it. You weren't to know.'

He couldn't think of anything to say that would put things right. 'Stopped raining at last, anyway. That's something.' He tried to sound cheerful. Whistled a bit. 'Probably be fine tomorrow.'

'So it has.' There was a pause. 'Does that mean you'll be flying, then?'

'I expect so.'

'I hope you don't, sir.'

'Oh . . . well . . . we have to jolly well press on.'

'Yes, I s'pose you do.'

'Peggy . . .'

'Yes, sir?'

'Look, I don't suppose there's *any* chance of you coming out another time, is there? I swear we wouldn't go anywhere like that again. It'd mean an awful lot to me.'

There was another, longer, pause. Unable to see her face in the darkness, he waited without much hope.

Her voice sounded soft and kind. 'Well . . . if you like.'

Charlie was sitting on his bed in the little upstairs room in the cottage and going through his poetry book. There hadn't been much spare time for a while and he didn't like to bring the book out in the hut too often. Stew would be bound to look over his shoulder and make one of his remarks. *Strewth, Charlie! Bloody rainbows again?* He'd slipped the book into his pocket today and brought it back with him, knowing he'd get the chance of a quiet moment to himself.

He turned the pages slowly, re-reading · old favourites.

> *Half a league, half a league,*
> *Half a league onward,*
> *All in the valley of death*
> *Rode the six hundred . . .*

Instead of thinking of soldiers and horses, he thought of bombers and airmen – just the same as when he changed *The Soldier* poem in his mind. Six hundred bombers charging into the Ruhr Valley and into a barrage of flak and fighters. *Was there a man dismayed?* Well, yes, there was. Himself, for one. And he wouldn't mind betting nearly everybody else as well, even though nobody showed it.

> *Theirs not to reason why,*
> *Theirs but to do and die . . .*

That was true enough. You didn't ask why. They told you at briefings. *Maximum effort required tonight, gentlemen. War factory . . . railway centre . . . important port . . . ship-building . . . submarine pens . . . vital target . . . England expects you to do your duty . . .* You did, and a whole lot of you died. Say twenty aircraft didn't get back, like on that last Cologne op. Multiply twenty by seven – if they were Lancs. One hundred and forty men.

> *Boldly they rode and well,*
> *Into the jaws of death,*
> *Into the mouth of hell*
> *Rode the six hundred . . .*

> *Cannon to right of them,*
> *Cannon to left of them,*
> *Cannon behind them*
> *Volleyed and thundered;*
> *Stormed at with shot and shell . . .*

Crikey, it sounded just like an op.

They that had fought so well
Came through the jaws of death,
Back from the mouth of hell,
All that was left of them,
Left of six hundred.

Just like the big raids. You'd think Lord Tennyson had been on one if you didn't know he couldn't have.

The rain was beating against the window panes but inside the cottage it was nice and cosy. The fire was lit downstairs and the smell of supper cocking drifted up to him. Something tasty. He could hear the wireless on in the sitting-room and Mum talking to Harry in the kitchen – hear her say something and Harry's low, slow rumble in reply. Charlie smiled to himself. She didn't have a clue that Harry was sweet on her but *he* could see which way the wind was blowing, plain as anything, and he didn't mind the idea of Harry as a stepfather. He was a good bloke: kind and decent, and he'd look after Mum. She needed somebody about the place. Someone to take care of her.

When they'd been stood down with the bad weather, Harry had come over to him, all casual, and asked if he'd be going to see his mum because he thought he ought to take a look at the wireless and see it was working properly. They'd biked over together and Harry had brought Sam because his one ear was starting to come off.

Of course there was nothing wrong with the wireless but Harry had spent a good bit of time fiddling about with it, while Mum had got out her sewing basket and sat down to mend Sam. When she'd finished putting the ear back on, Harry had said he wished he could sew neatly like that. If he sewed on a button it fell straight off, he'd said. And he always pricked his finger and got blood over everything. Then Mum had told him to bring over any sewing he needed done and she'd take care of it. Harry had gone all red, from his collar up, and said he couldn't do that, but Mum had insisted. It was to be in return for the wireless. And she'd asked him to stay for supper, too. Charlie grinned again.

He fingered a new pimple coming up on his chin – a great big lump of a pimple. He wished he wasn't always getting them. Covered with them, he was sometimes. More pimple than skin. There was a nice WAAF in Equipment, about his own age, that he'd kept noticing, and Bert was always going on at him to try his luck, but she'd never look at him with a face like his.

He'd never taken a girl out. Never kissed one. Let alone the rest of it. Maybe he never would. Maybe he'd never ever know what *that* was like.

'Charlie! Supper's ready.'

He closed the book and went downstairs.

The barmaid at The Saracen's Head seemed to know Sergeant Brenner well. He leaned across the counter and chucked her under the chin.

'The usual, sweetheart. And a lemonade for the lady.'

He'd been appalled when she'd asked for lemonade. 'Oh my word, that's not going to do you much good. Have a beer.'

'No, thank you.'

She found somewhere to sit and hooked her walking stick over the back of the chair, as out of sight as possible. She hated using a stick – it made her feel like old Mrs Mountjoy. Indoors she managed without it but outdoors, on uneven ground and in the blackout, it was too hard. Getting down Steep Hill had been tricky but she'd hidden that quite well and he'd carried the parcel.

He sat down opposite and raised his pint to her. 'Mud in your eye, Honor.'

'I beg your pardon?'

'Old Aussie saying. Good health.'

'Oh . . .' She lifted her own glass. 'Good health.'

'Cigarette?'

'No, thank you.'

He stuck one in his mouth, groped in his pocket for his lighter and flicked the flint wheel hard with his thumb. 'Well, what d'you know, it's working. Wonders never cease.'

As he bent his head to the flame she noticed his lashes in its glow – long for a man, especially a man like him. He kept the cigarette between his lips while he put the lighter away, talking through it. 'Seems to me they take advantage of you at that place. Give you the run-around. You ought to look for another job. Somewhere they treat you better.'

'I'm perfectly happy there.'

'Not from what I've seen.'

'Well, I don't suppose *you* enjoy what you do very much – whatever that is.'

He tapped the 'B' on his chest. 'I'm a bomb aimer. Can't say I *enjoy* dropping bombs on people but I'm willing to do it, since it's the Jerries. And I don't have any nightmares about it, if that's what you're thinking. They're *all* the enemy, far as I'm concerned: civilians, old people, the whole damn lot. They're in it together. Every man jack of them.'

247

'That sounds rather hard.'

'Yeah, well, we can't afford to be softies. Not the way I see it. They're not fussy who they kill over here, are they? Or anywhere else. I bet we don't know the half of what they've been up to in Europe . . . We've got to finish 'em off good and proper. Stop them getting up to any more of their nasty little tricks.' He muttered darkly into his beer. 'And I reckon some of us blokes're paying a pretty high price for having to do it.'

'I'm sorry. I didn't mean—'

'Forget it. Let's talk about something else.'

She thought rapidly. 'How about Australia?'

'What about it?' He was still frowning.

'Well, do you miss it?'

'Too right. Sun, surfing, decent food to eat . . . all kinds of things. Hated it here at first but you sort of get used to it. In spite of everything. God knows why.' He waved to a girl who was standing by the bar. She waved back, scarlet mouth smiling. 'Friend of mine.' He was smiling too.

'What about your family?' she said. 'You must miss them too.'

'Well, I've been away from home a good bit since I was eighteen. Took off for a couple of years, working my way round Australia – sheep-shearing, gold-mining, cane-cutting . . . Dad wanted me to get stuck into the family hotel business, but I wasn't too keen.'

'Your father runs a hotel?' She was very surprised. The background didn't seem to fit him at all.

'Yep. In Sydney. With my ma. Both of them run it, together. Like my grandparents did. They were Swiss, my grandparents. Emigrated to Australia from Berne

248

and started a hotel in King's Cross. Then Dad and Ma took over and made it bigger. Built another twenty rooms. You should see it. It's a bonza place. I've a big brother who works with them, too, but he's different. Settled down. Wife and a kid already. When I got back home from travelling around, the war had started so I joined up and took off again.'

'How did you get over here?'

'In an old cargo ship from Sydney. There were two hundred of us RAAF on board. We went to Christchurch, picked up some Air Force Kiwis and more supplies – oh, my word, she was loaded. One more thing and she'd've sunk. We sailed across the Pacific, through the Panama Canal, then up to Halifax and across the North Atlantic in a big convoy, dodging the U-boats.' He wove his hand, eel-like. 'Took us three months. We landed at Liverpool, just after the Luftwaffe had clobbered it the night before, so the first thing I saw of dear old England was piles of rubble.' He drew on his cigarette and flicked away the ash. 'That's one good reason why I'm not worried about giving it back to the Jerries.'

'I wanted to join up,' she said. 'To go into one of the Services. But they wouldn't have me . . . with my . . . my disability.'

'Yeah, what's wrong with your foot? You have an accident, or something?'

He didn't mince words. At home it was never discussed. Never even mentioned. Outside home, people looked away or pretended they hadn't noticed. 'I was born with it like that.'

'Bad luck. Still, you get around OK, don't you? Could be a lot worse.'

All very well for him to talk. To be so matter-of-fact

about it. Easy for him. She said stiffly, 'Yes, I suppose it could be a lot worse.'

'Couldn't the medics do something about it?'

'No.'

'Never go near them if I can help it, myself, but seems to me it'd be worth a try.'

'I did see a doctor – a few years ago.'

Too late, I'm afraid, Miss Frost. If your parents had only sought help when you were a child . . .

'No go?'

She shook her head.

'Still, you never know. I wouldn't give up, if I were you. They can do all sorts of things these days.'

She didn't want to discuss it with him. With anybody. She put down her glass and looked at her watch. 'I really must be going.'

'Hang on, you've only just got here.'

'My parents will be wondering where I am.'

'No, they won't. They're used to you being late. Besides you're over twenty-one, aren't you? You've got the key of the door.'

She was nearly twenty-two but she wasn't going to tell him that. 'I'm rather tired.'

'OK. Fair enough.' He lifted his mug. 'Soon as I've finished this I'll take you back. See you home.'

'I'd much sooner you didn't.'

'Yeah, but that's what I'm doing. And I'll carry the parcel. You forgotten about that?' He started to drink and then stopped, staring. 'Well, I'll be a monkey's uncle . . . Isn't that your little waitress at The Angel over there? Peggy.'

She followed his stare. 'And isn't that—'

'Our nav.' He grinned. 'Oh, my word. Wonder what his family'd have to say about that.'

250

Going back up the hill proved much harder for her than going down. She could only move at a snail's pace, dragging herself upwards with her stick while he dawdled along beside her.

'How about holding on to my arm?'

'I can manage, thank you.'

'Come on, it'd help.'

'No, *thank* you.'

'Suit yourself.'

Thank God for the dark, she thought, struggling on. He can't see what a crippled creature I really am.

At the top of the hill, she picked up as much speed as she could.

'Where's the fire?' he said. 'No need to be in such a rush.'

She turned down her road, shone her torch on the gate. 'This is where I live.' She clicked the latch open. 'Goodnight.'

'You're forgetting the parcel.'

'Oh . . .' She wedged it awkwardly under one arm, walking stick in the other hand. 'Thank you.'

'Sure you can manage?'

'*Perfectly* well.'

'I'll see you around, then. G'night.'

His footsteps rang sharply and quickly on the pavement. She listened to them fading away down the street. Normal footsteps.

She let herself in with her key and found her mother and father in the sitting-room – her mother knitting, her father reading the newspaper. It was always the same, every evening. Later, her mother would put down her knitting on the arm of her chair and go to make a pot of tea. At nine o'clock they would switch on the wireless to listen to the news. At ten o'clock they would go to bed.

She showed them the parcel and the tins of food.

'What an odd thing for a stranger to do,' her mother said, finishing another row. Her father peered over the top of his newspaper.

'He's not exactly a stranger. He stayed at the hotel.' Her mother picked up the tin of ham.

'Good gracious, all the way from Australia. It's bound to have gone bad. We'd better throw it away.' She took the brown paper on her knee, smoothing out all the creases carefully. 'This will come in very handy, though. And the string, too.'

Darling Cat,

I suppose this will reach you somehow, some day – if the bastards let it. Maybe you didn't even know if I was dead or alive – God knows how long they take to inform the next-of-kin.

I know I should be grateful to be alive, but being a POW is almost worse. A living hell. I know now what animals in cages must feel like. You don't realize how much freedom means until you lose it. All I can think about is getting out of this prison and getting back to England and you.

Write to me, Cat. Write to me often. I'm counting on you to give me a reason to live. To help me survive. I need to think of us with a future together when the war is over.

All my love, Peter.

Dear Peter,

I got your letter safely. Your mother phoned me as soon as she heard from the Red Cross. Until that moment it had been dreadful, not knowing if you were alive or dead. I

*think your mother suffered terribly. She was crying when
she gave me the news.*

*I'm so thankful, Peter, that you were spared. I under-
stand how hard it must be for you to find yourself a
prisoner but it won't be for long. Please try to be patient
and accept it. The war will soon be over and you will be
home again. I will write to you often and do everything I
can to help you get through it all. And when you come
back we will be able to talk about the future together.*

With my love, Catherine.

Dorothy had found the place by chance. Biking along
the road round the drome one day, she'd passed a
bit of the station boundary where there was a thick
patch of bushes as well as the barbed wire and hedge.
She'd hidden the bike in the ditch and wriggled her
way into the middle of the bushes so she could watch
what was going on without being seen. It didn't do to
hang about the perimeter openly, or they might think
she was a spy and arrest her.

A bomber had been standing a few yards away from
the boundary and men in overalls had been perched
high up on scaffolding, working on one of its engines.
She'd heard the clatter of tools, the high whine of an
electric drill and their voices talking to each other. It
was a Lancaster – she could tell that from the four
engines and the shape of the tail.

In spite of the cold she'd stayed there for a long
time. The bomber had awed and fascinated her. It
looked gigantic on the ground; the men like pygmies.
Maybe it was Charlie's bomber. Or one of the ones he
flew in. Maybe it was D-Dog – the one his crew liked
so much.

The next day, after dark, when she heard them

253

starting up at the drome, she got the bike out of the shed and rode round to the patch of bushes. The bomber was there again, standing in the moonlight. It looked even bigger: like some great black beast. Dorothy squeezed her way quietly into the bushes.

She could see a faint glimmer of light in the cockpit and another in the turret at the front, and torch beams flashing about on the ground. She waited and after a while there was a whining sound followed by popping noises like small explosions, and then an angry snarl that turned into a great roar. One engine was going, the propeller blades blurring into a dark circle. Soon the next started up. When all four of them were roaring she had to stop her ears. The earth was vibrating, her body with it. The roaring settled to a steady beat and the bomber rolled forward and swung round, the tail end skewing towards her. She tried to see if it was Charlie in the rear turret but a hail of dust and dirt blew in her face. In any case, it would have been too dark to tell for sure.

She watched the Lancaster turn onto the lighted pathway and rumble off into the distance.

Other bombers were starting up all over the drome. Other great beasts stirring and setting forth from their lairs. She listened to them bellowing their way into battle.

'Full power, Jock.'

'Full power, skipper.'

D-Dog, weighed down by her load of high explosives and incendiaries, guns and men and fuel, rose gallantly into the air.

'Undercart up.'

Jock's hand was there at the ready. Van would have

staked his life on it. *Did* stake his life on it. All their lives. They were a great double act now, he and Jock. Minimum talk, maximum efficiency. Clipped commands and responses. Perfectly attuned. It made him feel like a hell of a good pilot sometimes, until he reminded himself that Jock was a hell of a good flight engineer and that it took two to get a Lanc safely off the ground. And safely down again.

Van turned the bomber onto Piers' course. The Merlins droned away sonorously in his ears and that was the way he liked it: to hear them all functioning loud and clear. Singing to him. Once, coming back from over Norway on a long, straight, ass-numbing course, he'd fallen asleep for a few seconds and woken up in a shit panic thinking the engines had all stopped – until he'd realized he'd only stopped hearing them.

D-Dog went on climbing steadily. Jock, a bulky form in leather and sheepskin beside him, went on keeping a sharp eye for other aircraft. The only illumination in their confined, cockpit world came from the greenish flickering of the gauges before him and the eerie blue glimmer from the inner exhaust stubs outside.

After thirty minutes Piers gave him a course alteration. The target was Hamburg and the attack was to be from the north-east. They would cross the Danish coast north of Heide towards Kiel and then head south-east for Lübeck and finally Hamburg.

They always made it sound a cinch at briefing. A jolly old piece of cake. *Pop over the North Sea to Denmark, chaps. Bear right and breeze on down to Lübeck and on to Hamburg . . .* That sort of thing. *We're keeping you well away from the Jerries' beastly old guns, taking the home team by surprise, so no problems until you get to the target, where it could get a bit noisy.* Bitter comments from all over the briefing room. *Once you've pulled the plug, push off smartly and nip back across the coast here between Cuxhaven and Bremerhaven.* Casual tap, tap with the pointer. *Home again in time for your eggs and bacon.* Encouraging smile all round. *Good show. Any questions?*

He'd caught Catherine's eye but she hadn't been smiling. She knew the score too well. As the crews had left the briefing room he'd detoured so he passed close to her. She'd been talking to one of the Intelligence guys but she'd mouthed the words *good luck* at him. That was about as far as he could get with her. Friendly words. Polite conversation. Distance kept. Very British. Come on, with her guy a POW, what the hell else did he expect from a girl like her?

There'd been the usual send-off group by the runway – amorphous figures gathered in the darkness. Impossible to see more as D-Dog had roared past, but he'd had the feeling that she was there, watching and waving.

He snapped on his mike switch. 'Pilot to crew. Intercom check. Bomb aimer?'

'OK, skip.' Stew's voice came back instantly. No flies on him.

He called up the rest of the crew. All OK. Nobody'd blacked out with a faulty oxygen supply, or got shot up or fallen out without anyone noticing.

The dark indented mass of the Danish peninsula showed up clearly ahead under the moon. As they crossed the coastline, Piers gave him the course for Kiel. So far, so good. No gun flashes from below. No night fighter trails across the sky, or none that could be seen.

'Pilot to crew. Keep a sharp look-out for fighters.'

No need to remind them but it was his job to nag.

At Kiel they altered course again for Lübeck and then nosed south-west for Hamburg. As they approached the city a Brock's benefit awaited them: searchlights and flak and flames and flares lighting up the sky.

'Busy tonight,' was Jock's laconic comment.

Pretty soon, D-Dog was getting tossed about and the fun began. They went straight into the hellfire and Stew started his bit. The effort of holding D-Dog steady made the sweat pour on Van. A searchlight beam swept over one wing, wavered and tracked back. *Come on, Stew, for Chrissake. Those guys are onto us.*

'Bombs gone, skip. Bomb doors closed.'

Van yanked at the bomb door lever and dived the Lancaster away from the target, away from that searing white beam of light. They headed east for the German coast. He swiped his gloved hand across his forehead. It sure didn't get any easier.

He'd just made a course correction from Piers when they were hit. D-Dog staggered and reared and lurched crazily. He wrenched at the control wheel. *What the hell?* A dark shape twisting away to port below gave him the answer. An enemy fighter had attacked them from beneath. A JU88 trick. Sneak under the belly where nobody can spot you and fire upwards with the roof-mounted gun. Go for the jugular. Sonofabitch!

'Pilot to gunners. Enemy fighter rolling low to port. JU88. He got our wing. Watch for him coming back.'

'I can see him, skip.' Stew's guns fired in murderous bursts from the front turret. 'Out of range now, skip. He's pissing off.'

'OK, keep watching. He may be fooling. Pilot to crew, report any damage.'

257

There was no damage aft. The port outer had taken the hit. He could see the broken prop blades, whirling uselessly. Jock shut the engine down. 'He must have holed the port tanks badly, skipper. Got us right along the wing. We're losing fuel fast.'

'What about the auto seal?'

'I reckon the holes are too big.'

'How's the port inner?'

'Seems OK. And the starboard tanks are secure. We should be able to keep all three engines running if we cross-feed the starboards from the damaged tanks with the booster pumps and use up what's left there first. Then cross-feed the port.'

'OK, Jock. Let's try it. Pilot to gunners. Any sign of that guy?'

'Bomb aimer here, skip. Can't see the fucking bastard anywhere.'

'Mid-upper to pilot. Can't see him neither.'

'Are you sure?'

'Dead sure.' Bert sounded offended.

'Charlie?'

'Nothing back here, skipper. Very sorry I didn't spot him before.'

'You'd no chance, Charlie. None of us did. He came up beneath us. I'm going to tip the wings; try and see what's happening underneath. Take a good look.'

D-Dog responded obediently but there was no sign of the JU88.

'Must've gone home for breakfast,' Bert said.

Maybe that's just what he'd done. Maybe he was out of ammo, or short of fuel. Otherwise the guy would have made another run to be sure of finishing them off. Unless he thought he'd done that already . . .

He looked down at the moonlit landscape of

northern Germany – no lights to be seen, just the silver ribbon of a river far below, winding towards the sea. Going their way. But the enemy coast was still seventy miles distant and England three hundred miles across an icy and very unfriendly North Sea.

They flew on.

'Port inner's starting to over-heat, skipper.' Jock rapped the gauge with his knuckles.

Holy shit! *Come on D-Dog. Give us a break.* Maybe she didn't hear him. Maybe she hurt too much to care. The gauge needle went on climbing through the roof.

'We'll have to shut it down, skipper. No choice.'

D-Dog suddenly stopped being docile and acted like she was a tired and stubborn old lady with the ague who'd had a lot too much to drink. She staggered along lopsidedly, shaking all over, and it took all Van's strength, using full rudder and aileron trim, to keep the port wing up. The two remaining starboard engines kept tugging her round, and if he wasn't bloody careful they'd be flying in circles going up their own ass. He had to keep his right foot pressed hard on the rudder pedal to stop her turning. Pretty soon his legs and arms were aching and though he was managing to keep D-Dog more or less straight and level, they were losing height steadily. The land below was looking a whole lot closer now; he could make out the shape of fields and a line of pinpricks of light that probably belonged to an enemy army convoy on the move.

'Pilot to navigator. How far to the coast, Piers?'

'Eighteen miles, skipper.'

And after that, the sea.

'Do you reckon we can make it across, Jock?'

'Fuel's not going to last. Not at the rate we're having

259

to use it to keep her in the air. We lost too much from those damaged tanks. I'd say we might get three-quarters of the way – if we're lucky.'

OK, so it was a simple decision: hit the silk now or ditch later. He snapped on his mike.

'Pilot to crew. Looks like we're not going to make it back. Not all the way. You guys have two straight choices. Bale out now, while we're still over land, or we can ditch as close to England as I can take her and hope we get picked up by Air Sea Rescue.'

'Bomb aimer here. I'm not fucking spending the rest of the war behind the fucking wire, skip. Let's head for home and take our chance at getting picked up by our own blokes, not the fucking Jerries.' Spoken like a true-blue Aussie.

'I'm coming too, skip.' That was Bert.

'I absolutely agree.' Piers, of course.

'Aye, me too.' Harry.

'Charlie? What do you want to do?'

'Stay with the rest of you, skipper.'

Good kid. All alone back there. Probably shit scared.

'What do you say, Jock?'

'Same as the others.' Steady as a rock beside him. Eyes glued to the gauges.

'OK. If that's the way you all want it, we'll go for it. Get as far across as we can and I'll try and get her down in one piece. Harry, start sending a Mayday. Tell them we'll be ditching and we'll give them our exact position.'

He was soaked in sweat now and his legs and arms hurt like hell. Jesus, in another hour, or whatever time they'd got left in the air, he'd have run out of the strength to get her down any way at all. They'd had crew ditching drills at the conversion course, climbing in and out of a rubber dinghy in the local swimming baths. Nothing like the real thing. And landing a bomber on the open sea in mid-winter wasn't something you could rehearse. No circuits. No runways. Nobody helping from the ground. He could screw up so badly they none of them had a chance. And these guys were counting on him. If he'd've been them he'd have got out right now.

As they approached the German coast, a bright arc of tracer curved upwards at them. Some Hun coastal battery had a bead on them and at this height and speed they were a sitting duck. Nothing to be done but keep a-going. He hauled the bomber back to level flight yet again and they flew on through the barrage. The Jerry gunners must have been lousy shots, though, because they missed every time and D-Dog escaped out over the North Sea.

The vast expanse of water glinted in the moonlight. No way of telling how bad it was down there. Landing on a millpond in broad daylight would be a bastard, let alone on a rough sea in darkness.

His right leg and foot ached so badly now, he didn't know how much longer he could keep up enough rudder pressure to hold D-Dog on course. Hell, he *had* to. If he didn't keep her straight they could come down anywhere. They'd got to be on course, at the closest possible point to the English coast to stand a cat's chance of getting picked up. He gritted his teeth against the pain.

'Pilot to crew. We need to lose some weight, guys. Chuck out every damn thing you can. Guns, ammo, flares . . . Stew, get rid of the bomb sight. The lighter we are, the further we'll go.'

The altimeter needle was creeping round

anti-clockwise. At this rate they'd be down in the drink before they ran out of juice.

'Looks like the starboard inner's starting to over-heat, skipper.' Jock rapped the gauge with his knuckles.

Holy shit, if they had to shut another down they might as well forget the whole idea. He wouldn't have a prayer of getting her down OK on one engine. They'd be dead men.

'Do what you can, Jock. Let's get as far as we can.'

Crazy how calm his own voice sounded! Same as Jock's. Like they were out on some routine cross-country. D-Dog's nose was starting to swing round again; he forced his tortured muscles to get her back on course. *Come on D-Dog. Give us a break, for God's sake.*

She must have heard him this time and cared after all, because the starboard inner needle stayed where it was instead of climbing through the roof. They flew on some more vital miles.

'About another twenty minutes, skip. Not more.'

'OK, Jock. How far to the English coast, Piers?'

'A hundred and twenty-three miles, skipper.'

A whole lot of North Sea still between them and home. Too much. Much too much. Piers was giving their latest position to Harry but how in hell was any rescue launch going to get to them before they drowned or froze to death?

He could see white wave caps clearly now. Jesus Christ, that meant a Force four wind at least. Some guy who'd actually ditched once had told him it was like flying into a stone wall when you hit the waves. He wasn't going to be able to do it. Not a hope. D-Dog would break up on impact, or nose-dive and keep on going down.

'Pilot to crew. Crash positions. Keep sending our position, Harry.'

'Roger, skipper.'

Jock would stay in the cockpit with him, while the rest of them braced themselves against the main spar.

'Fifteen more minutes, skipper.'

'OK, Jock.'

'You'll do it fine.' Jock's head was turned to him, nodding. He wondered if the others felt as confident; he sure didn't. His heart was pounding, his mouth dry.

'Got some gum, Jock?'

He chewed on the stick of Wrigleys his flight engineer had passed him. Tried to kid himself that Jock was right. He'd got power still – so long as he didn't leave it until too late. He could choose his moment. He brought D-Dog down in a long, shallow, level approach, tail well down, slow as he could. The same guy who'd told him about the brick wall had said something about ditching along the swell, not across it. Or was it the other way round? *Shit!* Why the hell hadn't he paid more attention?

'Five more minutes, skipper. Mebbe less.'

'Pilot to crew. Standby for ditching.'

The port wing was dipping again and he summoned all his remaining strength to bring it up. The water was a black foam-flecked heaving mass coming at them fast. No hope of judging it properly. All he could do was his best.

Bert was praying – or what passed for it. *Christ all-bloody-mighty, get us down in one piece* . . . He'd never been much for God and all that stuff, but they needed some help from somewhere now. And getting down all right was only the start. They had to be able to get out of the hatches and the dinghy had to inflate. And if he fell in the water he'd better hope his Mae West worked because he couldn't bloody well swim a stroke. Never learned. He'd gone to the baths a few times when he was a kid, but he'd never fancied it after someone had pushed him in and then kept ducking him. If it hadn't been for the bastard who'd done that he might have stuck at it. Too late, now.

D-Dog was rocking like a rowing-boat, like the skipper couldn't hold her any more. Bloody hell, he'd *never* do it. Might as well face it, they were for it this time. This was going to be the Big Chop. He wondered if Emerald would mind a lot, or if she'd just find herself another bloke. And what about poor old Victor? Who'd look after him? Not Emerald. Not bloody likely. Still, he'd be a lot worse off if he'd brought him on this op, like that other time. The Committee of Adjustment blokes'd probably let him go free. Pity he wouldn't be around to see their faces when they opened the shoebox.

D-Dog had stopped rocking and felt like she was just hanging in the air – like she did when they were about to touch down on land. This was IT. Please God, help us. Don't let us die. Bloody well *help* us.

Bert shut his eyes tight.

Harry had clamped down the Morse key and stuffed the Very pistol, cartridges and torch inside his battledress jacket under his Mae West. He climbed over the main spar and went aft to get Sam and back to take up his ditching position, alongside Stew, Piers, Bert and Charlie – Sam tucked well inside his battledress jacket. They squatted down, hands behind their heads, backs braced against the spar. He made sure he was next to Charlie. Whatever happened he was going to see to it that the lad was all right. He waited. Any second now.

D-Dog hit the water nose first, and the impact flung him sideways so he hit his head hard. The Lanc was skidding along on her belly with a terrible grinding and tearing noise. Icy water gushed over him and his first thought, when he recovered his senses, was that they were already sinking, going down fast.

Then D-Dog finally came to a stop and Charlie was tugging his arm. He staggered to his feet and scrambled after the others to the roof escape hatch. The bomber was tilting forward at the nose but she was still afloat.

He was half-way out of the hatchway, when he realized he'd forgotten the pigeon. Couldn't leave the poor little bugger to go down with the Lanc, so back he went, sloshing his way through the fuselage. He squeezed his shoulders up through the escape opening again; wind and spray whipped at his face.

The moon lit the scene: the inky blackness of the ocean, the white-crested waves breaking over D-Dog. He played his torch over the bomber. She was rolling and pitching hard. Charlie and Bert were clinging to the starboard wing and Stew and Piers leaning over the trailing edge, hauling on the dinghy. The skipper and Jock were crawling towards him along the cockpit roof. All out safely, thank God. By the time he'd clambered out on the roof and slithered down onto the wing, the Lanc's nose had sunk further and the wings had tilted up so that the dinghy was now several feet below, bobbing around like a cork.

They had to jump for it: Charlie, himself with the pigeon in its carrier, Piers, Jock, Stew, Van. One after the other. But Bert hung back, still clinging to the wing for dear life with them all yelling at him, and when he finally got up the courage to jump, he missed the dinghy and fell into the sea.

He came up close by, choking and thrashing about wildly. The Mae West kept him afloat but the waves swept him away from the dinghy. Harry kept his torch beam trained on the yellow life jacket being carried off fast like a piece of flotsam, while Stew slashed loose the rope tethering them to the Lanc's wing and they paddled frantically after Bert. When they got close enough, the skipper and Jock, who were the nearest, leaned over the side and grabbed hold of Bert's arms. Little as he was, he must have weighed a sight more in sodden flying clothes, because they had a real job getting him on board, and he was kicking and struggling and choking and thrashing about, making things even worse. Each time another wave broke over the dinghy, swamping them, Harry thought they were going to lose their grip on Bert and that he would be gone for ever. Then a lucky wave lifted him up and, at the same moment, Van and Jock heaved him into the dinghy.

Bert had been snatched from the sea, but D-Dog was going. Stew shouted out and pointed and they all turned to see her twin tail fins rise up in the moonlight. None of them spoke as they watched her slide down into the dark depths like a sounding whale, leaving them alone.

Dorothy woke up suddenly. She sat bolt upright in bed, listening. She always heard the bombers coming back and listened to them circling overhead before they landed. Sometimes they'd circle for a long time and she'd picture Charlie up there, very tired and yet having to fly round and round and round. But there was no sound of any bombers. No distant rumbling drone, getting louder and louder. Nothing but the wind.

The luminous hands of her alarm clock showed it was only ten past eleven. They'd taken off at six in the evening – thirty of them – and they would probably come back around midnight, unless it was one of the very long trips.

She lay down again. No point in panicking. Getting herself into a state. Charlie might be safe in bed over at the station, sound asleep and dreaming. And yet, she knew he wasn't. She lay rigid in the darkness, eyes wide open, listening.

Aircraft: D. Captain: Pilot Officer VanOlden. *Missing*.

The WAAF sergeant was standing on a chair to reach the top of the ops board. Catherine watched her chalking the word in the space. Two other aircraft had failed to return and were seen going down in flames over the target, but nobody had seen what had happened to D-Dog. No news from any other station. The only hope left was that they'd bailed out or crash-landed safely somewhere in Germany or France. The sergeant finished off with a heavy dot after the 'g' and hopped down off the chair. She looked quite cheerful. Just another crew to her. One of the many. Nothing to cry about.

The Intelligence Officer wandered over. 'We've just had something in on VanOlden's crew. Apparently, an SOS was picked up from them. They lost two engines on the homeward leg and had to ditch in the North Sea. The rescue chaps are out looking for them, but no luck so far.'

A chance after all, but so slim. Not many crews who came down in the North Sea in winter survived.

'Do they know their position?' Catherine asked.

'They knew it just before they ditched. They were still sending then. Since then, nothing. The dinghy transmitter might be u/s, of course.'

Or they might all be dead, she thought bleakly. The Lanc might have sunk too fast for them to get out, or the dinghy failed to inflate, or the sea swamped them, or the cold got them.

'The weather . . .'

'Not too good, I'm afraid. A Force seven. It must be pretty rough and chilly out there. Doesn't make it any easier to find them either – if they're still alive. But we mustn't lose hope yet.' The squadron leader took a closer look at her and put a firm hand on her shoulder. 'Come on now, young lady. Chin up. It's not like you to let it get to you. You know you can't afford to do that. We none of us can. We have to get on with the job.'

'Yes, sir.'

'That's the spirit.'

Charlie didn't think he could last much longer. It wasn't so much the cold, which he couldn't seem to feel any more, it was the sea-sickness. Bit of a joke, that! Here he was floating around in a rubber boat in the middle of the North Sea in winter, soaked through, and the worst part of it was feeling sea-sick. He'd vomited over the side until he thought his insides would come up. Now all he wanted was to lie down at the bottom of the boat and die. Only they wouldn't let him. They kept shaking him and making him sit up and talking to him.

Poor old D-Dog! He'd hated to see her go like that – all by herself, down to the bottom. Nobody'd liked watching it. She'd been the best of the Lancs they'd flown in. Never failed them before and it hadn't been her fault this time. If only he'd spotted that Jerry, it might never have happened, but he'd never seen a blinking thing.

Bert was talking now, telling one of his stories, but nobody laughed, not even Stew. He'd thought Bert had had it when he fell in the drink like that. Nobody had known he couldn't swim a stroke. Still, Bert was the sort who always bobbed up somehow.

He wasn't sure how long they'd been drifting about, but it must have been several hours because it was getting light. That wasn't much comfort, though. There was nothing to be seen but miles and miles of empty sea. Cold, grey, heaving sea. No ships anywhere and no planes in the sky either. *Nothing*. Just the waves see-sawing them up and down, and round and round. Up and down and round and round. Up and down and round and round. He closed his eyes again.

'Wake up, lad.' Harry was shaking his shoulder roughly. Harry's face looked cold and grey as the sea, ringed by his yellow Mae West, and it was going up and down and round and round, too. 'Not long now before they find us.'

Some hope, Charlie thought. But he felt too ill to care. And if he was going to die, he didn't mind it so long as they were all together.

Stew thought, I'm buggered if I'm going to die. Not like this. Just waiting for it to happen. Giving up. Christ, he was cold, though. Couldn't feel his legs or feet at all. Could hardly move them. The spray stung his face and his eyes smarted from salt, lids stiff and sore with the bloody stuff, and every few minutes another bloody wave drenched them all again. They kept bailing out but as soon as they did, the water slopped back in. He'd've killed for a cigarette, but the pack in his breast pocket was a sodden pulp. He chucked it overboard in disgust and watched it swirl away and vanish.

Where the hell were those Air Sea Rescue wankers? The bloody dinghy transmitter was u/s, of course, but they'd known their position OK when they'd ditched, and they couldn't have drifted that far away for Christ's sake, so what the fuck were they doing? Having another cup of char? Stopping for a chat? Playing cards? Forget the bloody pigeon. About as much use as the transmitter. All it had done was fly round in circles over the dinghy before it'd finally pissed off in the general direction of Germany.

Jesus, the cold, the *cold* . . . If he ever got his hands on that bastard Jerry who'd done this to them, he'd fucking kill him.

He felt like he was falling asleep now, and that was a bad sign. Keep awake, you stupid sod. *Keep awake*. Eyes open, brain ticking. Think of something. *Anything*. Don't let go or you've had it. He thought of Bondi beach. Pictured himself there, walking barefoot along the hot sand. Blazing sun, blue sky, not a cloud, the rollers coming in, surfers riding them . . . a corker of a sheila coming towards him: long legs, blond hair, tanned all over, smiling. The picture faded. Dissolved into Miss Iceberg, frowning at him. Yeah, well, not much help there. That wouldn't warm his cockles. Back to Bondi. Only he'd lost it. It was gone. He couldn't see it any more. Just the flaming North Sea and the waves and the empty sky.

Van kept his eye on Charlie. The kid didn't look like he was going to make it. Hell, none of them were going to if they weren't picked up soon. They were all in real bad shape – teeth chattering like castanets, faces death-white and ominously patched with blue, limbs numb and near-useless, hands swollen. They couldn't last much longer. They'd start sliding into unconsciousness. Slipping away. Got to keep them moving. Keep them talking.

'Time to bail out again, you guys. Come on, Charlie. You, too, kiddo. Give us a hand.'

They scooped away slowly and painfully, tipping water over the side.

'Bert, how about another story?'

'Don't know any more, skipper.'

'Tell us the others again.'

'Aw, come on, skip, he'll bore us to death.'

'OK, Stew, you tell one.'

'Well . . . there was this bloke went into a bar . . .'

Jock counted as he bailed. One, two, three . . . up to ten to fill his forage cap. Another ten to lift it. Five to empty it. Then back to filling it again. Keep on doing that twenty times. Slow but steady. Move the arms. Never mind the pain. Keep going. One, two three . . . He went on scanning the sky and the sea. By a miracle his service watch was still working. Good old Omega. They'd been in the dinghy over nine hours. Somebody would have chalked *Missing* against their names on the ops board. He'd seen that a good few times. Stared at the names and wondered what had happened. *Missing* . . . until and unless somebody found them.

* * *

At dawn she dressed and went downstairs, unable to bear lying in bed any longer. Outside it was still blowing hard and starting to rain. Inside, the cottage sitting-room was dark and cold as a tomb. She put on her coat and went to let Marigold out of her house and feed her some mashed peelings and stale bread. When she came in again she switched on the wireless and stood staring at the oblong yellow light, waiting for the set to warm up.

This is the BBC Home Service. Here is the news and this is Alvar Liddell reading it. Last night the Royal Air Force attacked the German city of Hamburg, inflicting heavy damage and starting numerous large fires . . . Of the two hundred aircraft, seven failed to return . . .

She turned the set off and went and curled up in one of the easy chairs, still wearing her coat, arms wrapped round her shivering body. One of those missing aircraft was from Beningby. When the bombers had come back, she'd counted them: thirty had taken off, only twenty-nine had returned. She'd stayed awake for the rest of the night, listening for the thirtieth.

If it was Charlie's plane that was missing they'd come and tell her – as soon as they were sure. The padre would come down to the cottage, like he'd promised Charlie, and knock on the door and give her the news. She could go and stand at the window, watching the road, or she could stay here in the chair, listening for the knock. If nobody came it would mean that it wasn't his plane after all. She wanted to shut her eyes and stop her ears with her fingers so she couldn't see or hear anything at all, but that would be cowardly. Charlie wouldn't want her to be like that. He'd want her to face up to whatever happened.

She curled up even tighter, waiting.

*   *   *

Piers saw the aircraft first. It was only a small speck in the clouds but he kept his eyes fixed on it, not daring to hope. The speck grew bigger and his hope grew with it as he made out the short fuselage and twin rudders. It looked like a Hudson.

Harry had spotted it too and was trying to get the Very pistol ready, but his hands were so numb he couldn't pull back the firing pin. Piers put his thumbs over Harry's and they struggled desperately with the heavy pin, and then to squeeze the trigger together. His fingers had no life, no feeling, no strength. *Make them work before it's too late. Force them. Pull. Harder. Oh, God, we'll never do it . . . Oh God . . .*

The pistol went off and a brilliant star burst into the sky.

He watched the Hudson alter course towards them. *Thank God. Thank you. Thank you. Thank you.*

'Have a fag, mate.'

'Ta.'

The sailor stuck the lighted cigarette between Bert's lips.

What with that and the neat whisky, he was beginning to perk up quite nicely.

Once the Hudson had spotted them, they hadn't had too long to wait; it was the Royal Navy who picked them up. Blimey, had they been glad to see them coming over the horizon! He'd never seen a gladder sight in all his born days. The navy blokes had hauled them on board in a jiffy. Off with the wet togs, on with the blankets and they'd had them thawing out in front of a lovely hot fire. Bloody screaming agony for a bit, but he could move his fingers again now.

'Drop more whisky, old chap?'

Bert proffered his tin mug. 'Don't mind if I do, sir.'

'The Navy found them,' the squadron leader said. 'Picked them all up, alive and kicking.'

'All of them, sir?'

'*All* of them.' He looked at her. 'Pilot Officer VanOlden included.'

'That's very good news.'

'Yes, isn't it? Jolly good. They were damn lucky.'

Catherine fumbled blindly for her handkerchief.

'Here,' he said drily. 'You'd better borrow mine.'

'Those bombers kept me awake all night, Miss Frost. I'm going to complain to the RAF.'

'It's not all night, and they can't help the noise, Mrs Mountjoy. It's not their fault.'

'Not their fault? Of course it is. Who else is causing it?'

'They're going on bombing runs to Germany, surely you realize that? We should be extremely grateful to the RAF.'

'They may well be but there's no call for them to make such a racket about it. Or for you to be impertinent, Miss Frost.'

'Men are dying on those runs, Mrs Mountjoy.'

'That has nothing whatever to do with it. I can't think what's come over you lately, Miss Frost. Are you ill?'

'No, Mrs Mountjoy.'

'Well, I shall speak to Miss Hargreaves about your manner. It's most unsatisfactory. And by the way, that blackout blind in my room still isn't properly mended.

274

I can see daylight through the hole. I insist it's done today. Without fail.'

She was still curled up tightly in the easy chair when she heard the click of the garden gate, the sound of heavy footsteps up the path and a loud knock on the cottage door. She couldn't move. Her limbs were frozen, her heart pounding violently. More knocking, louder still. Important knocking. Urgent knocking. *Charlie, oh Charlie . . .*

She forced herself to stand up and walked slowly towards the door. Opened it.

'Mornin', Mrs Banks. Bit of a blustery day today. Looks like we'll be getting some heavy rain later.'

'Mr Stonor . . .'

'Anythin' the matter? You don't look too good.'

She clung to the doorpost. 'I'm all right, thank you. Just didn't sleep very well.'

'Dare say the planes kept you awake. Busy last night again, weren't they?'

She nodded.

The old man dug deep into his pocket. 'Mrs Dane asked me to give you this. Had a few just come in, she says, and she put one by for you. You can pay her later when you're next passing. She thought you'd like some for your tea. Nice on toast, they are.' He held out a tin. There was a picture of a fish swimming across the red label, one bright yellow eye, mouth open, tail waving merrily. 'Not worryin' about your boy, are you?'

She swallowed. 'One of the planes didn't come back last night.'

'So they say. No need to fret, though. Shouldn't think it was your lad's, but any road they're all safe.

Mrs Dane told me. Came down in the sea, she said, but they were all picked up. All safe and sound.'

She stared at him. 'Is she *sure*? How can she know?'

'Told you before. She knows everythin' goes on. Will you be keeping the pilchards, then?'

'Oh . . . yes, thank you.'

'Perhaps your lad'll like some too.'

Dorothy managed a weak smile. 'Perhaps he will.'

Twelve

Marigold was sulking. She pecked around in the far corner of the run, back turned.

'It's for your own good,' Dorothy told her through the wire netting. 'I can't let you out because if I do I can't catch you again and if I don't shut you up at night a fox will get you.'

She often talked to the hen. Whenever Charlie had done another op safely, she went and told her about it. Like people went and told their bees about important things, so she'd heard. Bees were supposed to mind and take an interest. She wasn't so sure about Marigold, who never took much notice.

The front gate latch clicked and she went round the side of the cottage to see who it was. Harry, the wireless operator, was standing there alone on the path and all her fears came rushing back. He must have seen it in her face because he said quickly, 'Charlie's fine. Got a bit of a cold, that's all, so he's stayin' in bed.'

'Just a cold?'

'Aye. Nothin' to worry about. He'll be right as rain in a couple of days. Told me to give you his love.'

He didn't look so good himself, she thought. Very white and weary.

He shifted his feet. 'We're stood down with the bad weather so I thought I'd bring Sam over again.' He took the bear out from inside his greatcoat. 'Needs some more mendin' – if you don't mind.'

'Of course not.'

'I'd've done it myself, but, like I told you, I'm no good with a needle.' He handed her the bear. 'Wondered if there's anythin' I could help with, while I'm here? Anything that needs doin'?'

'No, thank you, Harry.'

He looked a bit disappointed. 'How's Marigold gettin' along?'

'Well, she's not laying much. I think it's because she's sulking.'

'Sulkin'?'

'She kept getting out of the run – where she'd scratched a hole under the wire. Then she won't go in when it's time to shut her up at night, so I filled in the hole. She's very put out.'

'Shall I take a look? Make sure she can't do it again?'

He chopped some pieces of wood from the log pile and sharpened them into stakes, to peg down the netting tight all round. She watched him for a while, but it was too cold to stand about outdoors.

'Would you like some hot soup when you're done?'

'If it's not a trouble.'

'It's on the go. Easy.' She took Sam inside and left him on the armchair while she went to stir the vegetables in the pot on the Rayburn – carrots, potatoes, turnips, swede, onion, all simmering away in the stock she'd made from the marrow bones the butcher had given her. It made a good meal, with some bread. Harry came into the kitchen when she was setting out the plates and bowls on the table.

'Sit yourself down, Harry.'

He took off his greatcoat and hung it up and then

sat down, hesitantly. 'I don't think she'll be gettin' out again now. You won't 'ave any more trouble.'

'I don't suppose Marigold thanks you, but I do.'

'Aye, she didn't look too pleased about it. Gave me some dirty looks. Still, it's for her own good. She's safer in there.'

'That's just what I told her.'

'I chopped up some of the big logs for you,' he went on. 'Made them a mite easier to 'andle.'

'You shouldn't have bothered.'

'Didn't take a moment.'

She ladled the soup into the bowls and cut slices of bread. 'There's a bit of marg, if you'd like some.'

'Nay, I wouldn't take any of your ration, thanks all the same.'

The soup wasn't bad, she thought, considering. Anyhow, Harry seemed to like it because he finished the lot and said how good it was.

'I expect you get much better on the station. Charlie says you're never short.'

'They feed us enough all right, but it's nothin' like this. Most of the taste's gone out of it, seems to me. Don't know what they do, but whatever it is, it's not right. Not that I know owt about cookin'.'

She wondered how he managed when he went home on leave, without a wife to cook for him. Maybe he lived with his parents? She didn't like to ask.

He helped her with the washing-up afterwards, drying everything very thoroughly with the cloth. She noticed that he needed mending, like Sam: there was a button on his sleeve that was about to fall off any minute.

He hung the cloth up to dry tidily. 'Anythin' else I can do?'

'No, thanks, Harry. You sit down while I do Sam.' She picked up the bear and looked him over. His left arm was as loose as Harry's button, and there was a long, jagged tear in his stomach with the stuffing coming out.

'Goodness, he looks as though he's been in the wars.' She'd spoken lightly without thinking, before she remembered that Sam *had* been in the wars. He went to war every time with them. She went and got her sewing basket and sat down with the bear on her lap. She sucked the end of the cotton, threaded it through the needle and started work on the long tear, poking the stuffing back carefully. 'He feels all damp inside, Harry. *Soaking.* Whatever happened?'

'Got a bit wet in the rain while we were waitin' for the crew bus. Sorry about that. There's nowhere to get things dry at the camp – only if you put them right by the stove, and I didn't want him to get singed.'

She didn't believe him. Charlie had told her Harry was in charge of Sam and carried him to and fro, tucked safe inside his jacket. The others joked about how he fussed over him. It must have been them that had come down in the sea. Charlie's plane *had* been the one missing. She'd felt that all along. *Known* it somehow, deep inside herself. No good asking Harry about it, though, because he wouldn't tell her a thing – any more than Charlie would.

She did another stitch. 'Not to worry. I'll soon have him mended and we'll dry him off by the Rayburn. And I'll sew that loose button on your sleeve for you, if you like – while you're here.'

'I wouldn't want to trouble you, Dorothy.'

She smiled at him calmly. 'It's no trouble, Harry. None at all.'

280

*   *   *

The American Air Force Flying Fortress flew into Beningby, badly shot up. Catherine watched it make a shaky touch-down and skid at breakneck speed along the runway, fire engines and ambulances in hot pursuit. Eventually it slewed to a stop on the grass, mercifully without bursting into flames.

'They're learning it's not quite as easy as they thought,' someone said behind her. 'Maybe they won't be so cocky in future.'

Later, when she went into the Officers' Mess two of the B17 crew were standing at the bar, still in their leather jackets and flying boots. They had the same sort of stunned expression that she'd seen so often on the faces of RAF sprog crews returning from their first op. Van was talking to them, buying them drinks, and after a while they were joined by other RAF. She watched the Americans relax a little – even laugh at some joke, but half-heartedly. Poor things, she thought. Thousands of miles from home, come to fight a war in a foreign country that must seem a wretched sort of place to them: battle-scarred and dreary, cold and uncomfortable. And sometimes ungrateful, too.

Van came over to her. 'Can I stand you a shandy?'

'No, thanks. I'm fine.'

'I'd like to.'

She didn't want to sound ungracious. 'All right, then. Thank you.'

He never seemed to be short of money, and it couldn't be on RAF pay. He must come from a well-off family, back in Philadelphia. That bloody Yank, Peter had always called him. Still did.

Promise me you'll wait for me, Cat. Swear it. Don't let

anybody else take you away from me – especially that bloody
Yank. He'll be sniffing round now I can't see him off. Tell
him to go take a running jump. I'm counting on you. I
couldn't bear it if you let me down . . .

The bloody Yank came back, carrying two glasses.

'Thanks.'

'You're welcome.'

'Those Americans look pretty shaken up,' she said.

'Yeah. They got jumped by a pack of 109s. Only just
made it back on a wing and a prayer. Both waist
gunners were killed, and their bombardier's in bad
shape.'

'How horrible for them! Was it their first op?'

'Third. The first two were a breeze. This one kind've
took them by surprise. They'll soon get used to it.
Cigarette?'

He always had plenty of those, too. American
Chesterfields.

'Do your family send you these?'

'Regular as clockwork.'

'They must worry about you a lot.'

'Guess so.'

'Your last op,' she said, but tentatively in case he
didn't want to talk about it. 'When you had to ditch.
It must have been pretty awful.'

'Well, the North Sea's kind of cool for a dip at this
time of the year. I sure don't recommend it.' The
throwaway line was typical RAF. Catching.

'I'll remember that.'

He eyed her through the cigarette smoke. 'I'll bet
you thought we'd bought it.'

'I was rather worried for a while – till we got
the news that you'd been picked up.' She sounded
as casual about it as he'd been. They might have

been chatting about some day trip. 'Thank God you were.'

'Yeah, we were kind of lucky. I'm glad you were rather worried.' He smiled at her and she looked away.

'I've had another letter from Peter.'

'How's he making out?'

'He sounds absolutely desperate. I'm afraid he'll go and *do* something desperate – try and escape.'

'I'd probably do the same in his shoes. Not much fun being a POW.'

'He's depending on me. Totally. I can't possibly let him down.'

'Yep, I know, Catherine,' he said. 'I read you loud and clear. I've got a question for you, though. Are you in love with the guy? Were you *ever*?'

Before she could speak someone called to him from the bar.

'Hey, Van! How about tickling the old ivories? Cheering up these chaps of yours.'

He went over to the piano and sat down. She'd heard him play in the Mess before – jazz and swing – very well. This time it was neither. He played *The Star Spangled Banner*, slowly and quietly. When she glanced across at the two young Americans, one of them was brushing his hand across his eyes.

'It's after six o'clock, Miss Frost.' The colonel had shuffled past the reception desk a few moments ago en route to the Oak Bar and then shuffled back again. He was blinking at his hunter watch in the palm of his hand. 'Time for my gin and tonic.'

Ron was late again and there would be yet another of his made-up excuses.

'I'm so sorry, Colonel. I'll see to it for you.'

283

He cupped a hand behind his ear. 'What? What's that you said?'

She raised her voice. 'I said I'll come and open the bar for you at once.'

He followed her eagerly, like an old dog at mealtime, and she unlocked the bar, poured out his gin and tonic and settled him in his usual corner chair.

'There you are, Colonel.'

'Thank you, my dear. Your very good health.'

More people came into the bar – guests staying in the hotel. She was serving them their drinks when she caught sight of Stew Brenner, standing in the doorway. He strolled over.

'Do everything round here, don't you?'

'The barman's late, that's all. What can I get you, Sergeant?'

'Stew, remember? We've met before. I'll have a pint of bitter, please.' He unbuttoned his tunic breast pocket and took out a pack of cigarettes, knocked one out and tapped its end against the counter. 'How've you been, then?'

She set the pint in front of him. 'Quite all right, thank you.'

He'd put the cigarette in his mouth and was flicking the wheel of his lighter with his thumb. 'I'm still alive, as you see. In our line of business that's considered pretty good. No cause for complaint. This flaming thing . . . got any matches?'

She sold him a box of Bryant and May, and he lit his cigarette and tossed the dead match into the ashtray on the counter. What on earth was he doing here again? The Angel wasn't his sort of place at all.

'Are your friends joining you? Your crew?'

'Nope. I got a ride in with our navigator, the one who's sweet on your Peggy. He's come to see her.'

'Peggy's working this evening.'

He shrugged. 'Maybe he'll wait around till she's finished. I reckon he's nuts about her.'

Pilot Officer Wentworth-Young seemed very nice but, of course, that could never work. Maybe she ought to have a word with Peggy, because she might get hurt. Only it was really none of her business. She went to serve another customer further along the bar. There was still no sign of Ron, and more and more people were coming in. Out of the corner of her eye she noticed that the sergeant was taking his time over his drink, leaning one elbow on the counter, smoking and watching her. When she came near him again he leaned across.

'Want a hand? I know that side of the bar as well as I know this. Used to help Dad at the hotel in Sydney.'

She was about to refuse when she heard the telephone ringing in her office. It went on ringing and ringing because there was nobody to answer it.

He stubbed out his cigarette. 'Better get that, hadn't you?'

'I'm most frightfully sorry to barge in here like this, Peggy. Only . . . well, I just couldn't wait until next Wednesday to see you. And I might not even see you then.'

She could feel herself going all red in the face. What if Miss Hargreaves came in and found him there in the dining-room when she was supposed to be finishing the tables? She could lose her job. 'I'm a bit busy, sir—'

'I know. I'm sorry. The thing is, I wondered if I could see you when you've finished? This evening?'

She said doubtfully, 'I won't be done until after ten.'

'I'll wait for you. In the car – outside at the back. I'll drive you home.'

She couldn't really refuse, could she? Not with him being so kind. 'All right, then.'

'Gosh, that's super.' He went on standing there, staring at her.

'I have to finish the tables before I ring the gong at seven.'

'Yes, yes, of course – terribly sorry. I'll see you later, then.'

She hurried through the rest of the laying. Imagine someone like him being interested in someone like her. She still couldn't understand it.

'It's nearly seven, Peggy,' Miss Frost called to her round the dining-room door. 'Don't be late with the gong, for goodness sake. Mrs Mountjoy's waiting.'

'I'm seeing you home in this fog,' Stew Brenner told Honor. 'And you can save your breath arguing.' He switched on the torch but it was hard to see more than a foot or two ahead. 'I used to think England was always like this,' he said. 'Always foggy. Now I know it's only half the year. The other half it rains.'

They followed the white edge of the kerb. The fog was clammily cold, muffling every sound – even her dragging foot.

'Thank you for helping out this evening.'

'Don't mention it. I reckon he's no good, that little runt you've got in the bar.'

Ron had turned up an hour late with some story about losing the key to his bike padlock.

'It's not easy to get staff these days. All the men are called up or doing war work.'

'Why isn't he?'

'He's got knock-knees, or something.'

'Oh, my word. He ought to come along with us some time. That'd make his knees knock all right.'

'I should think he'd die of fright.'

'Yeah, save the Jerries the trouble of killing him. By the by, Honor, there's something I wanted to ask you. A while back we got diverted over Cornwall and I saw a real bonza-looking beach – just like back home. Had a good surf rolling in. Our nav said it was a place called Newquay. Know anything about it?'

'I do, as a matter of fact. My aunt lives there. She runs a bed and breakfast.'

'Well, stone the crows,' he sounded pleased. 'Think she'd have me to stay, next time I get some leave? I want to take a closer look at that surf.'

'I expect she would. But it would be much too cold to swim.'

'I know that.' He chuckled. 'Last trip we ended up in the drink.'

'Drink?'

'Not grog. The sea. We had to ditch.'

She said, shocked, 'That must have been dreadful!'

'Well, it was no picnic, I'll tell you. We were lucky, though. Got picked up in time. Could've been a lot worse.'

Could have been dead. Frozen to death, or drowned. Not walking along here beside her.

'I'll write to my aunt and ask her, if you like.'

'Thanks. I'd just like to see that place. Maybe I'll still be around over here when the summer comes. Or what you call summer.'

They turned down her street and followed the kerb as far as her house.

'Would you like to come in for a cup of tea?'

'You mean that?'

'Yes, of course.' She wasn't quite sure whether she did or not but it seemed rude not to make the offer. She fumbled for her key in her handbag and unlocked the front door. The hall light was switched off but the door to the sitting-room was ajar. She opened it further. 'This is Sergeant Brenner. Of the RAF. I asked him in for a cup of tea.'

Her mother's knitting needles halted in mid-stitch; her father's jaw dropped over the top of his newspaper. She'd never brought any man into the house before, and guests – apart from relatives – were never invited. Her mother had always remarked that they preferred to keep themselves to themselves.

'Well, I'll make the tea, then,' her mother said, recovering. 'Though it's twenty minutes earlier than usual.'

Her father took off his spectacles and laid aside his newspaper, prepared to make an effort. 'RAF, eh? What branch exactly?'

'Bomber Command, sir. Stationed at Beningby.'

'Oh yes . . . Beningby. They fly those Wellingtons, don't they?'

'It's all Lancasters now.'

'Lancasters . . . yes, of course. Two engines.'

'Four, sir.'

'Yes, indeed, four. And you . . . you do what?'

'I'm a bomb aimer. I aim the bombs at the target.'

'Oh. Very important, then. You've got to get it right, haven't you? Hit the target.'

'Yeah . . . they like it that way. The RAF, that is. Not the Germans.'

'Sergeant Brenner is from Australia, Father. From Sydney.'

'*Australia* . . . goodness me! That's a long way away.'

'Twelve thousand miles, sir.'

'Good gracious . . . *that* far?'

She went into the kitchen, where her mother was pouring boiling water from the kettle into the teapot. There was an extra cup and saucer on the tray, and a clean cloth.

'You ought to have warned us you were bringing a stranger back, Honor. We'd like to have known in advance.'

'He's not a stranger, Mother.'

'He is to us, dear. We don't know anything about him.'

'He walked me home in the fog and I thought it would be polite to ask him in.'

Her mother fitted the cosy over the teapot. 'However did you meet him?'

'He's been to the hotel a few times. He gave me those tins of food, remember?'

'The ones that I had to throw away?'

'You didn't need to. There was nothing wrong with them.'

'Well, you can't be too careful, that's what I always say. Better safe than sorry.'

'The sergeant is from Australia, dear,' her father said to her mother when they had gone back into the sitting-room and the tea had been poured and handed round.

'Really? That's a very long way away, Sergeant.'

'So people keep telling me.'

289

'I expect Australians think *England* is a long way from them, Mother.'

'That's not quite the same thing, Honor. Australia is a colony. They look to England as the mother country. *That* way round. Isn't that right, Sergeant?'

She held her breath but he said pleasantly, 'Well, we call it Home even if we've never set foot over here, so I'd say you have a point there, Mrs Frost. Myself, though, I look to Australia. That's my home.'

'Then I wonder what you're doing here, Sergeant.'

'Yeah, I often wonder that, too.'

'I expect you find England very different.'

'Too right I do.'

'You have no real history or tradition in Australia, do you? Not like us.'

Honor held her breath again.

'I wouldn't say that,' he answered slowly. 'We go back a fair number of years and we've got quite a few traditions. Matter of fact we got most of them from this country.'

'But that would be from the convicts, wouldn't it? Not quite the kind I meant.'

She saw his face darken. He opened his mouth, caught her anxious eye on him, and shut it again.

She changed the subject quickly and talked about the fog and anything else she could think of: inane, empty, safe conversation. After a while he drained his cup and stood up. 'I'll be off, then. Thanks for the tea, Mrs Frost.'

In the dark hallway she fumbled for his greatcoat and cap on the hooks and handed them to him. 'I'm so sorry about what my mother said. She didn't mean to be rude.'

'No worries. I'm used to it by now. Convicts,

kangaroos, upside down . . . I reckon I'm immune.' He was buttoning his RAF greatcoat, turning up the collar round his neck. 'Don't forget to ask your aunt in Newquay – about my staying with her.'

'I'll write to her tomorrow.' She was anxious to make amends.

'Ask her if she'll have you as well.'

'Me?'

'You heard. You could do with a holiday, I reckon. And you could show me the way.'

'You know where Newquay is.'

'That was from the air. Besides, I bet she'd like to see you. I'll bet you're her favourite niece.'

'I couldn't take the time off work.'

'Always excuses. Why not? Don't they give holidays?'

'Only in the summer.'

He put on his forage cap, tugging it down on his forehead. 'Tell them you're going with an Aussie and it *is* summer where he comes from.'

She closed the door after him and went back into the sitting-room. Her father was turning on the wireless; her mother looked up from her knitting.

'Has he gone? That's good. What a brusque young man! And that peculiar accent . . . Come and sit down, dear. It's time for the news.'

She'd been five minutes late ringing the gong, and Mrs Mountjoy had created a real fuss.

'Dinner is supposed to be at seven o'clock, girl. *Sharp*. I don't like being kept waiting.'

'I'm very sorry, madam.'

A big sniff as Mrs Mountjoy picked up the menu. 'Well, what is that man going to poison us with this evening?'

'It's cottage pie, madam.'

'*Cottage pie!* All the leftovers, you mean. Is that the best he can do?'

'There's spam fritters, if you prefer, madam.'

Mrs Mountjoy sniffed again. 'And this place calls itself a hotel. I might as well be staying in a boarding house.'

I wish you were, Peggy thought as she wrote down the order on her pad. I wish Hitler would drop a bomb on you. I really do.

She hurried with the clearing up as fast as she could, but the chef was in an even worse mood than usual and kept finding fault and more things for her to do, and poor Mavis had got a terrible cold and was feeling dreadful, so she helped her with all the washing up and putting away. When she finally went to put on her coat and scarf she was sure Piers would have given her up.

It was so foggy outside that she couldn't see a thing until a fuzzy beam of light came towards her.

'Is that you, Peggy? It's me, Piers.'

She made out the shape of him behind the torch. 'I'm sorry to be so late, sir. I couldn't get away sooner.'

'It doesn't matter a bit. You're here now . . . ' He took hold of her arm. 'The car's over here.'

'My bike—'

'Lord, I'd forgotten all about it. I'll put it in the boot, same as last time. You wait in the car.'

She slid onto the soft leather seat. He made her feel a real lady – just as important as someone like old Mrs Mountjoy.

'All done.' He got into the car beside her and started up the engine. 'The fog's pretty bad so we'll have to go jolly slowly.'

292

They crawled down Steep Hill and she opened the side window so she could see the edge of the pavement for him.

'You'd make a good navigator, Peggy,' he told her. 'Much better than me.'

He was teasing her, of course. She'd never be able to do anything clever like that.

Out of the city he had to go even slower because there was nothing to guide them and once they almost went into the ditch. Luckily, she saw it just in time. He stopped the car a little way from the house and turned off the engine.

'I wanted to talk to you, Peggy. While I've got the chance. To tell you something.'

'Did you, sir?'

'The thing is . . . well, what I want to say is . . . what I mean is . . .'

'Yes, sir?' She waited, wondering what on earth it was.

He took a deep breath. 'Actually, I wanted to tell you I love you – most terribly. I think you're the sweetest girl I've ever met. Absolutely terrific. Do you think you could ever possibly marry me . . . when my tour's over, of course . . . that's if I come through it all right. Do you think you could . . . possibly?'

She couldn't believe what he was saying. He was asking her to *marry* him. Her, Peggy Barton. Waitress at The Angel. People like her didn't ever marry people like him. Or if they did, she'd never heard of it. Things like that only happened in fairy stories. Or in films.

'Peggy? Won't you say something? I know it's the most awful cheek of me. You probably hate the whole idea . . . think I'm the most frightful chap—'

She found her voice at last. 'Of course I don't think that, sir. I think you're ever so nice.'

'Do you really? Honestly?'

'Yes—'

'I don't suppose that actually means you love me? I mean, liking someone's different, isn't it? Do you think, by any chance, you could ever come to *love* me? I mean, when you get to know me better?'

I love you now, she wanted to say. I love you ever so much. I know I do because of the way I feel inside whenever I see you.

'Peggy?'

'There couldn't ever be anything like that between us,' she said. 'It wouldn't be right.'

'Why on earth not?'

'Well, you being what you are . . . and me being what I am.'

'But you're absolutely *wonderful*, Peggy. And I'm a frightfully ordinary sort of chap.'

'You're not a bit ordinary,' she said. 'And I'm not a bit wonderful.' She felt like crying now; her throat was going tight and she could hardly speak. 'I knew I never ought to've gone out with you to begin with. I wish this had never happened.' The tears had started though she tried hard to stop them.

He put his arm round her. 'Gosh, please don't cry. I wouldn't have upset you for anything in the world. Please forgive me.'

'It's all right, really it is, sir.'

'The thing is, I thought you *did* care for me a bit. Jolly conceited of me to say so. I must have got it all wrong.'

'No, you didn't, sir. That's the trouble. You didn't.'

'Gosh, *Peggy* . . .'

Thirteen

Hark! the herald angels sing,
Christ, we've lost a bloody wing . . .

Bert eyed the group surrounding the Sergeants' Mess piano sourly. 'Dunno what they've got to be so cheerful about.'

Stew glanced over his shoulder from the bar. 'What's eating you, sport? Not like you to be down in the mouth.'

'Well, for one thing, I can't afford a beer.'

'Cripes, that's bad. I'll stand you one.'

'Wouldn't say no.'

He felt better with a pint in one hand and a Players – also thanks to Stew – on the go in the other. He lifted both to Stew. 'Cheers, mate. Up the Aussies.'

'Same to you. What's the other thing, then?'

'What other thing?'

'Yeah. You said "for one thing". So, what's the other?'

Bert hesitated. 'Well, since you ask, it's Emerald.'

'Dumped you?'

'No, wish she had. She's up the spout. In the family way.'

'Oh, my word. She sure about that?'

'I s'pose so. She says she thinks she is.'

'Thinking's not the same as being.' Stew took a drag

on his cigarette. 'I knew a sheila once spun me the same yarn and in the end it turned out to be a false alarm.'

'Well, Emerald's in a real old stew about it. She says she'll be kicked out of the WAAF in disgrace. Says I've got to do the decent thing and marry her.'

'You don't look like you fancy the idea too much.'

'I bloody don't, chum.'

'Thought you told us she was flaming marvellous.'

'To tell the truth, I've gone right off her lately. Well, see, she doesn't like Victor – hates his guts. Wants me to get rid of him, an' I don't reckon that's reasonable, do you?'

'Too right. Every woman ought to like having snakes around the place.'

'Come on, Stew, it's no joke. You know what I mean. He's only a little grass snake, after all.'

'Yeah, wonder what she'd have to say about a boa constrictor.'

'I told you, it's not funny, so you can take that grin off your face. An' it's not just Victor, neither. She's costin' me a fortune. Best seats at the pictures, chocolates, meals out an' all. I'm skint till next pay day, and then most of that's already owed to 'arry. Not even the price of a drink, at bloody Christmas.'

'Cheer up, sport. We'll soon be dead, anyway.'

'S'posing we're not? What the 'ell am I goin' to do then?'

'Not panic. That's what you're going to do. Wait till she's certain – one way or the other. And next time you dip your wick take more care. Strewth, haven't you learned that yet?'

All bloody fine for Stew, Bert thought miserably. He must've had more women than I've had hot dinners.

He wouldn't go and get nabbed like this. There'd only been one before Emerald. Well, one and a half if he counted that time with that girl in the one and nines, and he wasn't sure it did.

Joyful all ye Lancs arise,
Join the Jerries in the skies . . .

He didn't want to go and marry Emerald – not a bit. It'd be a fate worse than death. How could he ever have thought she was such a bloomin' smasher? Victor was better looking, and a lot better company – not to mention a whole lot cheaper to run. If he had to choose between spending the rest of his life with Emerald or Victor, he'd pick Victor any day. Straight off, he would. Well, maybe he'd get the chop soon, like Stew said, and that'd solve the whole problem. Right now, he almost wished he would.

Hark! the herald Angels sing
Christ, we've lost the other wing.

Bloody racket!

'Think it'll be a scrub, Harry?' Charlie was looking hopefully up at him.

'Wouldn't be surprised, lad.'

They'd been hanging around at dispersal, watching the weather out of the hut window for what seemed like hours. Trouble was, they were all dog-tired before they even started. Ops on two nights in a row and both of them shaky dos. He was getting too old for this sort of lark.

'Don't forget you're coming over next time we

get off. Mum's cooking a chicken for Christmas.'

As if he'd go and forget that! 'Bring Harry,' she'd said, so Charlie had told him. 'If he'd like to come.'

He'd sent Paulette's present off a week ago – posted it good and early to make sure she'd get it in time for Christmas Day. She'd like the doll a lot better than the luminous rabbit. Bit of luck the way he'd caught sight of it, tucked away behind a lot of junk in the shop. It was only second-hand, of course, but then you couldn't get brand new toys easily now, with the shortages. Everyone had to make do.

It was a nice looking doll, with a dress and bonnet you could take off, as the woman in the shop had shown him. She didn't have proper hair, just brown painted plaster waves on her head, and her eyes were only painted, too, and didn't open, but otherwise he thought that Paulette would surely be pleased with her. Maybe Rita would leave the present at the end of her bed – if Paulette still believed in Father Christmas. When she was two years old he'd dressed up in an old red blanket and a home-made cotton wool beard. He could still remember her face when she'd woken up and seen him standing there at the foot of her cot. She'd never guessed it was him.

The hut door opened, letting in a blast of cold wind.

'Take-off in thirty minutes, chaps.'

Harry let his hand fall on Charlie's shoulder. 'Not to worry, lad. It's another one chalked up for us. 'Appen we'll be stood down tomorrow for Christmas.'

'Come on in, Jock.'

'Guid of you to ask me, Mrs Gibbs.'

'Well, we thought you could do with a nice Christmas meal, though I'm sure they do you very well at the camp.'

He took off his cap and greatcoat and followed her into the kitchen. It smelled of roasting meat and pastry cooking. All the comforts of home, he thought: good food, warmth, hot water, dry bedding. Everything they lacked at Beningby. Things he'd lacked for most of his life.

'Ruth's outside somewhere, but she'll be in in a minute. Unless you want to go and fetch her.'

'No,' he said. 'I doubt she'd appreciate that.'

'You don't want to take any notice of the way she is sometimes, Jock. She really likes you, you know.'

'Then she's a funny way o' showing it.'

He'd been to the farm once or twice before in the past month and each time Ruth had more or less ignored him. Well, he could take a hint. She'd meant just what she'd said: it'd all been a game with her. He should have believed her the first time and not gone on trying, and making a bloody fool of himself.

He helped Mrs Gibbs set the table and fetched her home-brewed beer from the larder.

'We've killed a goose,' she told him, busy at the range, 'for a nice treat. I hope you like goose.'

'I've never eaten it.'

'Well, you'll soon find out. Dick'll be in to carve directly. Ah, here's Ruth.'

He turned round to see her standing in the open doorway. Same old tweed cap. Same old ragged hair. Same man's jacket and plaid scarf over her jersey and breeches. If she was trying to make herself look as plain as possible, it didn't work. Not with him.

'Happy Christmas, Ruth.'

She came into the kitchen, shutting the door

behind her. 'I didn't know you were going to be here, Jock.'

'Sorry,' he said tersely.

The meal was the best he'd ever eaten: roast goose, apple sauce, brussels sprouts, roast potatoes, with Mrs Gibbs' apple pie to follow.

'Must try some of the wife's beer,' Mr Gibbs had insisted. 'Seeing it's Christmas.'

He drank several glasses recklessly, one after the other. Why not? This was probably his last Christmas. The hell with everything.

'I see your lads are giving the Jerries a big dose of their own medicine,' Mr Gibbs told him. 'Saw some photos in the newspaper. They're getting it good and proper.'

'Aye. We're doing our best.'

Ruth put down her knife. 'I've heard they don't hit the target half the time. Don't even get near it. It's all pointless.'

He flushed angrily. 'That was at the beginning. It's different now. The photos prove it.'

'You can fake photographs.'

'Mebbe so. But we've no need to. The RAF's doing a grand job. At the cost of a great many men's lives.'

'I'd say it's wasting them.'

'I'd say differently. I'd say men are dying willingly in the cause of freedom. Your freedom.'

He gave Mrs Gibbs a hand with the clearing away and the washing-up. Ruth had disappeared outside again.

'I'll be getting back to the station, Mrs Gibbs.'

She put her hand on his arm. 'I wish you wouldn't. I wish you'd talk to Ruth. Knock some sense into her.'

It sounded painfully like something his father might really do. 'I don't think she wants to listen to me.'

'Well, don't go without saying goodbye to her. Give it a try, Jock. Please. We're fond of Ruth, Dick and I. It's been like having a daughter of our own.'

He knew the beer had taken effect because otherwise he'd have collected his cap and greatcoat, left without a word to her and never come back, no matter what Mrs Gibbs asked. Instead, he went out into the yard, his anger still smouldering away inside him.

He found her in one of the byres, laying down fresh straw, with a pitchfork. 'I'm off then.'

'Fine. Goodbye.' She tossed straw about, back turned.

The anger erupted. 'If you wanted to be rid of me, then you've succeeded, so you can stop your games now. It's nothing to me. What I don't care for is what you said about the RAF. Say what you like about me, but don't ever say things like that again. If you were a man I'd've knocked you down.'

She turned, pitchfork raised as though he really meant to. 'Go on, then. What's stopping you, Jock? You're like your father, aren't you?'

He wrenched the fork out of her hands and hurled it into a corner. Took hold of her and shook her so hard that her cap fell off.

'*Just* like your father!'

'That's enough, Ruth. You've said more than enough. I'm not going to hit you. I'd never do that – no matter how angry you try to make me.' He'd backed her up against the byre wall, still gripping her shoulders; her face was inches from his, mocking him. Daring him.

'So, what *are* you going to do, Jock?'

301

Maybe she was making a fool of him again; maybe it was another of her games. He couldn't help himself and he didn't give a damn.

'Happy Christmas, Harry.'

'Happy Christmas, Dorothy.' He stepped over the cottage threshold and produced Sam from inside his greatcoat. 'Didn't like to leave him behind. People'll pinch anything.'

'Take off your coat, Harry, and make yourself at home. Charlie's just getting some logs in.'

If only it *was* his home, he thought. The room was looking a picture. She'd decorated it with holly and ivy all along the mantlepiece and over the door lintels – must have gone out and gathered it – and there was a nice fire blazing away in the grate. Table laid all ready, and more holly with bright red berries in a jar in the middle. He could see she'd taken a lot of trouble.

He said awkwardly, 'I've brought you somethin'. It's not much, I'm afraid.'

'Oh, Harry . . . that's so nice of you.' She took the package from him. 'Shall I open it now?'

'If you like.' He watched as she undid it and wished he'd been able to get some fancy paper and ribbon to make it look nicer, like you could before the war. When she saw the vase inside she gave a cry of pleasure.

'It's lovely! You really shouldn't have. Wherever did you find it?'

'Oh, in a shop.'

It had been the same shop where he'd found the doll for Paulette. He'd spotted the green glass vase on a shelf, all dusty and dull, but he'd seen it was a pretty

302

shape and would clean up well. And he'd noticed she liked having flowers about the place. 'Hope you like it.'

'Oh, I do. I really do and it'll come in ever so useful. All I've got here is jam jars. Thank you, Harry. I've something for you, too, but you're to open it after we've eaten. I don't want the meal to spoil.'

She went off into the kitchen as Charlie staggered in with a big basket of logs and he gave him a hand with them. The lad had filled out a bit, but sitting cramped up in a gun turret for hours on end wasn't the way for a growing lad to build up his strength.

Dorothy called out from the kitchen that it was ready and he went to help her carry in the roast chicken and vegetables. A real treat.

'Will you carve, Harry? If you don't mind.'

Of course he didn't mind. He was proud to have been asked. It made him feel a part of the family, like the real head of it – though that was just stupid day-dreaming. Still, he could pretend, just for today. He picked up the carving knife and fork. The chicken looked golden brown, done to perfection. Dorothy was a wonderful cook, and no mistake. He prepared to make the first cut and then stopped, knife in mid-air.

'This isn't . . . it isn't . . . *Marigold*?'

She laughed at that. So did Charlie. 'Goodness, no, Harry. We couldn't ever eat her. It's one Mr Stonor brought me from the farm. Just an old one, he said, so I expect it'll be tough as anything.'

The bird didn't seem tough at all. Anything but. He guessed that Dorothy had really been given a nice young one, though she didn't know it.

She'd made a plum pie for the pudding – from plums off the tree at the back of the cottage that she'd bottled in the autumn. He thought it was the best pudding he'd ever tasted. The best dinner he'd ever had. The best Christmas.

Afterwards, when they'd cleared up everything – Dorothy washing-up, him drying and Charlie putting away – they sat down to listen to the King's speech on the wireless. His Majesty stumbled a bit over his words – well it must be a bit of a worry to think that millions of people were listening to you all over the country, taking heart from what you had to say. His Majesty wasn't allowed to fight in battles, like kings in the old days, but he was still their leader. He hadn't gone away to Canada to be safe from the Nazis. He and the Queen had stayed to face the music with everybody else. So had the Princesses. God bless them.

When they played God Save the King at the end of the speech, they got to their feet, and he and Charlie stood at attention. He felt a bit weepy, but he hid it.

'This is for you, Charlie,' Dorothy said, handing out her presents. 'And this is yours, Harry.'

He took the flat package uncertainly. He couldn't remember when he'd last been given a present. Charlie was unwrapping his and he saw that it was a book of poems. He looked right pleased with it and sat down by the fire and started reading it straight away.

'Aren't you going to open yours, Harry?'

'Oh, aye. Sorry.' He fumbled clumsily with the string and opened up the brown paper. Inside was a woollen scarf in RAF blue. He unfolded it to its full length.

'I hope you like it.'

'It's – well, it's just wonderful. Thank you, Dorothy. Did you . . . did you knit it yourself?'

'Yes. It's just like the one I did for Charlie, except

I made it a bit longer for you because you're so much bigger. He says his keeps him nice and warm when he's flying so I thought you might do with one too.'

She'd knitted it for him; her hands had formed every stitch.

'Thank you,' he said again. 'It's a grand present.'

'Well, let's see how it looks on you.'

He put the scarf around his neck and she came over and stretched up on tiptoe to adjust it. He stood still as a rock while she looped one end of the scarf over the other to make it lie neatly on his chest. She smiled up at him. 'There. It looks very smart on you.'

He tried to smile back, all natural and easy, too, but he couldn't manage it. Couldn't speak either for fear his voice would give him away. And his heart was thudding away so loud he thought she was bound to hear it.

'Listen to this,' Charlie said from his chair by the fire, and started to read out one of the poems from his book. It was all about bugles blowing and castle walls and lakes and glens, but Harry only half-listened. The other half of him was reliving the touch of Dorothy's fingers and allowing himself to hope. Just a bit.

It was Piers' idea that they should all go to the pantomime at the theatre in Lincoln. He'd been shocked to hear that Van had never seen one. 'Don't you have them in America?'

'I guess not. What are they?'

'Well, they're sort of Christmas plays, based on children's fairy stories. Things like Jack and the Beanstalk and so on. This one's Cinderella.'

'Jeez . . .'

'Actually, they're meant for grown-ups as well. They work on both levels. Jolly good fun sometimes. You'll enjoy it.'

Van doubted it, but Piers was so enthusiastic, he reckoned he ought to go along quietly. Do the decent thing. Stew, who had never seen a pantomime either, wasn't quite so gracious.

'My bloody oath, Piers, I'm not sitting through some kids' rubbish.'

'I told you, Stew, it's not just for children. They always put in jokes for grown-ups as well.'

'Blue ones, you mean?'

'Well, *doubles entendres.*'

'For Pete's sake, talk English.'

'You know, double-meaning ones. So the children don't understand but the adults do.'

'Still sounds bloody awful to me.'

'It's all tradition, you see. The Ugly Sisters will be played by men, dressed up as women, and Prince Charming will be played by a girl.'

'You *sure* this is for kids?'

'Yes, absolutely. The principal boy – who's a girl, of course – always has awfully good legs and there'll be Dandini, too, the prince's servant. He'll be played by a girl, as well.'

'With good legs?'

'Rather!'

'Hmm. OK, I'm on, then. Jolly good show!'

They squashed into Piers's car and drove into Lincoln for the afternoon performance. Van prepared himself for a boring experience. When the curtain went up, though, he found he was rather enjoying it all: the wobbly scenery, the simpering village maidens capering about to the gutsy little orchestra. And Piers had been right about the legs. There were piercing whistles from all the service men in the audience as Prince Charming came on and strode down to the footlights, dressed in a short gold tunic, fishnet tights and high-heeled shoes. She was flanked by half-a-dozen old guys in green, carrying long-bows, who looked like they'd strayed from Sherwood Forest. The orchestra struck up some bouncy tune.

> *Here we go, on our way,*
> *Heads held high and hearts afire.*
> *Forward men, so good and true*
> *On we go together.*

Prince Charming slapped her thigh and marched from one side of the stage to the other, tracked by a wavering spotlight.

> *Here we go, on our way,*
> *Off to fight and face the foe.*
> *Never daunted, never weary,*
> *On we go together.*

The spotlight was having a tough job keeping up with her and so were the old-timers. A bit of on-the-spot marching, centre stage, another slap of the fishnetted thigh and she was off again, relentlessly to and fro.

> *Here we go, on our way,*
> *Spirits soar and sinews stiffen,*
> *Forward men, so strong and brave*
> *On we go together.*

More piercing whistles and frenzied applause as she marched away, waving and smiling, her faithful band scrambling after her. Stew said something unprintable in his left ear.

The guys dressed up as the Ugly Sisters were funny and it was clever the way the old hag changed into a glittering fairy godmother, and Cinderella from her rags into a ballgown.

The crazy irony of it all struck Van as he watched Cinderella trying on her glass slipper. One night they were over Germany, flying through hellfire to bomb the crap out of the enemy, the next they were sitting here solemnly watching fairies and golden coaches and tinsel make-believe. *Crazy*.

Stew noticed the bunch of mistletoe hanging from the ceiling as soon as he walked into The Angel. Well, now . . . who'd've thought it? There were some coloured paper chains strung across and a Christmas tree in the corner decorated with glass ornaments and lights. Somebody'd given it a go. Nobody at reception. Or in the office either. He took a peek in the Lounge and saw the old colonel fast asleep in a chair by the fire, head lolling on his chest. Or maybe he'd snuffed it and nobody'd noticed yet. As he closed the door again, Peggy came out of the dining-room.

'Hallo, there.'

'Hallo, sir.' She looked at him with her big blue eyes – all innocence. He could see why Piers fancied her.

'Where's Miss Frost, d'you know?'

'No, sir. Shall I see if I can find her for you?'

'No, that's OK. I'll wait around.'

She hesitated. 'If you're sure there's nothing I can do, sir?'

'Yeah, you can come over here for a second.'

'What for, sir?'

'There's something on this carpet,' he pointed downwards. 'Just here. Take a look.'

She fell for it hook, line and sinker. As soon as she was standing under the mistletoe he caught hold of her in his arms and kissed her. He let her go soon, though. Well, she was only a kid. She ran off giggling.

'The bar isn't open until six.' He turned round. Honor was half-way down the stairs and he knew she must have seen him with Peggy. No chance now of pulling the same trick with her or he might have given it a try. Too right. He waved an arm round the hall. 'You do all this? The Christmas stuff?'

She nodded.

'Good on you. Cheers things up.' He nodded at the mistletoe. 'Specially that. Just been to the pantomime. Weirdest thing I've ever seen. Blokes dressed up as women. Sheilas dressed up as men—'

'It's traditional.'

'So they tell me. I thought you Poms were supposed to be civilized.'

'We are.' She came down the rest of the stairs and limped over to the reception desk, giving him and the mistletoe a wide berth. 'Did you want something?'

He followed her over. 'I came to see you. Wanted to know if you ever wrote to that aunt of yours in Newquay? I've got six days leave coming up soon and I'd like to go there, if I can.'

'Yes, I did.'

'Well, what did she say?'

'I had a letter from her yesterday. It would be quite all right for you to stay there.'

'That's bonza,' he said. 'How about you?'

'What about me?' She could be a bloody irritating sheila, no question.

'You know what I mean. Are you coming too? Like we arranged.'

'We didn't arrange anything of the kind.'

'Yeah, but she'd like to see you, wouldn't she? I bet she asked if you'd be showing up as well.'

She'd opened the registration book and was going through the pages like it was life or death. He'd got her rattled, he could see that. 'What's the matter? Got cold feet? Scared to come with me? Frightened I'll make a pass at you?'

'Don't be ridiculous.'

'I might – if I thought I'd get anywhere.'

She turned another page, running a finger down the entries, frowning. 'My aunt did ask me to visit her, as a matter of fact. I haven't been there for a long time . . .'

He leaned both forearms on the desk. 'So?'

'I really *ought* to go and see her.'

'Yeah, you really ought.'

'If I can get the time off work. Miss Hargreaves won't like it.'

'Say your aunt's ill. At death's door. And she wants to see you.'

'*Lie*, you mean?'

'Don't look so shocked. Don't you ever tell lies?'

'No, I don't, as a matter of fact.'

'Time you started. For your own good.' He leaned across and closed the registration book firmly. 'Right now. This minute.'

'I've had a letter from my mother, Van.'

'She OK?'

'Yes, fine. She wanted to know if you'd like to spend some of your next leave in York. Nothing exciting, she says, but if you've nothing else planned she'd be glad to have you.'

'That's real nice of her, Catherine, I'd be glad to go. Will you be there too?'

'I'm not sure. I've got a forty-eight due. I might get up there for that – if I can.'

He said levelly, 'I won't count on it.'

Fourteen

'I wouldn't worry about flying today, sir.' Mabel handed him his cup of tea and went over to undo the blackout. 'It's snowed. Nice and deep it is.' She came back and stood at the end of Piers' bed. 'You drink that up while it's hot.'

He did as he was told, just like he'd always done what Matron said. And Nanny too. *Eat up your crusts, Master Piers, they're good for your hair; sit up straight or you'll grow up with a hunched back; spinach will make you a strong man.*

When the batwoman had gone, he hopped out of bed to take a look out of the window. Yes, there it was – deep and crisp and even. A wonderful thick white blanket over the drome, barbed wire all white too – rather pretty, actually; everything stopped and silent. Three rousing cheers! He got back into bed and pulled up the covers round his neck. Bliss. He could stay here, curled up like an animal safe in its burrow, and he could think about Peggy.

God, it was absolutely amazing that she felt the same about him. Fantastic! He couldn't believe his luck. She'd let him kiss her and even began to kiss him back – once she'd got the hang of things. Not that he was any great shakes at it himself, it had to be said. He'd only kissed two other girls in his life and he hadn't even liked one of them all that much.

The best thing was that Peggy had finally agreed to let him take her home on his next leave. It had taken a lot of persuasion on his part. She'd kept repeating all that nonsense about not being good enough for him, how his parents wouldn't like her. Absolute rubbish, of course. You couldn't *not* like Peggy, and it didn't matter a jot that she was a waitress. His parents would just have to lump that. In any case, as he'd said to Peggy, there was no need to tell them if she didn't want to, if it worried her so much. She wouldn't go on being a waitress after they were married. He was going to take care of her so she'd never need to do work like that again.

He'd had to promise not to say anything about them being engaged, and she wanted it kept secret from her parents as well. From everybody.

'But I ought to ask your father's permission, Peggy. I'm supposed to do that.'

'You can ask him later,' she'd said jolly stubbornly. 'But not yet.'

Anyway, she was coming home with him and that was that. And he didn't care what his parents thought. He didn't want to marry the sort of girl they wanted him to marry. He wanted to marry Peggy.

Piers drifted off into a happy doze, imagining the future. He came into his trust fund from the grandparents at twenty-five and that was quite a bit, so there was nothing his parents could do, like cut him off without a penny. He'd be able to buy a decent house somewhere nice . . . in the country, perhaps, if Peggy liked the idea. He wouldn't go to Cambridge, as planned – no point in that if he was a married man. He'd get a job in the City, or something, and go up and down by train every day. He could picture himself coming back to Peggy in the evening. She'd be waiting for him with the children. A boy and a girl – maybe more, if she didn't mind – he'd quite like a big family, and they could get a good nanny, if there were any nannies left when the war was over. He opened his eyes. None of this could happen until the war had finished, until they'd beaten the Huns. It might be years before they managed that, at the rate things were going. He might have bought it long before. So he couldn't possibly marry Peggy yet: it simply wouldn't be fair on her.

Van stirred, groaned and came out from under his blankets. 'What's the weather like?'

'It's snowed. Pretty deep.'

'Thank Christ for that. Maybe we'll be left in peace.'

But they weren't. The station commander ordered everyone – desk-fliers and WAAFs included – out onto the runway with spades and shovels and brooms. By mid-afternoon the runway was cleared enough for ops to be on. And it was Essen.

Trust them to give us a stinker just before we go on leave, Charlie said to himself. Why couldn't we have a nice ice-cream op? Milan or Genoa, with the Eyeties waving a few searchlights around and not much else. Or an easy bit of gardening. Plant the vegetables off some coast and scarper.

He swivelled the rear turret and moved his guns up and down. There we were, all looking forward to a nice, well-earned rest, feeling quite bright and breezy for once, and they dump the Happy Valley on us. *Essen.* Sounded a bit like a snake hissing when you said it. Not Victor, though, he never made a sound. Just lay coiled up in his shoe box, nice and warm in his hay

314

bed, with regular room service. The life of Riley, he lived. Bert thought he was the cat's whiskers, though he couldn't really see it himself.

He shifted around a bit, making himself as comfortable as he could. His cushion had got to be like an old friend. They'd flown together since the third op. It'd been to Duisburg, Bremen, Stuttgart, Cologne, Frankfurt, Kassel, Kiel . . . all over the place, and now it was coming with him to Essen. If Two-Ton-Tessie didn't want it back when the tour was over, he'd like to keep it as a souvenir.

All four engines were roaring away, and K-King was shaking about like she was doing the hokey-cokey. They sounded good and healthy. The Merlins didn't usually let you down. They went on and on, whatever the weather – sun, rain, cloud, ice, sleet, snow. Mr Rolls and Mr Royce were clever blokes.

The Lanc was moving off now and turning out onto the peri track. The tail bumped along the concrete and he watched the amber and blue lights flicking past. He could see the lights on the opposite peri track where other Lancs were heading towards the control cabin from the other side of the drome. Pitch dark on a freezing cold snowy January night, taking-off for Germany! The things you did for England!

Bump, bump, bump . . . it was a fair way round to the start of the main runway. Plenty of time for the jitters to play you up if you let yourself think this might be your last few hours alive. He stopped himself thinking about that and thought about his new book of poems instead. Good for Mum, finding it for him at the jumble sale. It'd been printed in 1926, but it was in nice condition with brown leather like a shiny conker and gold lettering on the spine. *A Selection of*

English Verses. A bloke he'd never heard of had chosen his favourites and put them all together. He didn't think much of some, but there were others he liked a lot.

> *No coward soul is mine,*
> *No trembler in the world's storm-troubled sphere;*
> *I see Heaven's glories shine,*
> *And faith shines equal, arming me from fear.*

He spoke the lines aloud. Nobody could hear, so long as his mike wasn't switched on, so it didn't matter. He couldn't even hear himself for the noise of the engines, but he knew what he was saying. He might be afraid, but he didn't think he was a coward. You were only a coward if you ran away from doing your duty because you were frightened. None of them were cowards. He'd never seen anybody refuse to go on ops, even though they knew they were probably going to get the chop. They went off to their deaths and that was that. They even joked about it. Charlie wasn't sure whether they were armed from fear by Heaven's glories – couldn't see Stew thinking like that, for one. Most likely what kept them going was knowing they were on the right side, fighting for their country. *We must be free or die that speak the tongue that Shakespeare spake.*

The Lanc had stopped and they were waiting their turn to move onto the runway. The skipper and Jock were doing their final checks; Harry would be on the look-out in the astrodome, watching for the green light from the caravan, Bert in the mid-upper turret, Stew another pair of eyes in the front, Piers ready with his charts. Any minute now.

'Green, skipper,' Harry's voice crackled over the intercom.

K-King rumbled onto the runway, turning slowly for the take-off, swinging Charlie round in his goldfish bowl.

'Pilot to rear gunner. All clear behind?'

'All clear, skipper.'

A sudden bellow from the Merlins and K-King leaped forward. The flarepath lights zipped past and he could see great piles of dirty snow lining the runway. Then the tail went up, floating along with him, airborne, and he waited, breath held as per usual, for the rest of the laden Lanc to unstick and haul herself up into the night sky.

Good old K-King made it all right. She staggered a bit under the weight but up she went; the flarepath lights fell away below him. Mum was down there. She'd be listening to them taking off, standing at the cottage window or maybe out in the garden by the front gate – he knew she did that sometimes, even in the cold. But the good thing was that she never knew if it was him. For all she knew he was at the station, safe and sound. When they got back from Essen he'd try and get down to the cottage and make sure everything was OK with all the snow. No frozen pipes, or anything like that. He'd take Harry too. Play Cupid.

He'd watched Harry on Christmas day, standing there stiff as a statue and red as a beetroot while Mum had tied the scarf for him. The penny didn't seem to have dropped with Mum at all, but she liked Harry all right, and with a bit of luck things might work out between them. No sense in rushing it. Not in wartime.

The drome lights had vanished and there was only

317

blackness around him; no stars yet. He strained his eyes for other aircraft, keeping a constant watch.

They were up to fifteen thousand when they crossed the Lincolnshire coast and started the long trek across the North Sea – miles and miles of it ahead before they reached any land again. It made Charlie feel colder than he already was, just to think of it. Made him remember what it had been like down there in the dinghy. The heating in his suit must be on the blink because his legs and feet felt like blocks of ice, and so did his hands, and he wasn't too warm in the middle either. Trouble was, they'd taken out the centre Perspex panel which was always getting misted or frosted up. You could see better, but it made it a bit nippy in the turret, even with the heated flying suit working full blast, which it wasn't.

He could see the stars up above him now, keeping him company, like the cushion: Spica, Vega, Rigel, Polaris . . . Piers' helpers. Clear and bright as anything. Crikey, but he was cold. And another seven hours of this. One thing, it would warm up over Essen – in a manner of speaking. He listened to them talking to each other up front – the skipper and Jock and Piers and Harry and Stew. Nothing for him to do at the moment except keep on looking out for trouble. Bert would be doing the same, whizzing round in his turret on top of the fuselage. He and Bert didn't have to worry about their position or courses, wind, air speeds or marker flares, or anything like that, but they had to stay wide awake just the same. Keep their eyes peeled all the time.

Something was bothering Bert lately. He wasn't telling any of his stories or making any of his jokes. Women trouble, most likely. That WAAF he went about with looked like she could mean a whole lot of it. He didn't fancy women like that himself. Not that they'd fancy him either, though his spots had been a bit better lately. Not quite so many. That WAAF in Equipment had smiled at him the other day.

He heaved a sigh of relief when they crossed the Dutch coast, though that was a bit stupid because the really dangerous part was in front of them. Still, he felt easier, knowing they were over dry land.

'Nav from bomb aimer. Red marker flares ahead.'

'Thank you, Stew. Would you let me know when we're overhead, please.'

Funny to listen to those two talking to each other. Piers was always so polite. Lots of thank yous and would yous and pleases. Stew never bothered with all that. Just gave it to you straight. Charlie reckoned it didn't much matter how you said it so long as you'd got it right. When he came to think of it, it was funny, too, how they all got on so well. It didn't seem to matter how different they were. The seven of them had stuck together through thick and thin, and that's what counted. He reckoned the others knew him better than Mum did, really. And he probably knew them better than their mums did.

As they got nearer the target, K-King started to rock about in someone else's slipstream and the skipper took her up to clear it. You stooged along alone for hours and then all of a sudden the others were all around, heading for the target with you. It might have been a bit of a comfort if you didn't have to worry about colliding with them.

Flak was coming up and tossing them about all over the shop. The open panel in front of him let in the stink of cordite and made him feel sick. He peered

319

out. Bloody bedlam down there by the look of it. Flames and smoke, flares burning, gun flashes, lines of bomb bursts in fours and the brilliant single woomphs of exploding cookies. They were giving it to them tonight all right. He wouldn't like to be on the receiving end of that lot. There was another explosion nearby in the sky, so bright it blinded his vision. When he could see properly again, the explosion had turned into a gigantic firework shooting out stars of flame. He stared at them falling slowly to earth and fading. It didn't look like a bomber copping it. Maybe it was some new weapon Jerry had dreamed up. Whatever it was, it was scary.

Their turn now. Stew getting ready to pull the plug. 'Left, left. Steady, skip. Steady . . .'

They dropped their bomb load and the skipper got them out of there fast. Never wasted any time over that. They always headed straight for the dark, away from trouble quick as possible. Charlie reckoned that was one reason why they hadn't bought it long ago. Anybody who hung about was asking for it.

'Rear gunner to pilot. See that big explosion to port when we were over the target, skipper? I couldn't make it out.'

'I reckon it was one of those scarecrow flares they've been warning us about, Charlie. To frighten the pants off us.'

As if they needed to.

Stew spotted more flak ahead on the Dutch coast near Rotterdam but the skipper slipped round north of it and out across the North Sea. Now that they were on the home straight, so to speak, Charlie started to feel the cold again. The skipper and Piers were talking to each other about the bad head-wind that K-King was having to battle against. They were crawling along, it seemed to him, and it looked like it was going to take hours to get home. Hours squashed up in his Perspex prison in the bitter cold. Just got to put up with it, hadn't he? No use feeling sorry for himself. Only this time it was worse than it'd ever been. He found he was sobbing with the cold and the cramp and stopped himself quickly. That wouldn't do at all.

When they landed back at Beningby it was still pitch dark and snowing again. Charlie was so stiff that he could hardly crawl out of the turret; his body and limbs felt like they'd locked solid.

Harry helped him up onto the back of the crew lorry. 'You look done-in, lad.'

'Bit cold, that's all. The wiring in my suit's conked out, I think.'

Harry was shocked. 'We'll get that fixed, no danger.'

He thought he was going to fall asleep at debriefing and he was too tired to eat more than a few mouthfuls of his bacon and eggs afterwards. Three crews were missing – twenty-one empty places at the tables in the Mess.

He stumbled back to the hut and fell into bed. The sheets were icy cold and so damp they felt wet, but all he cared about was lying down. The last thing he saw was Harry leaning over him, laying his greatcoat over the top of the blankets, before he closed his eyes and slid into blessed oblivion.

PART IV

Fifteen

Jock found an empty seat in a Third Class Smoking. He hoisted his kit-bag up onto the rack and sat down, wedged between two army blokes who weren't fussy about taking up most of the room or about keeping themselves clean. It wasn't easy in a bit of tepid water, as he well knew, but these two couldn't have washed for weeks. Months, maybe. As well as that, the compartment reeked with cigarette smoke, but it was still a lot better than standing. The train jerked forward and steam clouded the windows. He was tired. So tired he'd probably sleep most of the way, bolt upright. He folded his arms and closed his eyes, ready to drop off. Instead, he started thinking about Ruth. No surprise in that. She was on his mind most of the time, except when he was flying. He didn't allow himself to think about anything else but the job in hand, then. Down on the ground, he thought about Ruth. He knew he was in love with her. Couldn't get her out of his mind, no matter how hard he tried. Or how hard she tried to put him off. Either she hated him, or what had happened to her had made her hate all men, never mind who they were. He didn't know the answer.

He wasn't too proud of what had happened at Christmas. She'd made him so angry he'd lost control of himself. It'd been close as anything to rape, except that she hadn't tried to stop him. Not that that made it any better or was any excuse. He'd behaved like a drunken lout. *Just like your father.* Aye, she'd been right about that, and that was the worst of it.

There'd been no chance to say he was sorry. To try to tell her how he felt about her. Mr Gibbs had come out into the yard and they'd had to scramble about with clothes and buttons and make out they were busy with the chicken feed. He was never alone with her after that until he left – Ruth had made sure of it.

One of the Brown Jobs had lit up yet another cigarette and the atmosphere was getting like pea soup. If it hadn't been so cold in the compartment already, he'd've reached across to the window strap and let some fresh air in, whatever anybody else said. He watched the countryside going by. Plenty of snow about still. He'd always reckoned he was pretty tough – inured to the bitterest weather – but it had been terrible at the station lately. The cold had got into everything: their clothes, their bedding, their very bones. They'd looted coke for the stove and when that had run out they'd chopped up chairs and shelves and used those instead. At night they wore flying clothing to bed and piled greatcoats on top of the blankets. Anything to get warm.

There was snow in Glasgow, too, and a wind that cut into him like a knife as he walked the blacked-out streets from the railway station to the tenement. When he knocked on the door his mother opened it a crack.

'Who is it?'

'It's Jock.'

'*Jock* . . .' She gave a sob and opened the door wide, heedless of the blackout. He went inside quickly and shut it behind him. The light bulb hanging from the ceiling showed him her face streaked with tears, eyes swollen and red, and a dark bruise on her cheek. He could feel his fists bunching. God help me, I'll kill that bastard. *Kill him.* She gave another sob and threw herself into his arms. He cradled her gently against him. He wouldn't let her stay in this place another day. He'd take her back with him. Find somewhere for her to live. His mind raced ahead. Maybe Charlie's mum might have her for a while . . . Then, as soon as his tour was over he'd find her somewhere to live, wherever they posted him next.

'I'll look after you, Mother. I'm taking you away from here.'

She stopped crying and lifted her head. 'It's your father, Jock.'

'Aye,' he said grimly. 'I know it's him.'

'No, you dinna understand . . . He's *ill.* They took him to hospital. It's bad. Very bad.'

That was why she'd been crying, why she was so upset. Not because the brute had been bashing her about but because he'd been taken sick. He stared at his mother.

'What's the matter with him?'

'They didna tell me. It was yesterday evening . . . he fell down – here in the kitchen.'

'Nothing unusual in that.'

'It wasna the drink.' She looked at him with anguish. 'He lay there moaning and moaning. I didna know what to do at first. Then I went next door and they went round for the doctor. And they took him away by ambulance. Oh, Jock . . .'

He held her again while she cried some more. 'Have you been to see him?'

'No. I had to go to work. I was waiting for you . . .'

'I'll take you,' he said. 'We'll go together.'

His father was lying in a long, green-tiled ward. The place smelled of Jeyes Fluid and the decrepit flesh of sick old men. It nauseated him, even more than the smell, to see the way his mother bent to kiss his father and to stroke his forehead tenderly. How could she, after the way he'd treated her? How could she care what happened to the pig?

'Come to gloat, then, have you?' His father's eyes had opened and focused blearily on him. His face was unshaven and a dirty yellow.

'No. I've brought Mother to see ye.'

'You'll no be sorry to find me like this.'

He wasn't, but he said nothing – for his mother's sake. Her hand went on with the stroking and he could scarcely bear to watch it: hardly stop himself thrusting it away.

'I'll leave you with him,' he said. 'I'll be back in a wee while.' He found the ward sister by the door: a starched Gorgon, with thin lips and a complexion like dried putty.

'Can you tell me anything about my father's condition? Donald McIntyre, last bed on the right.'

'He's as ill as he deserves to be.'

'What's that supposed to mean?'

'It's the drink. But I dare say you'd know that well enough.'

'Is he going to die?'

'It's not for me to say.' She nodded towards the corridor. 'Here's the doctor now. You'd better ask him.'

The doctor was in a hurry. 'Mr McIntyre? Yes, well it's not good news, I'm afraid. He must have been drinking a great deal over a great many years. In the end the body can't take it. His liver's destroyed. We'll do the best we can and he may go on for a while, if he's lucky, but the damage is done and can't be undone.'

'How long will he last?'

'Impossible to predict precisely – hours, days, a week. Not more. I'm sorry. Now, if you'll excuse me—'

He waited around in the grim and draughty corridor, unable to bring himself to go back to his father's bedside. Nurses passed by and one or two of them smiled at him; it was the RAF uniform that did it, he supposed. He didn't envy them with that old battle-axe of a ward sister. Or working in such a place. After what seemed a very long time, his mother came out. She was weeping again, handkerchief pressed to her face. He put his arm around her and led her away.

He spent that night on his old mattress bed behind the partition, listening to the vermin running about. It was almost as cold as the sergeants' hut at Beningby; he swore to himself that when the end came he was going to see to it that his mother didn't spend one more day there.

They went back to the hospital in the morning. This time there were screens put round the bed and his father didn't open his eyes. He left his mother at the bedside and walked the streets of Glasgow, hunched into his greatcoat against the wind. When he returned it was to find that his father had died half an hour earlier. His mother wept and wept.

He dealt with the death certificate and made the arrangements for the funeral – the best that could be done with the savings his mother had hidden away in an old jug, and with what he had to give from his pay. There was a delay digging the grave because of the frozen ground, and it was the last day of his leave before the burial could take place. It didn't surprise him to find there were no mourners except his mother and himself. Not that he counted himself a mourner. There wasn't a shred of regret in his heart as he watched the chipboard coffin being lowered into the cold earth. *Let him rot.*

'You're leaving here, Mother,' he told her when they were back in the kitchen. 'You're not staying in this place.'

She was putting the kettle on the hob to make tea and turned round, her face stained with all the tears she had shed.

'Och, no, Jock. I wouldna want to leave.'

'Why ever not? What's to keep you?'

'This is my home. It's where I lived with your father.'

'But now he's gone you've no need to stay. No reason at all.'

'It's still my home,' she said stubbornly, just like she'd always done. 'My married home. I dinna want to leave it.'

Nothing would change her mind and it was all he could do not to lose his temper. As long as he lived he'd never understand her. Never understand women. Never.

'Just be yourself, Peggy. That's all you have to do.'

But they weren't going to like herself at all. The very moment she opened her mouth they'd know her for what she was, that's if they hadn't seen it the minute they set eyes on her. She'd put on her best skirt and jumper and coat, and borrowed a hat from Mum. And she'd packed her best frock, a new pair of shoes, a blouse and cardigan she'd borrowed from Mum, too. None of it was going to make any difference, though, because they'd see it was all cheap make-do.

330

'Only a few more miles, darling,' Piers said, smiling at her as though there was nothing whatever to worry about.

She wanted to tell him to slow down. Not to drive the car so fast, so they would take longer to get there. *Never* get there at all. For part of the journey she'd been imagining what Piers' mum was going to look like. *Lady Wentworth-Young.* She'd never met a lady before. The nearest thing she knew was Mrs Mountjoy, and if she was anything like her then she'd turn tail and run. If Mrs Mountjoy knew about this she'd have a word or two to say. She could hear her saying it. *I don't know what the world is coming to. A common waitress thinking she's good enough for an officer and a gentleman . . .*

Of course, they wouldn't know Piers wanted to marry her. Perhaps they'd think she was just a friend? And then, when they'd got to know her a bit better, they might quite like her and not mind so much . . . No, no use hoping anything like that. They were going to hate her straight off.

They turned through a gateway and down a long drive. It went on and on.

'Here we are. This is it.'

Peggy gulped. She'd never pictured anything nearly as grand as this. She clung to Piers as they stopped outside the front door.

'I can't . . . I can't . . .'

'Of course you can, darling. There's nothing to be afraid of. They can't eat you. I'll be with you all the time. Just try to remember not to call me sir if you can.'

He got the luggage out of the boot – her father's old canvas bag with its rusty hinges and his own beautiful leather suitcase with his five initials on the top.

There was nobody in the huge hall. For a moment she hoped against hope that they'd all gone away somewhere, but Piers had put down the luggage and was opening one of the doors.

'They'll be in the drawing-room, I expect. Yes, here we are. Come on, Peggy.'

There were three of them sitting in a room even bigger than the hall: two ladies and a gentleman. The gentleman stood up slowly; the ladies stayed sitting. None of them smiled.

Piers put one arm under her elbow. 'This is Peggy.' He pulled her forward, else her feet might have stuck where they were. 'Come and meet my mother.'

The lady on the sofa was nothing like Mrs Mountjoy at all. Not to look at, anyway; much younger and ever so smartly dressed. Peggy just stopped herself bobbing a curtsey.

'Pleased to meet you.'

'And this is my sister, Pamela.'

The eyes were the same as the other lady's and stared at her in the same way. She hadn't known Piers' sister would be there as well, just to make matters even worse.

'Pleased to meet you.'

'And this is my father.'

He was the most frightening of all. He reminded her of the general who had once come to dinner at The Angel, shouting his order as though she was deaf and half-witted.

An old woman in a black dress and white apron, like her own waitress's uniform, appeared and led her up a big staircase and along a dark corridor. She showed her into a bedroom, and from the way she sniffed as she shut the door, Peggy knew what she thought of her and Dad's bag. She sat down on a chair because her legs were still shaking. The room was far grander than any of the ones at The Angel. All done in pale blue and with curtains that went right down to the floor. After a moment, when her legs felt stronger, she got up and went over to sit at the dressing-table by the window, gazing at her three reflections. She looked wrong in all of them, left, right and in the middle. Out of place. Sitting where she didn't belong and had no right to be.

'Come down in half an hour,' Piers had said. 'We'll be having a drink before dinner.'

She'd have to guess the time because she hadn't got a watch, and ought she to change into her frock, or not? Mrs Mountjoy changed for dinner every evening, decking herself out in jet beads like bits of shiny coal and a big cameo brooch. If Mrs Mountjoy changed, then she'd better, too.

She lost her way trying to find the staircase again and couldn't remember which door it was in the hall that Piers had opened. As she stood there, afraid to try any of them, he came out.

'*There* you are, Peggy. I was wondering what had happened to you.'

'I got lost . . .'

He put his arm round her. 'It's a bit muddling, this house, but you'll soon get used to it. You've missed the drink, I'm afraid. We're going into dinner now.'

There was no starched white cloth on the table, like at The Angel, just a wood surface so polished she could see her face in it; Piers seemed so far away. He kept smiling across at her and she tried to smile back, but her face felt too stiff.

The old woman came in and served the soup. After all the times she'd laid up the tables, Peggy knew which was the right spoon to pick up but she had to copy how to use it and how to break up the bread roll with her fingers. To her dismay the crumbs spilled over onto the polished table. She poked them under the rim of the side plate with her forefinger.

'Piers tells us that he met you in Lincoln,' Lady Wentworth-Young said in her drawly voice. 'Where was that?'

'At The Angel.'

'The Angel?'

'It's a hotel,' Piers said.

'Really? How interesting. Were you staying there, Peggy?'

'I work there.'

'*Really*? What do you do exactly?'

She looked at Piers in desperation.

'Peggy works as a waitress,' he said firmly. 'And she's a very good one.'

She saw the glance that passed between Lady Wentworth-Young and the sister.

'How fascinating. How long have you been doing that?'

'Only a few months.'

'I see. And you waited on Piers?'

'Yes. He came in – with some friends.'

'On my twenty-first birthday, actually.' Piers was smiling again at her. 'I'm afraid we all behaved most frightfully badly, didn't we Peggy?'

'Oh, no, sir—' The 'sir' was out before she knew it. 'No, you didn't really.'

It was the sister's turn now. 'Where do you live, Peggy?'

'She lives just outside Lincoln.'

'Do let her answer for herself, Piers. I'm sure she's capable of it. With your family?'

'Yes.'

'And what does your father do?'

'He works for a farmer.'

'Oh? What sort of work exactly?'

'Well, ploughing and hedging and ditching and things like that. Anything that needs doing.'

'And I'm sure he's *frightfully* good at it.'

It went on and on like that. Them asking questions and her stumbling over the answers and Piers helping her, and them being ever so polite all the time. But she could tell what they really thought underneath it all. Underneath the smiles and the *reallys* and the *how interestings*.

Somehow she got through the meal without spilling anything else or knocking anything over, but she was the last to finish for each course and they all had to sit waiting for her, watching every mouthful that she ate.

At long last she was able to escape up to the bedroom again. She undressed and put on her nightie and sat on the edge of the big bed with her hands over her face.

Someone tapped softly at the door. 'Peggy, it's me, Piers.'

She opened the door a little way.

'Are you all right?'

'Just a bit tired, sir.'

'I expect you are. The journey and everything. Can I possibly come in for a moment?' He shut the door behind him. 'You were absolutely marvellous this evening. Bit like the Spanish Inquisition, wasn't it?'

'Like what?'

'You know, having to answer all those questions. Anyway, they know all about you now so there's no need to worry any more.'

'They don't like me, Piers.'

'Of *course* they do. Mama said how sweet you were.'

'She's only pretending. She hates me.'

'You've got it wrong, Peggy. Honestly.'

'Didn't you see the way they kept looking at each other?'

'You're imagining it, darling. It's just that you're so awfully sensitive.' He put his arms around her and kissed her, and nothing seemed to matter then. Not even that she was only wearing her nightie. Not when it was Piers.

After a bit he whispered, 'I suppose I ought to go. I mean, I'd love to stay, but I mustn't . . . God, Peggy, I wish we could be married at once . . .'

When he had left her, tiptoeing away, she climbed into the bed and lay there in the dark with the bedcovers up to her chin. *It'll never happen, Piers. They won't let it.*

The next day, Piers showed her over the house. She trotted after him as he opened door after door. It was freezing cold everywhere. Not a bit cosy, like home.

'This is my old school-room . . . the nursery . . . the sewing-room . . . the library . . . the morning-room . . . my father's study . . . the billiard-room . . . the butler's pantry – of course we don't have one any more. Reynolds joined up. So did all the other staff, except our cook. She's too old to join, luckily for Mama.

I don't know how she'd cope without her.'

'It's ever such a big house, Piers.'

'Gosh, I suppose it is. Do you know, I've never really thought about it. Of course, we wouldn't live here, Peggy. We'll have our own home as soon as we can. I'm going to buy a house when I have the money, when I'm twenty-five, and you can make it however you want. What do you say to that?'

'A whole house? For us?'

'That's right. There'd be the children, too, of course. How many would you like?'

She blushed. 'I don't know—'

'Let's have at least four. Two boys and two girls.' He took hold of her hands. 'Look, Peggy, I want us to get engaged – *officially*. As soon as I've asked your father, of course. I want to tell my family and everyone that we're going to get married as soon as we can, the minute the war's over.'

'Not yet,' she said. 'Let's not say anything just yet. Let's wait a bit longer.'

He sighed. 'Well, if you *really* want . . . but I honestly don't see why.'

On the last day, he went off to see somebody in the village with the sister. 'Duty visit for Pam and me. Morrison, our old chauffeur. He's bedridden now, poor chap. I'd take you, darling, but it'd be terribly boring for you.'

She went and sat in the bedroom, waiting for him to come back. After a while there was a knock on the door and she ran to it, hoping it was Piers. The old woman stood there.

'Sir William wants to see you. In his study.'

She followed her fearfully down the staircase.

'Go on in, then.' The old woman gave her a shove

in the small of her back so that she almost fell into the room.

Sir William was sitting behind a big desk, wearing heavy spectacles which made him look even more frightening. He didn't smile; she'd never seen him smile.

'Sit down, then. No, not there. Over here. I want to have a talk with you – without Piers. Strictly between us. Understand?'

She nodded.

'You are not to repeat one word of this conversation to him. Is that quite clear?'

She nodded again.

'I'll come straight to the point. Lady Wentworth-Young and I are very concerned. Our son, Piers, appears to be quite infatuated with you.'

She didn't know what the word meant.

'Well? You must have something to say.'

'He loves me.'

'Has he told you that?'

She nodded again.

'Piers doesn't know what on earth he's talking about. He's taken complete leave of his senses. Behaving like a young fool.' The spectacles came off and were laid on the desk. Underneath, the eyes were like stones. 'My dear girl, you must see that it's quite impossible for this absurd liaison to continue.'

Another word she didn't know.

'I love him.'

'What absolute nonsense! The truth is you simply fancy yourself allied with someone like him. Someone far above your station. If you weren't so young and inexperienced I'd say you were nothing but a common fortune hunter. I'm giving you the benefit of the doubt. No doubt you were dazzled. Lost your head. Believed what he told you.'

'He did mean it. He did.'

'Of course he didn't. It's sheer infatuation. He'll come to his senses soon enough. Piers has a responsibility to his family. Traditions to uphold. Standards to maintain. He knows that perfectly well. He should never have brought you here. And you should never have come. We had no idea of your background or we would have put a stop to it. If you had any real regard for him, you'd leave him alone. I take it you wouldn't wish to ruin his life?'

'No, sir.'

'Well, then.' He pulled open a drawer of the desk. 'Now, I'm going to give you this on one condition – that you promise me never to see Piers again.' He was holding up a brown envelope. 'There are thirty pound notes inside this for you – if I have your undertaking never to have anything more to do with my son.'

She stood up and he held the envelope out to her. Shook it at her.

'Well, go on. Take it. Piers will never know.'

'No, sir.'

'You mean you want more? You've got some nerve, I must say.'

'I mean, I don't want your money. None of it. Not a penny.'

'So you refuse to give him up? You want to wreck his life?'

'I won't do that, sir. I told you, I love him.'

She turned and walked out of the room. He was calling her back, *shouting* after her, but she took no notice of him at all.

*　　*　　*

There were some boys playing with a toboggan in Sycamore Avenue, dragging it over the slushy snow by a long rope. As he passed them, Harry saw that the toboggan was made from old planks nailed crudely together. He'd made one himself once, he remembered, years ago, but he'd done a better job than that with proper shaped runners, waxed so they ran smooth. Maybe he'd make one for Paulette – if Rita would ever let her play with it.

He opened the gate to number sixteen and walked up to the front door. There was no sign of life at the windows, no twitch of the net curtains to tell him he'd been observed. When he knocked at the door it was opened by Len in his flash civvy suit, giving his oily smile.

'Oh, it's you, old boy.'

'Rita's expectin' me – to see Paulette.'

'Sorry, she's not here. Neither of them are. You're out of luck.'

'I wrote Rita I'd got leave and would be comin'.'

'Had to go and see her mother. The old girl's not well. Rita went this morning and took Paulette with her. They'll be back later. You can come in and wait, if you like.'

Harry hesitated. Rita's mother had the constitution of a ship's boiler, so it was very likely just another excuse of Rita's for not letting him see Paulette. On the other hand, he'd come all this way and he wasn't going to give up that easily. It'd be better waiting inside than out in the cold – even with Len. He followed Len inside.

'Drink, old boy?' Len was opening up the cocktail cabinet. The lights went on and the mirrors glittered, reflecting the rows of bottles.

'No, thanks.'

'I'll have one myself. I could do with it.' Len tipped up the Haig dimple bottle. 'Bit of bad luck, lately, I don't mind telling you. Nice little deal I'd been counting on went sour on me . . . Still, there's always the next one.'

'What's your line, then?' He'd never asked and Rita had never told him.

'Buying and selling. You'd be surprised what you can make – if you've got the right contacts. Know what I mean?'

'You mean you're a black marketeer?'

'Steady on, old boy. My business is strictly legit and you won't find anybody to say otherwise. Can I help it if people are willing to pay good prices for what they want? Besides, Rita costs a bit – as you'd know. Got to keep her happy, haven't I?' Len was lighting up a cigar. 'Go on, sit down and make yourself comfy.'

'I'd sooner stand, thank you.' He couldn't bring himself to sit down in company with a man who was making dishonest money out of the war. Thousands were giving their lives so that people like Len could line their grubby pockets.

'Suit yourself.' Len sat down on the sofa and crossed one leg over the other. He was wearing brown and white shoes with a lot of fancy punching and stitching. 'My feet are killing me. Fallen arches, see. That's why I failed the medical, or I'd be knocking Jerry for six, like you lot.'

He reminded Harry of a lizard: the slickness of him, the smooth hair, the small hands, the natty clothes. 'Doin' what?'

'Sorry?'

'What exactly do you think you'd do – in the Air Force?'

'Hard to say. Pilot, I suppose. Fighter, not bomber, though. No offence, but your kites are on the slow side, aren't they? What do they do? One-fifty? Just stooging along, aren't you? Sitting ducks. I'd sooner have a bit of speed myself. A Spit, say. Faster than a Hurry. Three-twenty – now *that's* what I call moving.'

He's been listening in on shop talk, Harry thought. One of those know-alls who butt in on conversations in pubs. 'I doubt they'd 'ave you.'

'Not with my feet, they wouldn't.' Len tapped his cigar. 'Frankly, old boy, I can't see what good you bomber blokes are doing. You don't seem to be hitting the *real* targets, do you? The ones that matter. Factories, docks – that sort of thing. What's the use of smashing up a whole lot of houses? Doesn't get you anywhere. Now, take the Yanks. They've got it all sorted out. Go in *daylight* so you can see what you're doing. Hit the proper targets. Precision bombing, they call it. No skulking around in the dark – '

Harry stepped forward. '*Skulkin'*?'

'OK, OK.' Len held up a hand as if he were a policeman stopping traffic. 'No offence intended. Bit touchy, aren't you? Rita always said you were. Doesn't do in this tough old world we live in. Sure you won't have that drink? Do you the world of good. No? Well, please yourself. You could have a long wait, I'm here to warn you . . .'

They'd played him for a sap, as usual. Rita and Paulette were most likely staying the night with her mother – anything to avoid him. Leave him to me, Len would have said. I'll soon get rid of him. Spin him a story, give him a drink and a bit of a chat and send

342

him on his way. He'd no choice but to leave. No sense in waiting hours for nothing. And if he tried it, he'd probably end up knocking Len's block off. He couldn't stay in the same room as him much longer.

'I'll be goin'.'

'Right you are, Harry. Just as you want. I'll see you out.'

In the hall he caught sight of Paulette's doll's pram by the foot of the stairs. He hadn't noticed it when he came in and he stopped to look now. There was a doll sitting inside it, a big doll, propped upright against the frilly pillow. Her blue glass eyes stared back at him: eyes with thick, black lashes, eyes that opened and shut. Real hair, curled and tied with a pink ribbon.

'Got it for Paulette for Christmas,' Len was saying. 'Cost me a pretty penny, I can tell you. Happened to run across a bloke who'd a few boxes of them put by. Pre-war manufacture. Nice quality. She plays with it all the time.'

He didn't need to ask where *his* doll was, or whether she liked it.

Len opened the front door. He clapped a hand on Harry's shoulder. 'Sorry you missed them, old boy.'

'Take your bloody 'and off me.'

'Easy now, Harry. Easy. No call to be like that.' Len took his hand away and smiled. 'Better luck next time.'

'The walls are nearly three miles long. We could walk along them almost all the way round the city, if you like.'

'Sure. It's a great way to see it.'

The Minster was beautiful in the winter sunlight, seen through bare branches from the narrow walkway on top of the medieval wall. They looked down onto

343

walled gardens and the backs of Georgian houses. The snow sparkled prettily.

'Guy Fawkes was born in York, did you know? In a house just by the Minster.'

'Guy?'

'Not your sort of guy, Van. Guy Fawkes. Haven't you heard of him?'

'Guess not. What did he do?'

'He tried to blow up the king and the Houses of Parliament with gunpowder in sixteen hundred and five.'

'You don't say. Couldn't have thought much of them. What was his problem?'

He was a fanatical Catholic and the king, James I, was Protestant. They found out about the plot just in time and hanged him. We burn effigies of him on the top of bonfires every year on the fifth of November, and call them guys.'

'Well, at least nobody's forgotten him. I figure that's worth a hell of a lot.'

She thought of Peter. *Your last letter took so long to reach here, I thought you'd forgotten all about me . . .*

'Dick Turpin's buried here too.'

'Another Englishman I've never heard of.'

'He was a famous highwayman in the eighteenth century. He used to ride round on a horse called Black Bess, robbing stage coaches. He was imprisoned here and hanged.'

'We had guys like that. Ever heard of Jesse James? Butch Cassidy?'

'Yes, I think so.'

'They came to a bad end too.'

They walked on along the wall, past the Minster towards Monk Bar. She showed him the old portcullis

344

still in place above the gate. 'They could lower it fast if necessary, and it's got spikes on the bottom.'

'You sure wouldn't want to get in the way.'

Further on he stopped and looked out over the wall away from the city. 'I guess they could see people coming a long way off.'

'Well, most of it was forest in those days, so it couldn't have been that easy.'

'PA's like that still. Forest for miles and miles. Cigarette?'

She shook her head and he lit one for himself, cupping his hand round it against the wind. He still looked tired, she thought. Spent. Like they always did towards the end of a tour. Her mother had told her he'd slept almost solidly for the first two days of his leave. Four more ops to go. Only four.

'You've never told me why you volunteered, Van.'

'To get away. To forget.' He stowed the Zippo away in his pocket and leaned on the wall again, head turned from her, smoking the cigarette. 'That makes me sound like some guy joining the French Foreign Legion. Real dramatic.'

'A girl?'

'Yeah. A girl. Only it wasn't to forget her, but what I'd done to her. I killed her.'

She stared at him, shocked.

'Not on purpose. Nothing like that, but just the same, I killed her.'

'What happened?'

'We were college kids, both nineteen. We'd been dating since high school. Known each other since we were small. I'd had pretty good grades that semester and my father gave me a brand new Packard for a birthday present. I thought I was the smoothest guy

345

around . . . a real swell. I took her to the movies in it and on the way home a truck came straight out of a side road and hit us. Carrie died in the wreck.'

'*You* didn't kill her, though. It was the truck driver's fault.'

He shook his head. 'I was driving much too fast. Showing off. One arm round her, finger on the wheel. Not paying attention or I'd've seen the truck in time.'

'It was still an accident.'

'That's what everyone kept telling me. Only as far as I was concerned it *was* my fault and I killed her. And that's the way I'll always see it. Putting myself in the line of fire seemed some kind of rough justice – self-administered, since nobody else would do it. So . . . that's why I joined. No heroics, not like the other guys. Just the only way I could deal with it.'

'Tragedies happen in life, Van.'

'Sure. I see them happening all the time now. *You* see them, Catherine. Kids of Carrie's age dying like flies. Only I'm not responsible for them, not the way I was for her. I can blame the war for it.' He smoked his cigarette for a moment. 'I guess it's kind of ironic that I've been flying bombers that have killed God knows how many people, but that doesn't seem to get to me either. I can blame the war for that, too. Blame the Jerries for dropping bombs on us first. Blame Hitler. Blame Butch Harris.'

'Have you ever thought of the lives you're helping to *save* when you're risking your own? The Germans have murdered thousands of innocent victims. A *million* Jews, it said in the papers. And if they're not defeated, they'll kill thousands more. And they'll murder people here, and people in your own country, if they ever get the chance. You're stopping that happening. It might help a bit if you thought of that.'

'I guess so . . . ' He turned round and smiled at her. 'Let's walk on, if we're going to get all the way round.'

When they returned to the house, her mother had gone out, leaving a note. *Gone to do a stint at the canteen. Pie in bottom oven, so help yourselves. Don't wait for me as I may be late.*

She wasn't deceived for a moment. Her match-making mama would leave them alone for as long as possible, but it wouldn't do any good. *Don't let me down, Cat. You're the only thing that keeps me sane and surviving this hell on earth.*

'We ought to eat that pie before it gets too dried up.'

'OK by me.' He followed her into the kitchen. 'Anything I can do?'

'Well, you could get some plates out of the cupboard over there.'

'Sure thing.'

When she turned round from the oven he was hunting in the wrong cupboard. 'Sorry, I meant the other one.' She put down the pie and went to show him. He came to stand behind her as she opened the door.

'These blue and white ones in here. Look—'

But when she turned round he wasn't looking at the plates at all. He was looking at her. She should have moved away at once, not gone on standing there like an idiot. Letting it happen.

'This is Sergeant Brenner, Auntie Barbara.'

He stepped forward and shook the aunt's hand. Not bad, and a damn sight better than her sister. A widow, Honor had said. She didn't look like most widows he knew. He smiled at her – his best-behaved smile, the one he used to charm older ladies. 'Stew's the name.'

'How do you do, Stew? Welcome to Newquay.'

Yep, she was a definite improvement on the mother, he decided, and so was her home. Nice little house with everything bright and cheery. No antimacassars or gloomy old furniture. And not a stag's head in sight. The sitting-room had a large window, and he went over and took a squint out. No snow down here, thank Christ. He'd had enough of that. To think he'd ever got excited at first seeing the flaming stuff. The house was part way up a hill with a good view of a beach. He looked approvingly at the wide stretch of sand – not as good as Bondi or Manly or Whalebeach, of course, but not bad. He frowned.

'Strewth, what's happened to the sea?' He could see the line of it bloody miles off in the distance.

The aunt laughed. 'The tide goes out a long way here, Stew. Don't worry, it will come right in at high tide.'

'That so? Never seen that much of a drop before.'

'I'm afraid it will be much too cold to swim at this time of year. In fact, I expect you'd find the Atlantic a bit chilly, even in summer.'

He could have told her the North Sea wasn't so hot either.

'Come upstairs and I'll show you your room.' The aunt led the way. 'Honor always sleeps in here.' She opened a door and he took a mental note of which one. 'And this is yours. I thought you'd like to have the view.'

It was the same view as from the sitting-room, only higher up, and he could see the sea better now. Grey, not blue: he'd never seen the sea over here properly blue. He stood, staring out of the window, when suddenly the homesickness got to him. It was like being socked hard in the guts. Jesus, it was midsummer back home. Probably up in the nineties. They'd be out on the beaches, soaking up the sun, fooling about . . . Indigo sea, golden sand, white surf, cold beers, big steaks . . . my word, it didn't do to think about it and that he might never see it again. He'd get all choked up like some kid. Must be because he was so bloody tired. He turned away from the window.

'It's bonza. Thanks a lot, Mrs – sorry, Honor never told me your other name.'

'It's Rowan, but just call me Barbara.' She smiled at him. 'I want you to enjoy your leave, Stew. Rest and recuperation, isn't that what leave's supposed to be about? I promise I'll do my best to see you get plenty of both. We owe you brave young Aussies an awful lot, coming from the other side of the world to help us. I think you're pretty special.'

That got him choked all right. He couldn't answer her for the life of him. Had to turn away quickly and take another dekko out of the window in case she noticed.

It was dark before the tide came in, so he didn't see it until the next day. The aunt brought him a cup of tea in bed.

'We left you to sleep as much as you could.'

He propped himself up on one elbow. 'Thanks, Barbara. Must have needed it. Where's Honor?'

'Downstairs. She thought you might like to go for a walk later. Take a closer look at the sea.'

'Too right.'

As soon as he'd finished the tea he got up and padded over to the window. Just like she'd said, the sea had come right in and there was a good surf breaking a couple of hundred yards out. He watched the rollers sweeping in, curling over and crashing onto the shore. Not bad. Not bad at all.

He got dressed and went downstairs and found that the aunt had gone out shopping and Honor was in the kitchen, stirring something on the stove. He liked the jumper and skirt she had on – a lot better than the old maid clothes she wore at the hotel. Her hair wasn't rolled up all tight either, just tied with a ribbon.

She gave him a bit of a smile over her shoulder. Things were really looking up. 'Did you sleep well?'

'Like a log.'

'I've made some porridge, and there's a sausage and an egg. Would that do?'

'An egg? I wouldn't want to take that.'

'Don't worry, my aunt keeps hens.'

While he started on the porridge, she fried the egg and sausage for him in a pan, together with some bread. She did a nice job, he reckoned. Funny to eat an egg without having to fly to Germany and back for it.

'Barbara said you're planning a walk.'

'Well, I thought you'd like to go along by the beach. That's what you came for, isn't it? To see the surf.'

'Yeah . . .' As he ate, he watched her washing up at the sink. No doubt about it, he fancied her. Hell, it was more than fancying her. He fancied women all the time. But this one was different. Everything was different. For a start, you didn't mess around with a sheila like Honor, same as you could with the Doreens. There were different rules, but he wasn't too sure how to play the game.

They took a road leading down to the beach and, as usual, he matched his pace to her much slower one. He breathed in the salty air. It made him feel good. Like a new man. And having her walking along beside him made him feel good, too. And a different sort of man. He wasn't sure what sort – yet.

The lameness didn't worry him but he reckoned it worried her a lot. She acted like she thought it was something ugly, something to be ashamed of. Some time he'd tell her she was all wrong about that.

They stood and watched the rollers coming in with a booming noise like ack-ack guns; the seagulls were screaming and wheeling about overhead same as a pack of Jerry fighters. He glanced at Honor. She'd got a scarf tied round her head, but the wind was blowing a lock of hair across her face. He liked that.

'Mind if we walk along a bit?'

'Fine.'

'Sure you're up to it?'

'Of course.'

It was too cold to go far anyway and they turned towards the town and found a café open. Steamed-up windows, grubby glass-topped tables, some old slag behind the counter. But it was warmer inside.

'My shout,' he told Honor.

The woman slopped the tea into the saucers as she poured.

'Got any biscuits, or something?'

She nodded towards a plate of curling sandwiches under a dome. 'Only them there.'

'That the best you can do?'

She glared at him indignantly. 'There's a war on, you know.'

'You don't say.' He carried the teas over to the table. 'Thanks for showing me the beach.'

'There are more of them along the coast. We could take a bus tomorrow . . . if you'd like.'

'Too right, I'd like.'

'It's a pity you won't see it in summer, but I expect you'll have gone back to Australia by then.'

'Doubt it.' Probably another bloody tour, he thought, stirring his tea. Forget about going home. Don't even think about it.

'What will you do when the war's over, Stew?'

No harm in dreaming. 'I know what I'd *like* to do.'

'What's that?'

'Have a vineyard. Grow grapes. Make wine.'

'In *Australia*. I thought that was only in Europe.'

He shook his head. 'Not any more. We've got the climate, see. I once worked for a man who'd planted a whole lot of vines – up north of Sydney. Beaut place. They were doing well. Making good wine. I reckon I'd like to have a shot at that some day. See if I can make a go of it. What do you think of the idea?'

'I really don't know anything about it, but it sounds exciting. Rather wonderful, to do something like that.' She was drawing circles with her finger on the table top, round and round on the glass. Hardly ever looked at him direct now, he'd noticed. Wouldn't meet his eyes. Was that a good sign or a bad one?

He wondered what she'd say if he told her straight out how much he fancied her, about all those sinful things he'd been thinking? How much he was building his dreams round her? And he wondered what she really thought of him, beneath the Pommie smoke-screen she put up. Sooner or later he was going to find out.

It rained solidly for the next three days. Jesus, he thought, staring out of the sitting-room window, what a sodding awful climate it is.

They went to the cinema in Newquay twice and walked some more in the rain and went to a couple of pubs where he knew he could have picked up any one of the girls hanging round the bar, easy as anything. With Honor, he bided his time, waiting for a chink to show in the armour. No luck. She was freezing him off. Keeping a safe distance. Making bloody sure he never got any chances. Doing a real Miss Iceberg.

The rain stopped so they took the bus along the coast and walked down to one of the other beaches. The surf was even better there. My word, he thought, it's almost as bloody good as Bondi.

When it started to rain again they took refuge in a bus shelter. It was littered with empty packets of Smith's crisps and fish and chip newspaper, and a used French letter that he kicked tactfully out of sight.

'I'm sorry,' she said. 'The weather's been awful for you.'

'Well, it's winter, isn't it?' He was trying to get his lighter to work and, as usual, the bloody thing was playing up.

'I've got some matches.' She took a box out of her handbag. 'You really ought to get another lighter.'

'It's my lucky mascot. Can't chuck it away yet. Not till the war's over.'

She struck the match and held it up close for him. Now *that* was a good sign, he thought, but don't count on it. Instead of putting his cigarette to the flame he stepped forward and blew it out slowly, giving her a long look over the match.

As soon as he kissed her he knew nobody'd been there before. Not even Postman's Knock. She hadn't a clue. Not the foggiest. She didn't push him away, though – not at first. When she finally did, just as things were getting going nicely, he stopped at once.

'Please, Stew . . .'

'Sorry.' He steadied his breathing. 'Got carried away there.'

'I don't want you to think—'

He retrieved the fag he'd dropped in the clinch. 'I don't think anything, Honor. Not a thing. Mind lighting me another match?' But he knew he was in with a chance.

After supper that evening – the last evening – she made some excuse and went off to bed early. She'd spent the whole time since the bus shelter not looking at him, but that didn't worry him. He knew now that she fancied him too.

The aunt got out a bottle of brandy, hidden away in a cupboard, and poured him a stiff tot. She was a great old girl, he thought. Must have been a real good-looker in her day. Still got nice legs and kept her figure. He might have gone for her himself when she was young. What was she now? Must be at least forty. Old enough to be his mother. Tough on her being a widow. He nodded towards a framed photo of a man in army uniform on her desk.

'Hope you don't mind my asking, but is that your husband?'

'Yes, that's David. He was killed in the First World War. In the trenches.'

'Sorry about that.'

'I was, too. Distraught. We hardly had any time together after we were married – only a few months.

One thing I learned was that in wartime people should make the very most of life while they can. Live every single day to the full.'

'I'll go along with that.'

She smiled at him. 'I thought you would, Stew. I wish Honor felt the same. She's in love with you, you know.'

'She tell you that?'

'No, but I know my niece well enough. She's had a dreary sort of life up to now. Very narrow. Very repressed. I expect you realize that.'

'Yeah, I met her parents.'

'It's not just them. It's her disability as well. She's convinced it sets her apart. Puts men off. So she puts them off first, herself. You're like a shining knight riding up on a white charger, hacking away the brambles to get to her.'

'Strewth!'

'A bit fanciful, I agree, but that's how it strikes me. Have some more brandy?'

'Thanks.'

She poured him another bloody great dollop. 'I'm off to bed now. Will you turn the lights out?'

'No fail.'

At the door she turned. 'Don't bother about disturbing me when you come up, Stew. I sleep very deeply and never hear a sound.'

He stared after her. Well, stone the bloody crows . . .

When he tapped on Honor's bedroom door it opened after a moment. She was standing there in a thin nightie and bare feet with her hair all loose. Nothing like Miss Iceberg at all. No point messing around. He remembered about being a flaming

shining knight and scooped her up in his arms. He
kicked the door shut behind him.

'Stew, I haven't ever—'

'Yeah, I know,' he whispered in her ear. 'No worries,
sweetheart. I have.'

Sixteen

'The target for tonight, gentlemen, is Essen.'

Bert's stomach looped-the-loop. Not *again*. Back to the bloody Happy Valley. He stared disconsolately at the map. There were groans and mutters going on all around him in the briefing room. He looked at the nasty red patches of flak along the coast and the great big red splodge of the heavily defended Ruhr. The Jerries didn't like you going anywhere near there, and they had vays of making you stop.

'Heavy industry, arms manufacture, communications . . . We'll be part of the first wave, supporting 8 Group's Pathfinder Force . . . take-off eighteen-fifteen . . . the Met chaps tell me there'll only be patchy cloud over the target and a full moon, so you'll be able to spot it easily . . .'

They'll be able to spot *us* easily, too, Bert said to himself bitterly. He'd sooner a nice bit of thick cloud any time so's the searchlights were buggered up.

'. . . so, let's put up a damned good show. Go out there tonight and rip the guts out of the Hun.'

Enough to make anyone queasy and he always felt that on ops days anyway. The minute he saw their names on the board, his body got up to its tricks. Sometimes he almost convinced himself that he wasn't well enough to fly. He'd feel hot and shivery like he was coming down with a bad dose of 'flu or something,

357

and once he'd even come out in a rash. But in the end he always went. Well, he couldn't let the others down, could he? Everyone knew it was bad luck to take a spare bod, and besides, the MO could spot a malingerer at twenty paces. When it came down to it, he was even more frightened of being thought windy than of going on the raid itself.

The Nav Leader stood up, pointer in hand. 'Assemble over Southwold at twelve thousand feet. Get up to eighteen thousand feet before you reach the yellow marker here on the Dutch coast . . . then turn towards the target. It's a straight run down . . .'

Bert's mind wandered. He thought of Emerald. What the hell was he going to do about her? She was still going on at him about getting married. Still swore she was expecting. The thought of being tied to her for the rest of his life was horrible. Imagine being a husband and father by the time he was twenty! Staying in every night. Never being able to go out with the lads. No pints down the local. No swapping stories, no darts, no bloody fun at all. Stuck with a crying baby and Emerald nagging away. And no Victor.

'. . . turn off the target and gain speed by losing height, but don't go below ten thousand. The route is plotted to avoid flak concentration at Rotterdam on the way out and Amsterdam on the way back.'

What about over the bloody target, Bert thought? Fat chance of avoiding *that* flak.

The Intelligence Officer was up on his hind legs now. Bert didn't like the bloke. He was too big for his boots and had a toff accent you could cut with a knife.

'OK, cheps, we're going to be bombing Essen tonight—'

Bert joined heartily in the whistles and catcalls.

'*You're* going to be bombing Essen, I should say. Bomb aimers, some of you cheps are still dropping your bombs early, short of the target. Take a good look at these slides.'

The lights went out and photos of a previous raid appeared on the screen.

'See, bomb aimers, the bombs are landing further and further away from the centre as the raid goes on. Bad show. Some people call this creep-back. I call it wind-up. And I don't want to see any of you cheps getting that tonight.'

Bert took a peek at Stew. Blimey, Stew didn't like that one bit. Face black as thunder. He was saying something to the skipper next to him, and it wouldn't be anything you'd want your maiden aunt to hear.

At the end of the briefing the Squadron CO gave them the usual pep talk. Bert could hardly see him for the fog of cigarette smoke.

'Nothing to add, gentlemen, except let's do our damnedest tonight. Stick to what you've been told, keep in the stream, and it'll be a piece of cake. Set your watches. It's sixteen-twenty-five . . . NOW. Good luck, all of you.'

He didn't fancy the flying supper much – not even the egg, and he always used to enjoy it, even the pre-op one. It wasn't so much Essen, he thought, but Emerald that'd taken his appetite away. If she was on duty this evening he'd be bound to see her when he collected his brolly. No getting out of it. He wasn't going without one.

By a stroke of luck she was off, and the WAAF who handed over the parachute wouldn't have tempted him if he'd been in the nick for forty years.

He used a penknife to open his locker, having long

since lost the key. Of course, someone had half-inched his gloves. Nothing for it but to beg, borrow or steal from somebody else. He emptied his pockets of anything handy for Jerry intelligence – bus tickets, cinema stubs and the like – and struggled into his flying suit and his heavy sheepskin boots. You could hardly turn round in the locker room for blokes zipping and buckling themselves in, getting all togged up like a lot of bloomin' chorus girls backstage – except they were putting on a lot more clothes.

'These yours, Bert?' Charlie was holding out his gloves. 'I found them mixed up with my things.'

A likely story he would have said, if it hadn't been Charlie, who'd never pinch anything from anyone. As he pulled his Mae West over his head, his sharp ears heard the familiar squeal of a crew bus brakes outside the hut.

Your carriage awaits without, sire . . . prithee step yonder.

Bert looped his harness straps over his shoulders and up between his legs and buckled them. He stuck his Fry's Sandwich bar in a reachable pocket and picked up his 'chute pack. Essen, here we bloody come. May as well get it over with.

They took off on time into a clear night sky. No delays or possible scrubs. No shilly-shallying. Straight out to the bomber, start up and go. Harry found that a lot easier on the nerves. No time for too many jitters, and after that you were too busy. He listened intently as they flew out over the North Sea. He always heard voices when he listened: the Pathfinders ahead sending out instructions, the Jerries gabbling away to each other, and sometimes the voices of men in bad trouble – lost or wounded or shot-up or low on fuel or

360

plunging downwards out of control. Men asking for help when they were beyond it. Some of them screamed and yelled, but most of them sounded quite calm, as if they didn't want to be a nuisance. He'd heard another wireless op who'd realized he and his crew were for it. *Not to worry. There won't be anything left to find . . .*

He'd be that glad when this tour was over. Maybe it was because he was older than the rest of them, but it was taking its toll. He felt sick to his soul. Sick of the whole horror of war. When it was over all he wanted to do was settle down somewhere and lead a nice, quiet, peaceful life. With Dorothy.

Somehow he'd got to get up the courage to speak to her. Tell her how he felt. She seemed to quite like him or she'd never have knitted him the scarf, so maybe there was some hope. He'd got to find out. If the weather held they could have finished their tour in the next few days, which meant they'd all be going their separate ways. Charlie would be posted away and Dorothy would be going back home to Kent. He might never see her again.

But first he ought to ask Charlie whether he minded. That was the right and proper thing to do. Only fair. He'd put it to him when they got back from Essen. Find a quiet moment to have a word.

'Navigator to pilot. Twenty minutes to the Dutch coast.'

'Roger, Piers. I'm trying to get some more height out of her.'

This kite was sluggish as hell. Van had coaxed her up close to seventeen thousand – still way short of where they should have been. If she'd been R-Robert they'd have reached their height long ago, but R-Robert was being serviced so they'd been handed this bastard. She reminded him unpleasantly of S-Sugar and that trip to Duisburg.

He'd wheedled another couple of hundred feet out of Z-Zebra by the time they crossed the coast and Piers had given him the final course for the target, but they were still beneath the stream. Bad news if they were there when the others started dropping their bombs. They'd soon know what it felt like to be flying in a Stirling if that happened: the low, slow Cinderella on mixed raids, drawing the worst of the flak and dodging the bombs raining down from above.

'Flak ahead, skip.' Stew, reporting from the front turret below.

Van could see it, too. Firefly flickers in the distance, hundreds of them. This was going to be some party. They flew on towards the target.

'Mid-upper to skipper, there's a Lanc dead above us.' Bert's voice was squeaky with horror.

'OK, mid-upper. I can see her.' He let the Lanc above draw ahead and saw her bomb doors open and the five-hundred pounders dropping out, well clear. Then the heavy cookie followed, falling much slower and swinging straight towards them in a lazy arc. *Jesus Christ!* He flung Z-Zebra to port as the four-thousand pounder sailed past on its way earthwards.

Jock held up his hands with a couple of feet or so between the two.

'That much, I reckon, skipper.'

That much between seven men living and seven men dying. He gripped the control wheel and straightened out. Stew called him up. 'Bomb aimer to pilot; ready skip?'

'OK, Stew, let's do it.'

They dropped their bomb load on Essen and he dived Z-Zebra away from the target. They droned their way home without further trouble and crossed the coast in darkness. He was dead beat: forcing himself to keep awake and concentrating.

They had to circle over Beningby with the other homecomers, waiting for another Lanc that had been badly shot up to go first. He watched the faint blue glows from its exhausts as it went in to land. The guys in there would be saying their prayers. A bright stream of tracer streaked across the darkness, dazzling his eyes, and the blue glows exploded into fire. Control screeched in his ears.

'Disperse! Disperse!'

At the same moment Charlie yelled, 'Enemy fighter, closing port.'

Van wrenched Z-Zebra in a steep turn to starboard away from the drome, jinking and weaving violently. Out of the corner of his eye, he saw another arc of tracer curve close by. Lancs were fleeing in all directions.

'The bastards must've tailed us in,' Jock said. 'They got that crippled Lanc.'

'Rear gunner to pilot. Looks like they're shooting up the drome, skipper. Several of them. Giving it a real pasting. I can see fires everywhere.'

God, he thought, Catherine.

Control diverted them to land at another station seventy miles away. He tried, but failed, to get through to Beningby and it wasn't until the following day that they were able to return.

The Jerry night fighters had left a real mess behind them. As well as the crippled Lanc, they'd shot down three others and strafed the drome thoroughly, damaging the hangars and several buildings, including the Ops Block. Apart from the bomber crews killed or wounded, a couple of ground crew guys had copped it. No WAAFS had been hurt.

He saw Catherine in the Mess when she came off duty. 'Christ, I was worried about you.'

'I was much more worried about *you*. They got four Lancs, you know.'

'We were OK. Vamoosed like scared rabbits. I guess they'll be trying it on again. Sneaking in just when everyone thinks they're home and dry. Catching us with our pants down.'

'They did several other dromes, too, apparently. Pretty successfully.'

'I wish you weren't here. How about putting in for a transfer?'

'You know I couldn't.'

'Stupid of me to suggest it, I guess. England expects . . . even the women.'

'This is our war as well, isn't it? Everyone's. Men, women and children.'

He looked at her. 'Meantime, how about us?'

'We've been through all that, Van. I told you, I can't write a "dear John" letter. I just can't.'

'You also told me you loved me. As I remember. And you know I love you. Sooner or later you'll have to tell Peter.'

'But not now. Not yet. Not while he's a POW.'

'The war could go on for years. Are you going to go on keeping it from him? He's a grown-up man. It's not as if you're married to him. You're not even engaged to him, for Christ's sake.'

'I *can't* tell him, Van. You don't understand. His

letters are awful. He's desperate. Suicidal. If I wrote and told him about us, I don't know what he'd do. I think it would finish him.'

'He's writing like that on purpose, Catherine. Trying to scare you. Hang on to you, that way. *Any* way he can. And he's been playing that sort of game for a good while, far as I can tell. Can't you see that?'

'No,' she said. 'I can't. I see that he's a prisoner-of-war in Germany. Shut up like an animal in a cage.'

'So are thousands of other men.'

'Well, how would *you* like it?'

'I'd hate it. But that's not the point—'

'It *is* the point. If you were in his shoes would you like to get a letter like that? How would it make you feel?'

'Hell, I'd sooner have the truth than some girl stringing me along. Just to spare my feelings. It's plain crazy.'

She said angrily, 'I'm not stringing Peter along.'

'Sure seems like that to me.' He was angry now, too. Resentful. 'Or is it *me* you're kidding?'

'There's absolutely no sense in us discussing this any further, Van.'

He watched her walking away from him.

'Can I have a word with you, lad? If you've got a moment.'

''Course you can, Harry.' Charlie halted on the concrete pathway outside the station cinema. He was still galloping across the Wild West with John Wayne, six-shooters blazing. 'What is it?'

'Look, could we go somewhere a bit private like?'

There wasn't such a place on the camp, not that

Charlie knew of. 'How about we just walk about a bit?' It was dark and cold as charity, but he could tell it was important to Harry.

'If you don't mind.'

''Course not.' Anything for old Harry. He was the best. Charlie turned up his collar and thrust his hands into his pockets. They went along another path, away from the cinema crowd, feet crunching across left-over patches of frozen snow. Crikey, it was cold. He waited hopefully for Harry to speak up.

'I wanted to ask you something,' Harry said after they'd walked a good bit.

'Yes?'

They walked on. Come on Harry, spit it out. Whatever it is.

'It's about your mum.'

Aha, so *that* was it. He might have guessed. Still, it would be best to pretend he hadn't noticed anything. More tactful. 'What about her?' He could swear he heard Harry gulp.

'The thing is, lad, I've – well, I've come to have a great regard for her . . . if you understand me.'

Charlie smiled in the darkness. 'I understand, Harry. You don't have to explain any more.'

'You don't mind?'

''Course not. Why should I?'

'But – but how about if I asked her to marry me? Would you mind then?'

'Not a bit.'

'You really mean that? Because I wouldn't want to do anythin' to upset you or your mum. Not in any way.'

Charlie stopped walking. 'I'd be chuffed as anything if you asked her, and she said yes. You go ahead.

Far as I'm concerned, I wish you all the luck in the world.'

'Thanks, Charlie.' But Harry still sounded anxious. 'Do you think she'd have me?'

He wasn't sure of the answer to that one. 'I don't know, Harry, but I certainly hope she does.'

Seventeen

Heavy cloud and torrential rain put paid to flying for a week. The frozen ground turned to thick mud with puddles like small duck ponds. Tin roofs leaked, gutters blocked, stoves smouldered, spirits sagged.

Jock wandered about restlessly, peering out of windows and drumming his fingers on panes, willing the weather to lift. Cursing it under his breath. Only one more op, but they couldn't get it decently over and done with. He wanted the tour finished. To get away from Beningby. To find Ruth. He'd been over to the farm soon after he'd got back from leave, and found out that Ruth had gone. Mrs Gibbs had been upset.

'I'm sorry, Jock. She's left to work on another farm down south. She went to see the local Land Army person and got herself transferred. Just like that. I don't know what story she told them but I don't mind telling you Dick and I were quite put out about it at first. But then I said to Dick, there's more to this than we know. Ruth's not the sort to let us down without some good reason. And we wondered if it was something to do with you, Jock?'

'I wish I knew, Mrs Gibbs. I've never understood Ruth.'

'Well, if it was to get away from you, then she's a very silly girl in my opinion.'

'Do you know where she's gone? Her address?'

'She made us promise not to give it to anyone.'

'I see.'

'But I can tell you that it's down in Devon. She's on a farm near a place called Hatherleigh. That's all I'd better say.'

'Thank you, Mrs Gibbs.'

'You're welcome, Jock. You'll be near the end of your tour, then?'

'Aye. Just one trip more to do.'

'Good luck for it. God bless you and take care of you. And I hope you find Ruth.'

No sign of the cloud lifting. If anything it was getting worse, hanging low over the drome and no wind to shift it. Jock went on cursing and drumming his fingers.

'No, Freda, that's not how you do it. Look, I'll show you. The smaller knives and forks go on the *inside*, with the dessert spoon in between the two knives and the soup spoon on the outside. You work inwards with the courses. Do you see?'

'Yes, Miss Frost.'

But she could tell by the new waitress's face that she didn't, and, worse, that she didn't care. Peggy had always wanted to learn but this one wasn't remotely interested.

'I'm afraid you'll have to re-lay all the places and you'll have to hurry. There's only twenty minutes until lunch.'

The girl pulled a face. She was going to be hopeless, Honor thought. She looked as though she'd modelled herself on some Hollywood film star, with her dyed blond hair all swept up, and her bright red lipstick. She'd done something to her uniform, too –

shortened the skirt to her knees and nipped in the waist. She started to lay another place carelessly – knives in the wrong place. 'I'll bet you get the Yanks coming in here, don't you?'

It was becoming clearer why Freda had taken the job.

'Sometimes. It's mainly RAF, though.'

'Raff?' Freda's face brightened. 'Some of them are all right. You don't happen to know if a bloke called Stew Brenner ever comes in, do you? He's an Aussie.'

'I really couldn't say.'

The girl patted her hair. 'Hope he does. I met him in The Saracen's a while back. Picked me up, he did. Fastest worker I ever met.'

'Those knives should go the other way round.'

'What? Oh?' Freda picked one up and put it down again crooked, leaving a thumb print on the blade. 'Smashing, he was. A real heart-throb. And ever so good with women . . . if you know what I mean. 'Course, I didn't believe half of what he said. You don't want to take a bloke like that seriously, do you? Bound to get lots of girls, isn't he? All he wants. He had my friend, Betty, too, matter of fact. I didn't find that out till after. Still, he was gorgeous—'

'You'd better get on with the other tables.'

'Oh, all right.'

'And don't forget to ring the gong on time.'

'*Gawd . . .*'

Honor went back to her office. She sat down in front of her typewriter, staring at a half-finished letter.

Dear Sir, Thank you for your letter of the 14th instant. I have pleasure in enclosing our tariff, as requested.

She'd been a fool. A gullible, pathetic fool.

Strewth, Honor, I've never felt like this before about any girl . . . my oath, I haven't.

Oh, Stew . . . I love you. I love you.

A girl like Freda wasn't so stupid. *'Course, I didn't believe half of what he said. You don't want to take a bloke like that seriously . . . he had my friend Betty, too . . .*

She put her face in her hands. Fool, fool, *fool.*

After a while, she pulled herself together and got on with her typing. She was in the middle of another letter when she heard the reception bell ring. When she went out of the office, Pilot Officer Wentworth-Young was standing by the desk. And Stew was with him.

The pilot officer said very politely, 'I'm frightfully sorry to bother you, but I wonder if I could possibly have a word with Peggy?'

'I'm very sorry but she's not here.'

'Oh.' He looked crestfallen. 'I thought she would be. She hasn't changed her day off, has she?'

Oh dear, she thought, he doesn't know. Peggy didn't tell him. 'As a matter of fact, she doesn't work here any longer. She left her job last week.'

The grandfather clock was striking, and out of the corner of her eye she saw Freda coming along, hips swinging, to ring the gong.

He stared at her. 'But she couldn't have done.'

Freda had gone straight up to Stew and she could hear Stew saying something to her and Freda giggling.

'I'm afraid she did.' She tried to soften the blow. 'It was all rather sudden. I think she'd decided she wanted to do something else. Some kind of war work.'

'I see.' He was looking utterly baffled.

'I should think you might find her at home.'

His brow cleared. 'Yes, of course. Jolly good idea.'

371

The dark, squat shape of Mrs Mountjoy was looming behind the Residents' Lounge glass doors. Mercifully she seemed to be having trouble with the handle.

'Freda, the gong! Quickly.'

'I'm just *going* to.'

As the girl sauntered over to the brass gong, Mrs Mountjoy burst forth like a grizzly from its lair.

'You're late, girl. Two minutes late.'

'No, I'm not. The clock's only just struck.'

'Are you arguing with me?'

'Well, see for yourself,' Freda said cheekily.

Stew came up to the desk. 'Aren't you going to say hallo to me?'

'I'm rather busy at the moment.'

'Come on, Honor, you won't even look at me.'

'I'm busy, I told you.'

'That's a load of rubbish.' He put his hand on her arm. 'What's up?'

She took her eyes off his hand. Stepped back away from it, out of reach. 'Nothing.'

'I don't believe you. What's bitten you?'

'Nothing,' she said again.

He said quietly, 'You forgotten Newquay?'

'Surely you didn't expect me to take that seriously?'

Freda started banging the gong, drowning his answer and as the booming died away, Mrs Mountjoy waddled up to the desk, elbowed Stew aside and rapped her stick on the counter.

'Miss Frost, I *demand* that you fetch Miss Hargreaves this instant. That new creature has just been grossly impertinent to me. I won't stand for it.'

Stew rounded on her. 'I'll be more than that, lady, if you don't shut up. Go and put your nosebag on.'

Freda clapped her hand over her mouth and let out

a loud snort of laughter. Mrs Mountjoy turned a livid red.

'How *dare* you! Miss Frost, are you going to just stand there and let this oaf insult me?'

'It's all right, Mrs Mountjoy, Sergeant Brenner is leaving.'

'Hell, no I'm not—'

'Please go, Stew. You've done quite enough damage.'

He looked at her. 'You really want me to go? You mean that?'

'Yes. Now, please. At once.'

He went on looking at her for a moment longer, and then shrugged. 'OK. If that's the way you want it. Come on, Piers, let's get out of here.'

The revolving door went on racketing round and round and round after them. Mrs Mountjoy's bosom swelled.

'*That's* what comes of letting riff-raff in.'

Piers left Stew, still fuming, in the car outside Peggy's house.

The door was answered by a man dressed in labourer's clothes who looked him up and down.

'You'll be Pilot Officer Wentworth-Young, I don't doubt.'

'Yes, actually—'

'I'm Peggy's dad. I dare say you've come lookin' for her, then.'

'Well, yes—'

'Sorry, sir, but she won't see you.'

'But I don't understand—'

'No, I can tell you don't. And I don't think you ever have. She's a good girl, our Peggy. Just lost her head

for a bit, that's all. Got too fond of you, sir. Nothin'
to be ashamed of, so long as it didn't go no further.'

He said, dismayed, 'I want to marry Peggy, Mr
Barton. I was going to ask your permission.'

'I know. She told me that. But I'd never've given it.
I knew she'd come to her senses in the end. You'll
have to forget all about her, sir. Peggy's goin' away to
live in a hostel. She's goin' to get work in a factory.
I'm not against that. A sight more useful'n waiting
tables, to my way of thinkin'. She's written you a letter.
Asked me to give it to you.' He tugged a crumpled
envelope out of his pocket. 'Here you are, sir.'

She'd written his name on it in pencil. *Pilat Officer
Peers Wentwerth-Young.*

'Not your fault,' Peggy's father was saying. 'You
meant well, I'm sure. But it'd never have done. Not
for her, and not for you.'

'Could I see her? Just for a moment, at least.'

'Sorry. Much better for you both if you don't.' Mr
Barton looked at him quite kindly. 'Goodbye, lad.'

The door shut in his face. He put the letter away in
his pocket and walked down the path.

'Flaming bloody women,' Stew growled as he
opened the car door. 'Let's go and get soused.'

'I gave him the letter, Peggy.'

'Thanks, Dad.'

'It was for the best.'

'Yes, Dad.'

'He's a nice lad, I can tell that, but it'd never've
done.'

'I know.' She peered round the edge of the window.
The car was just going and she caught a glimpse of
Piers and another RAF gentleman with him. Only a

374

glimpse. She'd scarcely been able to see him at all really – just the back of his head and the cap – and now she would never see him again. Tears started trickling down her cheeks and she wiped them away with the back of her hand. The letter had taken her hours to do. She wasn't sure how to spell some words and her writing wasn't very good, but the hardest part was saying it right. She'd begun it over and over again and kept tearing up sheets out of the pad, wasting paper.

> *Dear Peers,*
>
> *I'm very sorry but I do not want to see you agane. It's my falt, because I never ought to have come out with you. I knew from the begining that it was not right.*
>
> *I could never marry you because we are to diferent and so we would not be happy together.*
>
> *Please do not try to come and see me any more.*
>
> *I hope you finish your tour safly and have a happy life.*
>
> > *from,*
> > *Peggy.*

The car was a black blur through her tears. She watched it moving away down the lane until it went round the corner out of sight.

'I'd like to give notice, Miss Hargreaves.'

'What?'

'I'm leaving your employment.'

'You can't do that.'

'I'm afraid I can, Miss Hargreaves. I'll stay and work for the two weeks notice required, of course.'

'You're deserting me? Just like that? I call that

375

extremely inconsiderate of you, Miss Frost. Most ungrateful.'

'I rather feel it's you who should be grateful to me.'

'I don't know what you mean. You've had a free rein. Every latitude. Excellent conditions and pay. You won't find it easy to find another post as good, you know.'

'I shan't be looking for a post anything like this. I'm going to do some kind of war work.'

'The Services won't have you – you realize that? You'd never pass the medical with your crippled leg.'

'I know that perfectly well.'

'They'll put you in a factory. Munitions work.'

'Very likely.'

'Well, don't expect my blessing. Or a good reference. You've let me down, Miss Frost. I'm *most* displeased.'

Dorothy was standing in the rain feeding stale bread crusts to Marigold. She was a picky old thing all right; didn't seem to think much of them at all.

'You'll just have to make do. There's no corn left. Don't you know there's a war on?' She emptied the bowl and hurried back to the cottage, head bent against the rain, and ran slap into Harry.

'Sorry, Dorothy. Didn't mean to startle you. I've been knockin' at front door.' He looked soaked, like a big dog that had just been for a swim.

'You'd better come inside and dry off a bit or you'll go and get a chill.'

He followed her into the cottage, wiping his feet carefully. She was touched to see that he was wearing

376

the scarf she'd given him. 'Take your coat off and I'll make you a cup of tea. It'll warm you up a bit.'

'I don't want to keep you. You'll be busy.'

'No, I'm not. I'm on the last shift this week so I don't have to go to work till later.'

She went into the kitchen to put the kettle on and he came and stood in the doorway, like he usually did. Watching her. 'How's the job goin', then?'

'Not so bad. They let me do some cooking once in a while. Fry the sausages and the chips. It makes a change from peeling the vegetables, like I do mostly.'

'You won't be sorry to leave? When we're finished.'

She turned round to him. 'Oh, Harry . . . just one more op to do. That's all.'

'Soon be over,' he said. 'Not much longer and you won't have to worry about Charlie. You'll be goin' back home then?'

'Well, I won't try and follow him, if that's what you're asking.'

'Nay, I didn't mean—'

'I know you didn't, Harry. But I mustn't do it any more. Charlie's got to live his own life. I thought I'd try and join the NAAFI down in Kent. I saw an advertisement in a magazine. Cooks urgently needed, it said. I've got the address in London to write to about it. See if I can be a real cook.'

'You already are. The best I've ever known.'

'That's nice of you.'

He coughed, as though he really might be getting a chill. 'It's meant a lot havin' you here, Dorothy.'

'That's nice of you, too.'

'It's true.'

She poured some hot water to warm the pot, swirling

it round. 'You've been a wonderful friend to Charlie. He's always telling me how kind you've been.'

'I've done what I could. It hasn't been much.'

'Well, he thinks the world of you, you know.'

'Dorothy, I—'

'Could you pass me that tea tray there, Harry?'

'Oh, aye . . .'

She took the cups and saucers out of the cupboard and put them on the tray, together with the milk jug and the teapot. 'We'll take it through.'

He carried the tray into the sitting-room for her and set it down on the table. She started to pour the tea.

'They give you all leave as soon as you've finished, don't they, Harry?'

'Aye. Two weeks.'

'You'll be going home yourself, then?'

'I don't know what I'll do,' he said.

'Well, if you've nothing special, you must come and stay with Charlie and me. You're always welcome.'

'I couldn't do that.'

'Why ever not?'

'Well . . .'

'We'd be glad to have you.' She smiled at him. Dear Harry, he was looking as though he couldn't believe she meant it. 'Really we would.'

'Dorothy, there's something I wanted—'

'Here's your tea. I haven't any sugar, I'm afraid. It's all gone.'

'I don't take it.'

'You're sweet enough, Harry.'

He went a bit red. 'I was going to say—'

'Bother! There's somebody knocking at the front door. I'd better go and see who it is.'

It was Mrs Dane from the stores, standing there with her big black umbrella over her head, rain running off it like a waterfall.

'I've brought a nice bit of bacon for you, Mrs Banks. Had some in unexpected and I thought of you and Charlie.'

'That's very kind. Will you come in and have a cup of tea. I've just made some.'

She nosed past Dorothy's shoulder. 'I wouldn't say no, but I see you've got company.' She would have spotted Harry's bike by the gate. Nothing would escape her eagle eye.

'Sergeant Green from Charlie's crew called by.'

'Is that so? Well, I'll only stop a moment.'

She was more likely to stay an hour. Poor Harry sat there hardly saying a word while she prattled on. What a shame, Dorothy thought. It would have been much nicer to talk to Harry alone. She wanted to tell him properly how grateful she was about Charlie.

But she didn't get the chance. As soon as Mrs Dane drew breath he stood up.

'I ought to be goin', if you'll excuse me. Must be gettin' back.'

She saw him to the door. 'It was good of you to come by, Harry.'

'Thank you for the tea.'

'I meant to ask you, was there anything you wanted?'

'No. Just passin'.'

'I'll see you again, before you go on leave. When it's over?'

'Aye, of course.'

'Well, just in case I don't, thanks for everything,

Harry. For all your help. And for looking after Charlie.'

On an impulse she stood on tiptoe and kissed him on the cheek. He went red as a brick this time.

'Goodbye, then, Dorothy.'

'Goodbye, Harry. Good luck.'

She waved as he cycled away in the rain.

Eighteen

'We're on tonight, Jock. I've just seen the names.'

'Thank God.'

'Speak for yourself, mate.' Bert was jumpy as a jack-in-a-box. 'I'm in no rush.'

They air-tested R-Robert in the morning. With no heavy load to carry, the Lanc soared into the air like a free spirit. Jock felt his own spirits lift with her. Their last op. R-Robert would see them through. She was a good kite. Gremlin free.

They flew straight and level for a bit while Stew levelled the bomb sight, and then the skipper put her through her paces. Everything OK. All systems go. All they needed now was a decent target. Something nice and near and not too well defended. They could have finished their tour in a matter of a few hours.

It was Berlin. The Big City. Old Yellowstripe. The worst one of all. Jock stared at the long, long red tape marking the route on the map. Of all the mean, dirty tricks for fate to play on them . . . He listened to the briefing with bitter resignation. Over a thousand miles there and back. Flak, flak and more flak. Night fighters. Radar tracking devices. Decoy targets. Everything the enemy could throw at them.

'Maximum effort required, gentlemen. Three hundred aircarft. This is an all-out attack at the heart of the enemy. I'm counting on all crews to do their utmost.'

They'd been doing just that twenty-nine times and they wouldn't be doing anything less for the thirtieth. The question was, would their luck hold out for them one more time? He didn't think he was a superstitious man. He didn't carry any mascot, and he only touched Sam because he didn't want to be odd-man-out. Nothing could help you if your number was up. It was all fate. Nothing to be done, except maybe pray – if he'd been a praying man, and he wasn't that either.

They shared the bus out to dispersal with another crew.

'You lucky people,' their bomb aimer said to him. 'All over for you lot soon.'

You could take that two ways, Jock thought dourly.

If we come back safe, Bert said to himself as the crew bus swayed and bumped along the peri track, I swear I'll marry Emerald. He didn't know when he'd ever been so jittery about an op. Somehow he'd got the idea in his head that they were going to get the chop on the very last one and nothing would shift it. *Please God, if you let us come back safe, I promise I'll marry her.*

He used to say that sort of thing as a nipper, only about things that didn't matter half as much. *Please God, don't let me get found out and I'll be nice to sis for ever more. Please God, I'll never nick anything again if they don't catch me.*

The other crew was watching them, he knew that. Envying them, but knowing they weren't done yet, not by a long chalk. Not till they'd been all the way to bloody Berlin and back. Crews could go missing on

382

their last trip just as easy as on their first. It didn't even have to be a bastard like Berlin. Taffy Davis's crew had got the chop on an ice-cream.

He couldn't see what the skipper was looking like because he was sitting up front with Two-Ton-Tessie, but the rest of them weren't counting any chickens. Jock was grim as a wet night in Glasgow, Stew frowning as he tried to make that useless lighter of his work, old Harry hadn't said a dicky-bird for hours and Piers had a face miserable as sin – something to do with that girl of his dumping him, lucky sod. What he wouldn't give to be foot-loose and fancy free again! Charlie had his head turned away, staring out of the back of the Bedford, though there was nothing to see in the dark. Nobody looked full of the joys of spring, like they thought they were going to make it. He fumbled for his matches, scraped a light for Stew sitting opposite and offered it across the gap between them.

'Wouldn't 'ave one of those spare, mate?'

'Cripes, Bert, don't you ever have any of your own?'

Stew lobbed him a fag and he lit up from the same flame and took in a slow, deep lungful.

He didn't want to die. Be snuffed out like a bloody candle, for ever. Blimey, he'd only just got started. Anything was better than that. *If I get back safe, I swear I'll marry Emerald.*

Last time we do this, Charlie thought. One way or another. Whatever happens, we'll never be together again as a crew. Maybe, when the war's over, we'll meet up one day, and maybe we won't. One thing's for sure, none of us'll ever forget. Not even when we're old men. He couldn't imagine any of them being old – maybe they never would be.

383

They'd given them a real snorter to finish on. *Berlin*. The name was enough to give you the willies. Goose-stepping storm troopers, burning torches, hordes of chanting Nazi loonies. *Sieg Heil! Sieg Heil! Sieg Heil!* It didn't bear thinking about what might happen to you if you baled out over that lot. He'd heard blokes say they'd seen the Jerry night fighters shooting at parachutists coming down, which was probably a lot better than what would happen to you if the mob below got you.

Two-Ton-Tessie was taking them at a fair old lick. Too fast for his liking; they'd be there before you could say knife. Still, sooner there, sooner off and sooner back. The Bedford drew up with a squeal of brakes and he picked up his cushion, his ration box and the chute pack parked between his feet and jumped down to the ground. R-Robert was there, ready and waiting.

'Hey, Charlie!'

He turned to see Two-Ton-Tessie waving at him from the driver's window. She flashed him a big smile and stuck her thumb up before she drove on with the other crew. He'd forgotten to ask her if he could keep the cushion.

'Ready, you guys?'

The tail wheel got its final ritual dousing and they picked up their gear ready to climb in.

Chiefy raised a hand. 'Bring her back in one piece, sir.'

'I'll do my best.'

Van touched Sam as he passed him and made his way up the slippery incline of the fuselage, Jock behind him. They ducked under the mid-upper turret

384

and clambered over the mainspar. For once he didn't bark his shins. Thanks for that small mercy, R-Robert. He settled himself in the cockpit, fastened his harness and flexed his gloved hands on the control wheel.

'OK, Jock, let's start her up.' He reached for the buttons in turn and the Merlins spluttered and growled and then roared. Jock crouched at his panel as they ran them up. He opened up the throttles, in turn, in a deafening crescendo, testing boost, revs, pressures, temperatures. No snags.

He clicked on his mike switch. 'Pilot to nav. Can you hear me OK, Piers?'

'Absolutely fine, skipper.'

'Bomb aimer?'

'Loud and clear, skip.'

He finished the intercom check and slid open the side window of the cockpit, grabbed a few lungfuls of clean cold night air before he snapped it shut, sealing off the cockpit from the world.

At 1930 hours he taxied R-Robert out of dispersal, with a quick burst of power on the port engines to turn her onto the peri track. She purred sweetly round to the take-off point, where he slowed her to a gentle halt, tweaking the brake lever on and off. He went through the final checks with Jock for the last time. The green light blinked at them from the control cabin. Harry's voice confirmed it.

'Well, here we go, flight engineer.'

Jock gave him a brief nod, a grim grin. 'Aye, skipper. Here we go.'

He rolled the Lanc forward and heaved her round. The flarepath glittered beyond the windscreen.

'Pilot to crew. Stand by for take-off.'

With a roar R-Robert sprang forward. Thundered

385

down the runway, tail up. On and on. Faster and faster.

'Full power, Jock.'

'Full power, skipper.'

Jock's hand slid under his own to take over the throttles. Van eased back the control wheel and felt the Lanc lift smoothly into the air. All that fuel, all those bombs, and seven men, and up she went like the real lady she was. A class act.

Berlin lay more than six hundred miles away, a nasty chunk of that over enemy territory. And the Germans would be waiting for them.

Stew lay flat on his stomach in the front turret, looking down as R-Robert climbed upwards. Too dark to see anything much, but it was still a hell of a sensation. After a few minutes they flew into some cloud and he kept a sharp look-out for any other jokers around. If they were going to cop it this last trip he'd just as soon it was some Jerry got them and not another Lanc.

'Navigator to pilot,' Piers' voice said formally in his ears. 'Would you please set course zero nine four degrees in two minutes, skipper.'

Jesus Christ, you'd sometimes think Piers'd never even met the skip.

'Roger, nav.'

R-Robert was still climbing steadily through patches of cloud. Within half an hour they'd crossed the Lincolnshire coast at seventeen thousand feet and headed out over the North Sea on course for Denmark. Stew switched on the tiny masked light and took a quick look over his box of tricks again. All set to give the Berlin Jerries something to think about. 'Do us a favour, drop one on Adolf for me,' one of the fitters had shouted to him. Not much chance of that, he reckoned. The bastard probably hid down in some nice safe shelter underground, along with Goering and Goebbels and Ribbentrop – the whole bloody mob of them. It wouldn't be them that got clobbered. He switched off the light.

The stars were shining away merrily overhead but there was a layer of solid cloud below, like a bloody great thick carpet. Looked like you could get out and walk right across it. The sky was a weird and wonderful place, no question.

'Pilot to bomb aimer. Any sign of that cloud breaking up, Stew?'

'Not a chink, skip.'

They'd forecast clear skies over the target, but the buggers had probably screwed up. If they got back in one piece he was going out to get blind drunk, soon as he'd had a kip. And after that, when he'd sobered up, he was going straight round to The Angel to find out what the fuck Honor was playing at. What the hell had gone wrong? For Christ's sake, they'd been talking about her coming to Australia after the war. About making a go of that vineyard together. Getting flaming well married . . . *married*, for Chrissake! Him. Stew Brenner! But that's what he wanted: Honor and the vineyard and a future.

He stared into the darkness. 'Bomb aimer to pilot. Think I can see the cloud cover breaking up ahead, skip.'

'Thanks, Stew.'

He went on watching.

'Pilot to rear gunner. You OK, Charlie?'

'Yes, thanks, skipper.'

'Give your guns a try, will you?'

'Roger, skipper.'

The Brownings were all ready, loaded and cocked. Charlie pressed the trigger and yellow flashes spurted from the muzzles with an ear-splitting clatter. The bullets curved away from him in a shining arc, disappearing into the dark. The smell of burning cordite filled the turret.

'Rear gunner to pilot. All OK, skipper.'

'Great. Pilot to mid-upper. Give yours a go, Bert, will you.'

He listened to Bert's guns rattling. Everything working. That gave them a good chance.

'Navigator to pilot. Would you turn onto one six two degrees, please.'

'Roger, Piers. One six two.'

From the Danish coast they had flown east and by Piers' dead reckoning they were on their turning point for the final long leg to Berlin. No night fighters yet and the only flak they'd seen had been flickering away in the far distance. It couldn't last – he knew that. It was too good to be true. They would be over the target in forty-six minutes.

Forty-six minutes left to live, most probably. He wasn't sure he cared all that much. Not since he'd read Peggy's letter. Obviously she'd never loved him like she'd said. She couldn't have done. None of the differences had mattered a jot to him, so why had she minded so much? Maybe Stew was right and she'd met somebody else and decided to give him the push. Maybe she'd had another boyfriend all the time, and that was why she hadn't wanted them to get properly engaged. It was the only thing that made any sense. All his dreams shattered. The house, the four children, *everything*. Oh, Peggy . . .

'Bomb aimer talking. Route markers going down to starboard, skip.'

'OK, Stew.'

R-Robert swung towards the markers.

Piers clicked on his mike. 'Navigator to pilot. As soon as you're over them, skipper, would you turn onto one five zero for the target.'

'Roger, nav. One five zero.'

Not long now. Funny how calm he felt. As though he really *was* past caring.

Lucky he'd picked up that wind velocity broadcast for Piers, Harry thought. Looked like they were dead on course. It wouldn't do to wander off the route and run into a flak barrage. There'd be plenty of trouble over the target without going hunting for it. Twenty-two minutes to go. He'd got the jitters again, but never mind so long as nobody else knew. What worried him most, as usual, was Charlie on his own back there. Nothing to be done about it, though. Just hope they got through all right.

He wished he'd said something to Dorothy. Lost his nerve, hadn't he? He should have spoken out boldly when she was making the tea, before that other woman had arrived and gone on and on with her gossiping. Now he'd have to wait till there was another chance.

R-Robert had started rocking about – either somebody else's slipstream, or the flak had already started.

'Bomb aimer to pilot. Target indicators going down to port, skip.'

'OK, I see them, Stew. Thanks.'

Harry felt R-Robert alter course slightly to port as they headed for the indicators. Into the jaws of death, he thought. God help us.

Stew had never seen anything like it, and that was bloody saying something. Strewth, they must have every ack-ack gun in Germany down there, blasting away. The whole flaming sky was just that – *flaming*. Jesus, they'd never get through this lot. R-Robert didn't like it one bit either, plunging about all over the place, and you couldn't blame her when they were swatting bombers down like flies. He'd counted three in the past minute. Christ almighty, *another* one – a Lanc spinning down slowly, both wings on fire, tail section breaking off as she went . . . *Holy shit!*

Yeah, but they were getting it back down there. Too right they were. The whole bloody city looked like it was burning. A whole bloody sea of fire and smoke and explosions. Flaming hell down there, too. Serve 'em right. He settled himself good and steady. He was going to make fucking sure this last lot were right on target.

'Bomb doors open, skip.'

'Bomb doors open.'

Eyes fixed on the sight, hand ready on the release tit, tracking the target indicators. The skip was keeping R-Robert straight and level, God knew how. Good on him.

'Right . . . right . . . left, left a bit . . . steady . . . ste-ady . . .'

The TIs were smack on the intersection. Beaut!

'Bombs gone, skip . . .'

Take that from me, Adolf and the rest of you bastards down there. And there's plenty more where it came from. Take that from all of us!

Charlie got a grandstand view of the city burning as the skipper took R-Robert away in a tight diving turn. Although he knew it would wreck his night vision, he

390

couldn't drag his eyes away from the leaping flames. They had a horrible fascination.

> *About, about, in reel and rout*
> *The death fires danced at night.*

Don't think about the dead or the dying. Don't think about the old people or the kids down there. Think about London and Coventry and Liverpool and Southampton. Think about Hitler and the goose-stepping storm troopers. Think about what they want to do to the rest of the world.

They left the flak behind, and R-Robert went like the clappers, heading west across Germany. Charlie's eyes readjusted to the dark and he scanned the night skies for enemy fighters. If you didn't have the flak you had the fighters.

'Pilot to rear gunner. Keep a sharp look-out.'

'Roger, skipper.'

Up in the mid-turret, Bert was keeping his eyes skinned too, spinning his turret round. So far, so good, but it was still a bloody long way home. *I'll marry Emerald if we get back safe.*

With a bit of luck we might make it, Harry thought. That was all they needed now. A little bit of luck.

'Navigator to pilot. I'm rather worried about the wind strength. It keeps pushing us off course. I think I'll try a couple of shots.'

'OK, I'll hold her level.'

Harry waited while Piers stood up in the astrodome to use the sextant. There was a cold feeling in the pit of his stomach now. Something was going to go wrong – just when they thought it was nearly over. Steady on, he told himself. No cause for alarm. Piers'll put us right. You've got the jitters for nothing.

'Pilot to nav. I can see flak ahead. Where do you reckon that is?'

'That'll be Bremen, skipper.'

'Right, I'll go south of it.'

Van altered course. Another hundred miles and they'd be over the coast with only the North Sea between them and England. Hallelujah!

'Fighter, fighter! Corkscrew starboard! Go!'

As Charlie's voice shouted over the intercom, Van shoved R-Robert's nose hard down, foot jammed against the rudder. He could hear Charlie's guns firing crazily. When he came out of the dive they had fallen silent. 'Pilot to rear gunner. Have we lost him?'

No answer.

'Pilot to rear gunner. Any damage, Charlie?'

No answer. Jesus, not the kid.

'Pilot to mid-upper. Any sign of that fighter still around?'

'Can't see him, skip. I'm watching. Is Charlie OK?'

'Go take a look will you, Harry?'

He clambered over the mainspar, cracking his head on the escape hatch in his frantic haste, squeezed past the mid-turret and Bert's feet, and stumbled on down the vibrating, roaring darkness of the fuselage, between the ammunition ducts, past the main door and over the Elsan to the rear turret doors. Yanked them open.

At first he thought Charlie was already dead. He could feel the blood warm and sticky on his hands as soon as he touched him and the lad didn't move or say a word. Then, when he groped desperately for his heart, he found it was still beating. 'Wireless op to skipper. Charlie's wounded. Unconscious. I'm not sure how bad. I'll have to move him. Get him out of here somehow.'

'OK, Harry. Get him on the rest bed if you can.'

Just as well the boy was unconscious. He had to drag him out of the turret backwards. No choice. Just as well he was only a shrimp, too, or he'd never have been able to carry him all the way back down the length of the fuselage. He laid Charlie down gently on the bed and hurried back to fetch the first aid box from beside the crew door. Sam was hanging in his place there and, on impulse, he grabbed hold of him too.

He shone his torch on Charlie, fearful of what he would see. There was blood running down the lad's face and when he eased back his helmet he could see a wound above the left temple. Not deep, just a long gouge where a bullet must have clipped him. He'd been wounded in the left shoulder, though, and that looked bad. There was a lot of blood and a deep hole. A few inches lower and it would have got his heart. Harry tried to remember the first aid he'd learned. Staunch the wound, that's what he'd got to do first. Stop the bleeding. Bandage it tight. Keep him warm. Blankets . . . where were the blankets? Give him a shot of morphine if necessary to stop the pain.

He fumbled with the first aid box, tearing open dressings and bandages with shaking fingers. Hurry, for God's sake! He'd let Charlie bleed to death if he didn't get a move on.

'Pilot to wireless op. How's he doing, Harry?'

'I've got him on the rest bed, skip. He's still unconscious. Nasty wound in the left shoulder but I think I've stopped the bleeding.'

'Well done. Think he'll be OK?'

'I hope so.'

'Take over in the rear turret, Harry, would you? Soon as you can. That fighter could still be around.'

'Right-o, skipper.' He drew the blankets over the boy, tucking them in carefully, and checked his mask and oxygen supply. He'd done the very best he could for him. One more thing, though: he laid Sam beside him – for company.

He felt his way back to the rear turret and hauled himself in by the overhead handles, feet first, landing on the cushion Two-Ton-Tessie had given Charlie. It was a tight fit for someone of his size but he managed it, and he knew where everything was. Jack-of-all-trades, wasn't he? Sometimes it paid off. He swivelled the turret, aiming the Brownings up and down. If that bugger who'd got Charlie came back again he'd let him have it and no mistake.

Glory be, it was cold back here, with that open panel right in front of his face and the wind whistling in from the bullet holes. He didn't know how Charlie stuck it, but then in his heated suit it wouldn't feel quite as bad. He was only wearing his battledress, being so warm where he was himself in the kite. Hadn't thought to stop and put on his Irvin or his gloves in the rush. Lucky he was wearing his scarf. Too late now to go back for the gloves and jacket. Mustn't leave his post in case that Jerry turned up again. He looked hard into the darkness, concentrating. His night vision wasn't too good so he'd have to stay extra lively. He rotated the turret again, quartering the sky. There wasn't anything out there except the stars.

He saw the tracer before he saw the enemy night fighter. Bright beads of fire snaking towards him.

'*Fighter! Fighter!*' He got the words out just before the bullets ripped into the tail plane, and he fired his own guns as they hit.

Bert's voice crackled urgently, 'Mid-upper to rear turret. He's coming about port. Watch for him, Harry.'

He could see the 110 coming for them again, head on. Still too far away. Steady. Steady. Wait till he's in range. Get him in the sights. Go for the prop. The German and he fired together. The fighter's propeller disintegrated at the same time as its bullets tore at the rear turret, smashing Harry back against his seat.

Bert's guns were blasting away. 'Mid-upper to skipper. We got 'im! We bloody well sodding got 'im! Got 'is bloody prop. The bastard's going down.'

'Well done, Bert. Well done, Harry. Keep watching. There could be more of them. You OK, Harry?'

Harry fumbled with his mike switch. 'OK, skipper.'

Must have been hit somewhere, though nothing was hurting. No sense in saying anything. Making a fuss. It wasn't much. Couldn't be, as it didn't hurt. He could get it seen to when they got back. And he could still keep a look-out – enough to warn them anyway. Keep watching. Keep watching. He listened to them talking as R-Robert flew on. He tried to sit up more so he could see better but couldn't seem to manage that. Just have to do the best he could. He heard Stew sighting the Dutch coast and then they were out over the North Sea. Not so much likelihood of a Jerry catching them now. They'd got a chance of making it. A good chance. Not too long, if only he could hang on. He was very cold, though, with all the air coming in. It was a bit like sitting in a sieve out on an icefloe in the Arctic. And there was a nasty taste in his mouth.

'Pilot to rear turret. OK back there, Harry?'

It took him an age to press the switch this time. His hands looked like two dead fish and his fingers refused to do what he wanted. Like when he'd tried to fire that Very pistol in the lifeboat. No Piers to help him this time. 'OK . . . skipper.' He leaned his head back and closed his eyes. It was no good, he couldn't keep a proper watch any more . . . ought to tell the skipper, but he'd never manage the mike switch again. He couldn't speak but he could still listen. When Piers picked up the G-signals from England it meant they were on the final straight. He listened to the strong, even pulse of the Merlins taking them home.

He knew now what the foul taste was – blood – and his mouth was full of it. He could feel it trickling out from under his mask and running down his neck all over Dorothy's scarf. Not that it really mattered, because the blood meant he was a goner. No point in pretending to himself, but he'd like to last till they got back so he knew the others had made it safely and that Charlie was all right. He opened his eyes and looked at the stars. Charlie'd always said how they kept him company and he could understand it now. He went on watching them. Crossing the English coast now. Soon be home. Just as well because he didn't think he'd be able to last much longer. It was hurting now. Hurting a lot. He didn't know how he was going to stand it. *Jesus* . . .

He could feel the Lanc sinking lower and lower. The skipper was bringing R-Robert down so they'd be almost there. She was coming in nice and steady and he heard the heavy *clunk* as her wheels locked down into place. They were going straight in – the skipper would have warned Control about Charlie so they'd have priority. They'd be ready down there with an ambulance.

The rear turret skimmed over the boundary lights. He watched the flarepath unrolling in a blur and felt the tail wheel beneath him touch down at the same time as the other two. A greaser! Well done, skipper. That was the way to finish. In style. Thirty ops. They'd made it. *They'd bloody well made it.*

'Pilot to crew. Thanks for everything, you guys.'

He heard them answer in turn.

'Och, you're welcome.'

'Good on you, skip.'

'Thanks most awfully.'

'Ta, skip.'

And then Charlie's voice – a bit weak but OK. 'Thanks, skipper.'

He'd like to have said something to them all, too. *You've been bloody marvellous, the lot of you. God bless.* But he couldn't speak. Not to worry. Main thing was, Charlie'd be all right now. Soon as R-Robert stopped they'd have the door open and get him out on a stretcher. He'd be in hospital in a jiffy and they'd look after him. He'd be all right. He shut his eyes again. He didn't think they'd be able to do much for himself. Not to worry about that either. Rita wouldn't care tuppence and Paulette wouldn't miss what she'd never known. I wish I'd told Dorothy how I felt though, he thought. Too late now. But perhaps it's just as well.

Nineteen

'Someone to see you, Charlie.'

He turned his head to see Mum coming down the ward. He could tell she was worried stiff, in spite of the smile.

'Charlie . . .'

'I'm all right, Mum. Honest. It's nothing to fuss about.'

'They said you'd been wounded—'

'It's only the shoulder, and they took the bullet out. I'm fine.'

'What about your head?'

'That's nothing. Just a scratch.'

She sank down on the chair beside the bed and managed another smile. 'Thank God. Were any of the others hurt?'

'Harry was.'

'Oh, poor Harry.' She looked round the ward. 'Is he in here too?'

'He's dead, Mum.'

She looked shocked. Went white as anything. '*Charlie!* Oh, no! What happened?'

'He got me out of the turret after I was wounded, and took my place, then the Jerry fighter went and copped him. I'd've been the one to get it otherwise.'

There were tears welling up in her eyes. 'Poor Harry. Oh, Charlie! *Charlie . . .*'

He swallowed hard. Wiped his own eyes quickly. 'Yes, I know. Anyhow, he shot the Jerry down, or Bert did. They're not sure which one of them did it. Mum . . . did Harry ever say anything to you?'

'What about?'

Maybe he should tell her, but then what good would that do? Nothing could come of it now, and it might upset her more. 'Oh, never mind.' Instead, he pulled Sam out from his hiding place under the pillow. Blood-stained and battle-scarred Sam. The other blokes in the ward had been giving him a real leg-pull about having a teddy bear.

'Could you take him back with you?'

She looked at Sam, and then up at him. Her eyes were shining with tears. 'I'll give him a wash, shall I, Charlie? And a bit of a mend.'

'I'm so very sorry about Harry, Van.'

'We're pretty sorry ourselves.'

'He was a nice man.'

'Yep. One of the very best.'

Keep it off-hand. Mustn't show how cut up you were. He'd learned that, if nothing else, in the past months. Dashed bad form, as Piers would say.

'Congratulations on finishing your tour.'

'Well, we were one of the lucky ones in the end . . . except for Harry.'

'And on your DFC.'

'How did you hear about that?'

'News travels fast in a place like this. I heard Piers has one too.'

'Can't get anywhere without a good navigator and that's a fact. Stew gets the DFM, did you hear that? I've kept on at them since we had that hang-up.'

'He deserves it.'

'Sure does. And they're giving the same to Harry. Pity he won't he around to collect it himself.'

'I know . . .'

'They should *all* have got gongs. The whole damn crew. *Every* crew.'

'I know.'

They were standing outside the ops block in a wind like a razor's edge.

'Look, Catherine, can we go somewhere inside and talk a minute?'

'I'm on duty in five minutes.'

'That's all it'll take.'

In the corridor, people kept pushing past, staring. He took no notice. 'You were right about Peter,' he said. 'I'm sorry I was such a jerk.'

She looked up at him. 'I was going to tell you, Van. I've had a letter from his mother. Peter tried to escape – made a dash for it over the wire. The guards shot him dead.'

'Hell . . . I'd no idea. That's bad.'

'It's what I was always afraid of: that he'd go and do something crazy like that.'

More people went past. He could see them nudging each other.

'I guess I've been even more of a jerk than I thought.'

'No, you haven't, Van. You didn't know Peter. I did. And I never wrote that letter, thank God. I would have blamed myself for ever if I had.' She looked at her watch. 'I've got to go now.'

'When will I see you?'

'I don't know. You'll be posted, won't you?'

'I've got two weeks leave. Then the US Air Force

want me to switch over to them. I'll be converting onto B17s or 24s.'

'A change of uniform as well.'

'Yep, I'm getting the Yank one in London.' He touched his RAF wings on his chest. 'I get to keep these, though, and wear them. They mean a hell of a lot to me.'

'And your DFC?'

He nodded. 'That, too. So they say. What I want to know, though, is what happens to *us*?'

'I'm not quite sure.'

'Supposing we start over?'

'You mean back to square one? Like snakes and ladders?'

'Snakes and ladders?'

'Don't you have it in America? It's a board game, played with dice. You go up ladders and come down snakes. Sometimes you have to go back and start again at the first square.'

'I guess that's pretty much what I meant.'

She smiled and held out her hand. 'Assistant Section Officer Herbert, Women's Auxiliary Air Force. Delighted to meet you.'

He took her hand in his. 'They're moving me up a notch. First Lieutenant VanOlden, United States Eighth Army Air Force. How about dinner tonight?'

Bert was clearing out his locker and whistling while he worked. Blimey, the rubbish there was in there! Sweet papers, empty cans of orange juice, squashed fag packs, old magazines, half a bar of mouldy chocolate, part-chewed wads of gum, a crumpled pin-up of Rita Hayworth lying about in straw with her jumper sliding off one shoulder . . . He studied it for a moment with reverent approval – she was a smasher all right – and then stuffed it into his kit-bag. He'd take her with him. He groped some more in the locker and found a pair of women's knickers and a brassière right at the back. Emerald's. He held them gingerly aloft, at arm's length. To think he'd carried those around with him in his pockets. Must have been off his bloomin' trolley.

One of the new crew came into the hut. All sprogs, just starting out, and this one was the rear gunner – only a nipper, like Charlie. Turned bright red when he saw the undies. He'll see worse sights than that before he's finished, Bert thought. He tossed them into the rubbish bin and went on whistling. He felt like a man reprieved from the gallows. Saved at the eleventh hour. It'd all been a false alarm – just like Stew had said. All right, I'll marry you if you want, Emerald, he'd told her, like he'd sworn to do if he got back safe. Ready to sacrifice his whole life. Do the right thing. Thanks very much, she'd snapped back, but you needn't trouble yourself now. And furthermore I wouldn't marry you if you was the last man on earth. He'd almost hugged her, he was so relieved. Couldn't help grinning, just to think of it.

What with that and getting the Jerry fighter – well, he was sure it'd been him, not Harry who'd got the bugger – *and* finishing the tour, well, everything'd come up roses after all.

His grin faded. No roses for Harry, though. He didn't feel quite so chuffed when he thought about that. He'd been a good bloke. Poor old Harry. Sticking to his post like that. Must've been in agony, yet he'd never said a bloomin' word. First they'd known was when he didn't come out after they'd landed and got

Charlie away in the ambulance. And when they'd gone and found him it was too late. The skipper'd got to him first. Been holding his hand when he'd gone. Could've been Harry who'd nabbed the Jerry – he'd got to admit that. They'd never know.

The sprog kid was watching him the way they always did. He'd been just the same himself at the start, wondering what it was like, wanting to ask the old hands, thinking they knew all the answers. He was shit-scared, this one, all right. White face, goggle eyes, gulping. Bert started whistling again, ever so carefree. Thirty ops. Piece of cake. The locker was empty. He picked up his bulging kit-bag, swung it over his shoulder and tucked Victor in his shoe box under one arm. The sprog was still watching. He gave him a cheery thumbs-up. 'Good luck, mate. You'll be all right. Nothin' to it.' Sez me, he thought, as he left the hut. What a bloody joke!

'Jolly decent of you to give us a lift, old boy. Frightfully sporting.'

'Don't mention it, Stew.'

He didn't mind Stew taking the mickey. In fact, he was going to miss him doing it. He was going to miss them all. And Harry – well, that was the worst of it. The rest of them might meet up, with luck, but without Harry it wouldn't be the same. Six, not seven. Not a full crew. Not the same.

Bert and Jock and Stew shoved their kit into the Wolseley's boot. They looked strangely clean and tidy in their best blue, shoes polished, faces shaved, hair well brushed. It reminded Piers of the end of term at boarding school, with everyone going home, passed by Matron.

Lord, dismiss us with thy blessing,
Thanks for mercies past received . . .

Let thy Father-hand be shielding
All who here shall meet no more . . .

They'd gone and said goodbye to Charlie in hospital and to Van who was getting his transfer to the American Air Force sorted out. Shaken hands all round, promised to keep in touch and have regular reunions. He wondered if they really would. Whether any of them would even survive the rest of the war.

They'd said goodbye to Harry, too. The station had given him a jolly good send-off – all properly done with flowers and a rifle salute over the grave. The five of them had stood together: Van, Jock, Stew, Bert, and himself. And he, for one, had had the most awful lump in his throat. He thought the others had been pretty cut-up, too, though, of course, they hadn't shown it. Harry's parents had been there and Charlie's mother had come in his place, which seemed right. No sign of the ex-wife or daughter, though.

He shut the boot. 'Right, chaps. That's it.' He drove out of the station gates for the last time. It was raining hard, the cathedral a hazy blob on the horizon. Bert told one of his stories to entertain them on the journey – something about the Pope and a Mother Superior. Piers hardly listened.

They dropped Stew off at The Angel. 'Well, so long you jokers. See you around.'

As he walked away, Bert wound down the car window and called out something rude. Stew must have heard because he turned and grinned.

At the station Piers hung about. 'I'll come and wave you chaps off.'

'Och, no,' Jock said. 'You'll be wanting to get on home.'

'No, honestly, I've got lots of time.' He hated the thought of saying goodbye to them. Wanted to put it off as long as possible, though naturally he couldn't possibly say so.

They went onto the crowded platform. Among the khaki and the RAF blue he caught sight of a girl, back turned, wearing a scarf exactly the same colour as Peggy's. For a second or two he thought it *was* her and then she turned round and he saw that it was somebody else, a much older woman, nothing like Peggy at all.

As the train came in, Jock shook his hand. 'Well, good luck, laddie.'

'Good luck to you, Jock. Good luck, Bert.'

'Same to you, mate. Don't do anythin' I wouldn't do.'

He waited, watching them get on board and fight their way down the corridor. The whistle blew and he raised his hand in farewell as the train carried them off. There was a last glimpse of Jock giving him a casual salute and Bert holding up Victor to wave. Then they were gone. He went on standing there long after the train was out of sight.

'Excuse me, was that the London train?'

She came running down the platform, one hand clamped to her WAAF officer's cap, a suitcase in the other.

'I'm afraid it was.'

'Oh, *lord* I've gone and missed it. And I suppose the next one won't be for simply *hours*.' She put down

405

the case and straightened her cap, panting hard.

'Have you got far to go?'

'To Peterborough and then I'm getting a bus from there. A place called Woodthorpe. I'm going home on leave.'

'How extraordinary! I live frightfully near there. Only about five miles away.'

'Gosh . . . amazing!'

'I say, I don't suppose you'd like a lift, would you? I mean, I've got a car here and I'm just going home on leave myself. If it isn't the most frightful cheek of me . . .'

'Are you *sure*?'

'Absolutely.'

She smiled at him. He'd never seen eyes quite that colour grey before – sort of like storm clouds. Awfully attractive.

'Well, that's terribly kind of you. Thanks.'

'The Wolseley's just outside. My name's Piers, by the way. Piers Wentworth-Young.' He picked up her suitcase. 'There's masses of room in the boot.'

She heard the revolving door squeaking and looked up to see him striding in, kit-bag across his shoulder. He came straight over to the desk, dumped the bag down and leaned an arm on the counter. 'I'd like a room, please.'

She opened the book. Her heart was hammering away, her knees weak, but she was blowed if she'd let him see it. 'Single or double?'

'Double.'

Double. Well, what else would she expect? Get a grip on yourself, Honor. Show him that it's fine by you whoever he's with. 'How long for?'

'Tonight. Maybe longer. It depends.'

On the girl in question, presumably.

'Number twelve is available.'

'Good-oh. I'll sign in.' He scratched away with the pen. 'When're you going to get that door oiled?'

'I really couldn't say. Anyway, it's not up to me any more. I'm leaving soon.'

'What happened? You get the sack?'

She said stiffly, 'I handed in my notice, that's all.'

He grunted. 'About time. What're you going to do next?'

'Whatever the Labour Exchange tell me's needed.'

He stuck the pen back in the holder. 'I'm off, too. Finished my tour.'

'Congratulations.'

'Two weeks' lovely leave and then I'll be teaching sprogs. Then maybe another tour.'

Another tour? She wanted him to live, not die.

'Here's the key to number twelve.'

'I'll never find it.'

'Upstairs. Turn right. Third on the left down the corridor. You can't miss it.'

'That's what you Poms always say. I miss it every time. You'll have to show me.'

She went up the stairs ahead of him, moving as quickly as possible. She still had her pride, after all. As they reached the top Mrs Mountjoy came out of the Residents' Lounge below.

'Miss Frost, Miss Frost . . . where are you? The coal scuttle is empty and the fire's going out. Miss Frost . . .'

He leaned over the banisters. 'Get it yourself, lady. She's busy.'

She unlocked the door to number twelve.

'After you,' he said, with a bow and a sweeping gesture.

The blackout blind was still in place, so she went over to raise it, revealing the room in all its shabby gentility. She couldn't imagine why he wanted to bring some girl to The Angel. Surely a hotel in London would have suited his purpose better? Something ritzy and glamorous.

He shut the door and set down his kit-bag, took off his greatcoat and cap and tossed them on the bed. 'This'll do.'

There was a striped ribbon sewn above the left breast pocket of his tunic. They'd given him a medal. She had no doubt he'd earned it.

She handed over the key. 'I must go down and see to Mrs Mountjoy.'

'The old girl can wait. We've got things to discuss, us two. You and I. Here, in private.'

'What things?'

'I've been doing a spot of thinking, wondering what the hell you were playing at last time I was here. Know what I came up with?'

'No.'

'I reckon you got the idea I was messing you around. Giving you a whole lot of boloney, like I've given other sheilas. That so?'

She looked away.

'Yeah, I can see you did. Can't you tell when a bloke's serious?'

'How could I, with someone like you?'

'Well, why the hell d'you think I'm here now?'

'I've no idea.'

'To see you. Why else would I come back to this dump?'

She said slowly, 'You really meant it, Stew? Everything you said about Australia after the war . . . and the vineyard . . . and us?'

'Every flaming word. Dinkey-die.'

'But this double room . . . I thought . . . someone else . . .'

'You and me, sweetheart. You and me.'

She could hear Mrs Mountjoy screeching away below like an angry parrot. *Miss Frost, Miss Frost, Miss Frost.*

'Stew, I really ought to go and see to her.'

'No, you didn't.' He locked the door and dropped the key into his pocket. 'You're not leaving. We haven't finished yet, see. Not by a long chalk. Matter of fact, we've only just begun.'

At Exeter Jock hitched a lift with an empty army lorry and when the driver heard that he'd just finished a tour with Bomber Command he went out of his way to drop him within a few miles of Hatherleigh.

'Don't mention it, mate. Anything we can do for you blokes.'

He walked into the village and found a small post office and stores. He waited his turn in the queue at the counter beside a small pyramid of tinned spam, baked beans and beetroot slices in vinegar.

The old woman serving was impatient. 'There's farms all over. If you don't know the name I can't help you.'

'I'm looking for one with a land-girl working on it.'

She gave him a disapproving look. 'Land-girls are all over, too. And if you want my opinion, we'd be better off without them.'

As he walked out of the shop another woman called after him. 'Try Pennyman Farm – that way. They've a land-girl there. Seen her out in the field.' She was old, too, and gave him a near toothless smile in a wizened face. Looked him up and down. 'RAF, eh? Brave lads.'

He thanked her and set off. It was raining. Not the hard, cold, driving rain of Lincolnshire but a soft drizzle he could barely feel. Everything was gentler down here: gentle slopes, sheltered fields, enclosed skies.

He heard the tractor in the distance but because of the high hedge he couldn't see it until he reached a gap where there was a gate. He leaned on the wooden gate, watching the tractor ploughing steadily to and fro, making good, straight furrows in the red earth. A V of white gulls streamed out behind like a ship's wake. He could hear their cries. The field was more than half done when the engine suddenly faltered and choked to a stop. He watched as the driver got down and started fiddling about with it. After a while, he climbed over the gate and walked across the un-ploughed ground. A few yards away he stopped and called out.

'D'you need some help?'

She swung round. She wasn't showing it, but he knew damn well she was glad to see him. 'How the hell did you find me, Jock?'

'Why the hell did you go?'

She shrugged. 'That's my business. Can you mend this bloody thing?'

'Mebbe.'

'What do you think's the matter with it?'

'Dirt in the fuel, most probably. Same as before. I told you not to let it run low.'

'I don't need a lecture, thanks. Just *do* something.

410

You're supposed to know all about engines, aren't you?'

He stood there, not moving. Staying exactly where he was. 'I'll give it another try, Ruth. But not unless you really want it to work. To give it a proper chance. If you don't, I'm leaving right now. And I'll never be back.'

She stared at him. Under the cap's brim her mouth twitched into a grin. Another shrug.

'May as well, Jock,' she said. 'Since you're here.'

Mr Stonor stopped by the cottage on his way home.

'How's that boy of yours?'

'Mending well, thank you.'

'Finished his thirty, didn't he? Expect you'll be goin' home, then?'

'As soon as Charlie's out of hospital and fit to travel. I'll return your bike before we leave.'

'No rush. No rush. How about the hen? Will I wring her neck for you? Wouldn't take a moment.'

'No, thank you, Mr Stonor. I'll be taking her with us.'

'An old thing like that? Not much use to you.'

'I'm fond of her and she still lays eggs sometimes.'

He shook his head. 'Well, you can always put her in the pot.' He went on his way in the dusk.

Dorothy fetched her coat and went to shut Marigold up for the night. She fancied the hen looked at her anxiously. 'Don't worry. I'd never do anything like that to you,' she told her. 'You can stay with me always.'

She could make her a new run at the end of the garden in Bromley. Copy the same sort of thing Harry had done for her. Maybe even get some more hens as company.

As she wired up the henhouse door, she heard an engine start up suddenly out on the drome. A Merlin. She knew the sound as well as anything: could have told it easily from any other engine. Another one started. And another. And another. Four of them roaring away. The sound of a Lancaster. She stood still, listening. Presently more engines started. And then more. They were going.

Charlie was safe, for the time being at least, but other young men were risking their lives and some of them would never come back. It would go on and on – men replacing men, crews replacing crews – with no end to it. Not until the war was over.

She waited to hear the bombers take off, one after the other, and to watch them climb into the evening sky and turn towards the east. When the last one had gone and it was all quiet again she went inside and closed the cottage door.

THE END